SUMMER VAMP

VIOLET CHAN KARIM

SCHOLASTIC INC.

This is a work of fiction. Names, characters, places, and incidents either are the product of the author's imagination or are used fictitiously. Any resemblance to actual persons, living or dead, events, or locales is entirely coincidental.

ISBN 978-1-5461-4228-7

12 11 10 9 8 7 6 5 4 3 2 1 24 25 26 27 28 29

Printed in the U.S.A. 40

First Scholastic printing, September 2024

Editors: Whitney Leopard & Danny Diaz

Designer: Juliet Goodman

Summer Vamp was illustrated in Clip Studio Paint on an iPad, and the lettering was done in Photoshop.

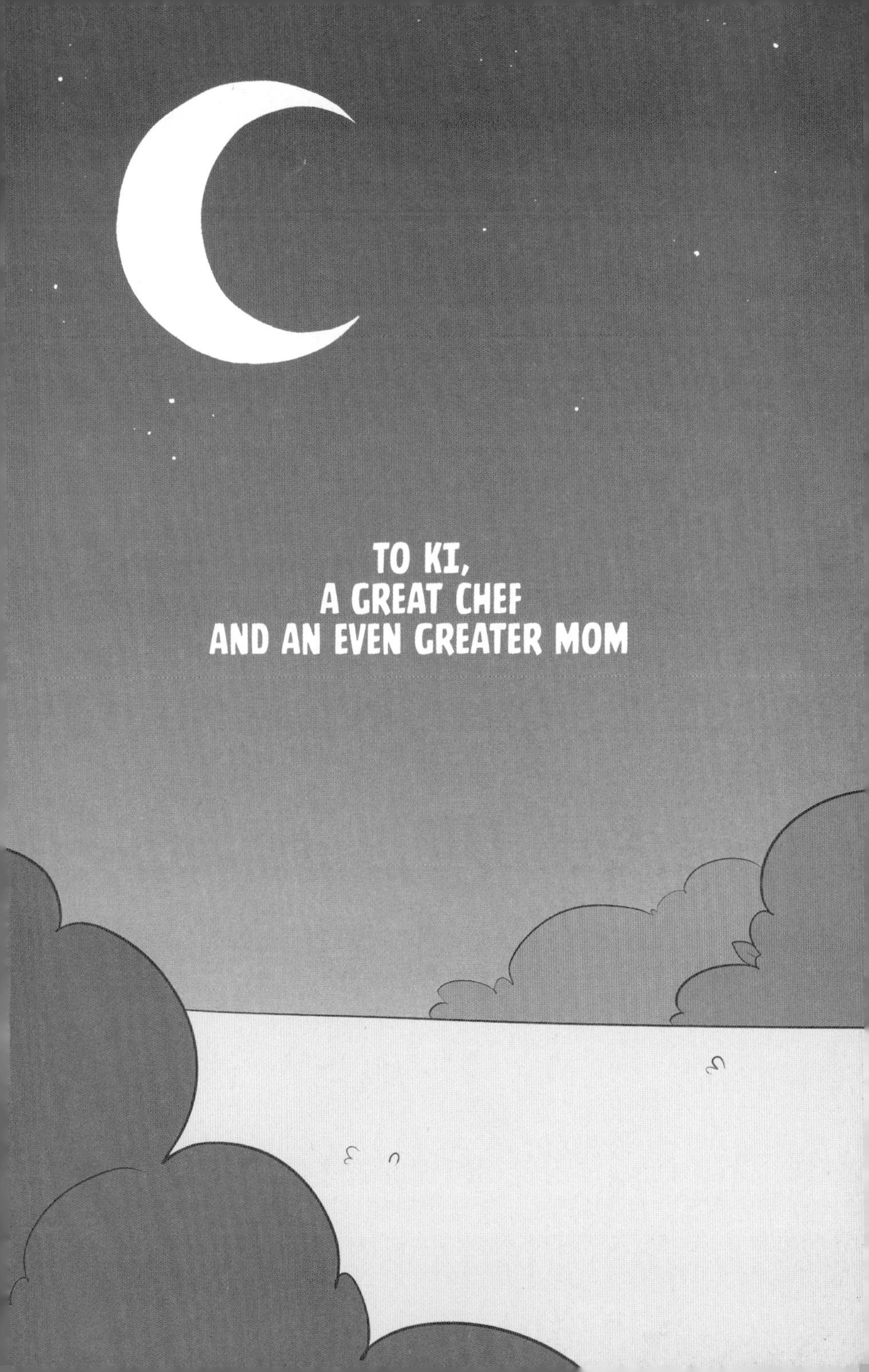

TO KI,
A GREAT CHEF
AND AN EVEN GREATER MOM

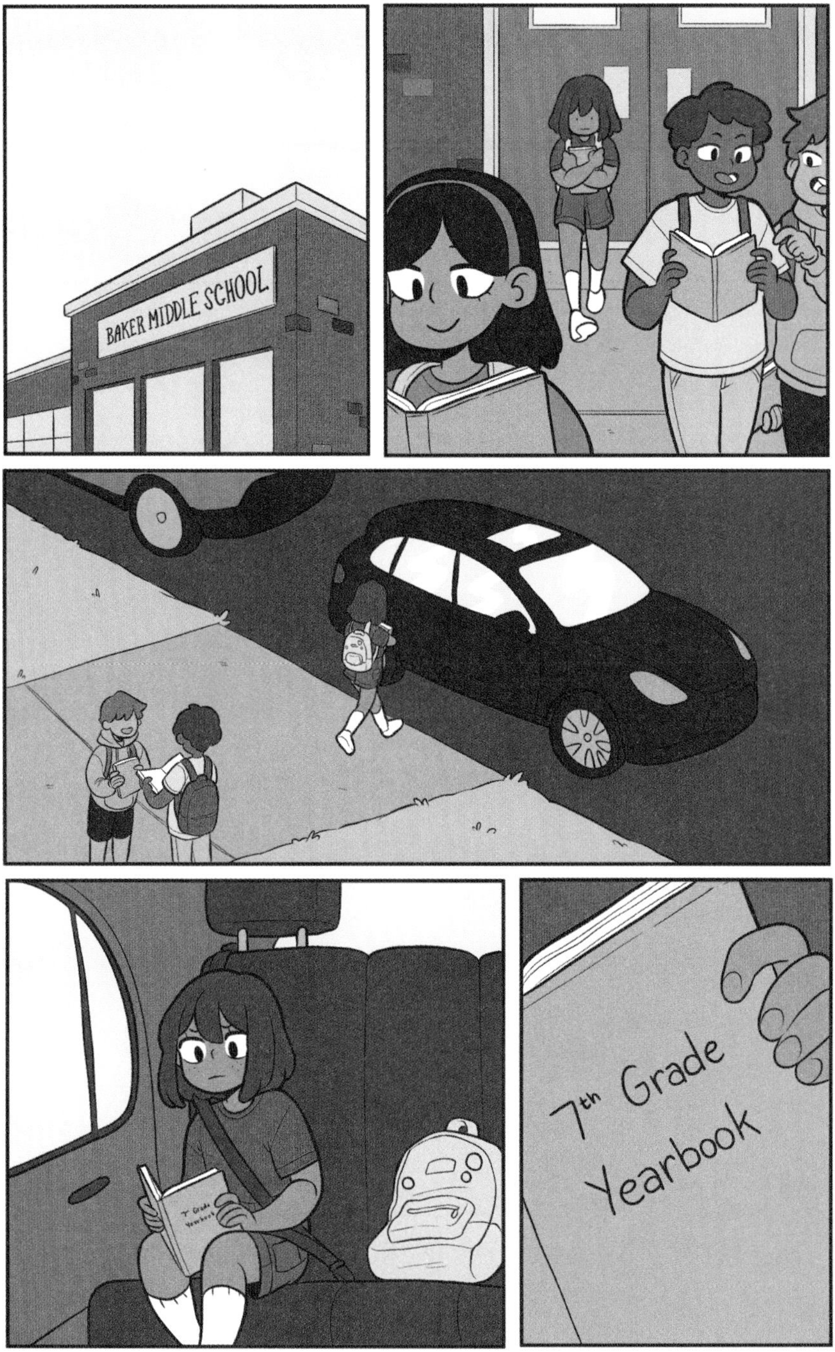
BAKER MIDDLE SCHOOL
7th Grade Yearbook

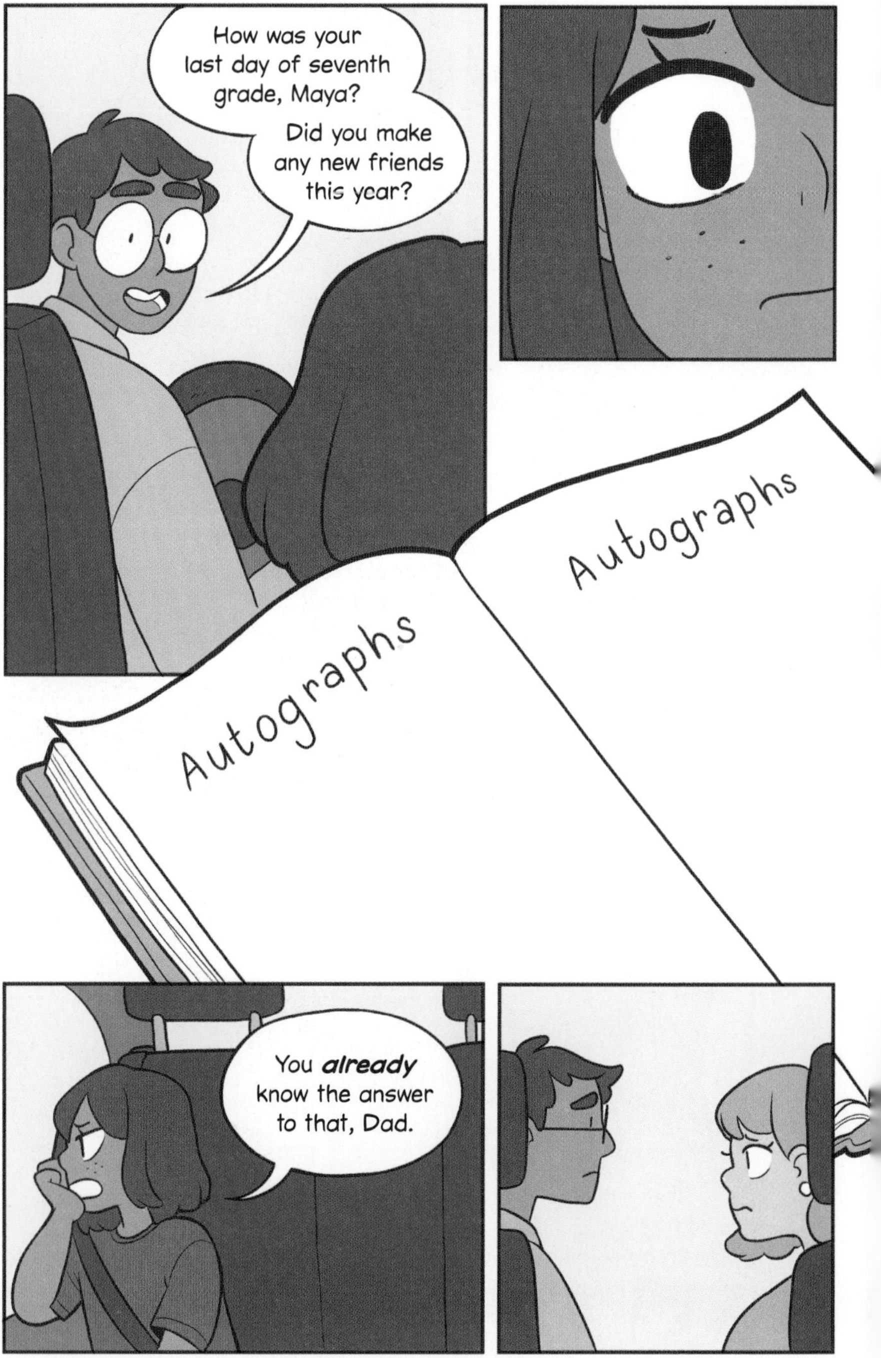
How was your last day of seventh grade, Maya?
Did you make any new friends this year?
Autographs
Autographs
You ***already*** know the answer to that, Dad.

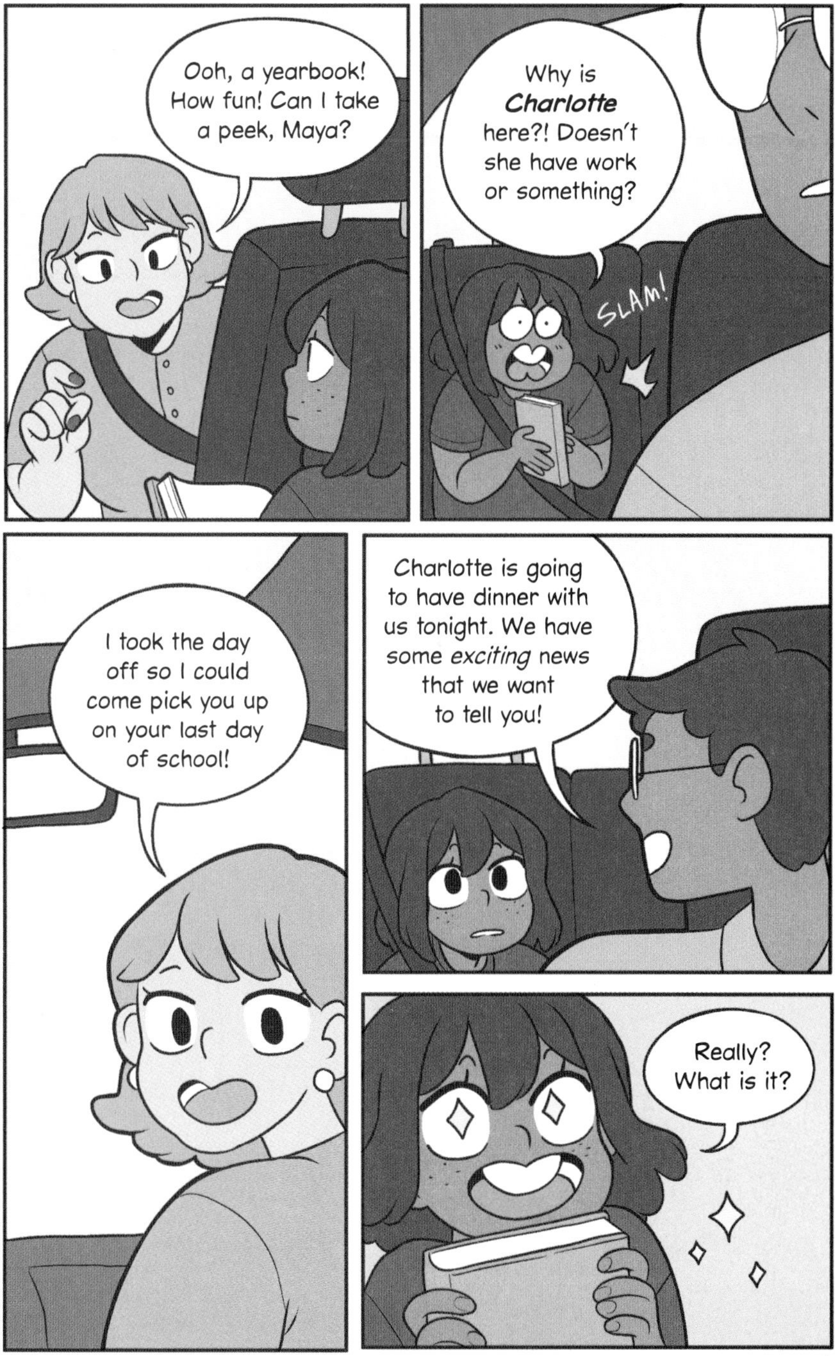
Ooh, a yearbook! How fun! Can I take a peek, Maya?
Why is **Charlotte** here?! Doesn't she have work or something?
SLAM!
I took the day off so I could come pick you up on your last day of school!
Charlotte is going to have dinner with us tonight. We have some *exciting* news that we want to tell you!
Really? What is it?

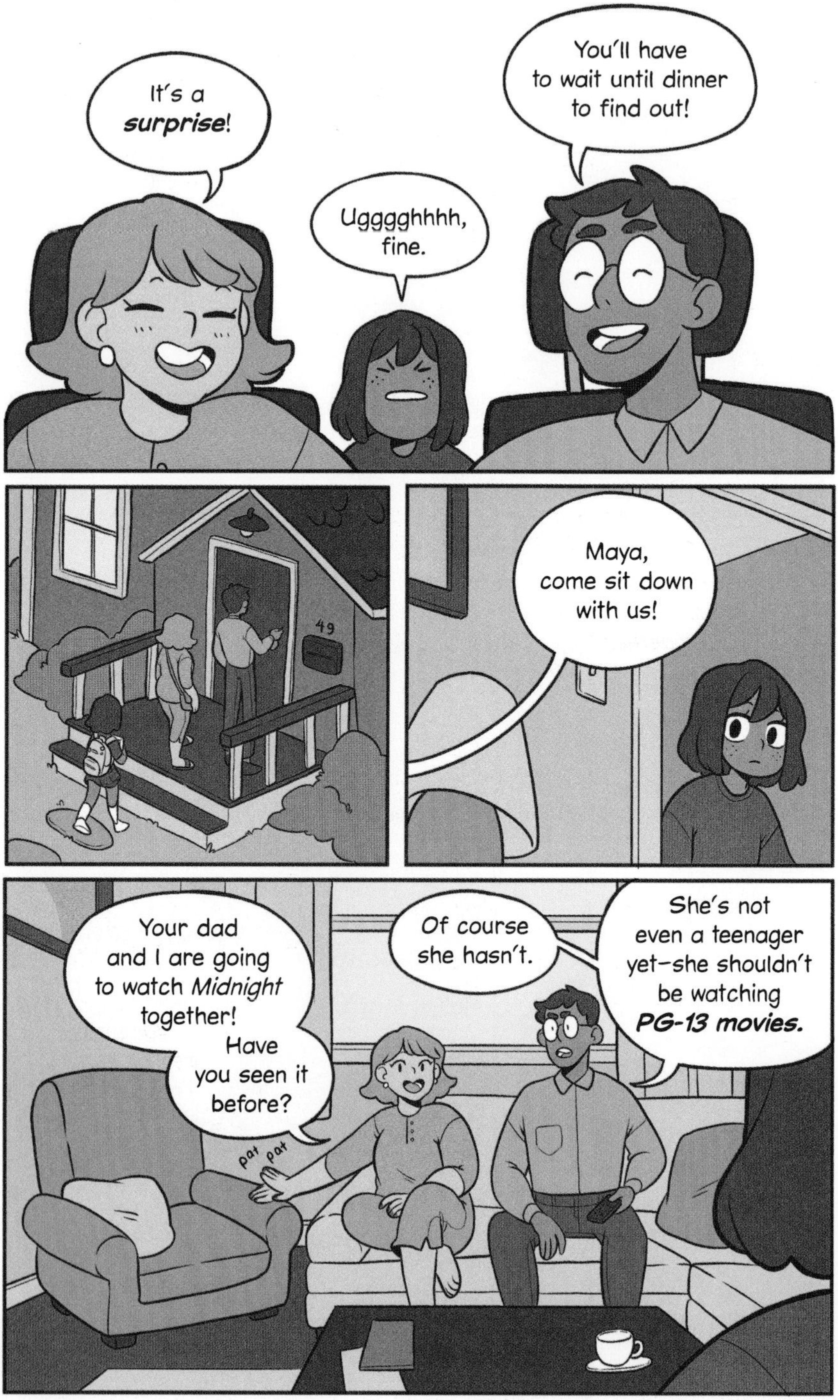
It's a *surprise*!
Ugggghhhh, fine.
You'll have to wait until dinner to find out!
49
Maya, come sit down with us!
Your dad and I are going to watch *Midnight* together!
Have you seen it before?
pat pat
Of course she hasn't.
She's not even a teenager yet—she shouldn't be watching **PG-13 movies.**

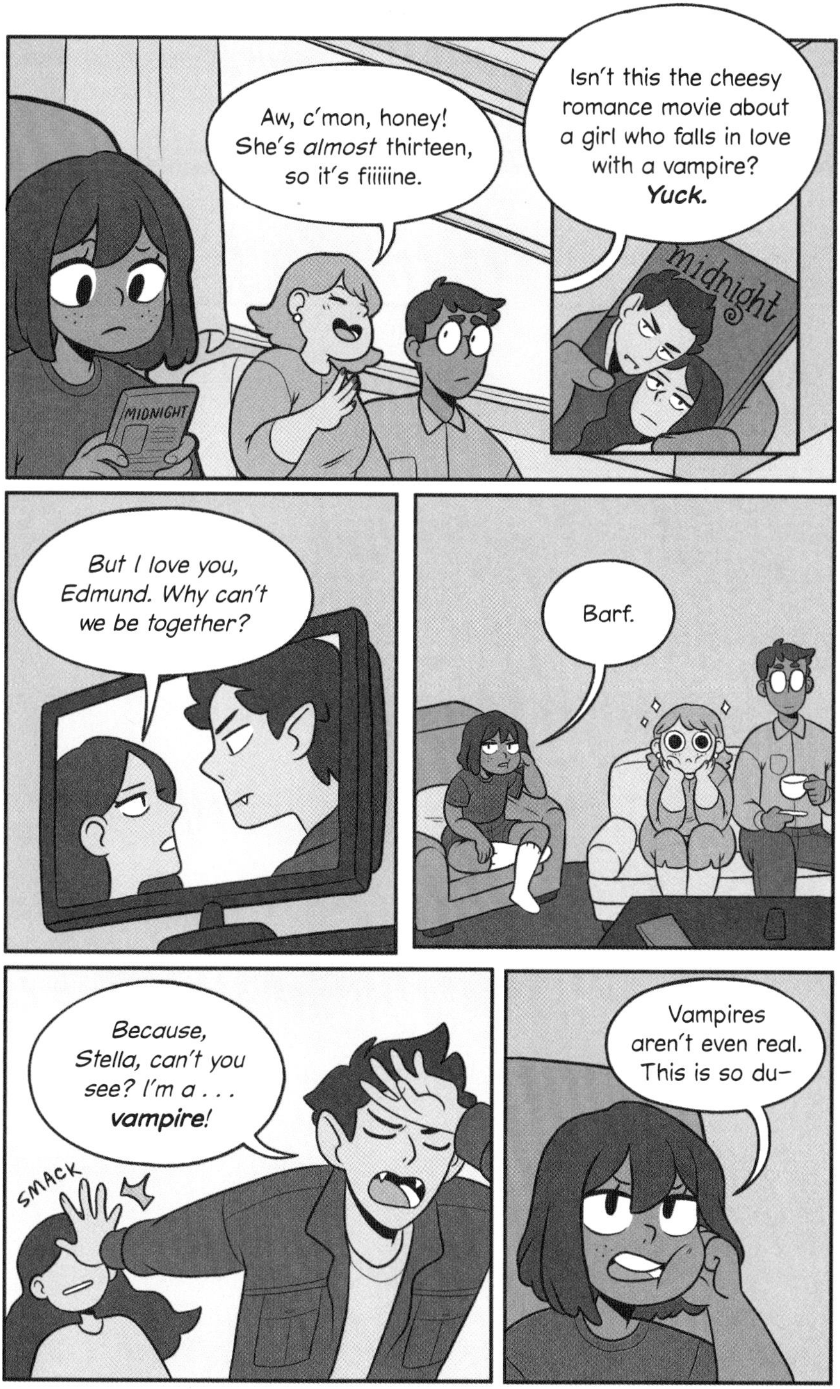
Aw, c'mon, honey! She's *almost* thirteen, so it's fiiiiine.
Isn't this the cheesy romance movie about a girl who falls in love with a vampire? **Yuck.**
MIDNIGHT
midnight
But I love you, Edmund. Why can't we be together?
Barf.
Because, Stella, can't you see? I'm a . . . ***vampire!***
SMACK
Vampires aren't even real. This is so du–

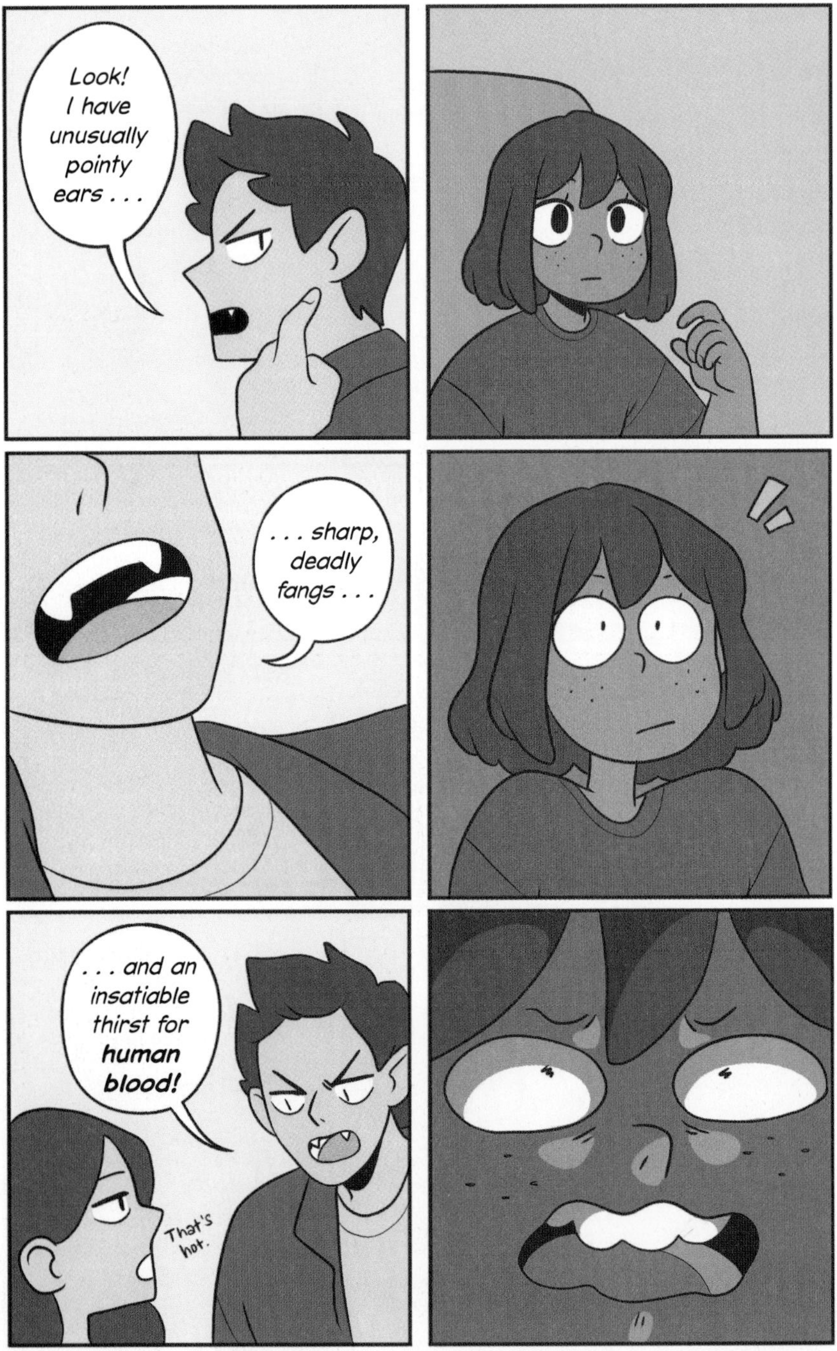
Look! I have unusually pointy ears . . .
. . . sharp, deadly fangs . . .
. . . and an insatiable thirst for **human blood!**
That's hot.

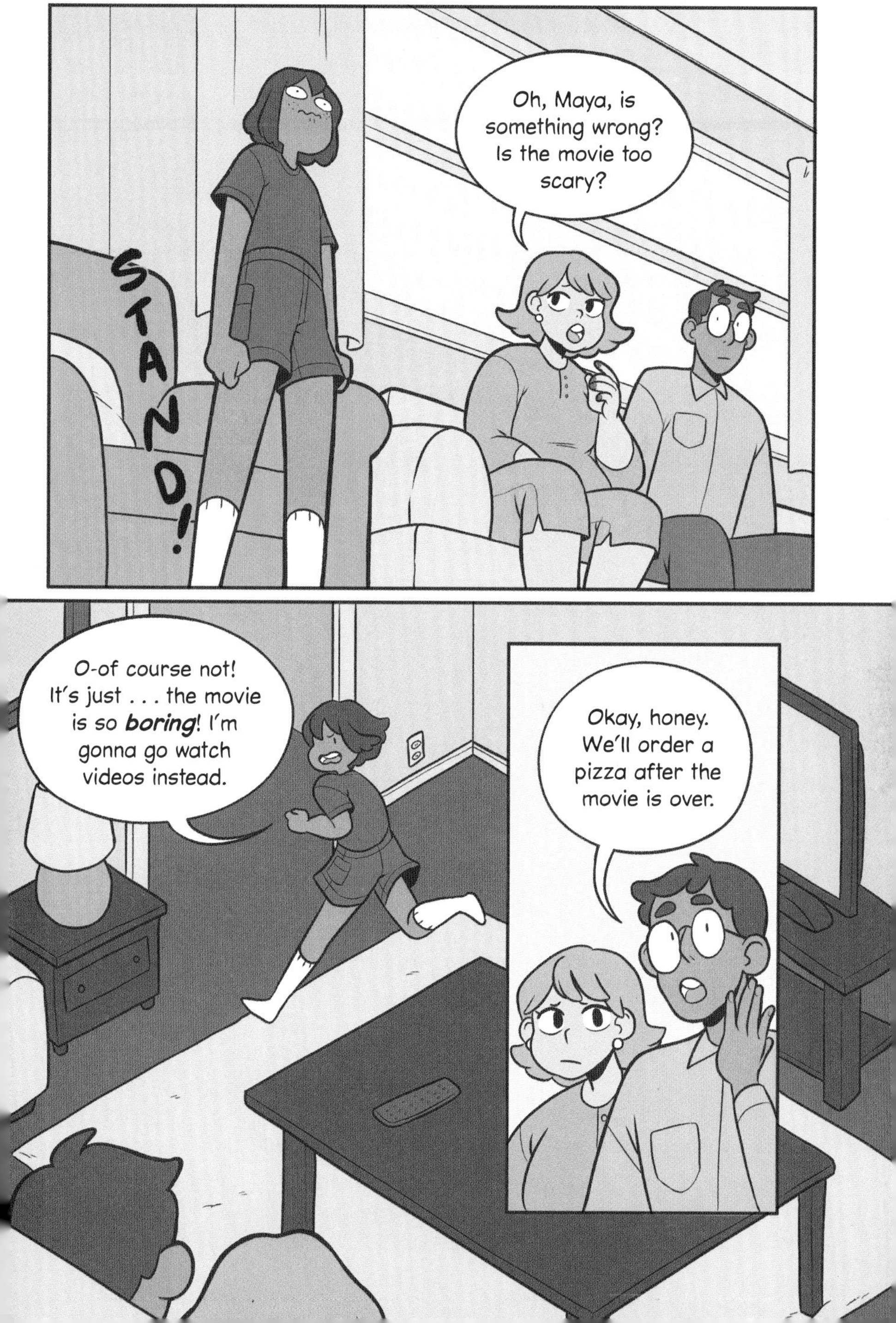
Oh, Maya, is something wrong? Is the movie too scary?
STAND!
O-of course not! It's just . . . the movie is so **boring**! I'm gonna go watch videos instead.
Okay, honey. We'll order a pizza after the movie is over.

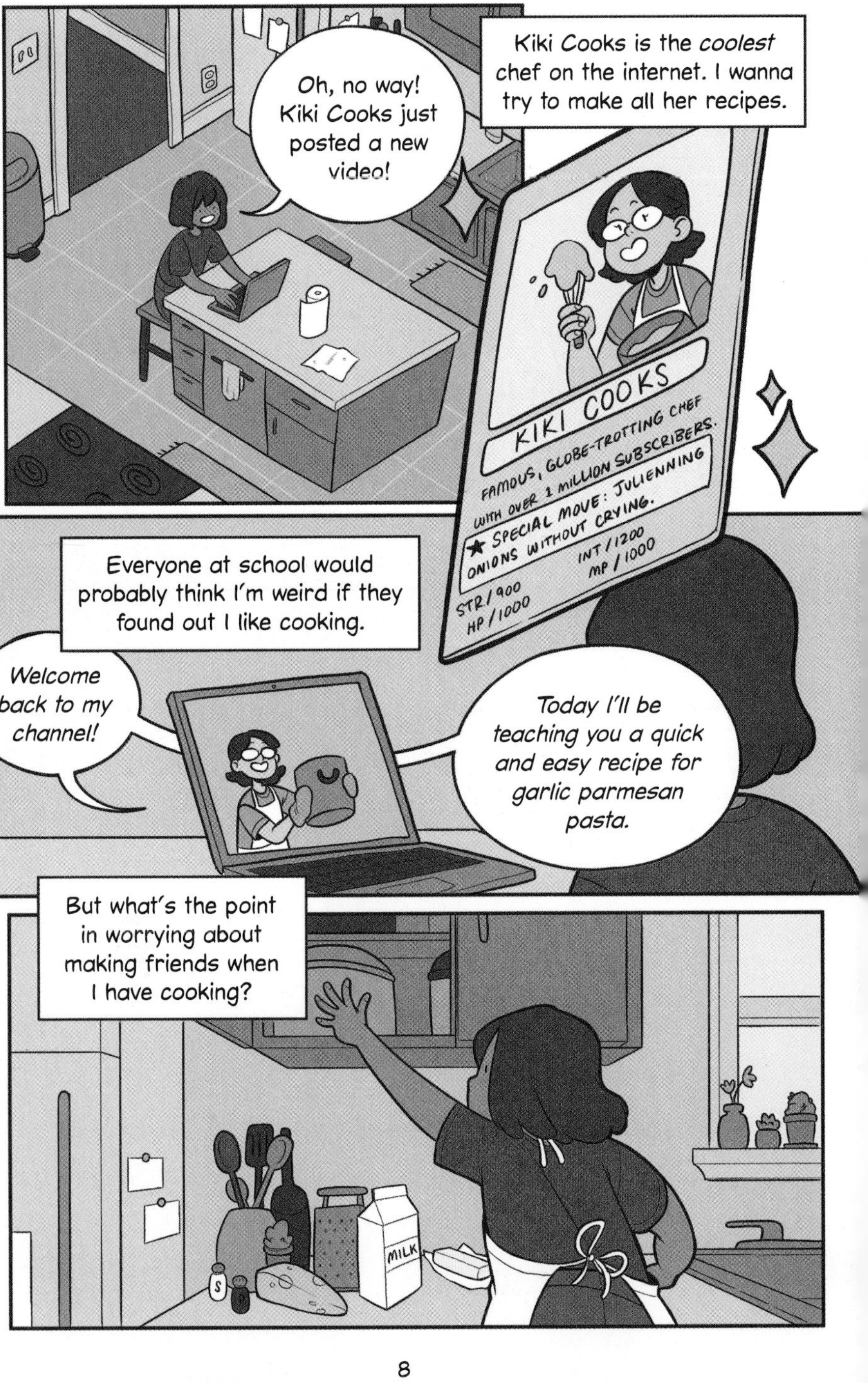
Oh, no way! Kiki Cooks just posted a new video!
Kiki Cooks is the *coolest* chef on the internet. I wanna try to make all her recipes.
KIKI COOKS
FAMOUS, GLOBE-TROTTING CHEF WITH OVER 1 MILLION SUBSCRIBERS.
★ SPECIAL MOVE: JULIENNING ONIONS WITHOUT CRYING.
STR / 900
HP / 1000
INT / 1200
MP / 1000
Everyone at school would probably think I'm weird if they found out I like cooking.
Welcome back to my channel!
Today I'll be teaching you a quick and easy recipe for garlic parmesan pasta.
But what's the point in worrying about making friends when I have cooking?
MILK
S
P

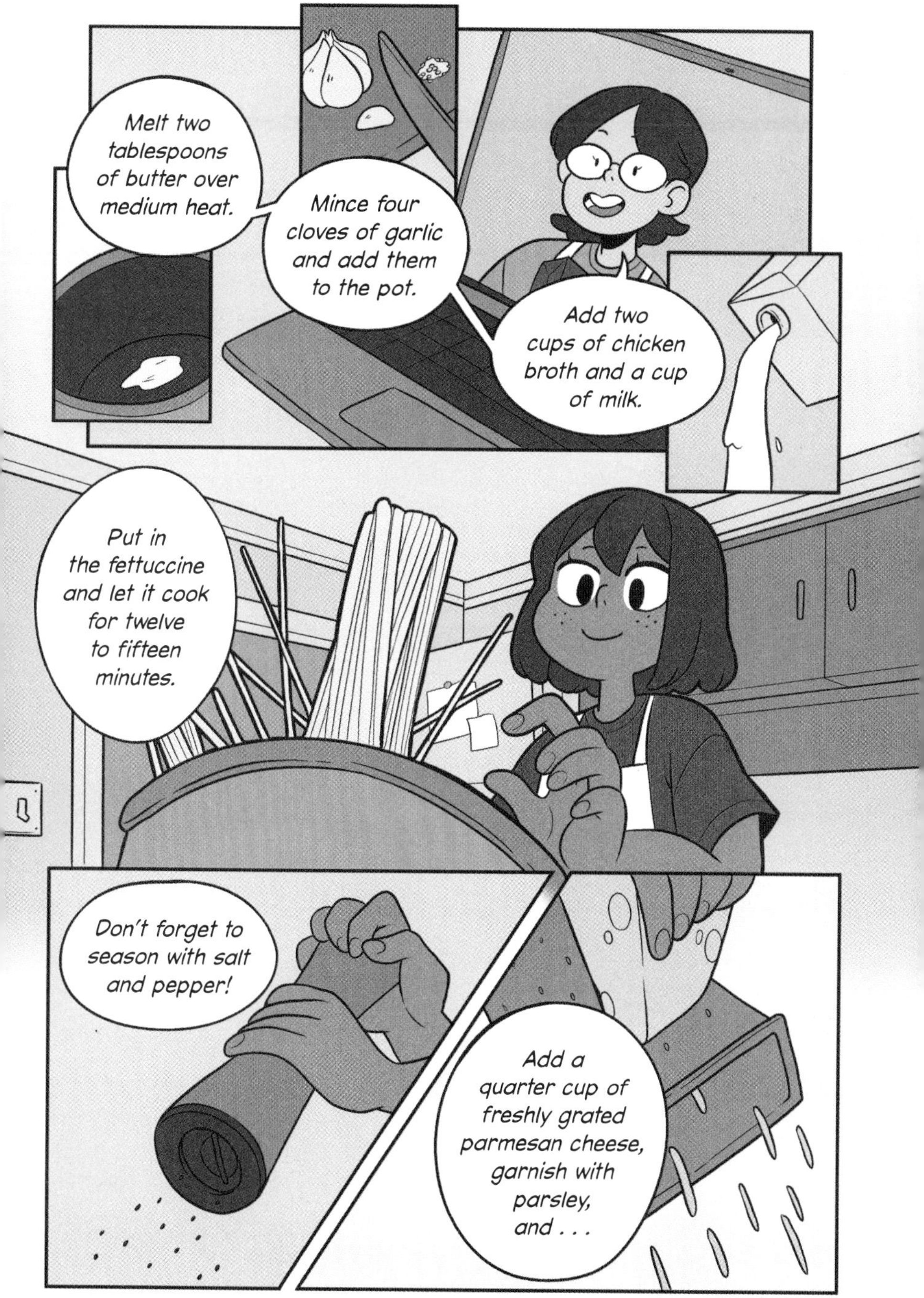
Melt two tablespoons of butter over medium heat.
Mince four cloves of garlic and add them to the pot.
Add two cups of chicken broth and a cup of milk.
Put in the fettuccine and let it cook for twelve to fifteen minutes.
Don't forget to season with salt and pepper!
Add a quarter cup of freshly grated parmesan cheese, garnish with parsley, and . . .

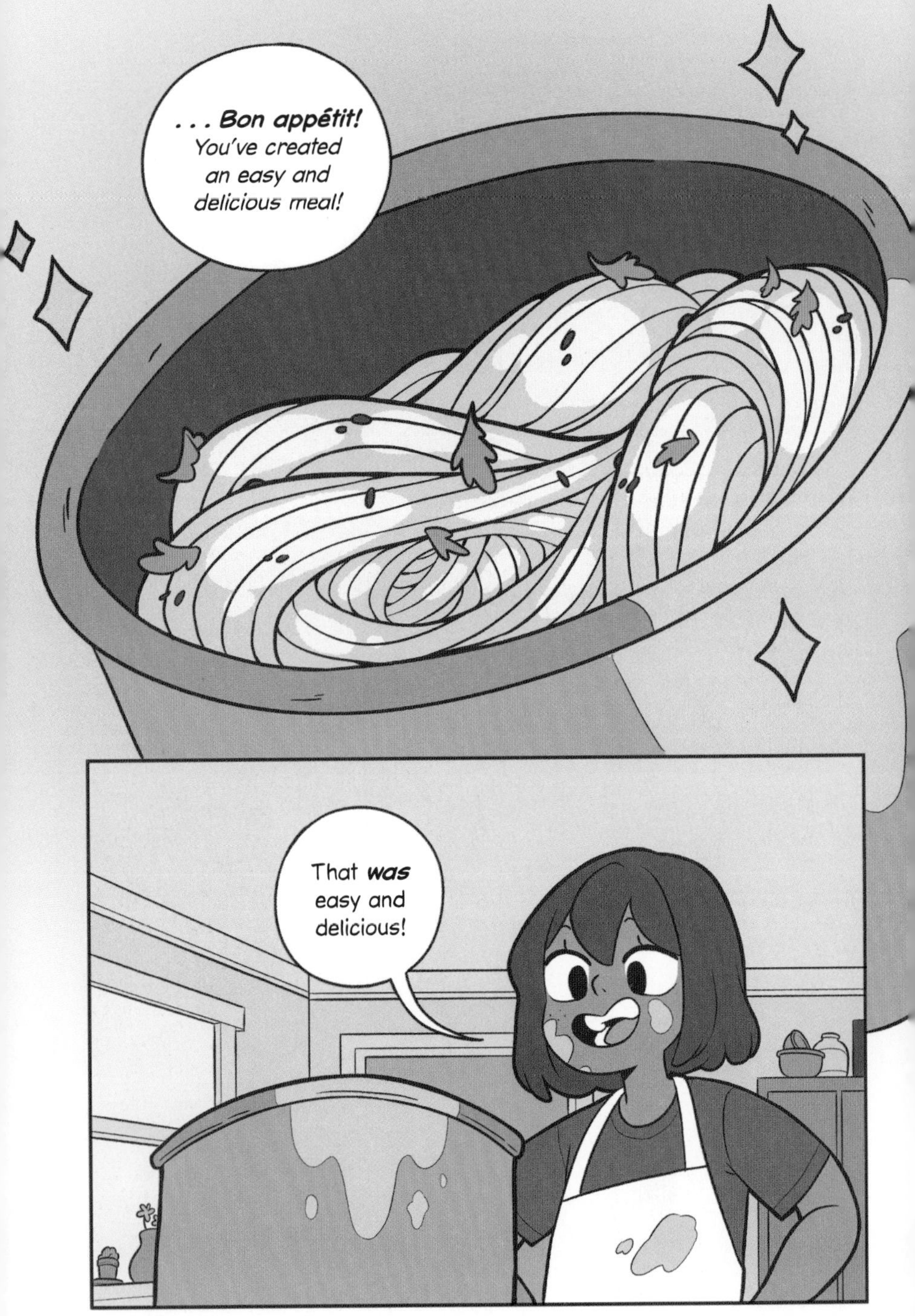
. . . Bon appêtit! You've created an easy and delicious meal!
That was easy and delicious!

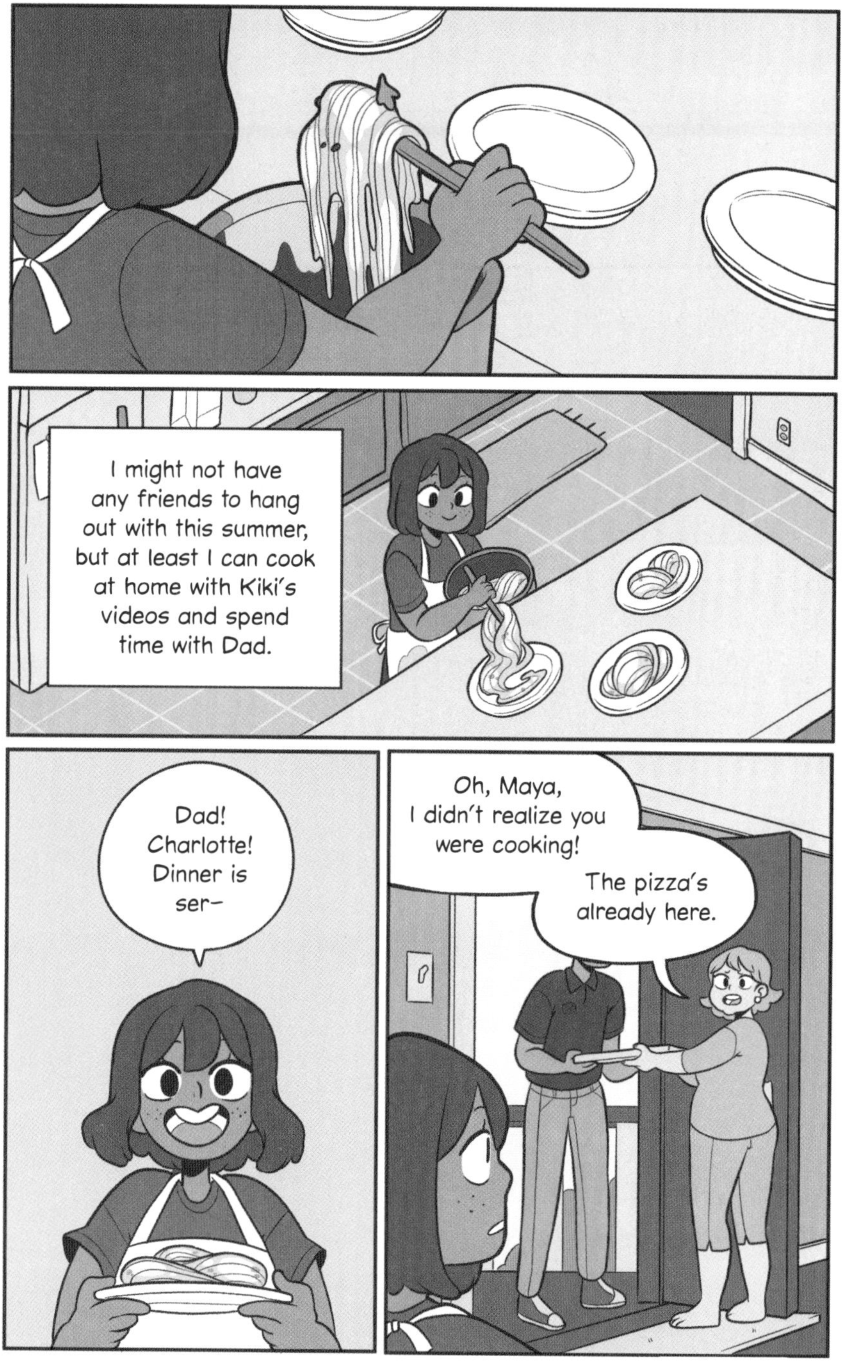
I might not have any friends to hang out with this summer, but at least I can cook at home with Kiki's videos and spend time with Dad.
Dad! Charlotte! Dinner is ser–
Oh, Maya, I didn't realize you were cooking!
The pizza's already here.

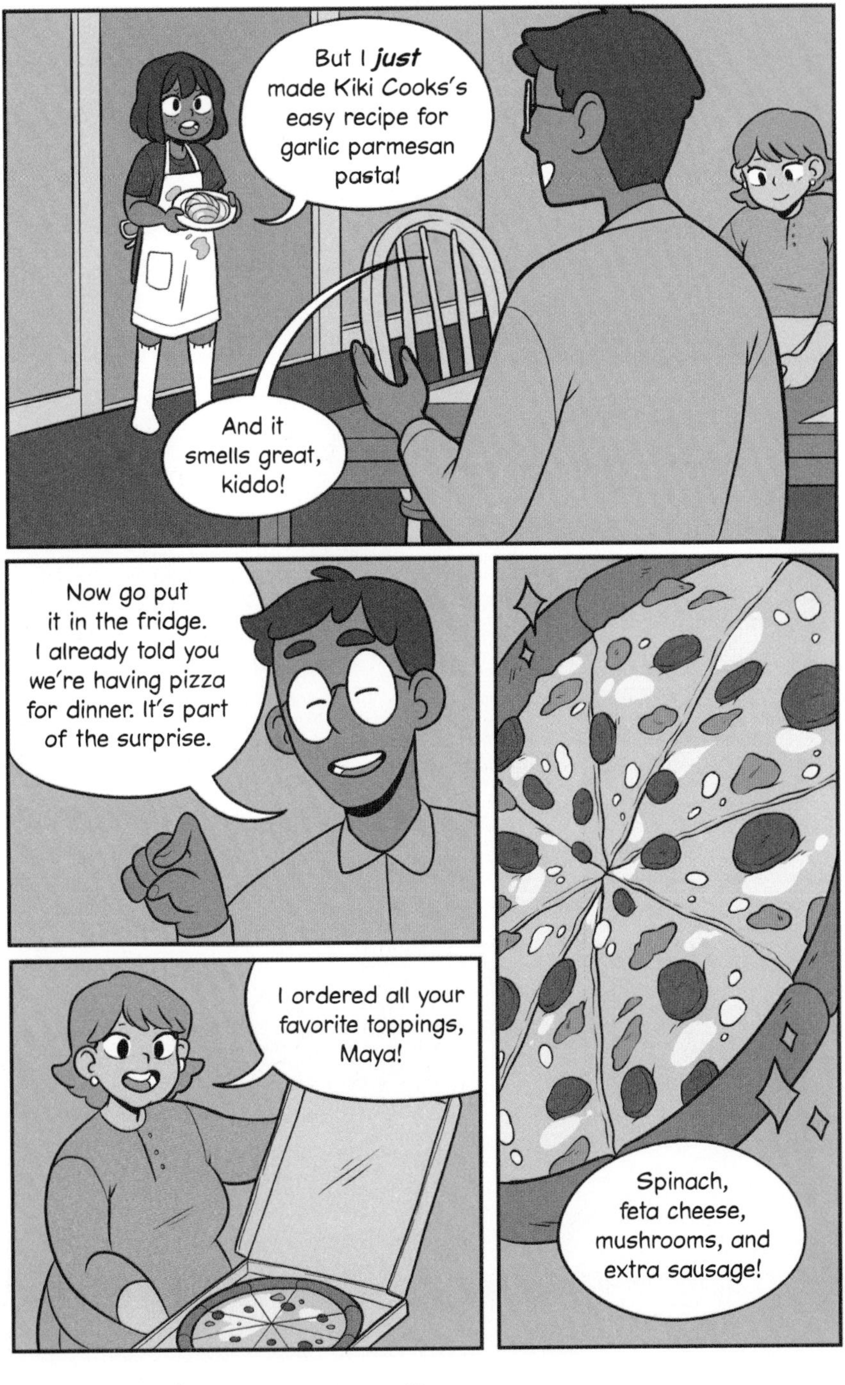
But I ***just*** made Kiki Cooks's easy recipe for garlic parmesan pasta!
And it smells great, kiddo!
Now go put it in the fridge. I already told you we're having pizza for dinner. It's part of the surprise.
I ordered all your favorite toppings, Maya!
Spinach, feta cheese, mushrooms, and extra sausage!

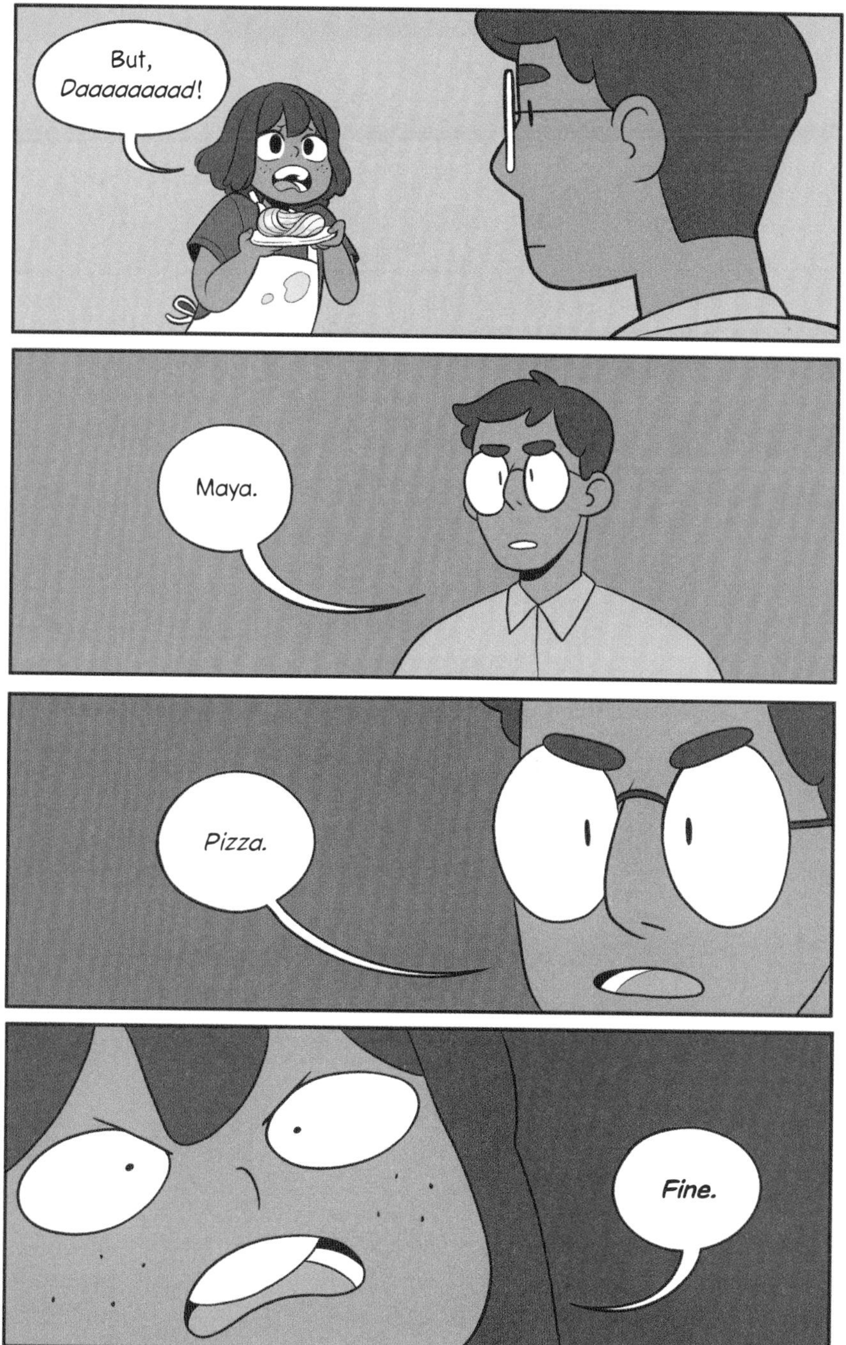
But, *Daaaaaaaad*!
Maya.
Pizza.
Fine.

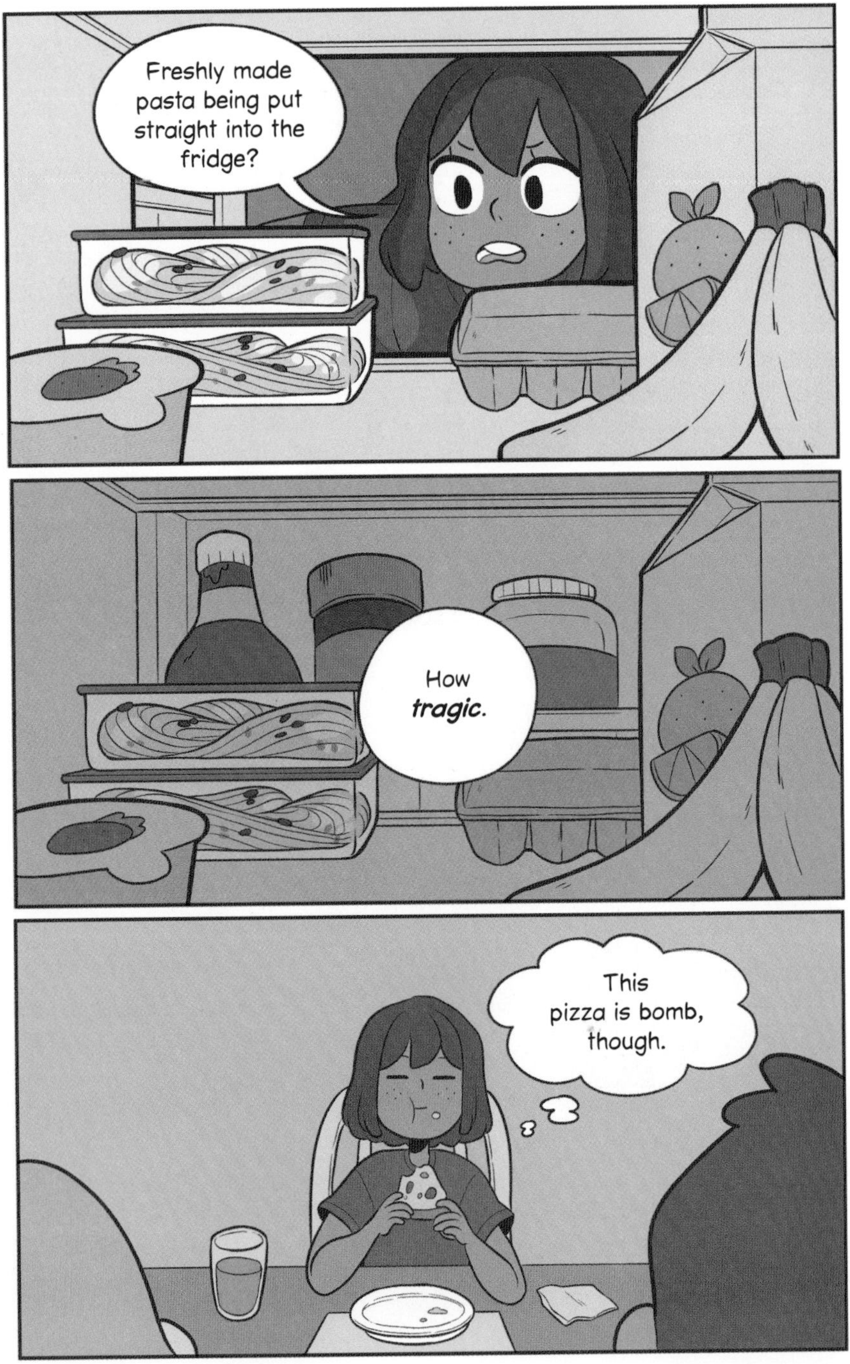
Freshly made pasta being put straight into the fridge?
How *tragic.*
This pizza is bomb, though.

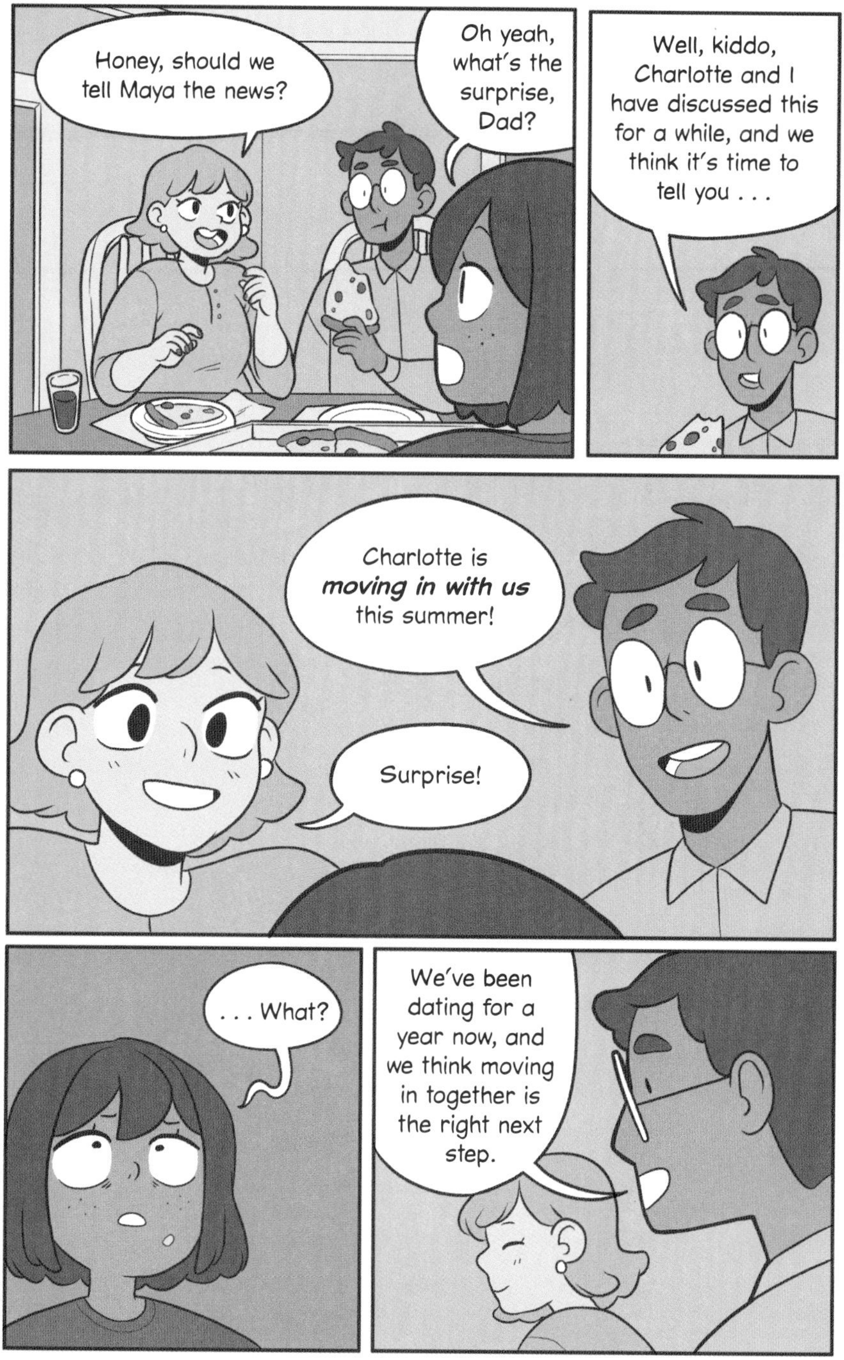
Honey, should we tell Maya the news?
Oh yeah, what's the surprise, Dad?
Well, kiddo, Charlotte and I have discussed this for a while, and we think it's time to tell you . . .
Charlotte is ***moving in with us*** this summer!
Surprise!
. . . What?
We've been dating for a year now, and we think moving in together is the right next step.

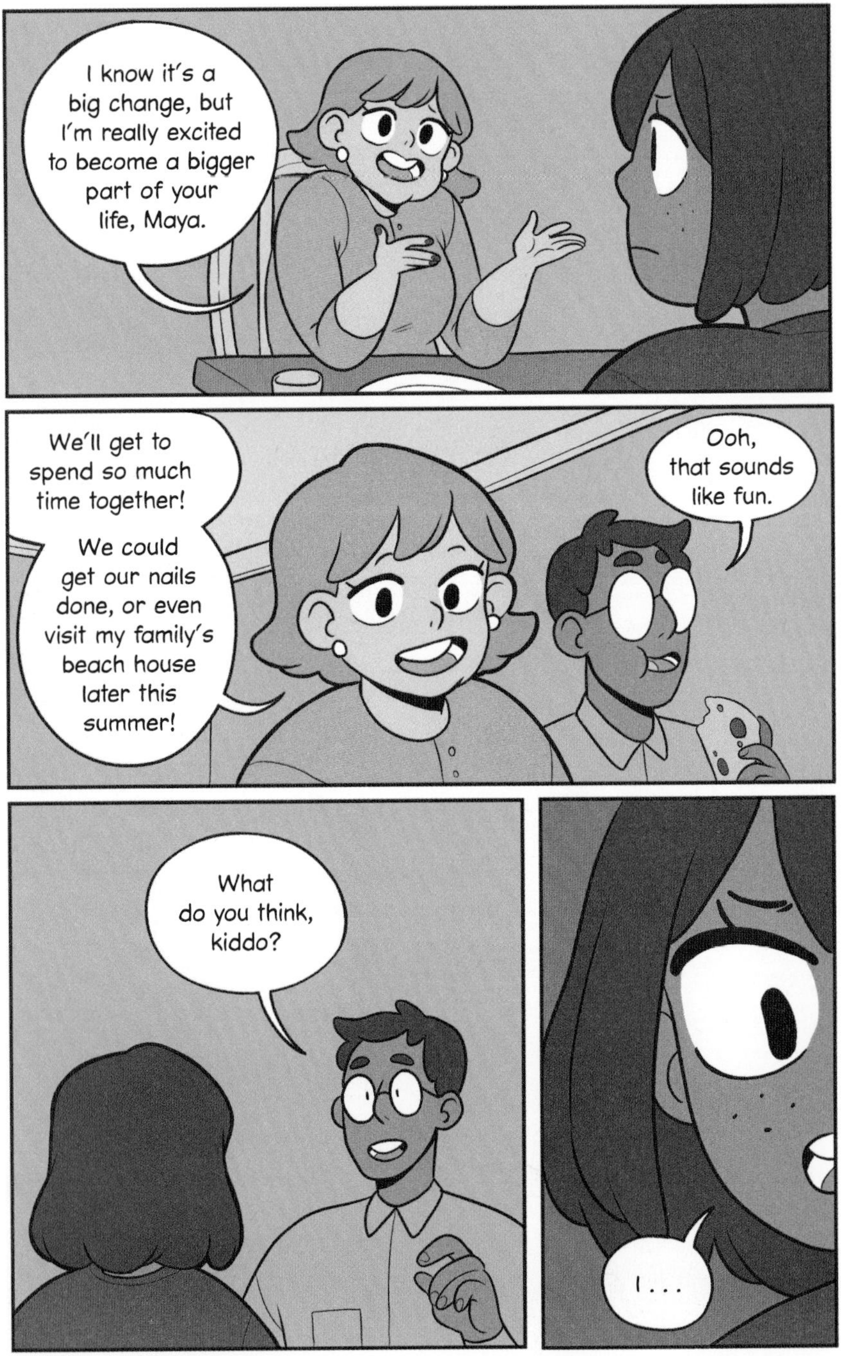
I know it's a big change, but I'm really excited to become a bigger part of your life, Maya.
We'll get to spend so much time together!
We could get our nails done, or even visit my family's beach house later this summer!
Ooh, that sounds like fun.
What do you think, kiddo?
I...

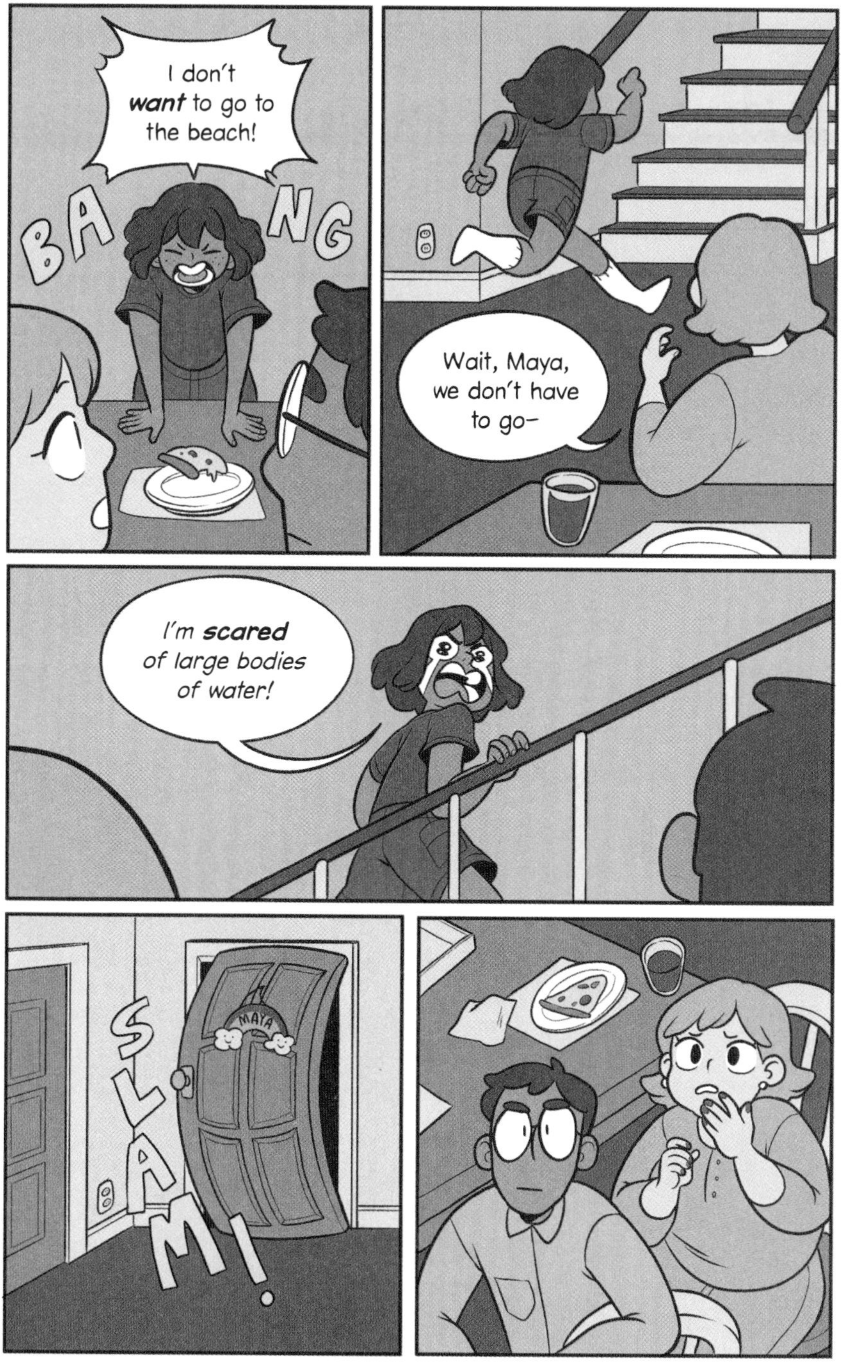
I don't **want** to go to the beach!
BANG
Wait, Maya, we don't have to go–
I'm ***scared*** *of large bodies of water!*
SLAM!
MAYA

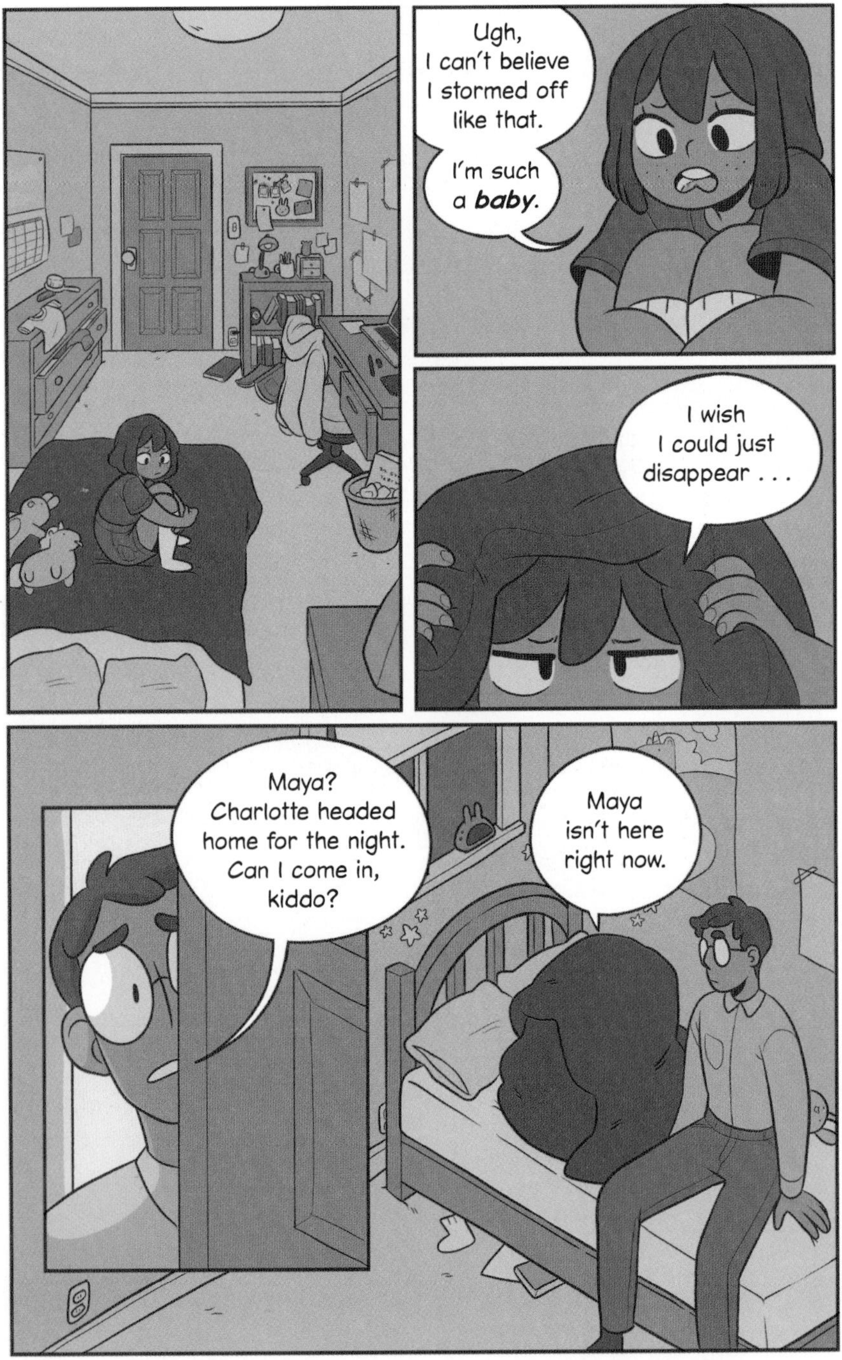
Ugh,
I can't believe
I stormed off
like that.
I'm such
a **baby**.
I wish
I could just
disappear . . .
Maya?
Charlotte headed
home for the night.
Can I come in,
kiddo?
Maya
isn't here
right now.

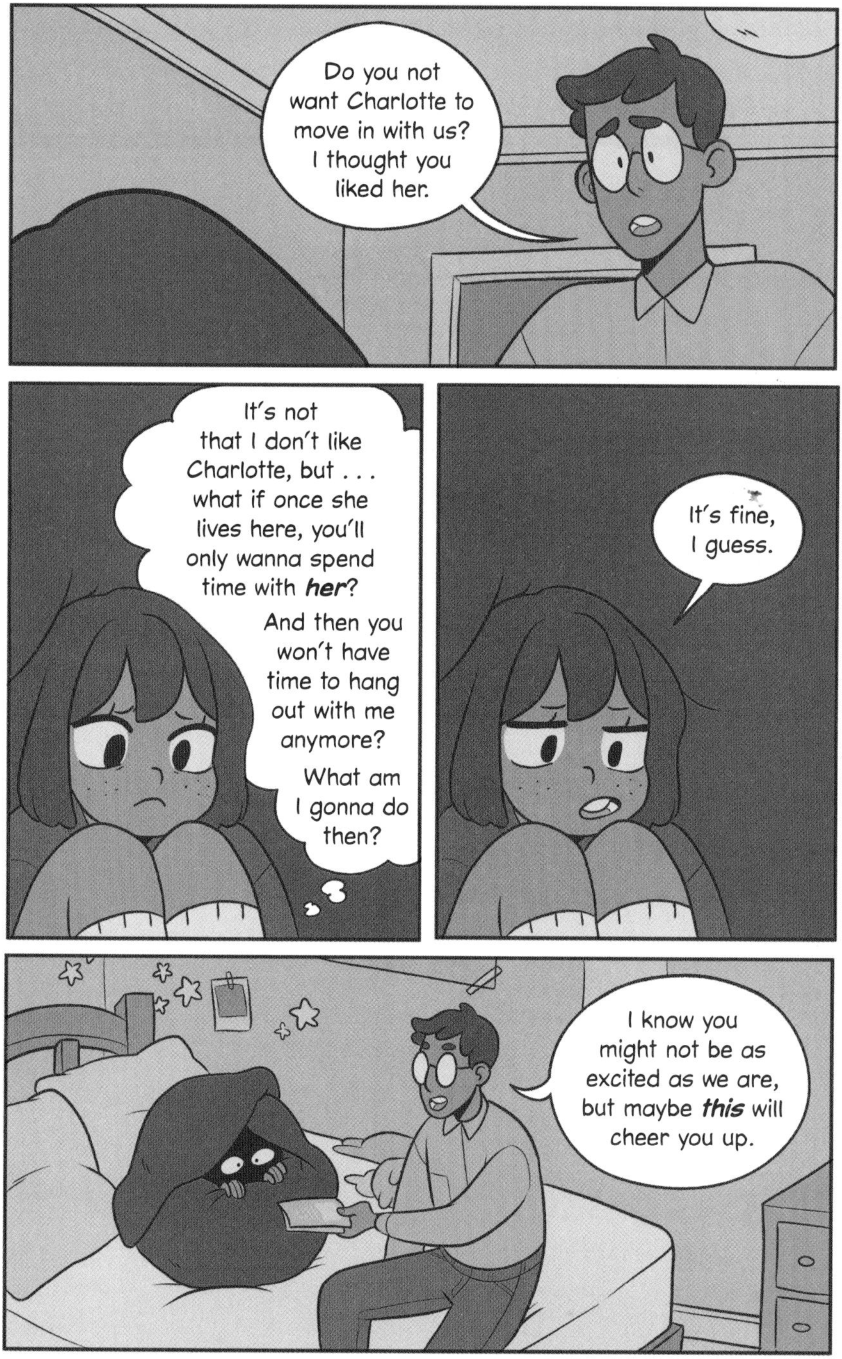
Do you not want Charlotte to move in with us? I thought you liked her.
It's not that I don't like Charlotte, but . . . what if once she lives here, you'll only wanna spend time with ***her***?
And then you won't have time to hang out with me anymore?
What am I gonna do then?
It's fine, I guess.
I know you might not be as excited as we are, but maybe ***this*** will cheer you up.

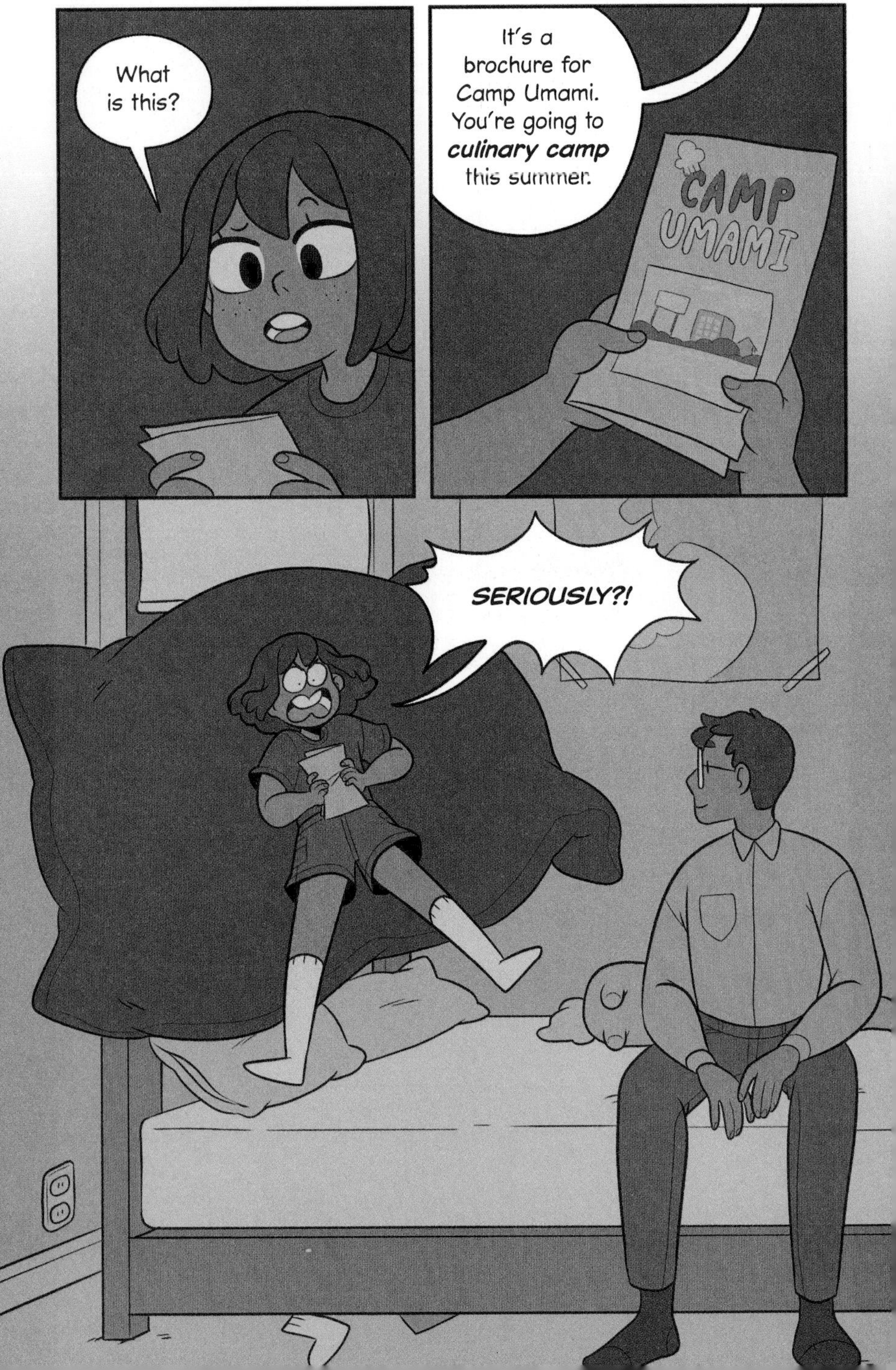
What is this?
It's a brochure for Camp Umami. You're going to ***culinary camp*** this summer.
CAMP UMAMI
SERIOUSLY?!

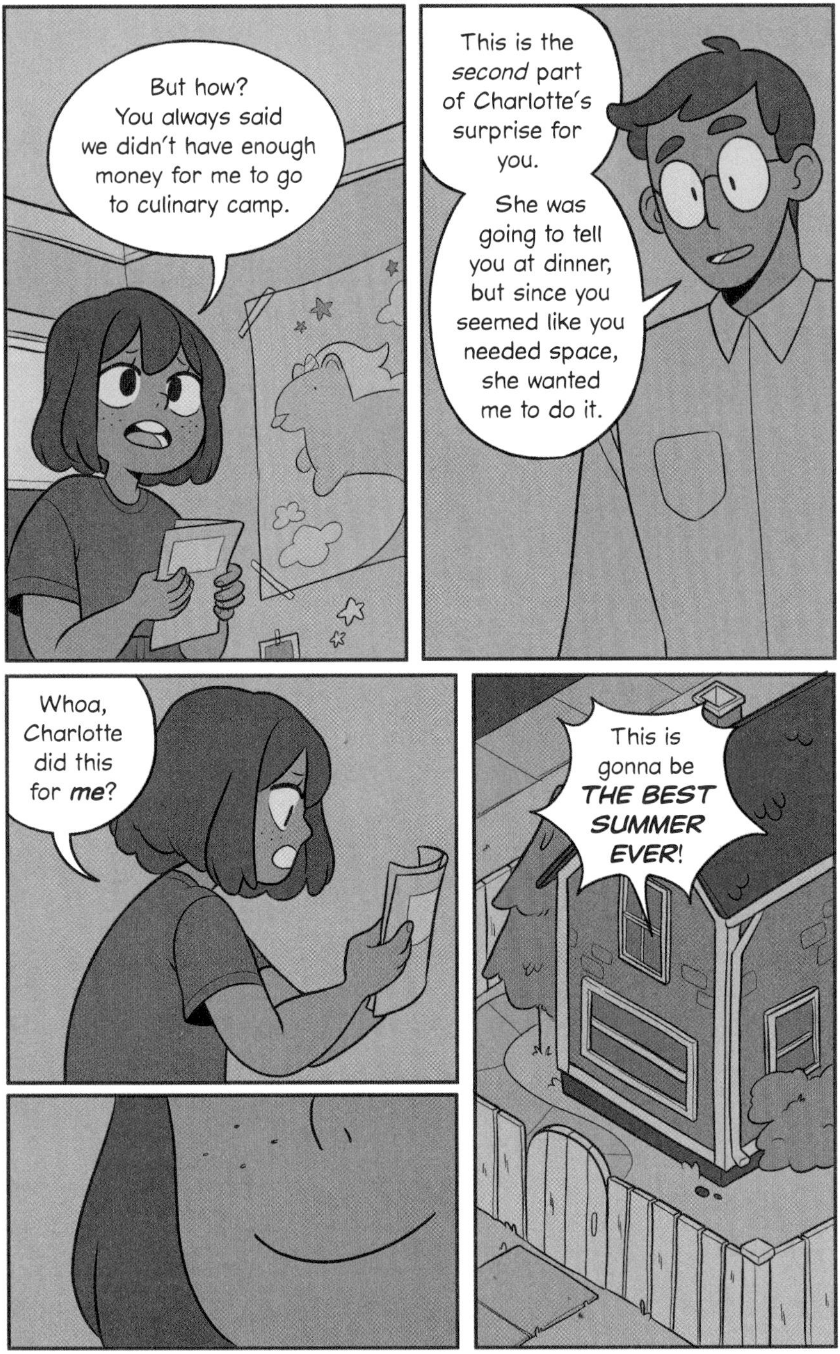
But how? You always said we didn't have enough money for me to go to culinary camp.
This is the *second* part of Charlotte's surprise for you.
She was going to tell you at dinner, but since you seemed like you needed space, she wanted me to do it.
Whoa, Charlotte did this for ***me***?
This is gonna be ***THE BEST SUMMER EVER***!

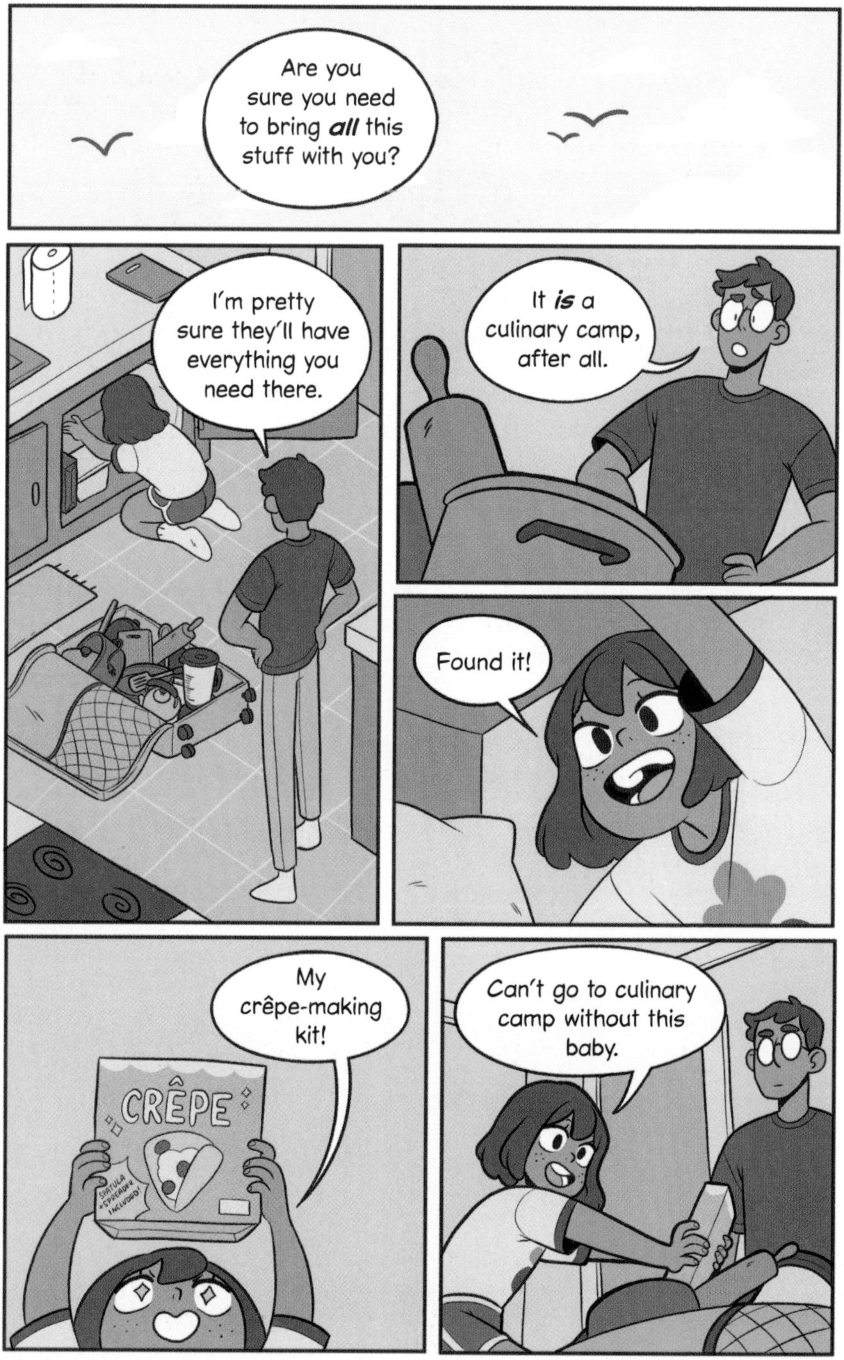
Are you sure you need to bring ***all*** this stuff with you?
I'm pretty sure they'll have everything you need there.
It ***is*** a culinary camp, after all.
Found it!
My crêpe-making kit!
CRÊPE
SPATULA + SPREADER INCLUDED!
Can't go to culinary camp without this baby.

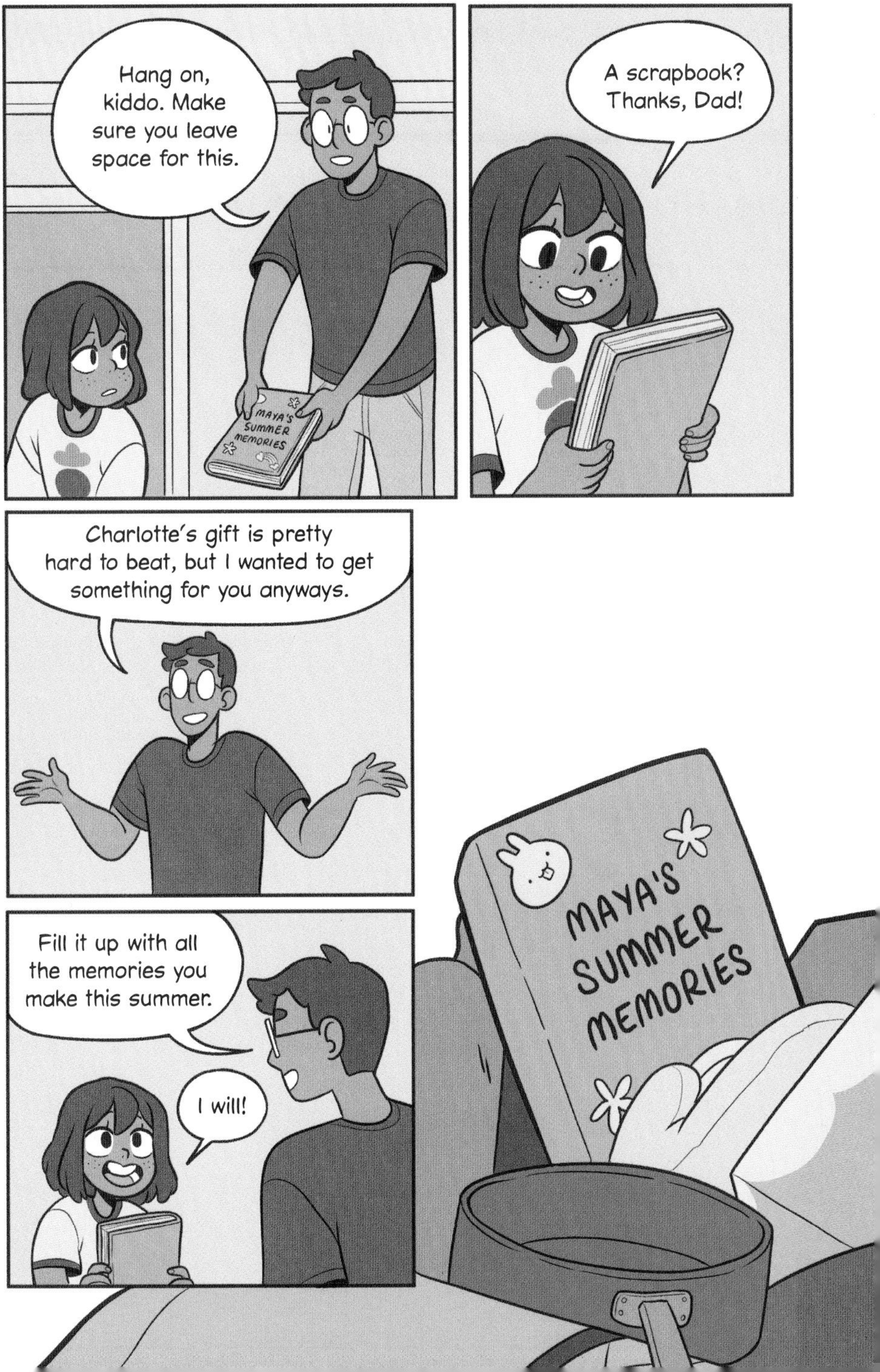
Hang on, kiddo. Make sure you leave space for this.
MAYA'S SUMMER MEMORIES
A scrapbook? Thanks, Dad!
Charlotte's gift is pretty hard to beat, but I wanted to get something for you anyways.
Fill it up with all the memories you make this summer.
I will!
MAYA'S SUMMER MEMORIES

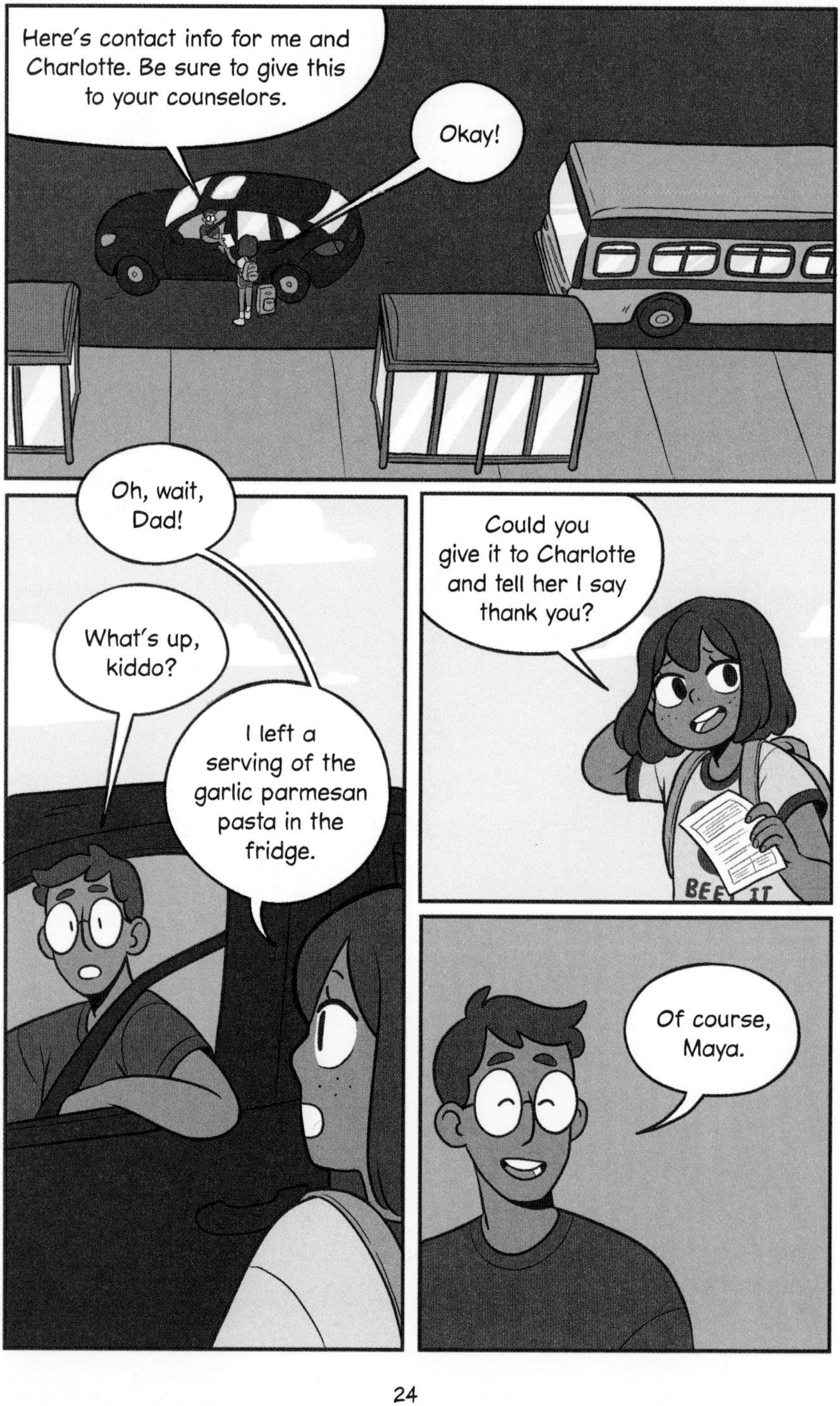
Here's contact info for me and Charlotte. Be sure to give this to your counselors.
Okay!
Oh, wait, Dad!
What's up, kiddo?
I left a serving of the garlic parmesan pasta in the fridge.
Could you give it to Charlotte and tell her I say thank you?
Of course, Maya.

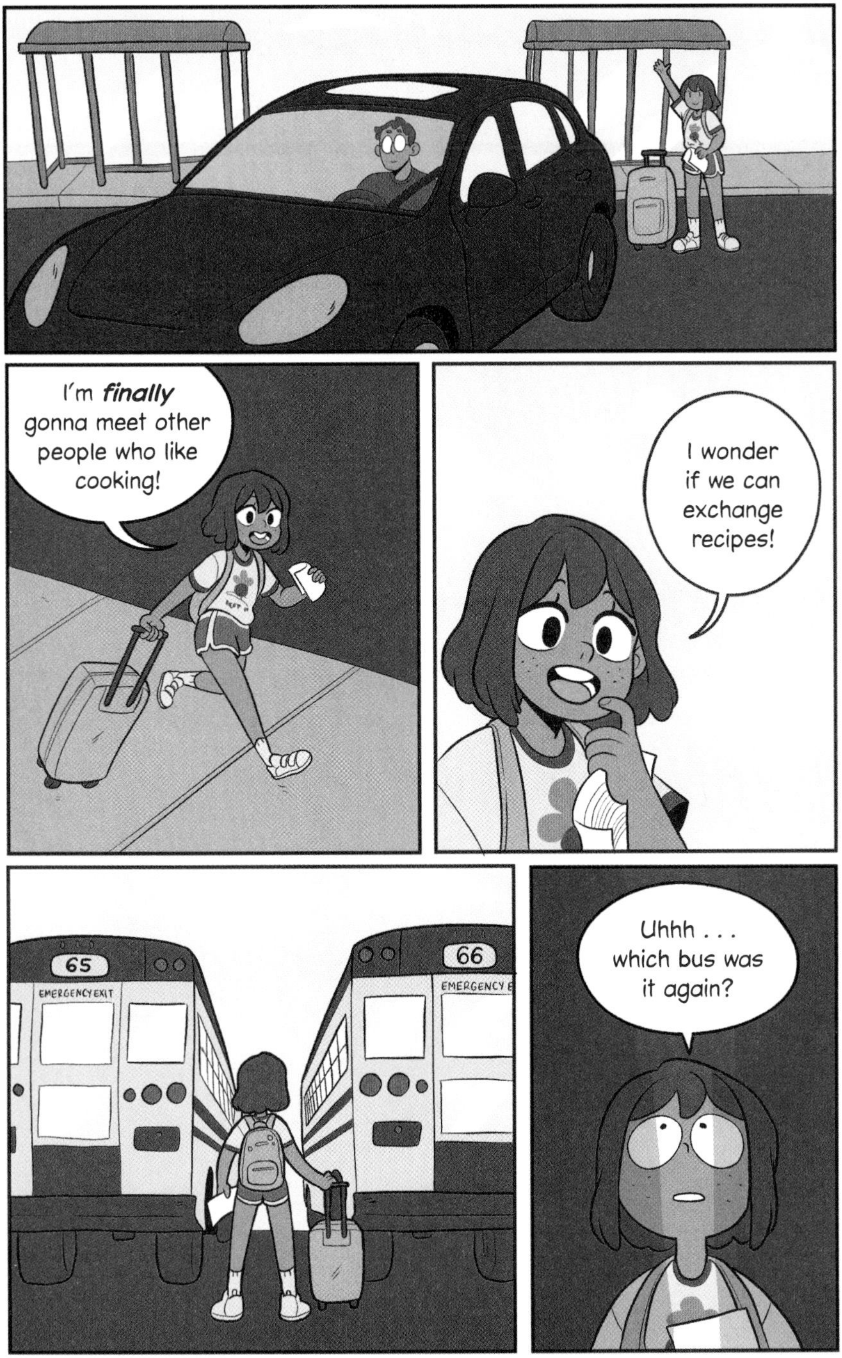

I'm *finally* gonna meet other people who like cooking!
I wonder if we can exchange recipes!
65
EMERGENCY EXIT
66
EMERGENCY E
Uhhh . . . which bus was it again?

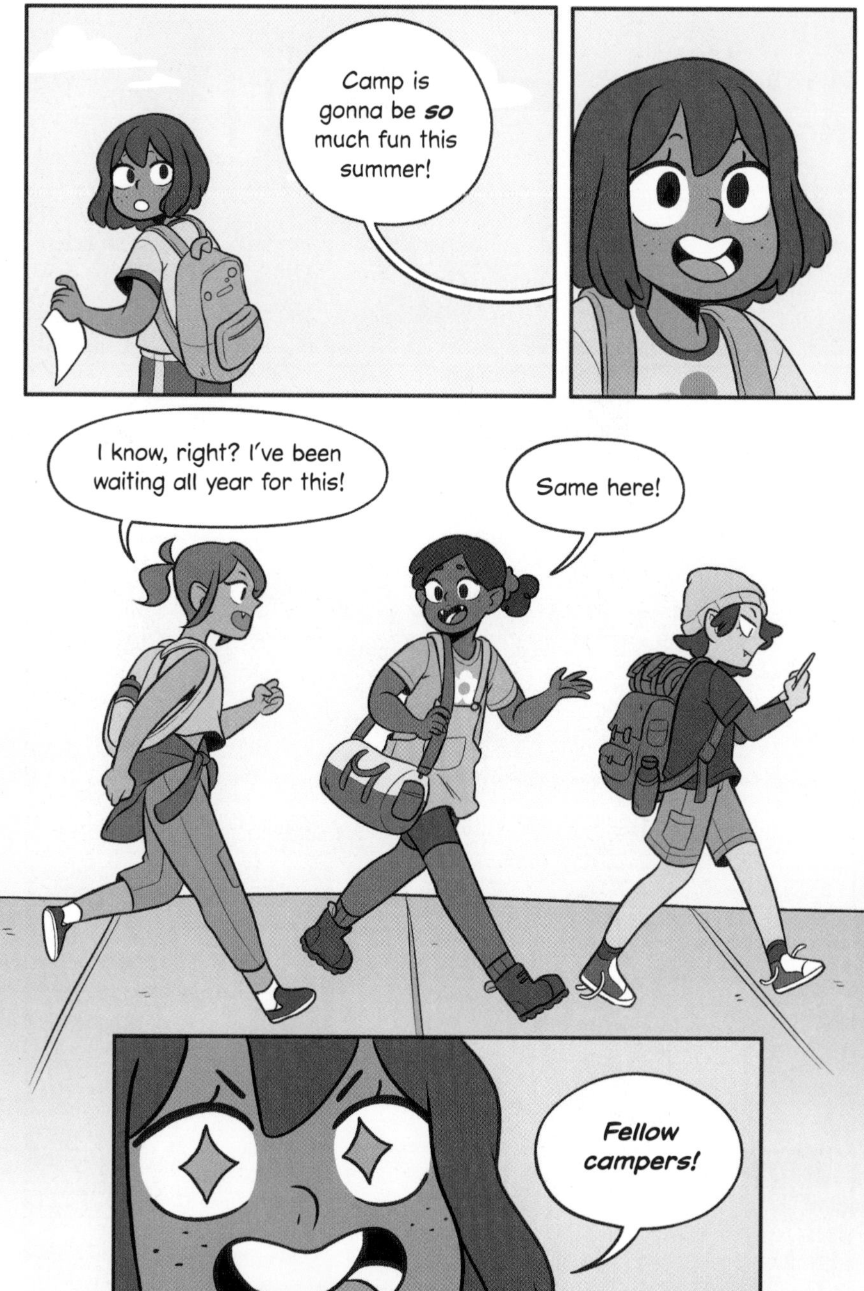
Camp is gonna be *so* much fun this summer!
I know, right? I've been waiting all year for this!
Same here!
Fellow campers!

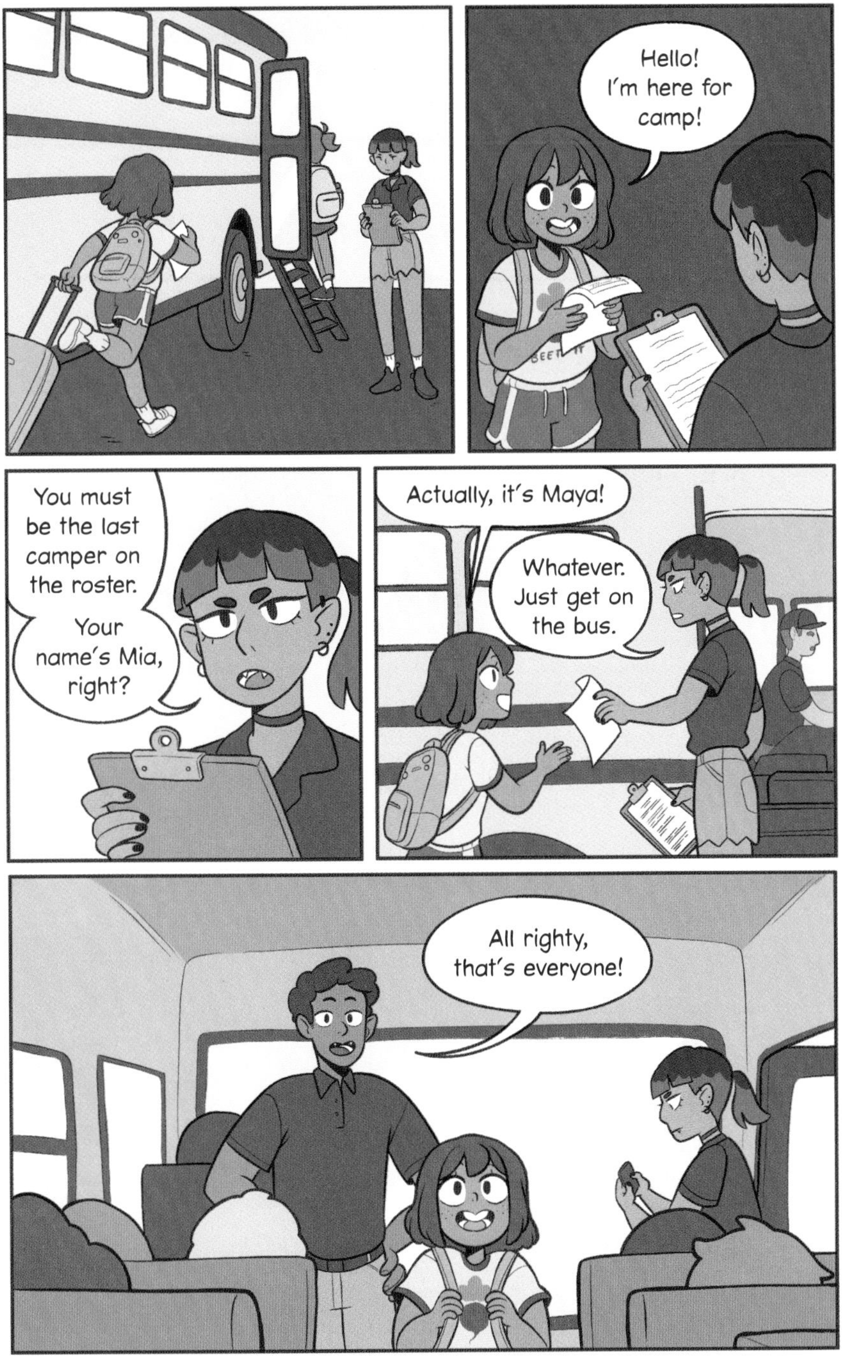
Hello! I'm here for camp!
You must be the last camper on the roster.
Your name's Mia, right?
Actually, it's Maya!
Whatever. Just get on the bus.
All righty, that's everyone!

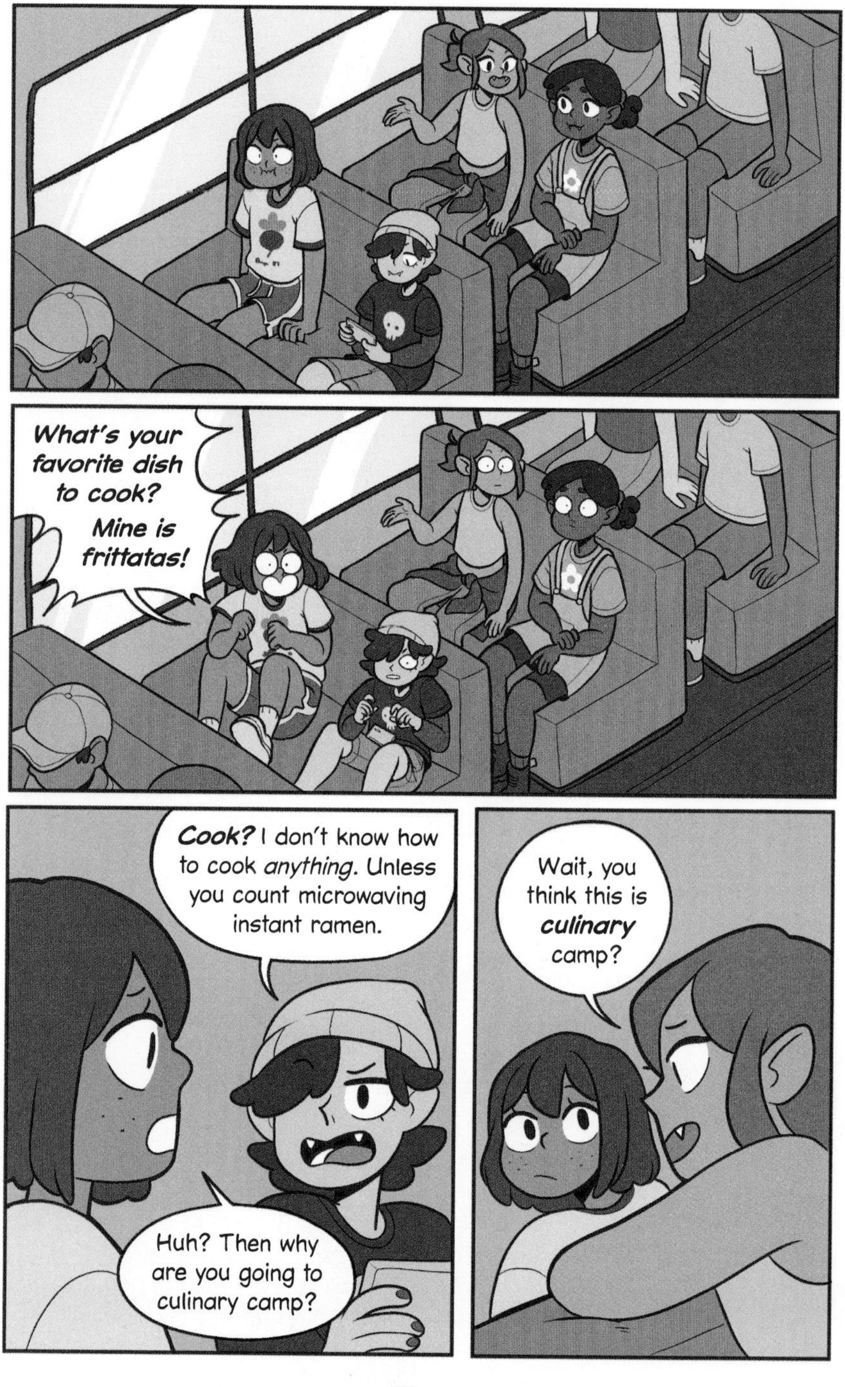
What's your favorite dish to cook? Mine is frittatas!
Cook? I don't know how to cook anything. Unless you count microwaving instant ramen.
Huh? Then why are you going to culinary camp?
Wait, you think this is culinary camp?

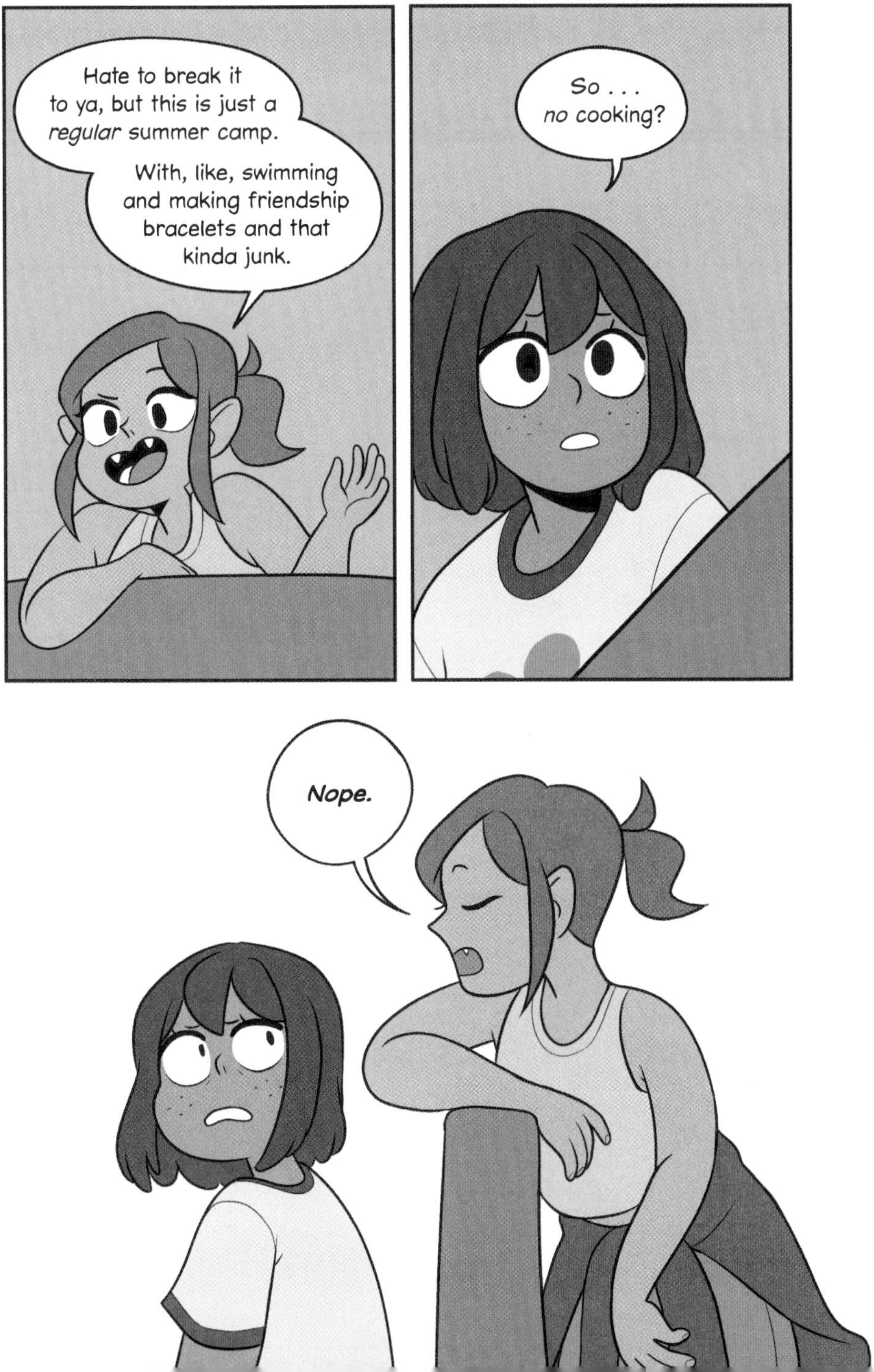
Hate to break it to ya, but this is just a *regular* summer camp.
With, like, swimming and making friendship bracelets and that kinda junk.
So . . . *no cooking?*
Nope.

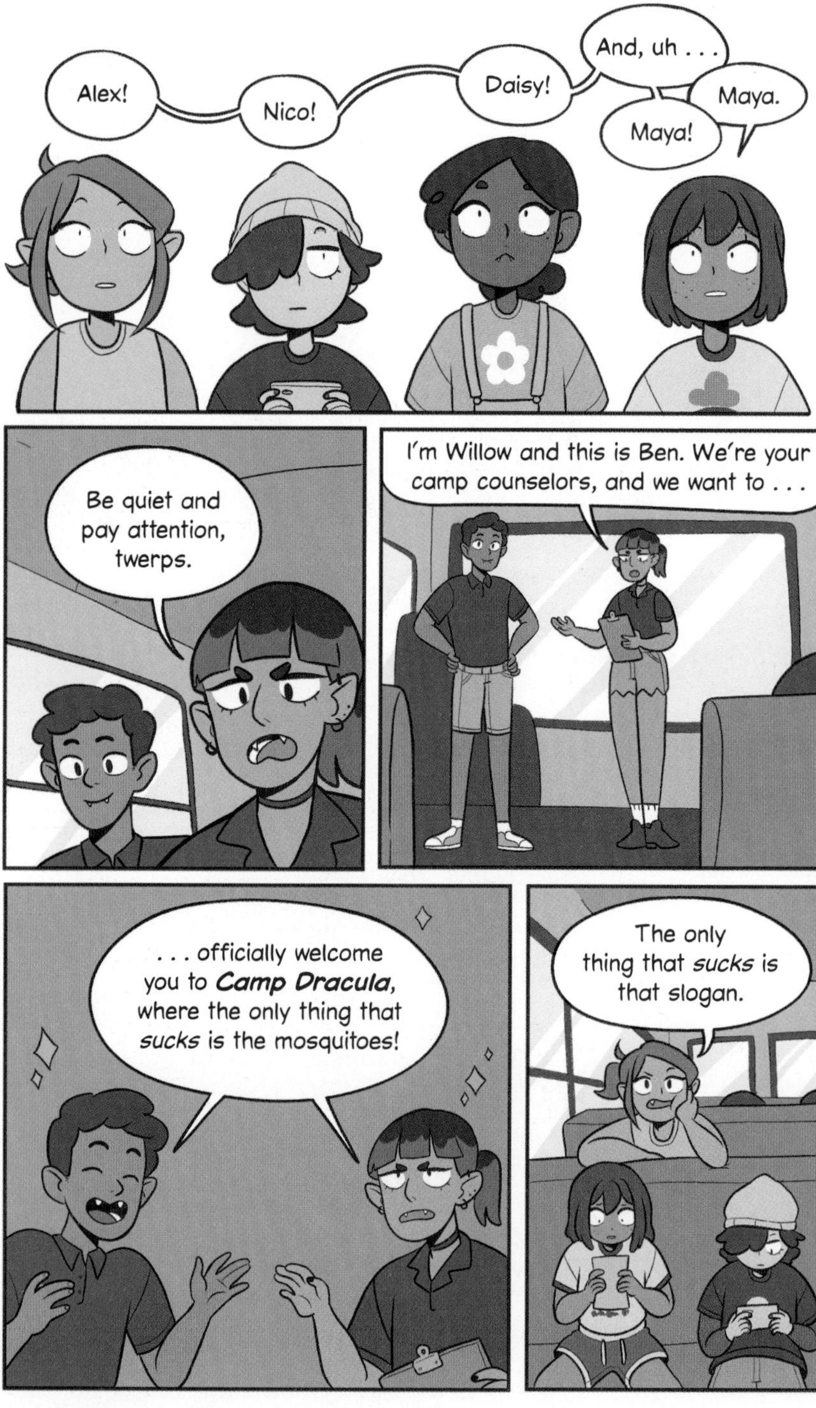
Alex!
Nico!
Daisy!
And, uh . . .
Maya!
Maya.
Be quiet and pay attention, twerps.
I'm Willow and this is Ben. We're your camp counselors, and we want to . . .
. . . officially welcome you to **Camp Dracula**, where the only thing that *sucks* is the mosquitoes!
The only thing that *sucks* is that slogan.

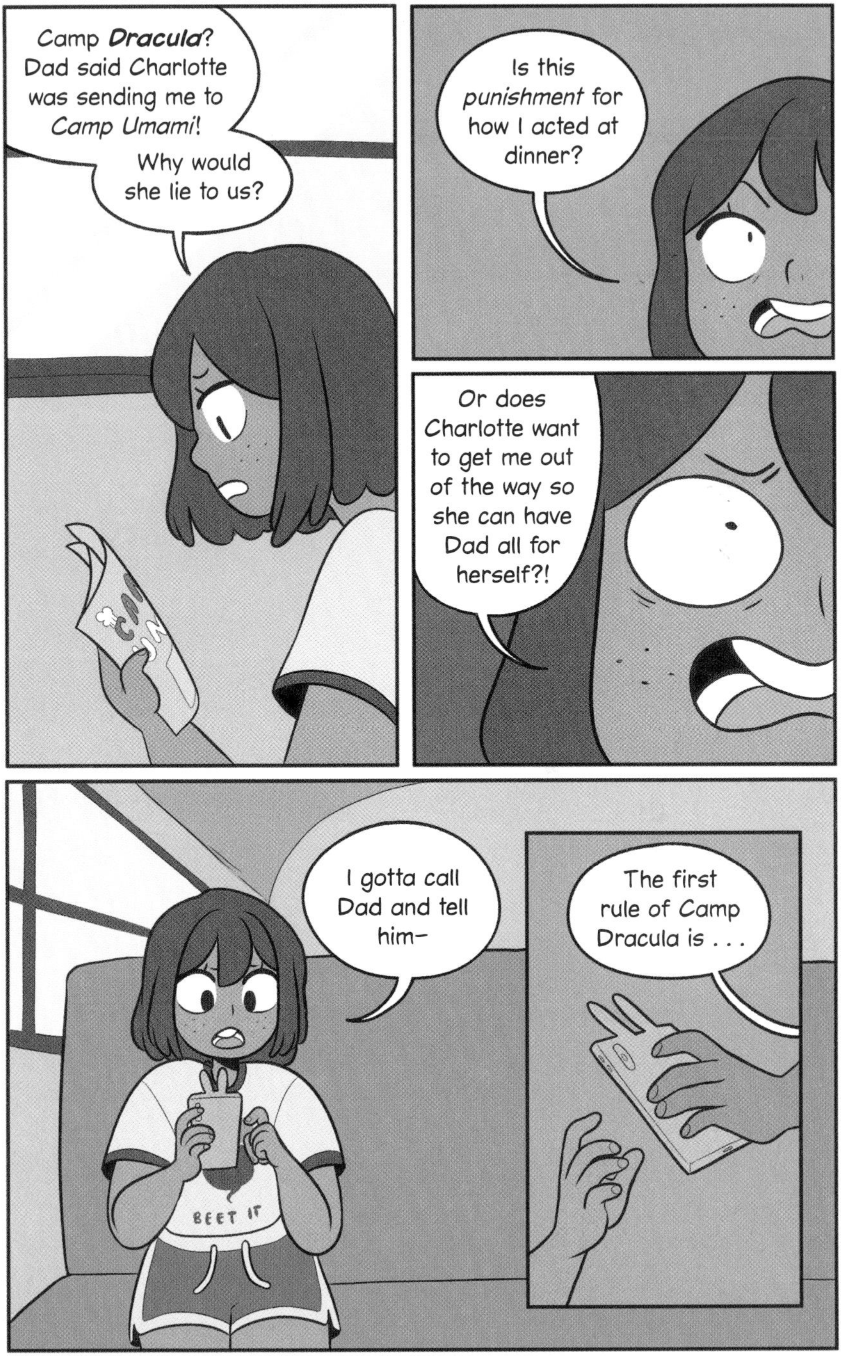
Camp **Dracula**? Dad said Charlotte was sending me to *Camp Umami*!
Why would she lie to us?
Is this *punishment* for how I acted at dinner?
Or does Charlotte want to get me out of the way so she can have Dad all for herself?!
BEET IT
I gotta call Dad and tell him–
The first rule of Camp Dracula is . . .

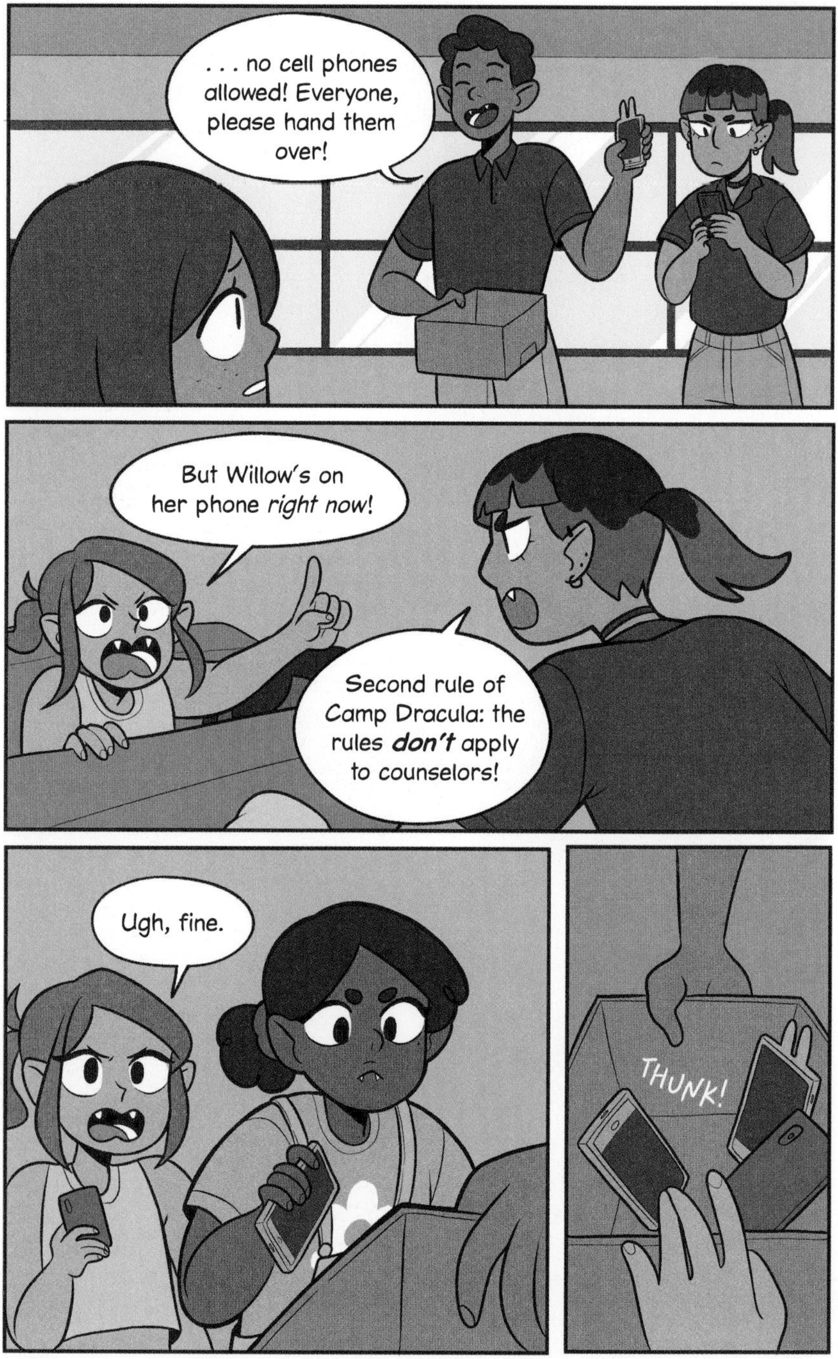
. . . no cell phones allowed! Everyone, please hand them over!
But Willow's on her phone *right now*!
Second rule of Camp Dracula: the rules ***don't*** apply to counselors!
Ugh, fine.
THUNK!

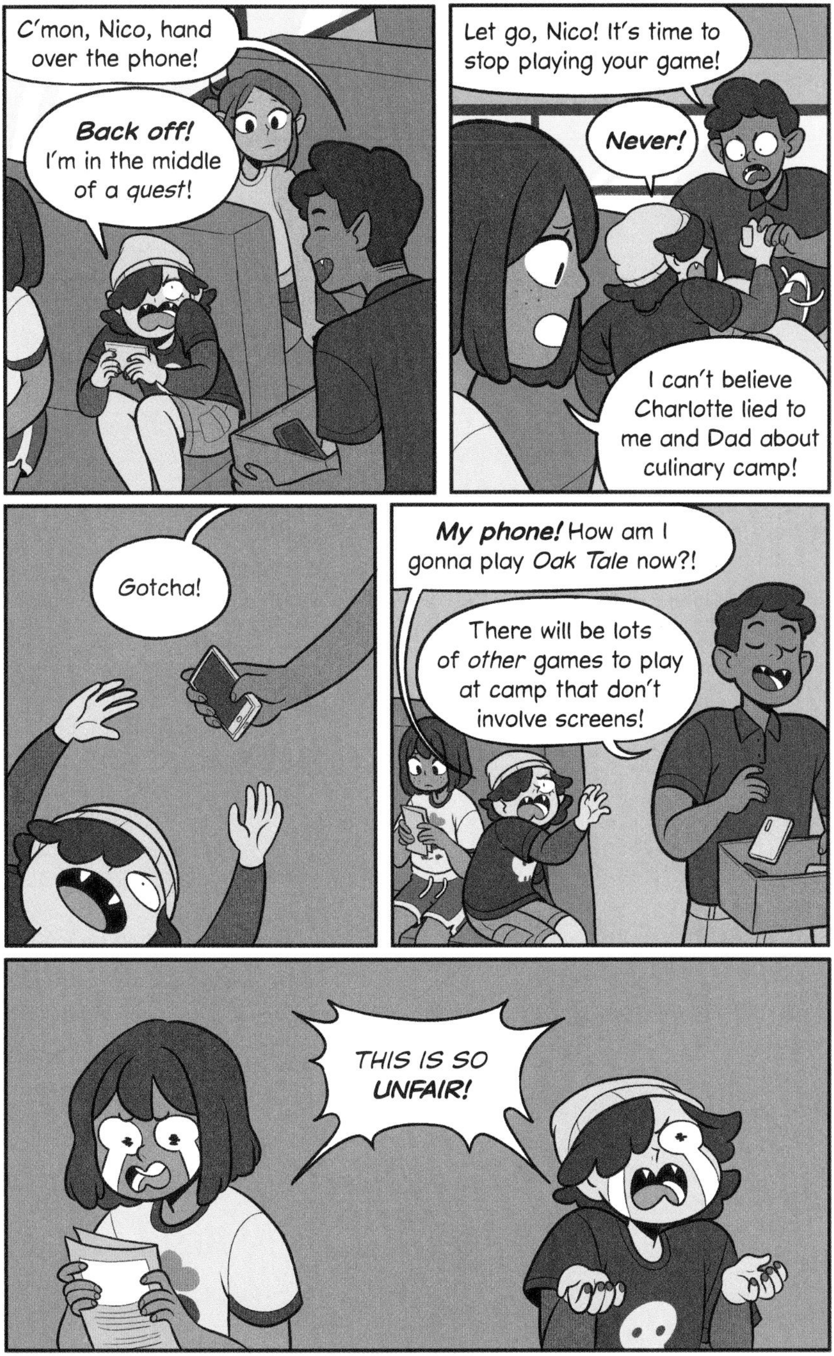
C'mon, Nico, hand over the phone!
Back off! I'm in the middle of a *quest*!
Let go, Nico! It's time to stop playing your game!
Never!
I can't believe Charlotte lied to me and Dad about culinary camp!
Gotcha!
My phone! How am I gonna play *Oak Tale* now?!
There will be lots of *other* games to play at camp that don't involve screens!
THIS IS SO **UNFAIR!**

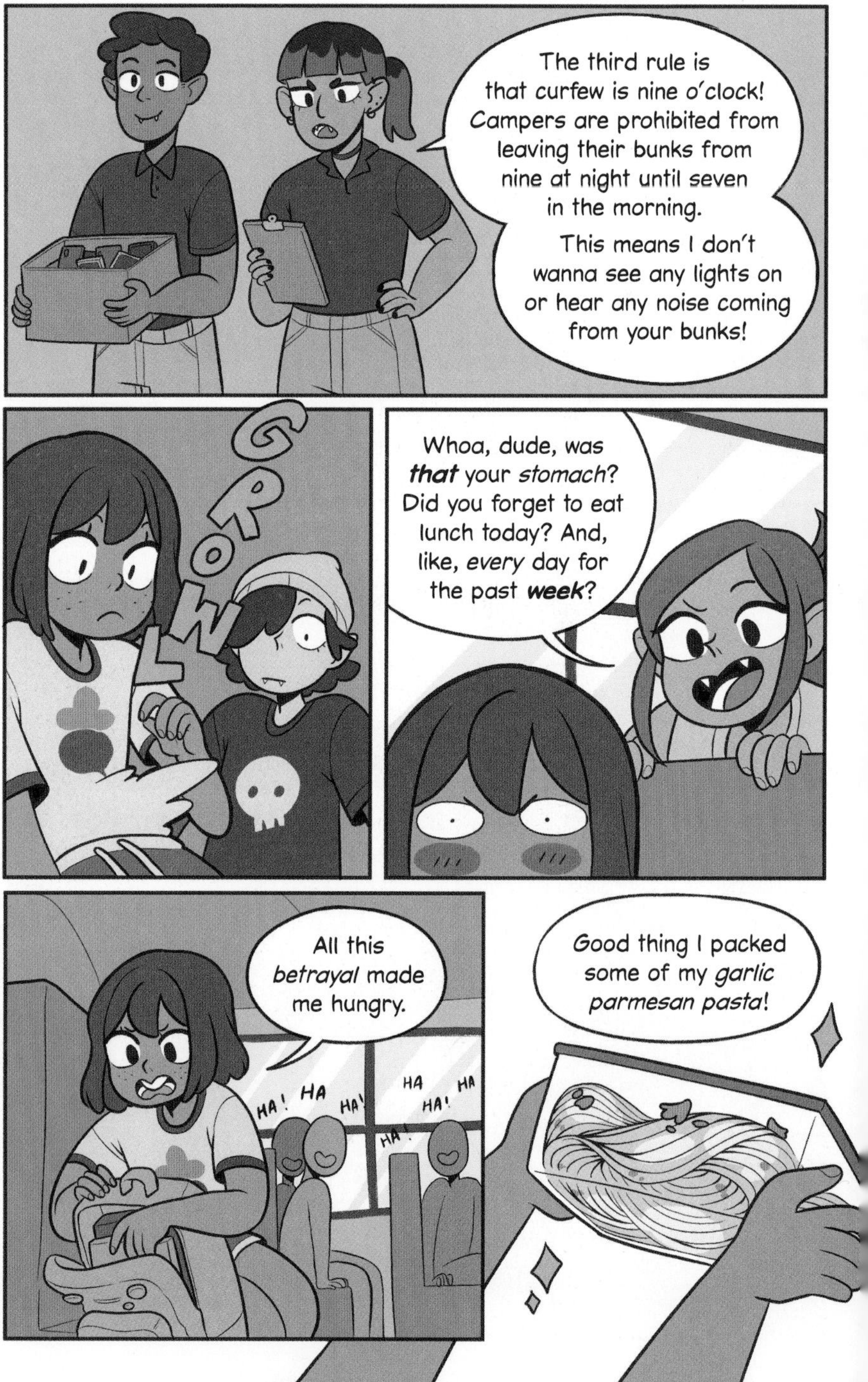
The third rule is that curfew is nine o'clock! Campers are prohibited from leaving their bunks from nine at night until seven in the morning.
This means I don't wanna see any lights on or hear any noise coming from your bunks!
GROWL
Whoa, dude, was *that* your *stomach*? Did you forget to eat lunch today? And, like, *every* day for the past *week*?
All this *betrayal* made me hungry.
HA! HA HA! HA HA HA! HA!
Good thing I packed some of my *garlic parmesan pasta*!

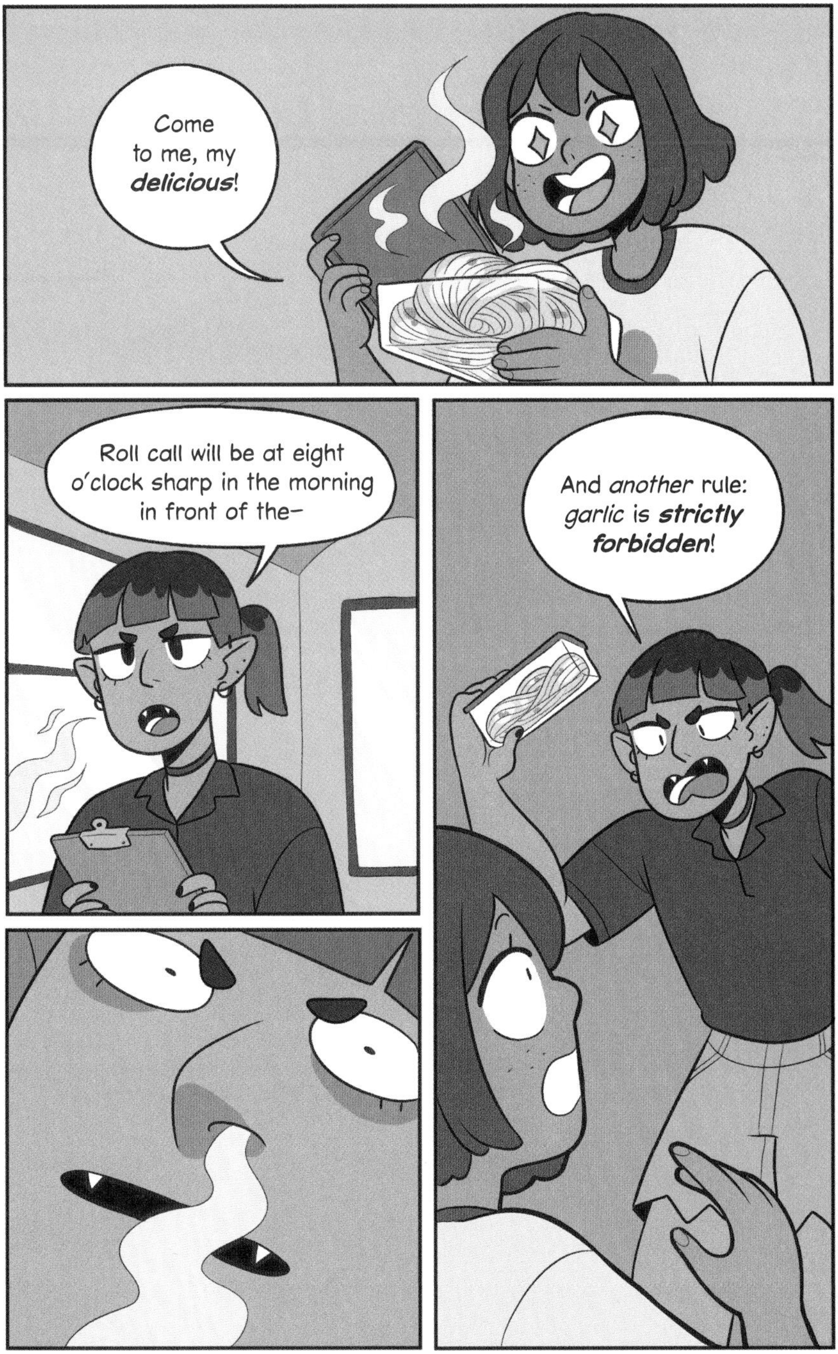
Come to me, my ***delicious***!
Roll call will be at eight o'clock sharp in the morning in front of the–
And *another* rule: *garlic* is ***strictly forbidden***!

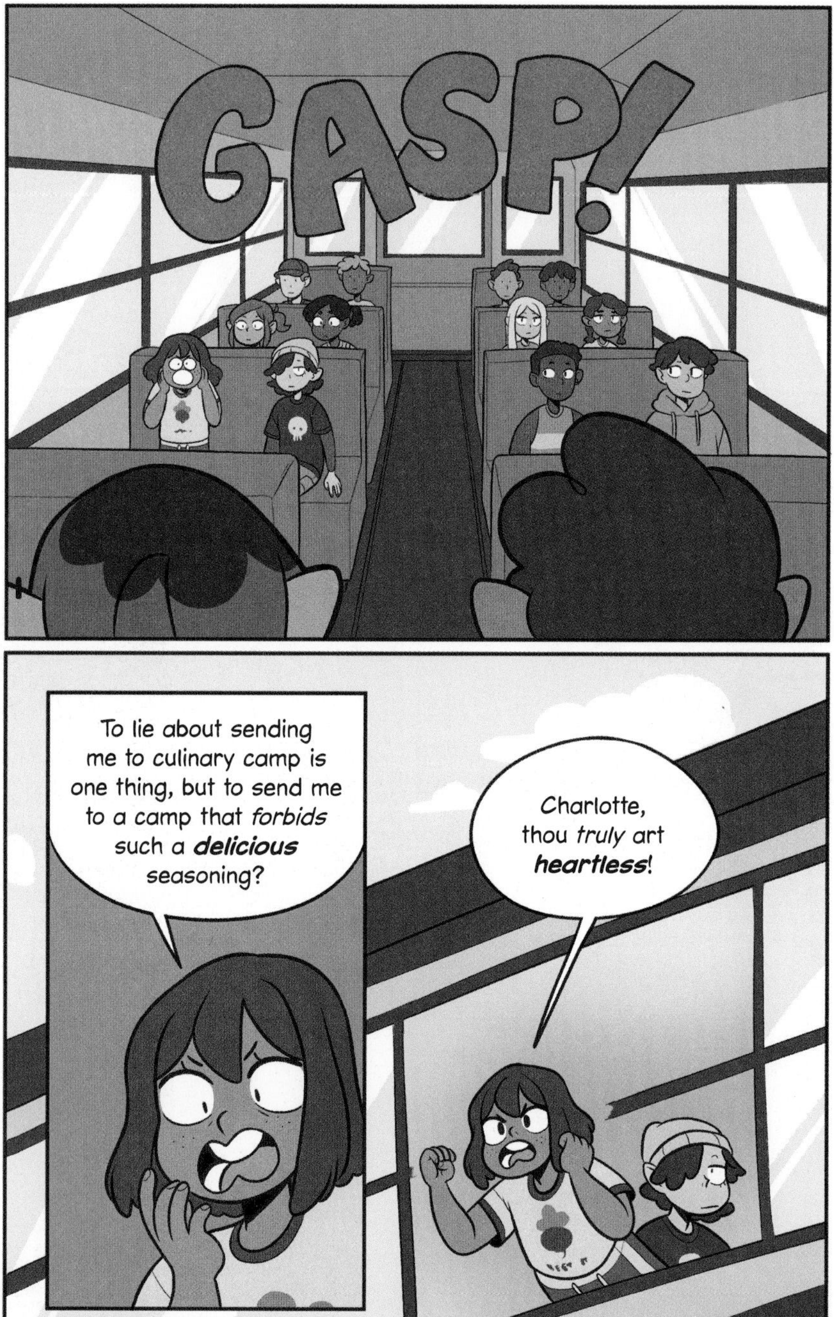
GASP!
To lie about sending me to culinary camp is one thing, but to send me to a camp that *forbids* such a ***delicious*** seasoning?
Charlotte, thou *truly* art ***heartless***!

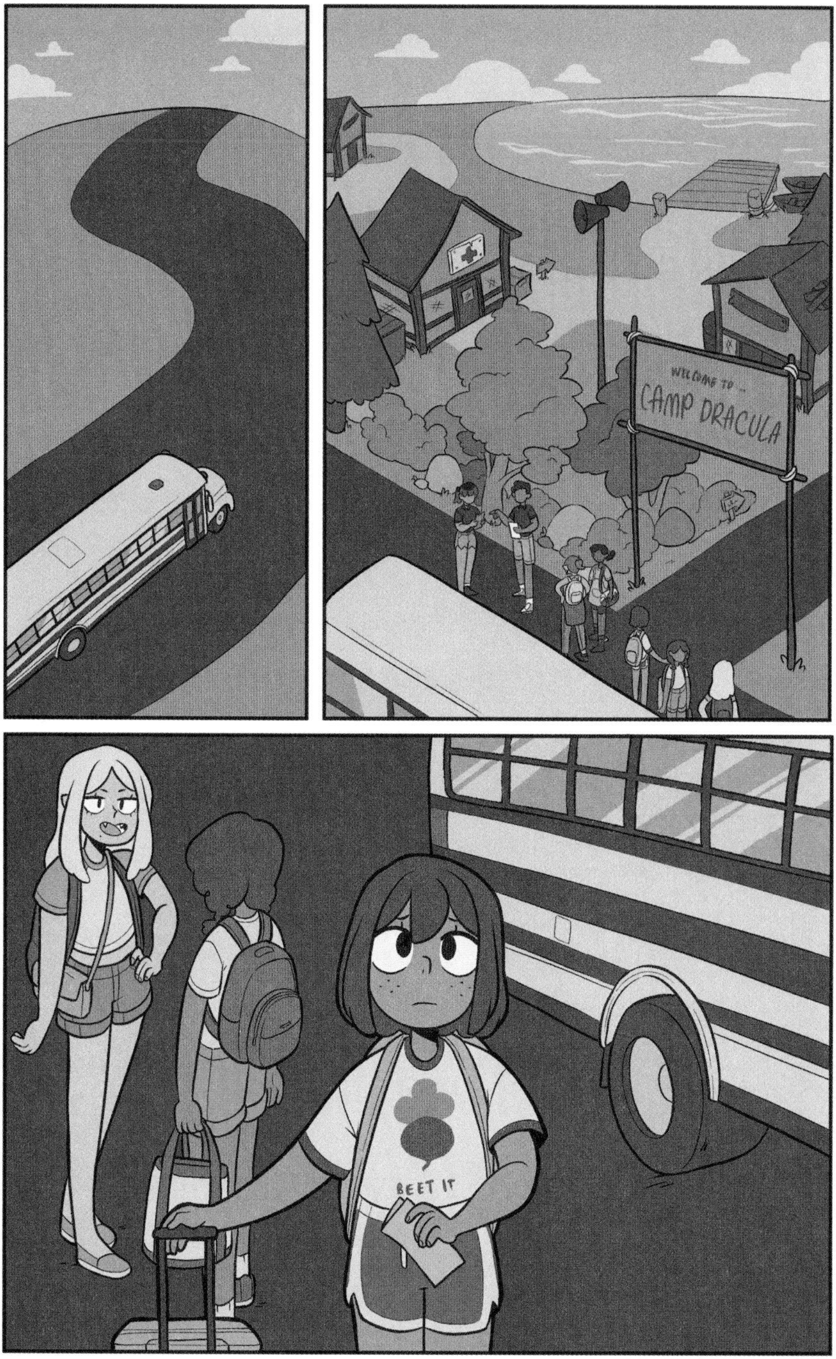
WELCOME TO ...
CAMP DRACULA
BEET IT

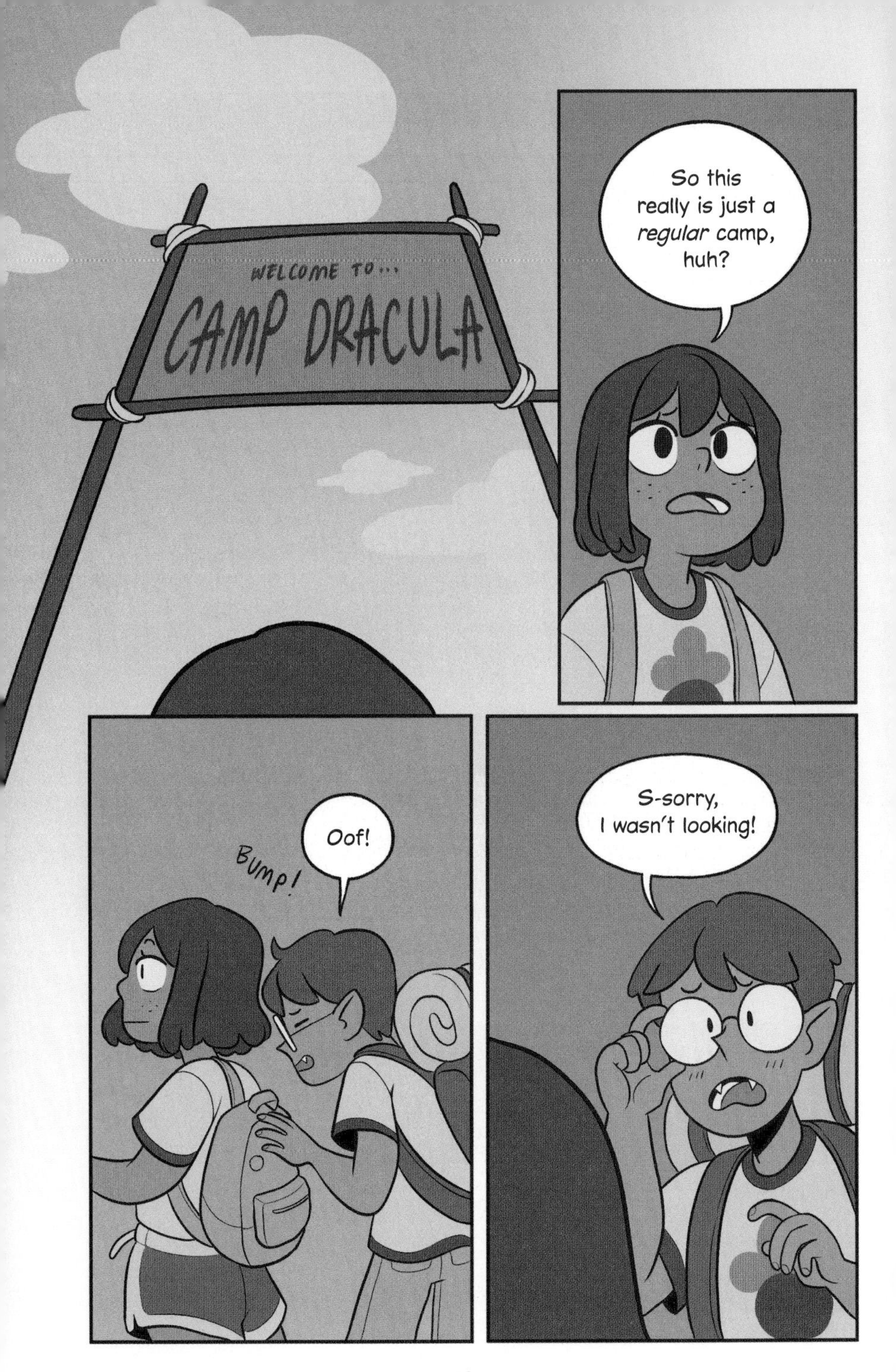
WELCOME TO...
CAMP DRACULA
So this really is just a *regular* camp, huh?
BUMP!
Oof!
S-sorry, I wasn't looking!

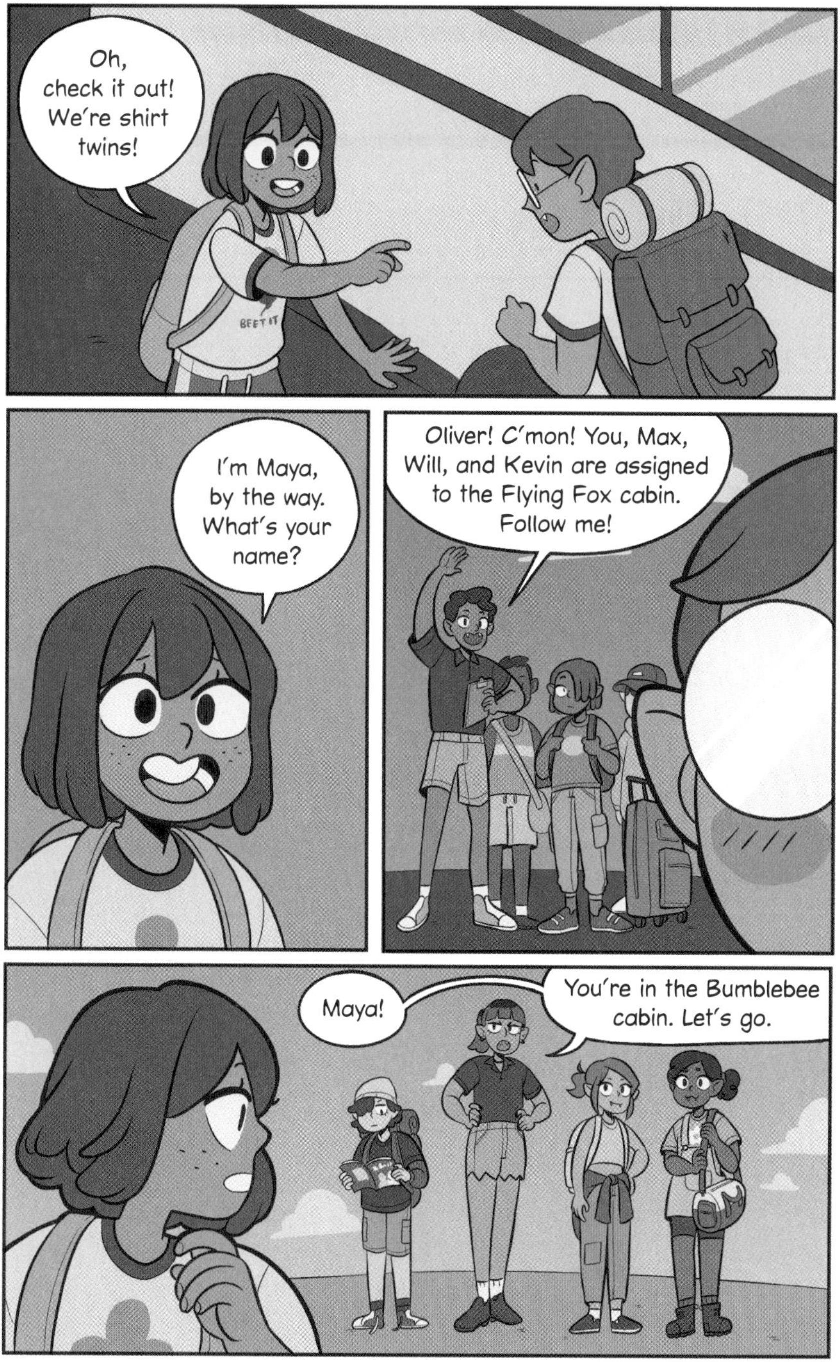
Oh, check it out! We're shirt twins!
BEET IT
I'm Maya, by the way. What's your name?
Oliver! C'mon! You, Max, Will, and Kevin are assigned to the Flying Fox cabin. Follow me!
Maya!
You're in the Bumblebee cabin. Let's go.

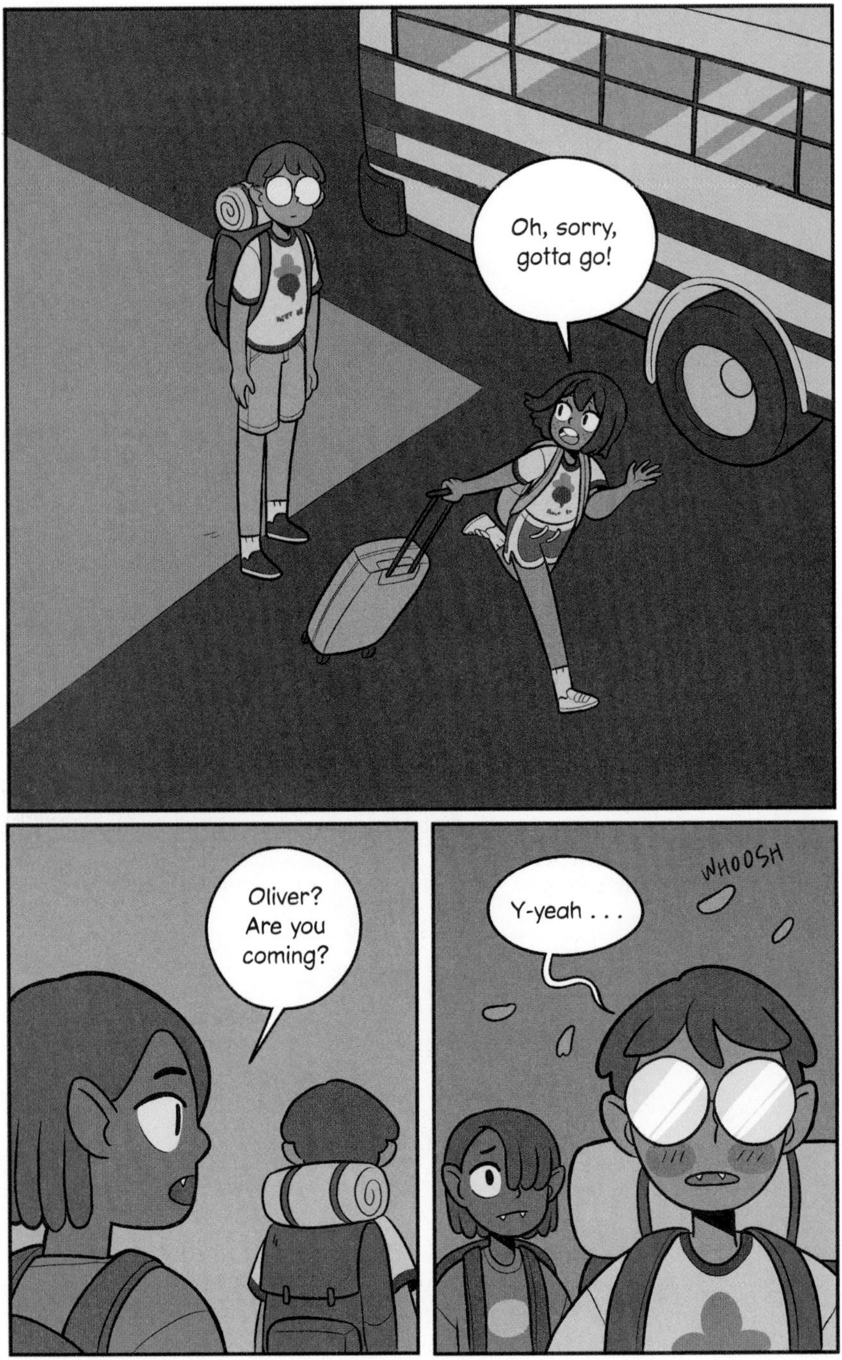
Oh, sorry, gotta go!
Oliver? Are you coming?
Y-yeah . . .
WHOOSH

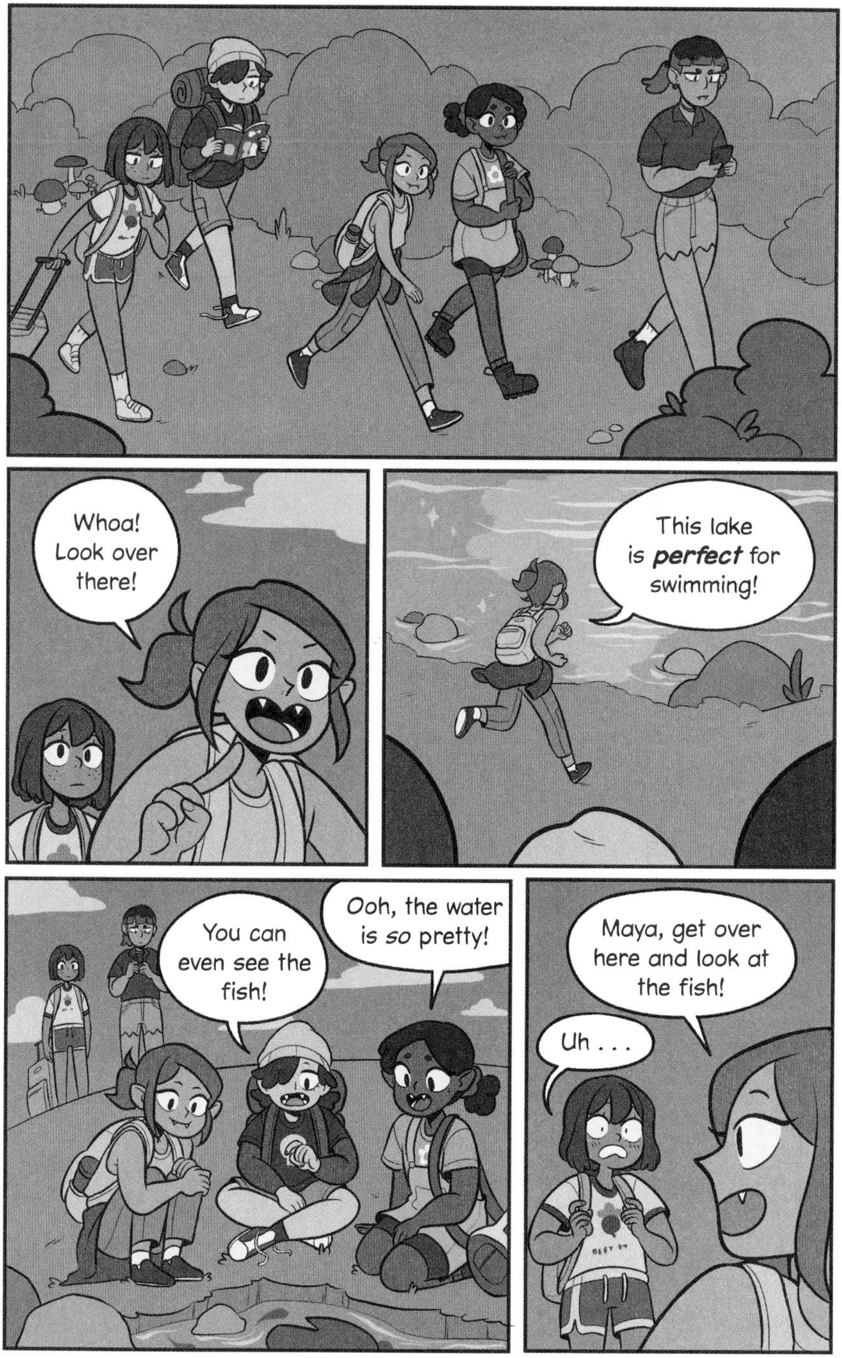

Whoa! Look over there!
This lake is ***perfect*** for swimming!
You can even see the fish!
Ooh, the water is *so* pretty!
Maya, get over here and look at the fish!
Uh . . .

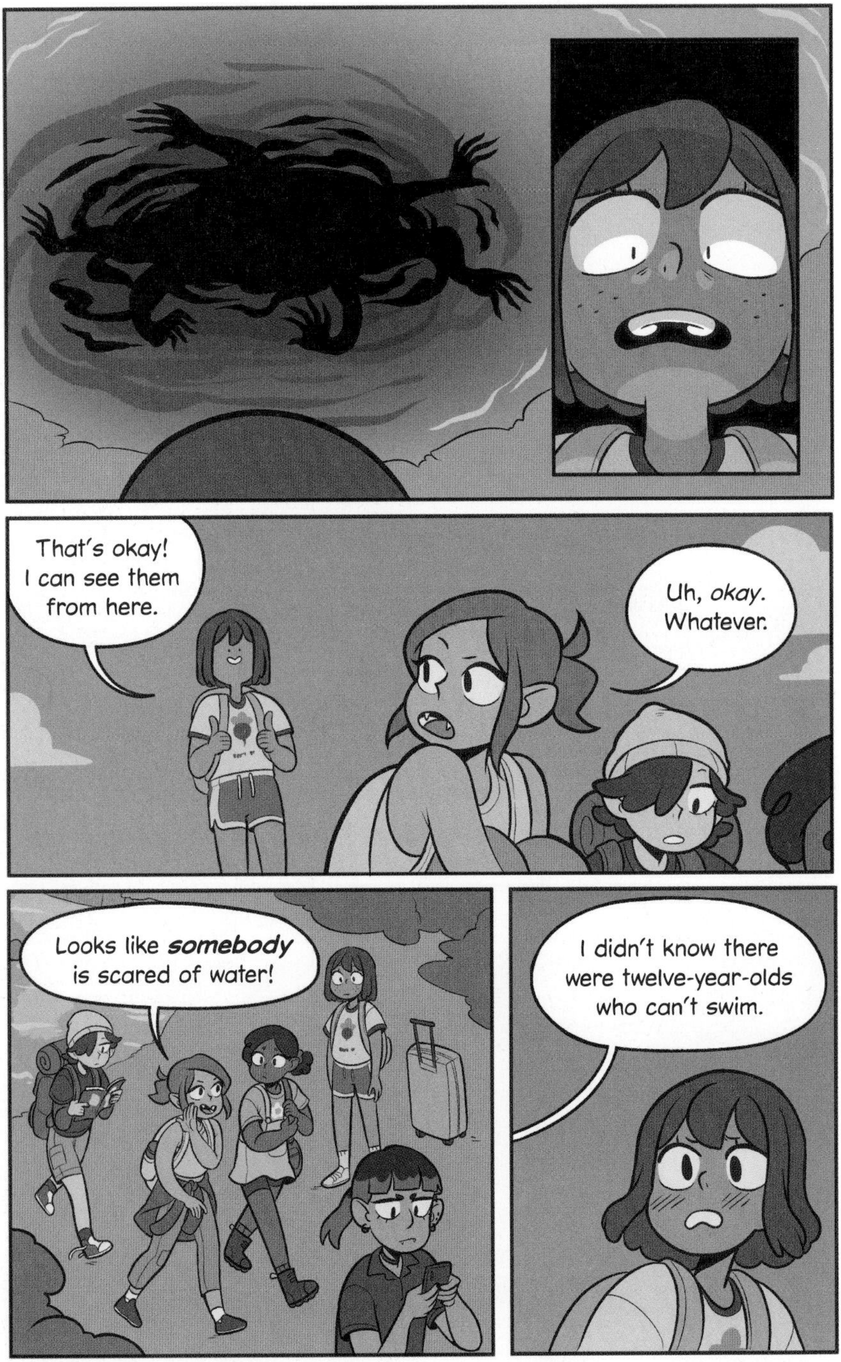
That's okay!
I can see them
from here.
Uh, *okay*.
Whatever.
Looks like ***somebody***
is scared of water!
I didn't know there
were twelve-year-olds
who can't swim.

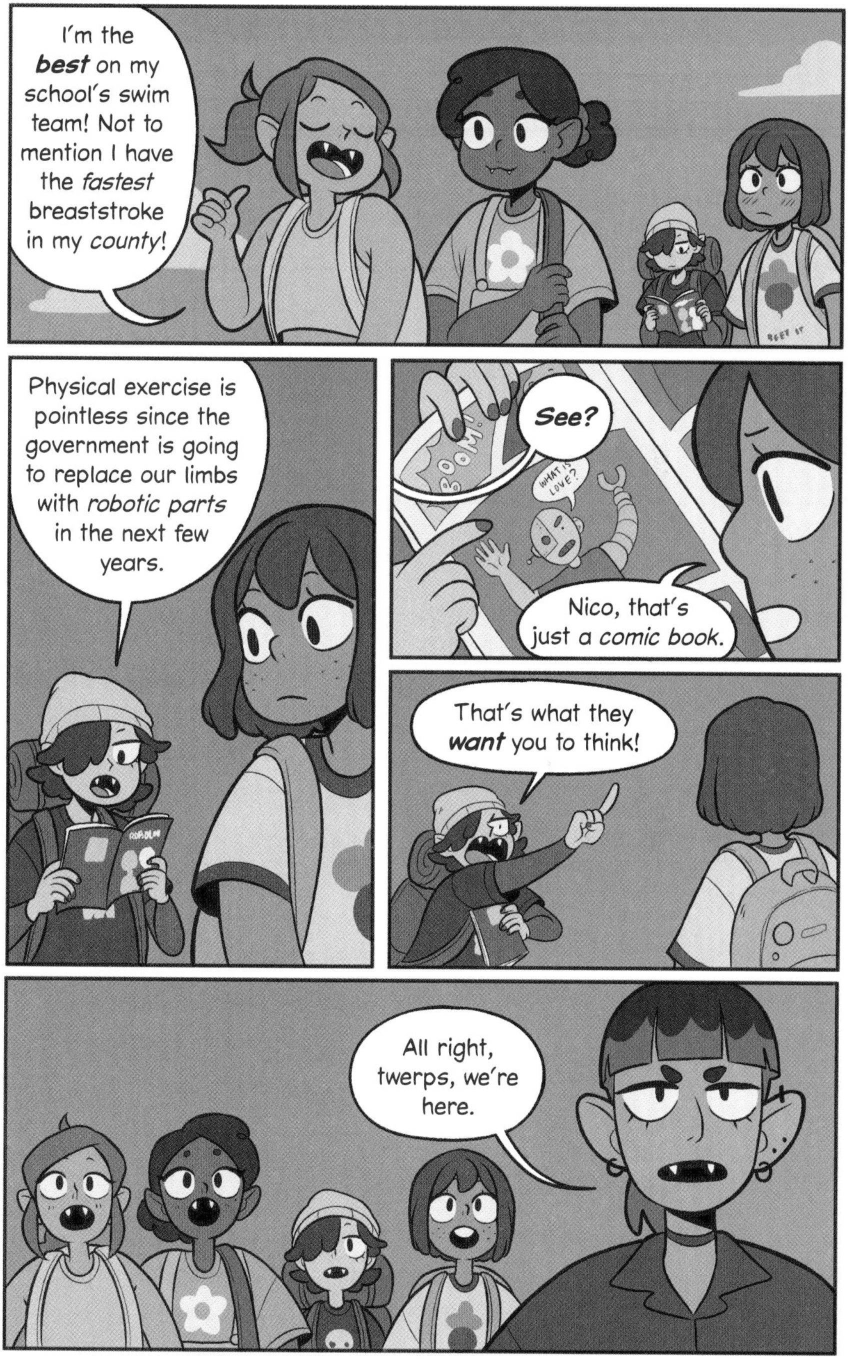
I'm the **best** on my school's swim team! Not to mention I have the *fastest* breaststroke in my *county*!
Physical exercise is pointless since the government is going to replace our limbs with *robotic parts* in the next few years.
See?
BOOM!
WHAT IS LOVE?
Nico, that's just a *comic book.*
That's what they **want** you to think!
All right, twerps, we're here.

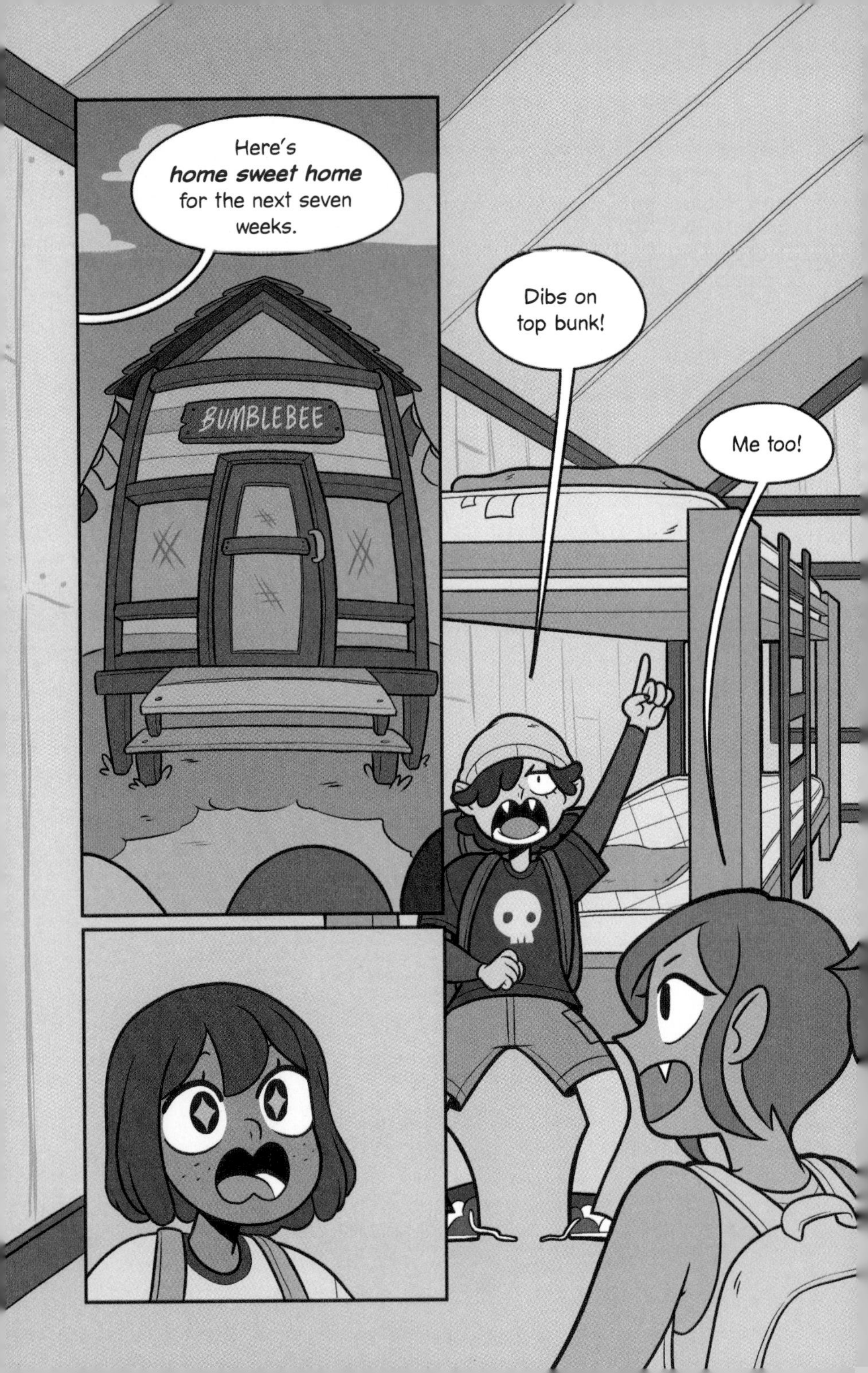
Here's *home sweet home* for the next seven weeks.
BUMBLEBEE
Dibs on top bunk!
Me too!

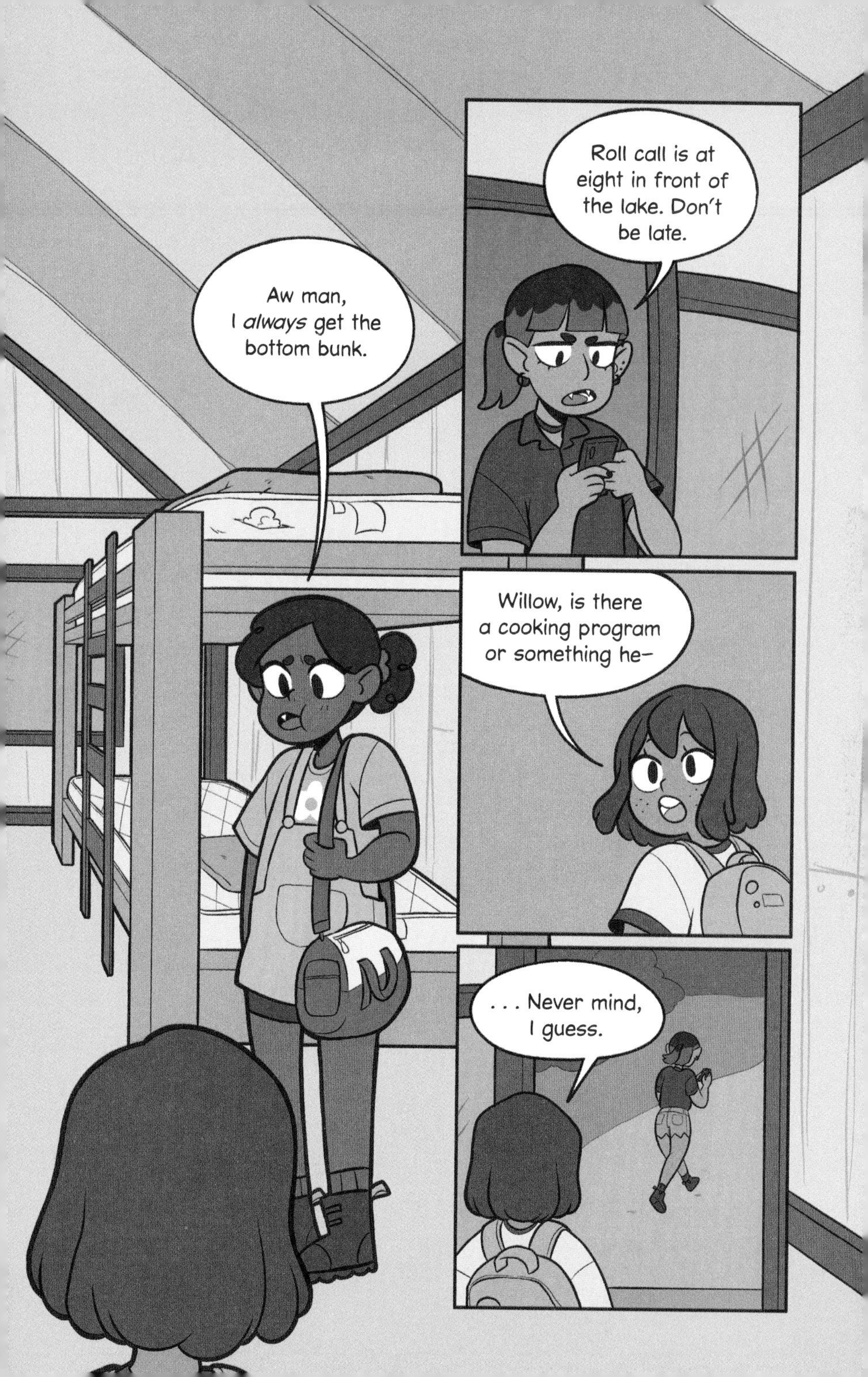
Aw man, I *always* get the bottom bunk.
Roll call is at eight in front of the lake. Don't be late.
Willow, is there a cooking program or something he–
. . . Never mind, I guess.

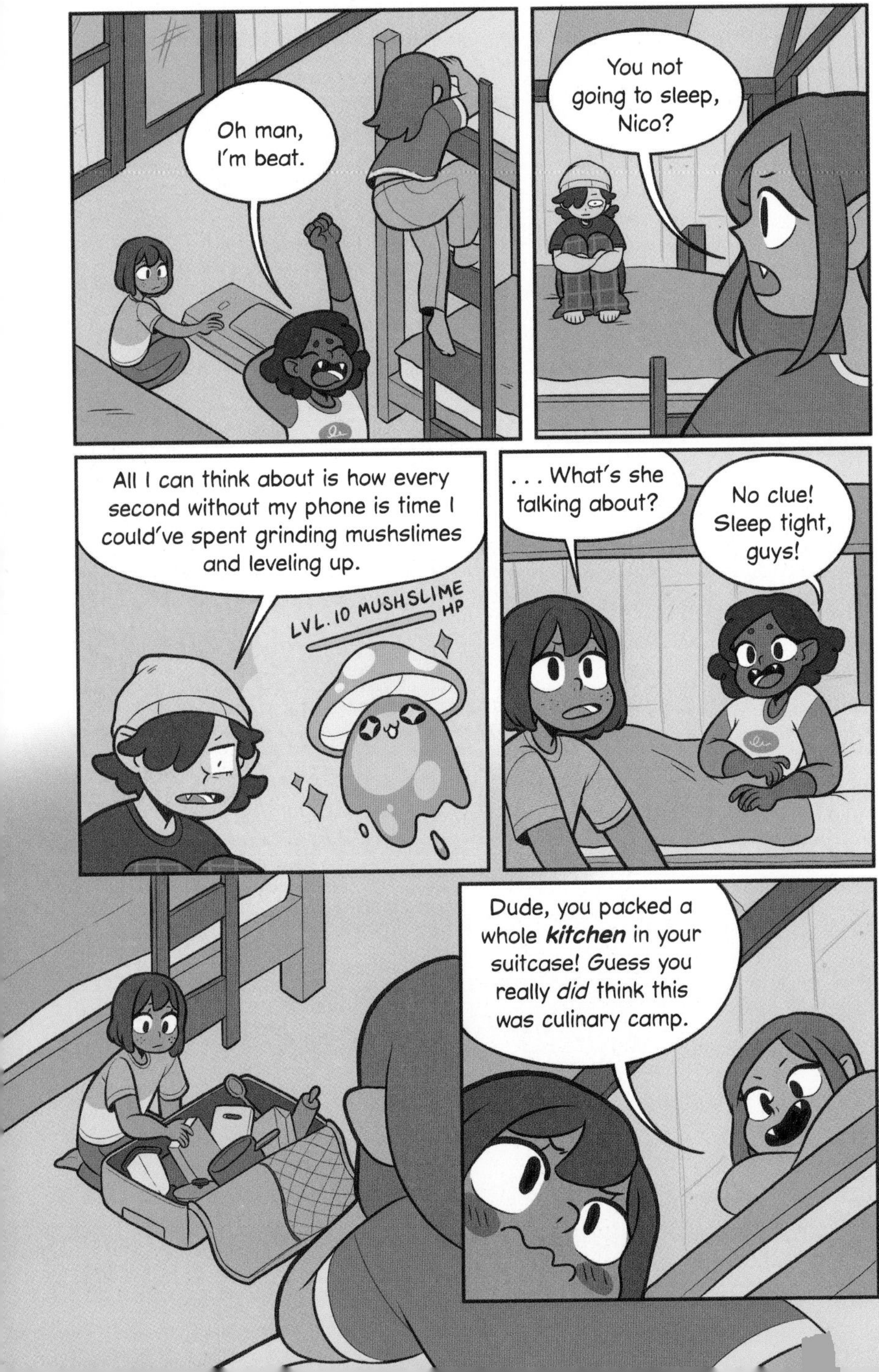
Oh man, I'm beat.
You not going to sleep, Nico?
All I can think about is how every second without my phone is time I could've spent grinding mushslimes and leveling up.
LVL. 10 MUSHSLIME
HP
. . . What's she talking about?
No clue! Sleep tight, guys!
Dude, you packed a whole **kitchen** in your suitcase! *Guess* you really *did* think this was culinary camp.

Maybe Charlotte made a mistake and thought Camp Dracula was a culinary camp?

What's up with that name anyways? It's so weird. Almost as weird as the rule forbidding *garlic*!

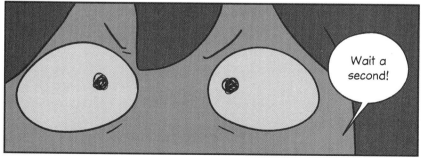

Wait a second!

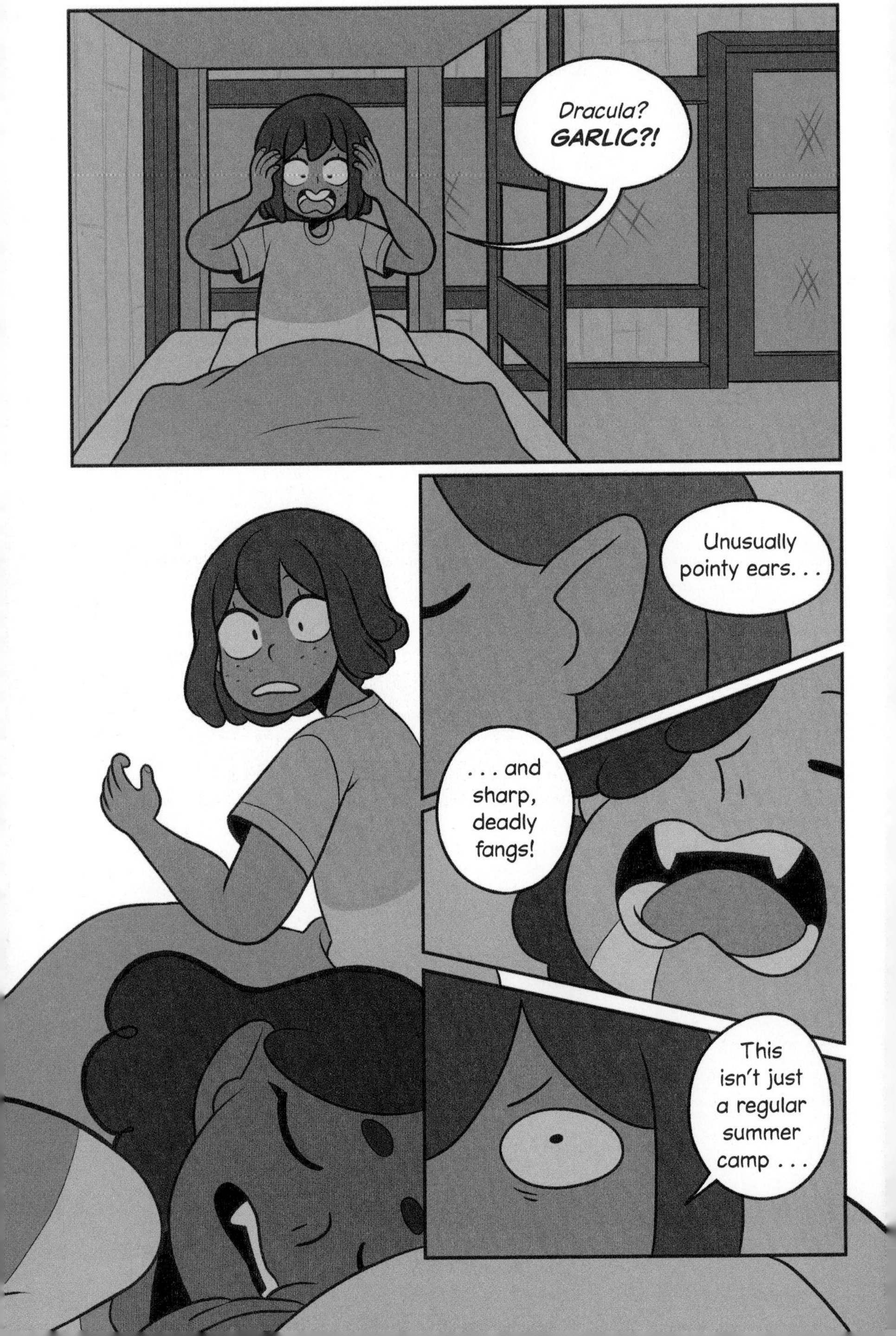
Dracula? GARLIC?!
Unusually pointy ears. . .
. . . and sharp, deadly fangs!
This isn't just a regular summer camp . . .

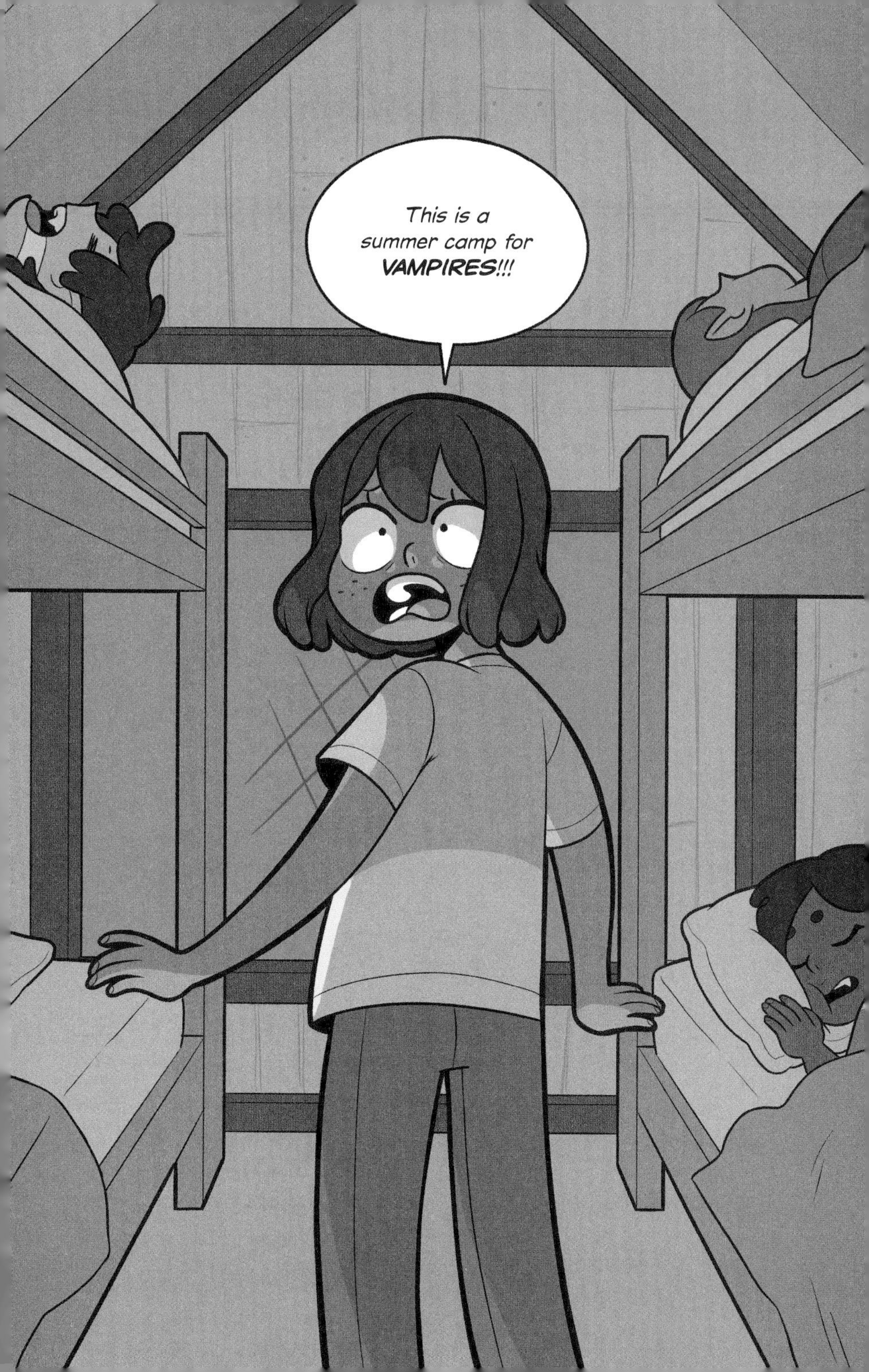
This is a summer camp for **VAMPIRES!!!**

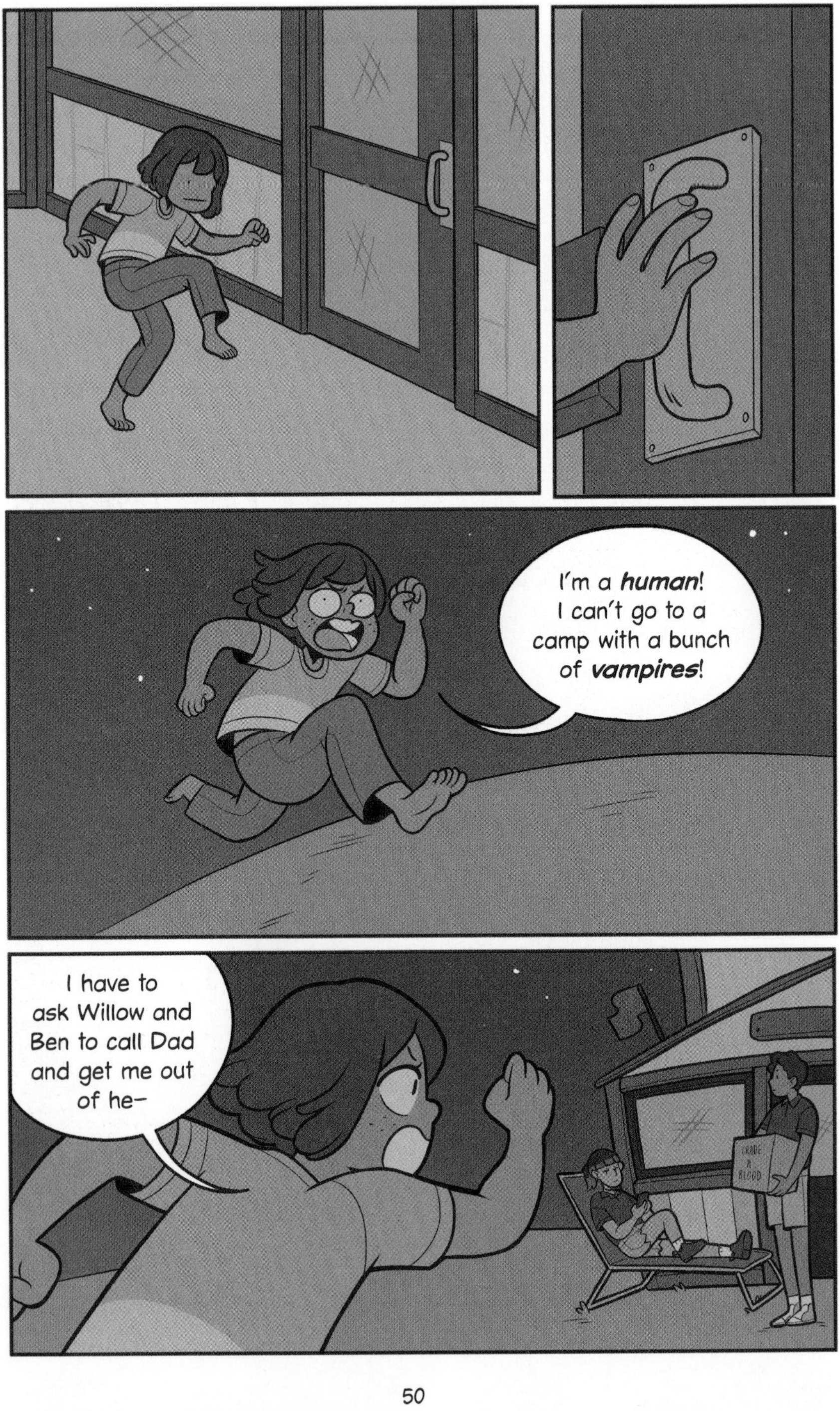
I'm a **human**! I can't go to a camp with a bunch of **vampires**!
I have to ask Willow and Ben to call Dad and get me out of he–

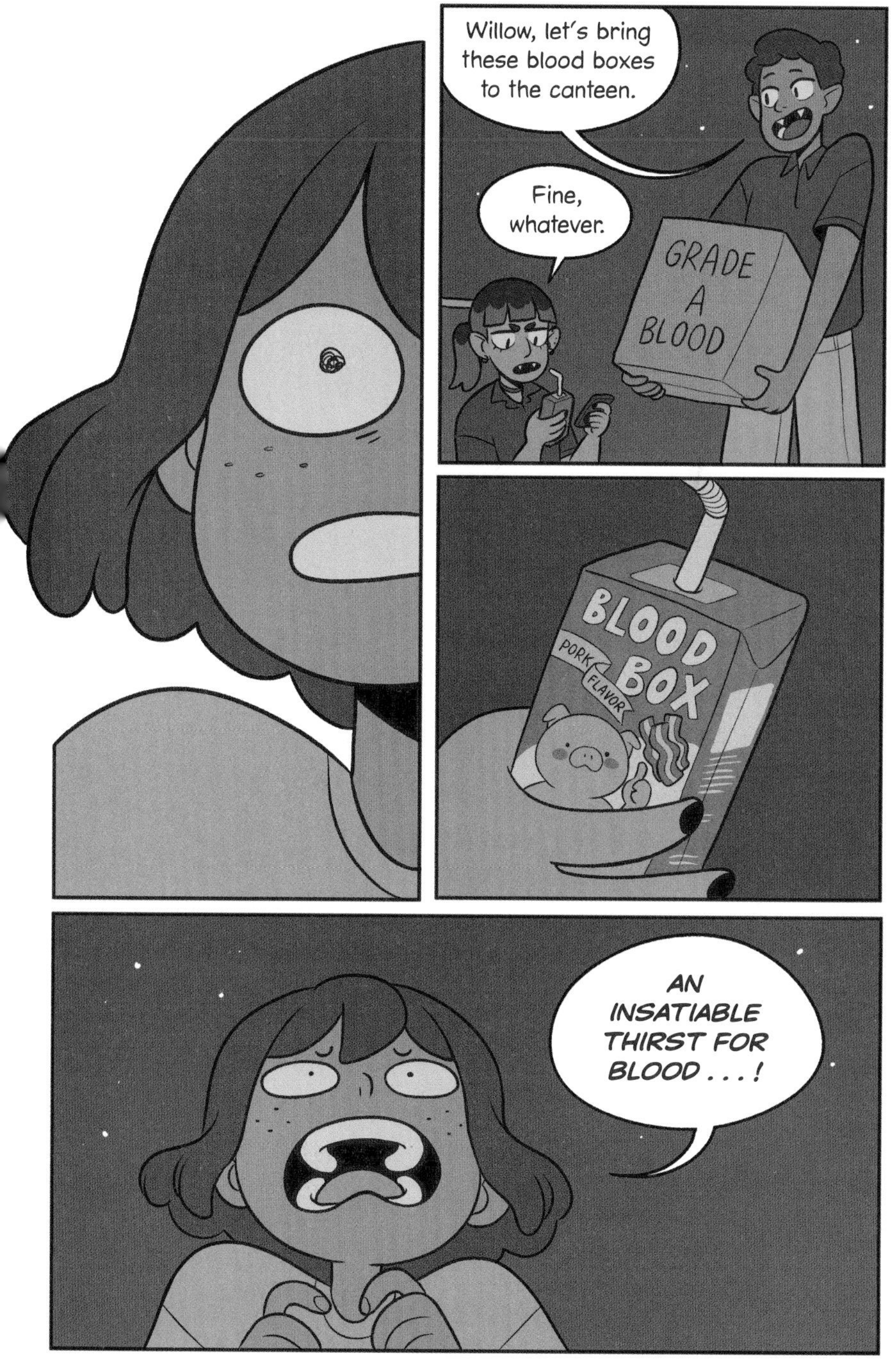
Willow, let's bring these blood boxes to the canteen.
Fine, whatever.
GRADE A BLOOD
BLOOD BOX
PORK FLAVOR
AN INSATIABLE THIRST FOR BLOOD . . . !

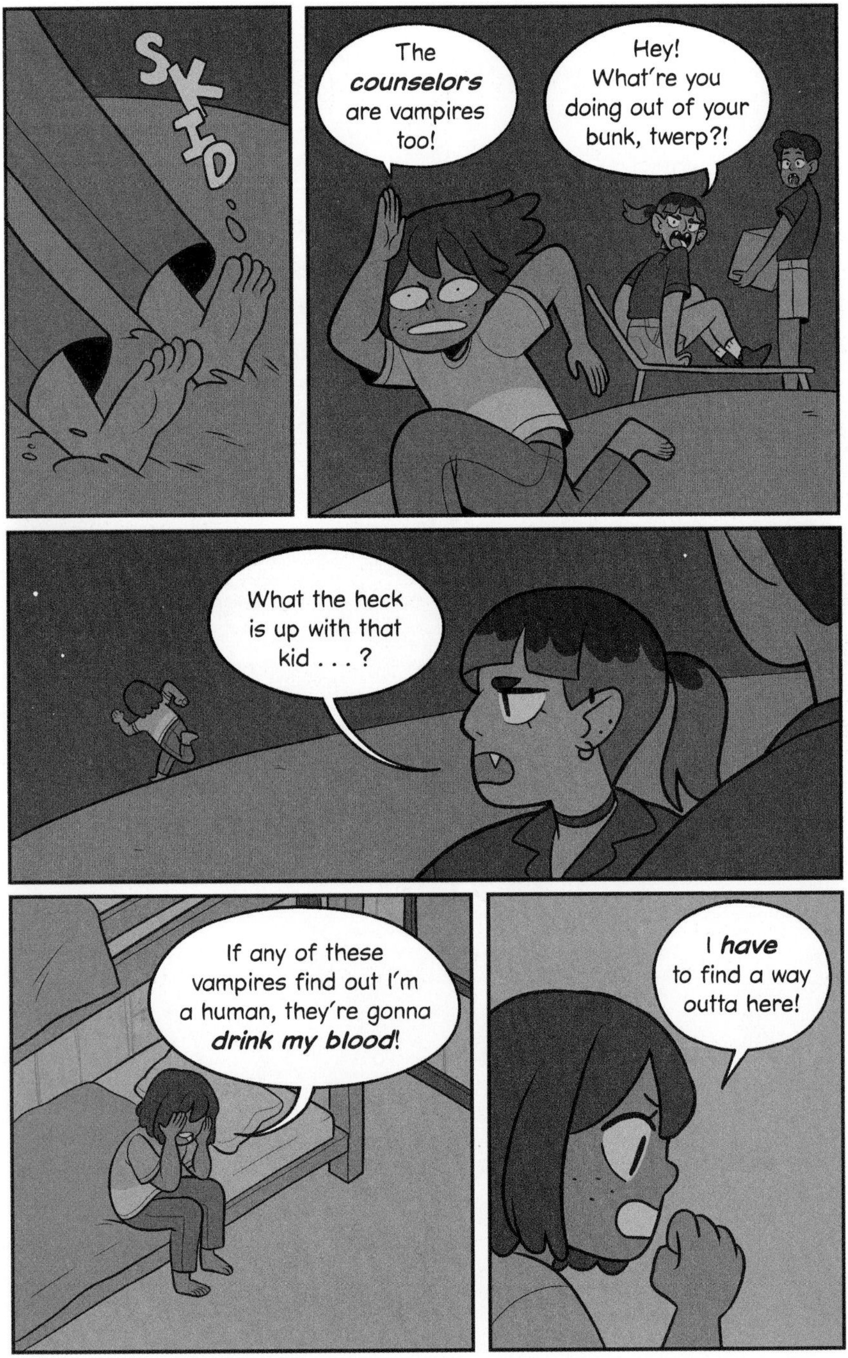
SKID
The *counselors* are vampires too!
Hey! What're you doing out of your bunk, twerp?!
What the heck is up with that kid . . . ?
If any of these vampires find out I'm a human, they're gonna *drink my blood*!
I *have* to find a way outta here!

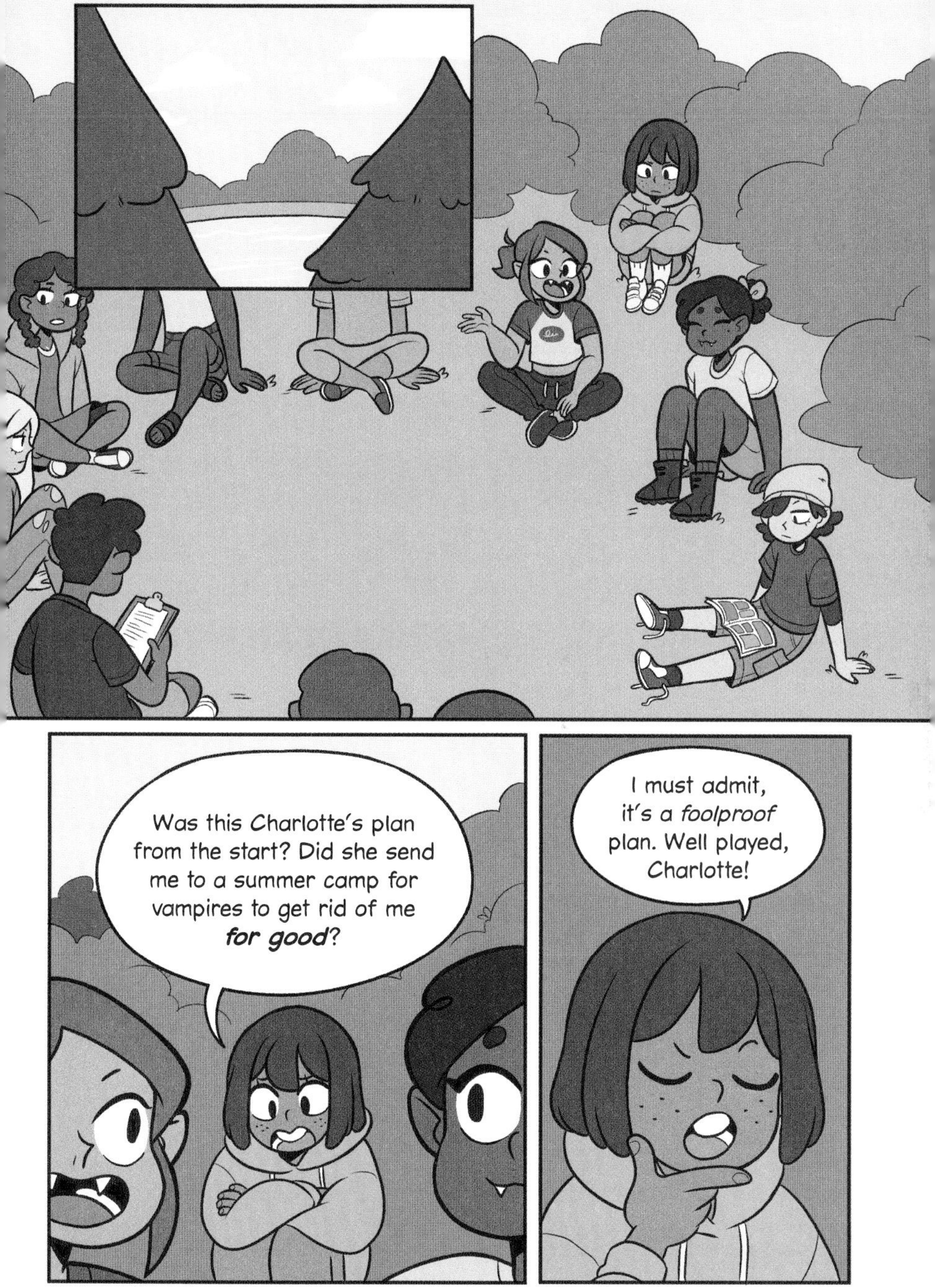
Was this Charlotte's plan from the start? Did she send me to a summer camp for vampires to get rid of me ***for good***?
I must admit, it's a *foolproof* plan. Well played, Charlotte!

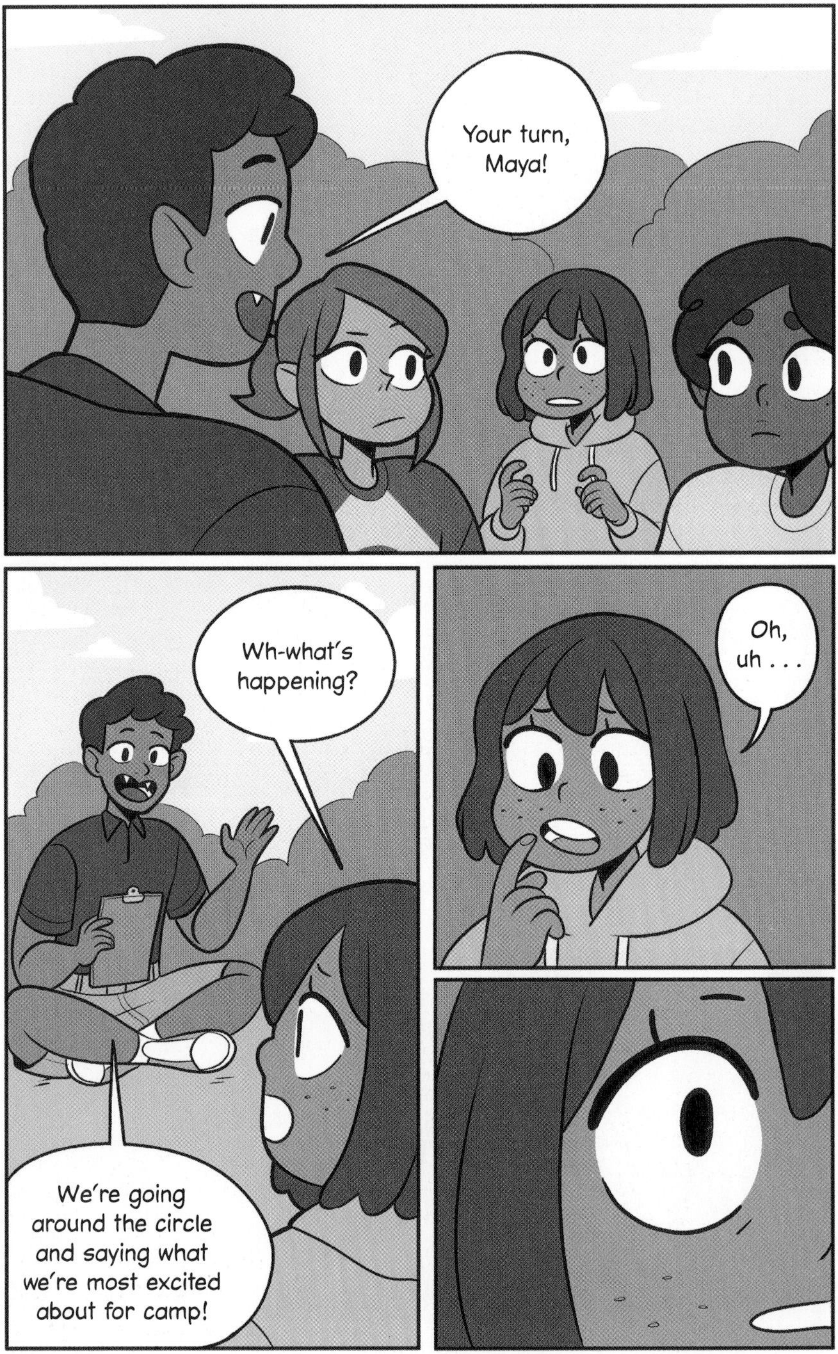
Your turn, Maya!
Wh-what's happening?
We're going around the circle and saying what we're most excited about for camp!
Oh, uh . . .

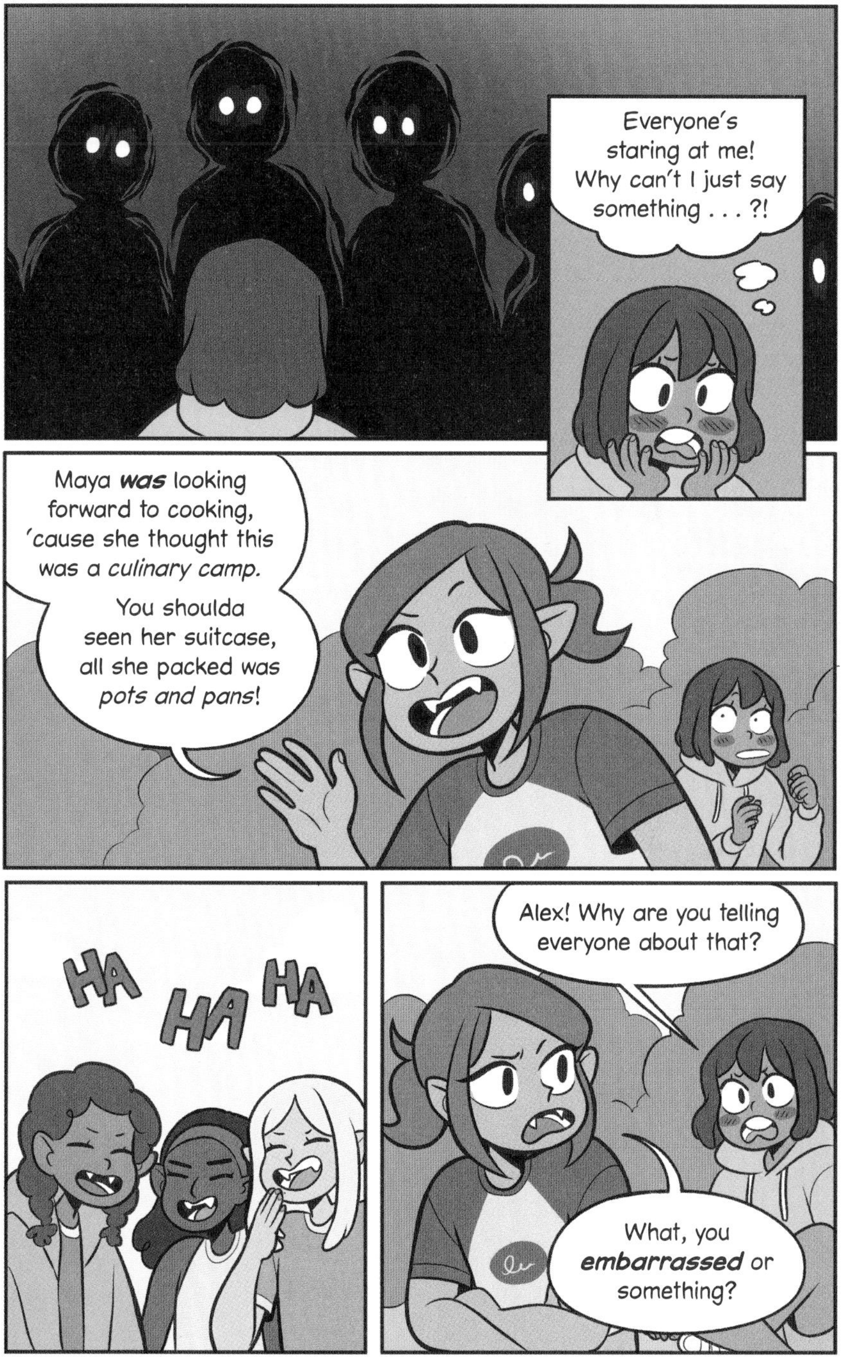
Everyone's staring at me! Why can't I just say something . . . ?!
Maya **was** looking forward to cooking, 'cause she thought this was a *culinary camp.*
You shoulda seen her suitcase, all she packed was *pots and pans*!
HA HA HA
Alex! Why are you telling everyone about that?
What, you **embarrassed** or something?

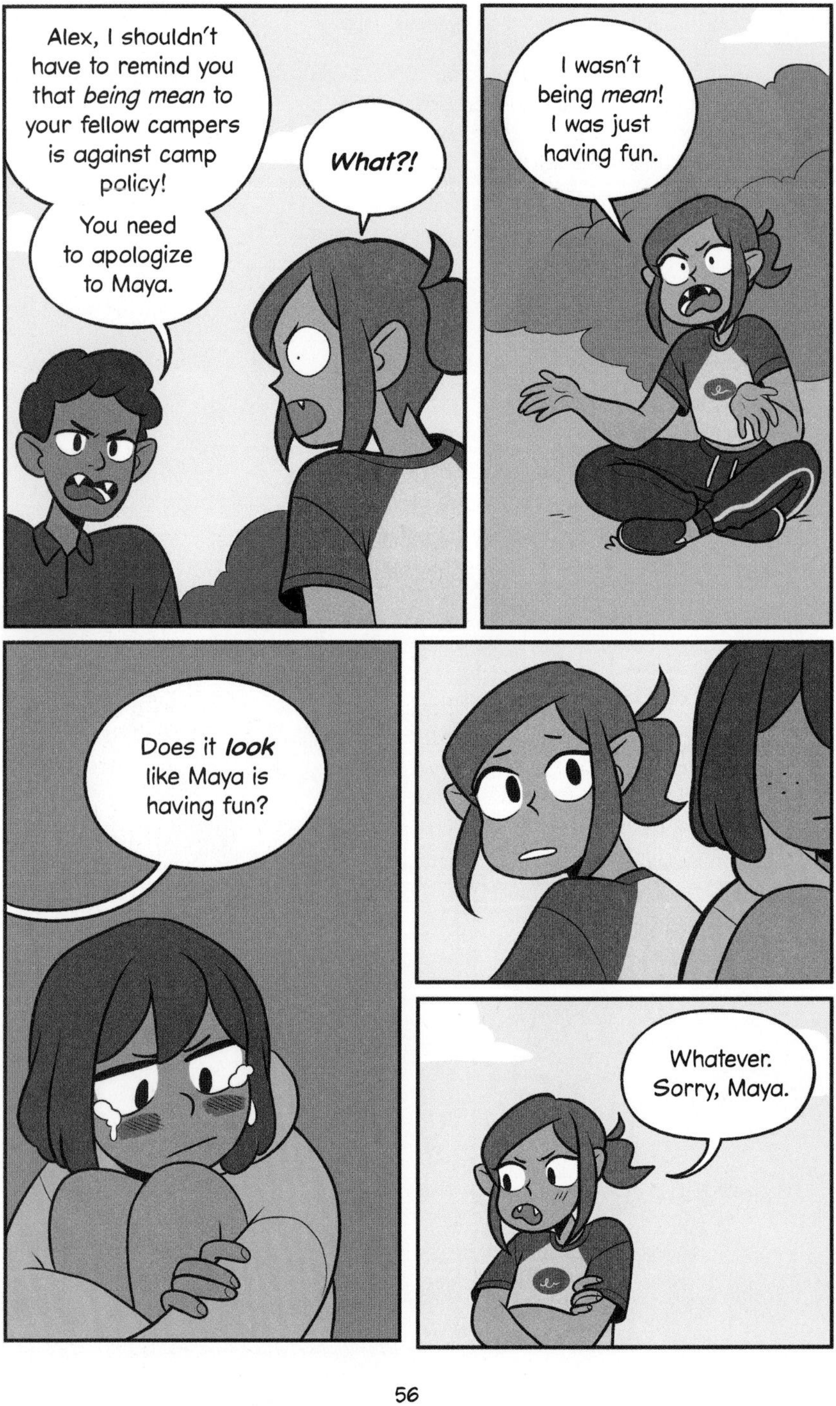
Alex, I shouldn't have to remind you that *being mean* to your fellow campers is against camp policy!
You need to apologize to Maya.
What?!
I wasn't being *mean*! I was just having fun.
Does it ***look*** like Maya is having fun?
Whatever. Sorry, Maya.

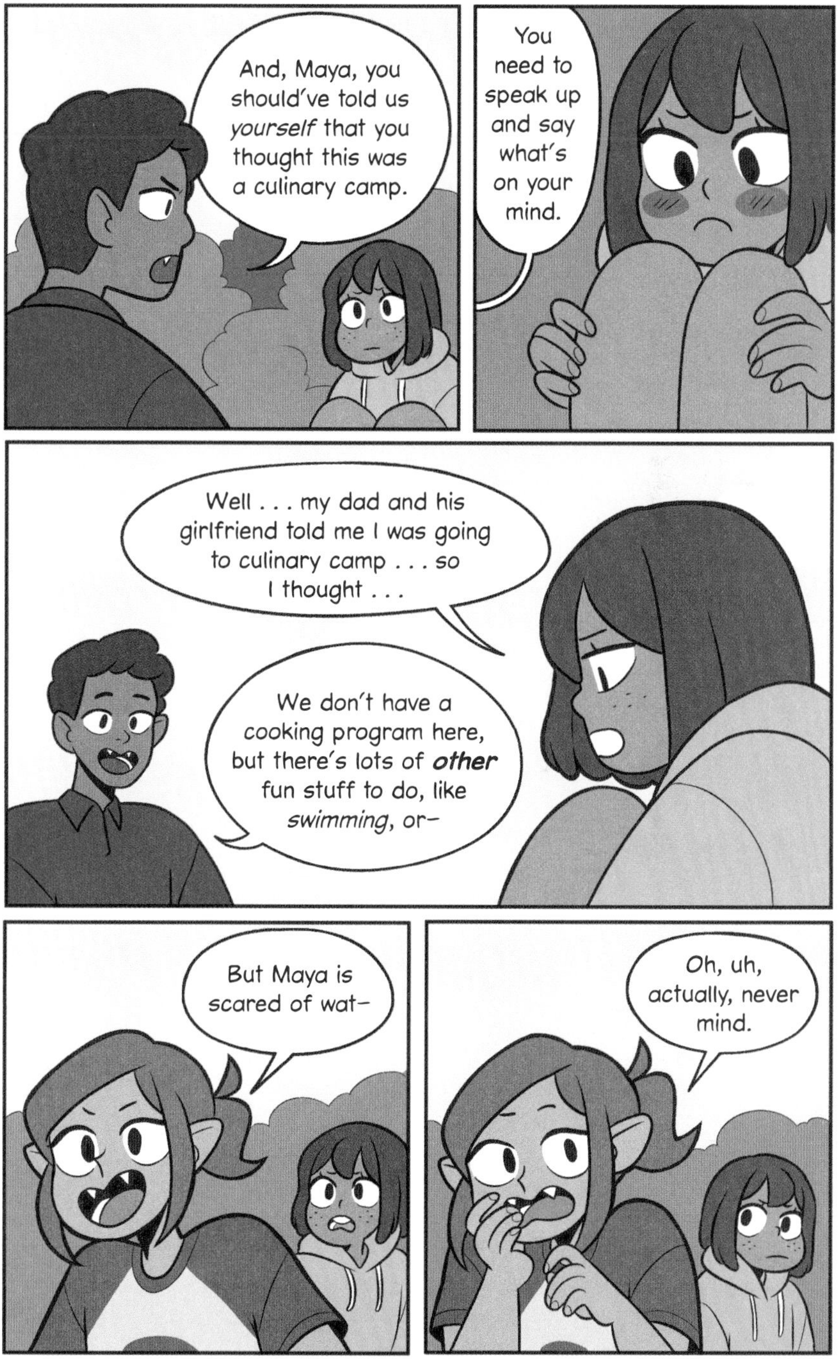
And, Maya, you should've told us *yourself* that you thought this was a culinary camp.
You need to speak up and say what's on your mind.
Well . . . my dad and his girlfriend told me I was going to culinary camp . . . so I thought . . .
We don't have a cooking program here, but there's lots of ***other*** fun stuff to do, like *swimming*, or–
But Maya is scared of wat–
Oh, uh, actually, never mind.

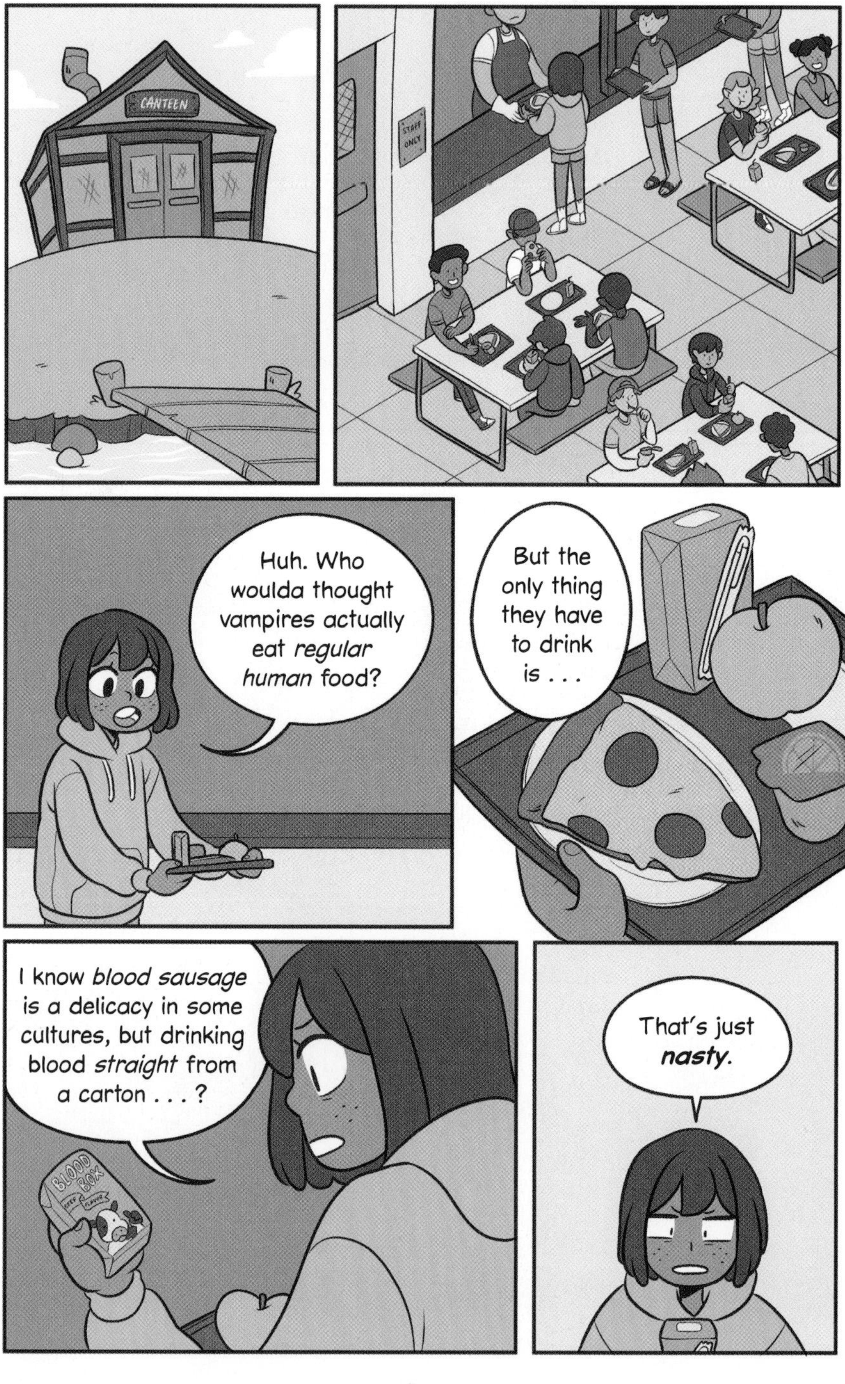
CANTEEN
STAFF ONLY
Huh. Who woulda thought vampires actually eat *regular human* food?
But the only thing they have to drink is . . .
I know *blood sausage* is a delicacy in some cultures, but drinking blood *straight* from a carton . . . ?
BLOOD BOX
BEEF FLAVOR
That's just ***nasty***.

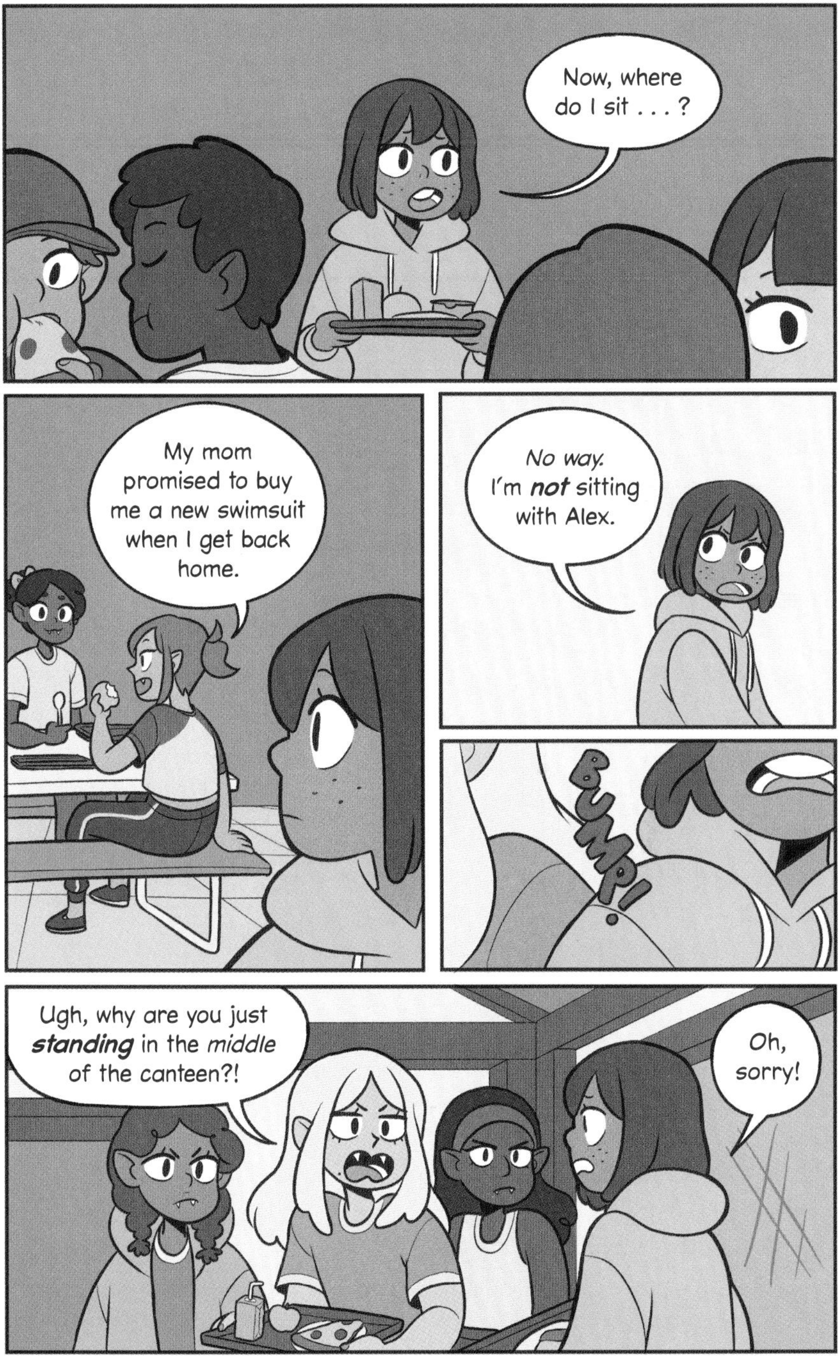
Now, where do I sit . . . ?
My mom promised to buy me a new swimsuit when I get back home.
No way. I'm ***not*** sitting with Alex.
BUMP!
Ugh, why are you just ***standing*** in the *middle* of the canteen?!
Oh, sorry!

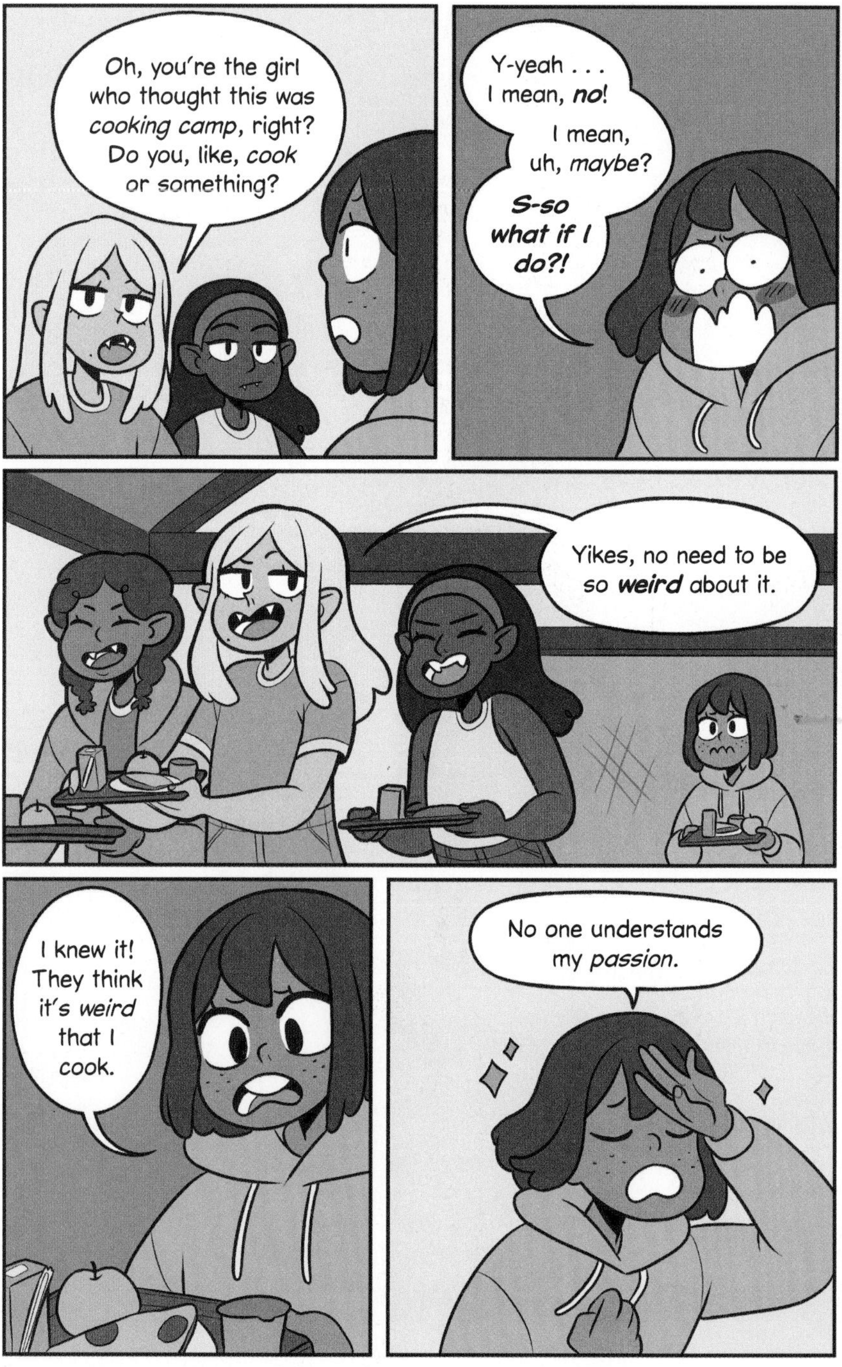
Oh, you're the girl who thought this was *cooking camp*, right? Do you, like, *cook* or something?
Y-yeah . . . I mean, ***no***!
I mean, uh, *maybe*?
S-so what if I do?!
Yikes, no need to be so ***weird*** about it.
I knew it! They think it's *weird* that I cook.
No one understands my *passion*.

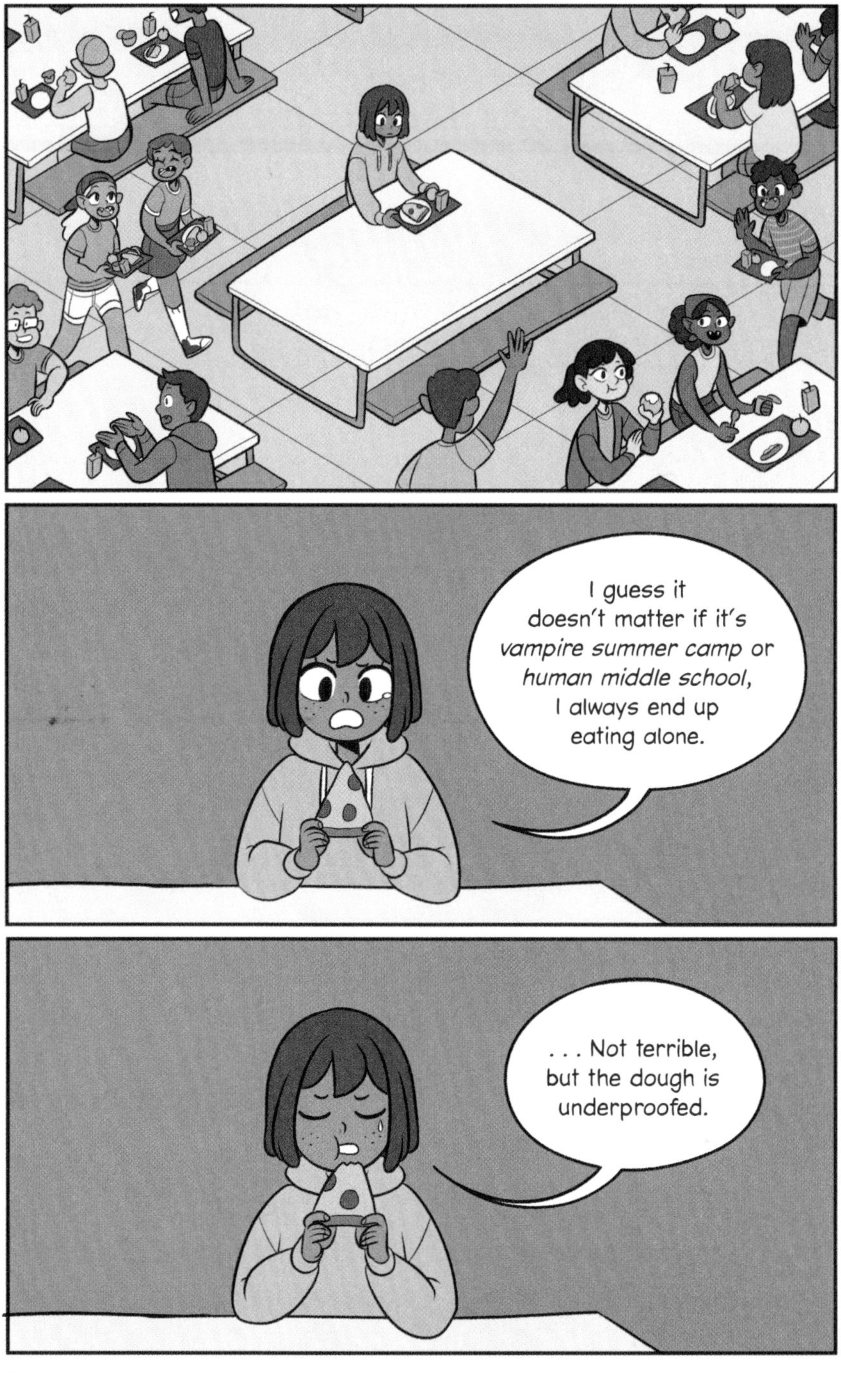
I guess it doesn't matter if it's *vampire summer camp* or *human middle school*, I always end up eating alone.
. . . Not terrible, but the dough is underproofed.

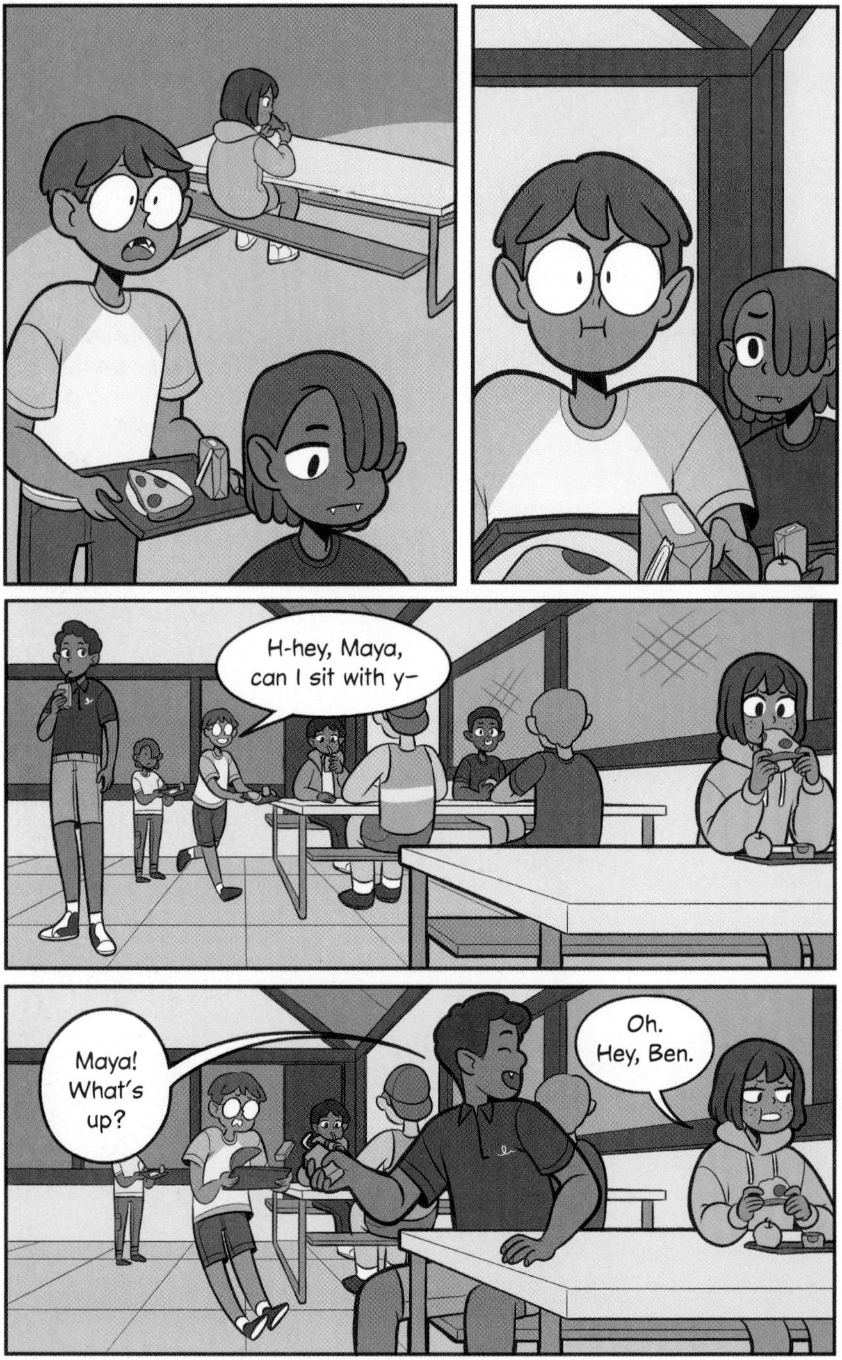
H-hey, Maya, can I sit with y-
Maya! What's up?
Oh. Hey, Ben.

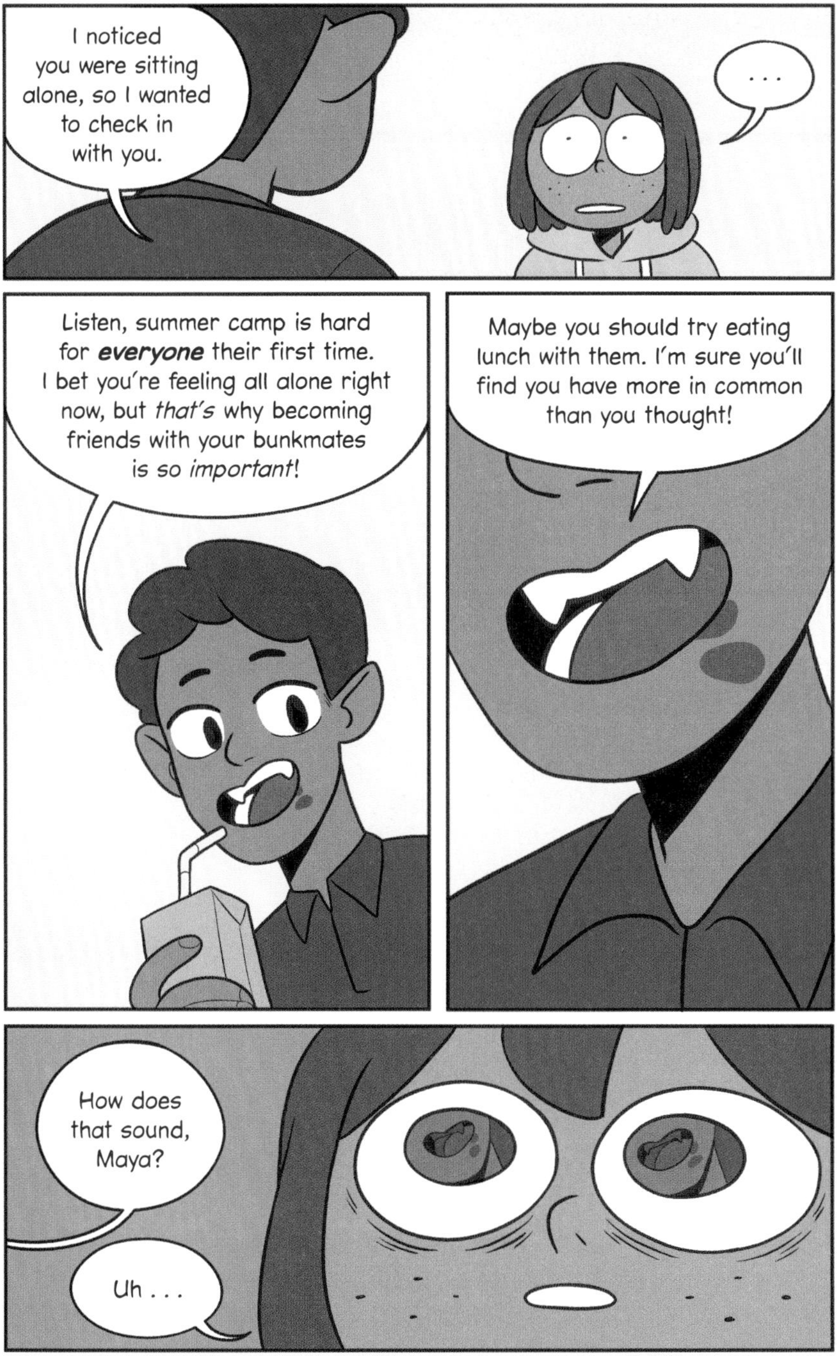
I noticed you were sitting alone, so I wanted to check in with you.
. . .
Listen, summer camp is hard for **everyone** their first time. I bet you're feeling all alone right now, but *that's* why becoming friends with your bunkmates is so *important*!
Maybe you should try eating lunch with them. I'm sure you'll find you have more in common than you thought!
How does that sound, Maya?
Uh . . .

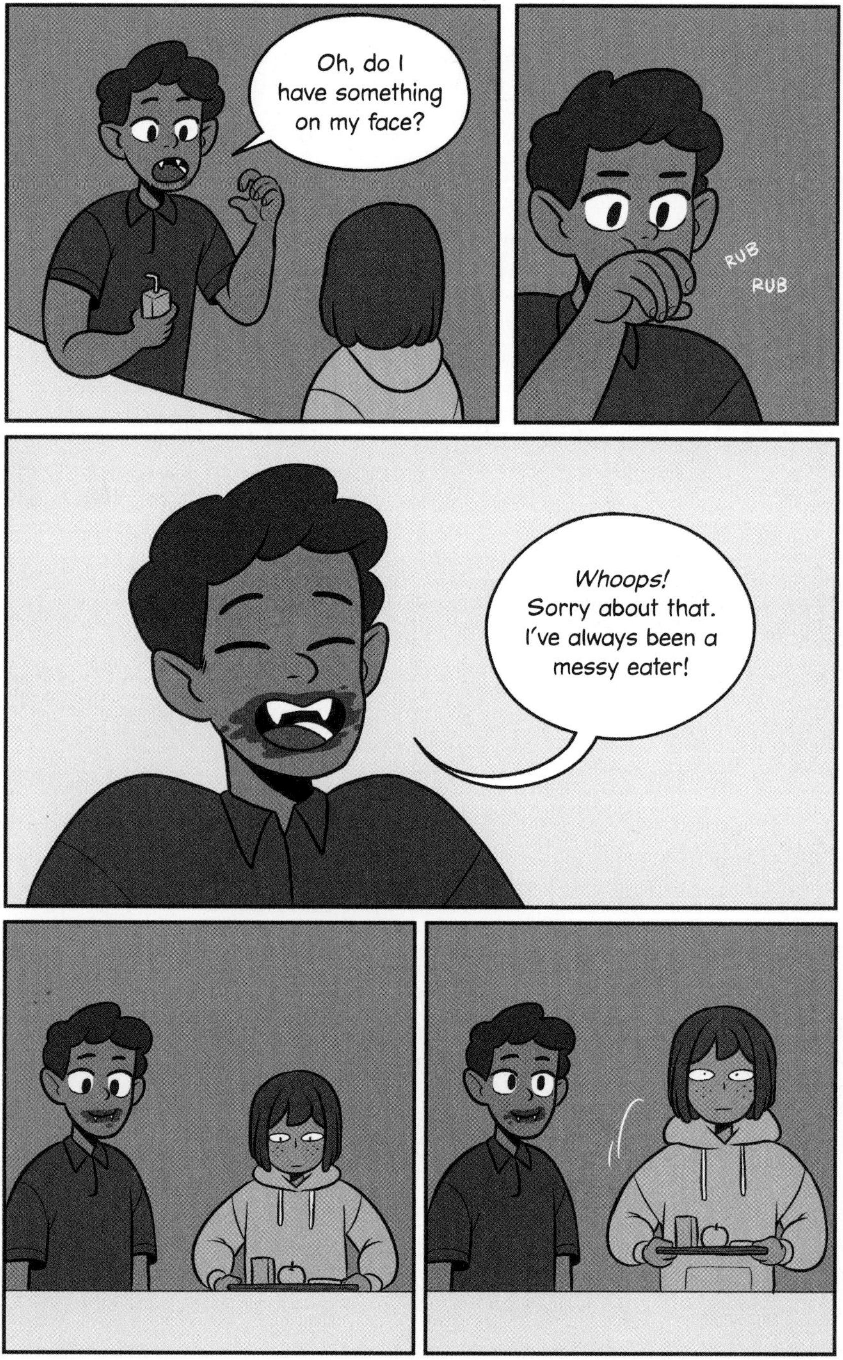
Oh, do I have something on my face?
RUB
RUB
Whoops! Sorry about that. I've always been a messy eater!

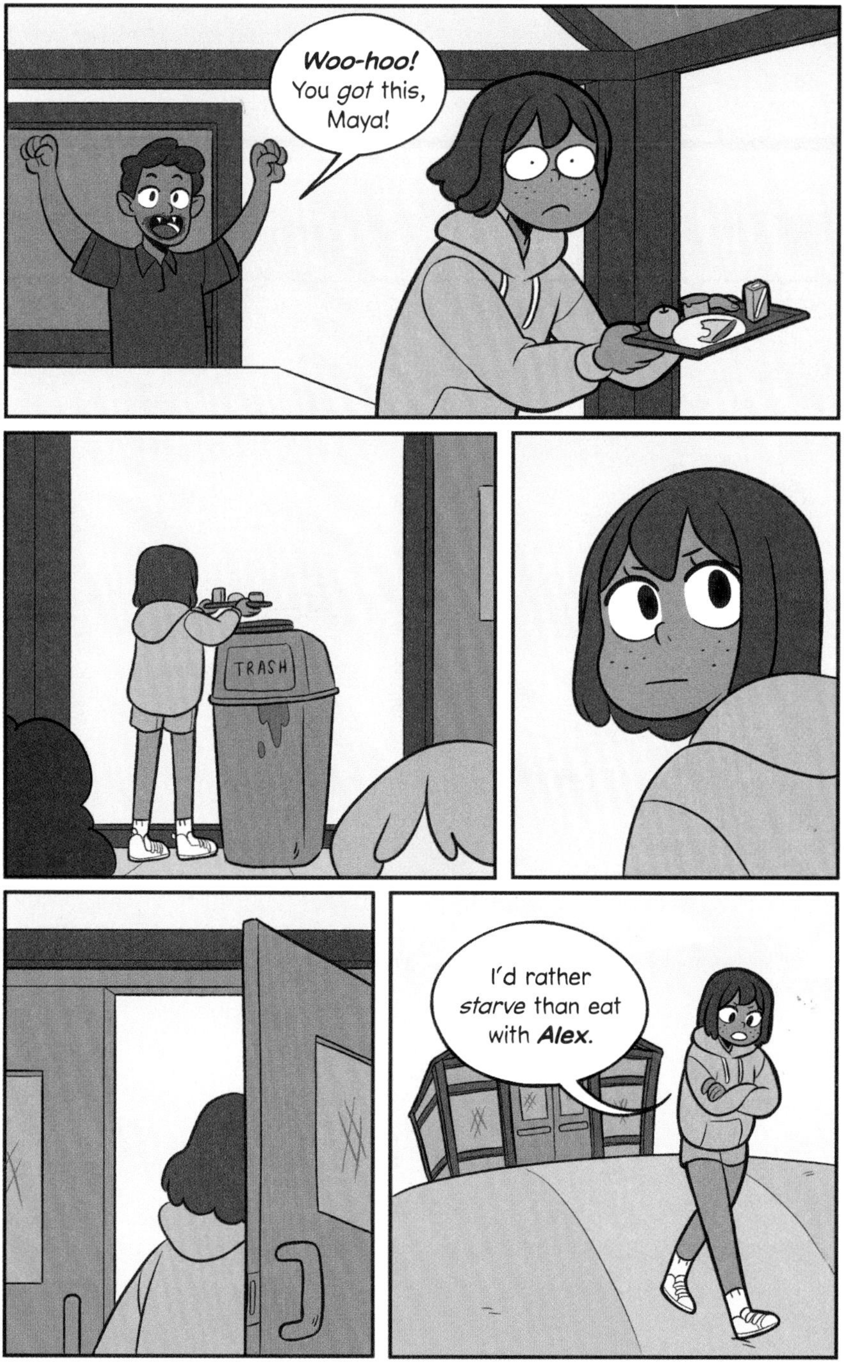
Woo-hoo! You got this, Maya!
TRASH
I'd rather starve than eat with Alex.

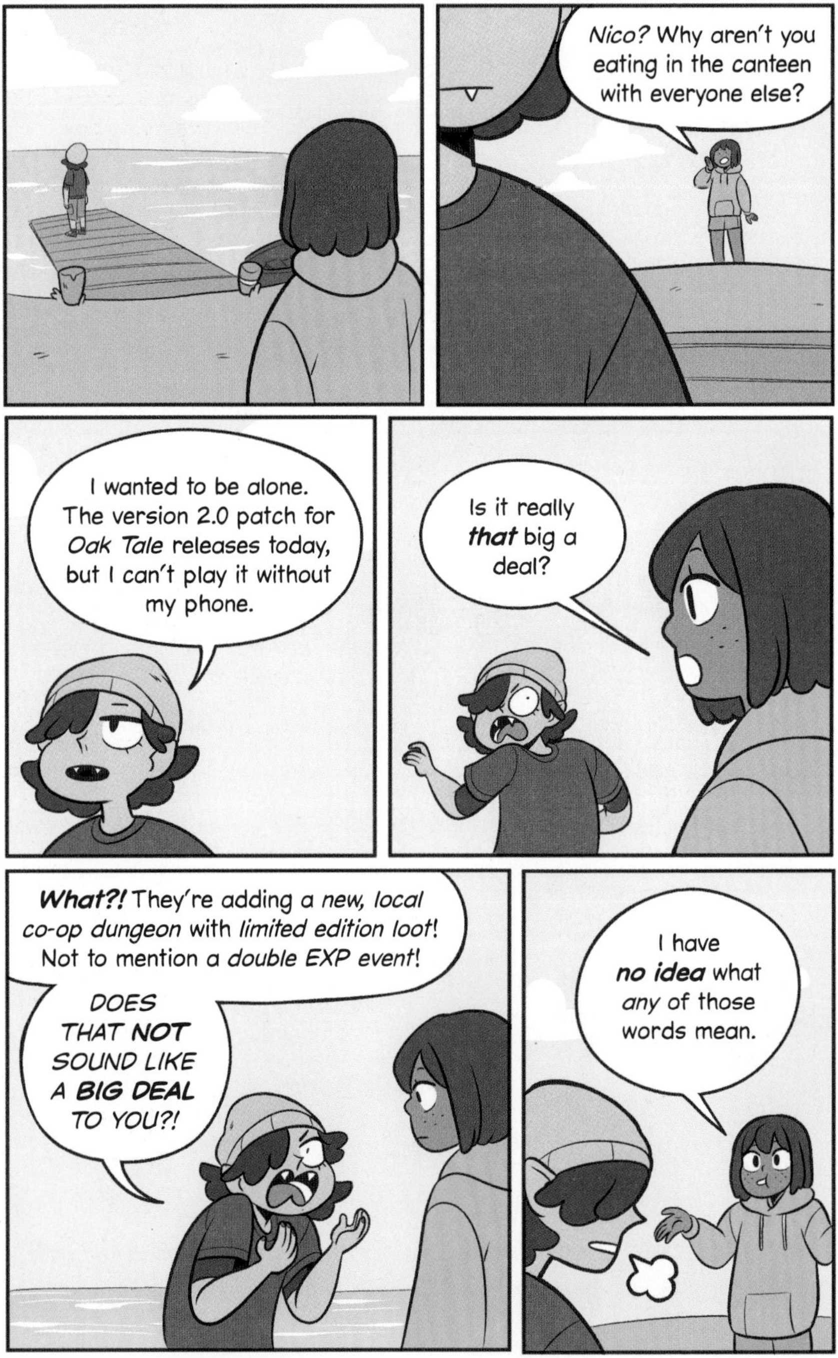
Nico? Why aren't you eating in the canteen with everyone else?
I wanted to be alone. The version 2.0 patch for *Oak Tale* releases today, but I *can't* play it without my phone.
Is it really ***that*** big a deal?
What?! They're adding a *new, local co-op dungeon* with *limited edition loot*! Not to mention a *double EXP event*!
DOES THAT ***NOT*** *SOUND LIKE A* ***BIG DEAL*** *TO YOU?!*
I have ***no idea*** what *any* of those words mean.

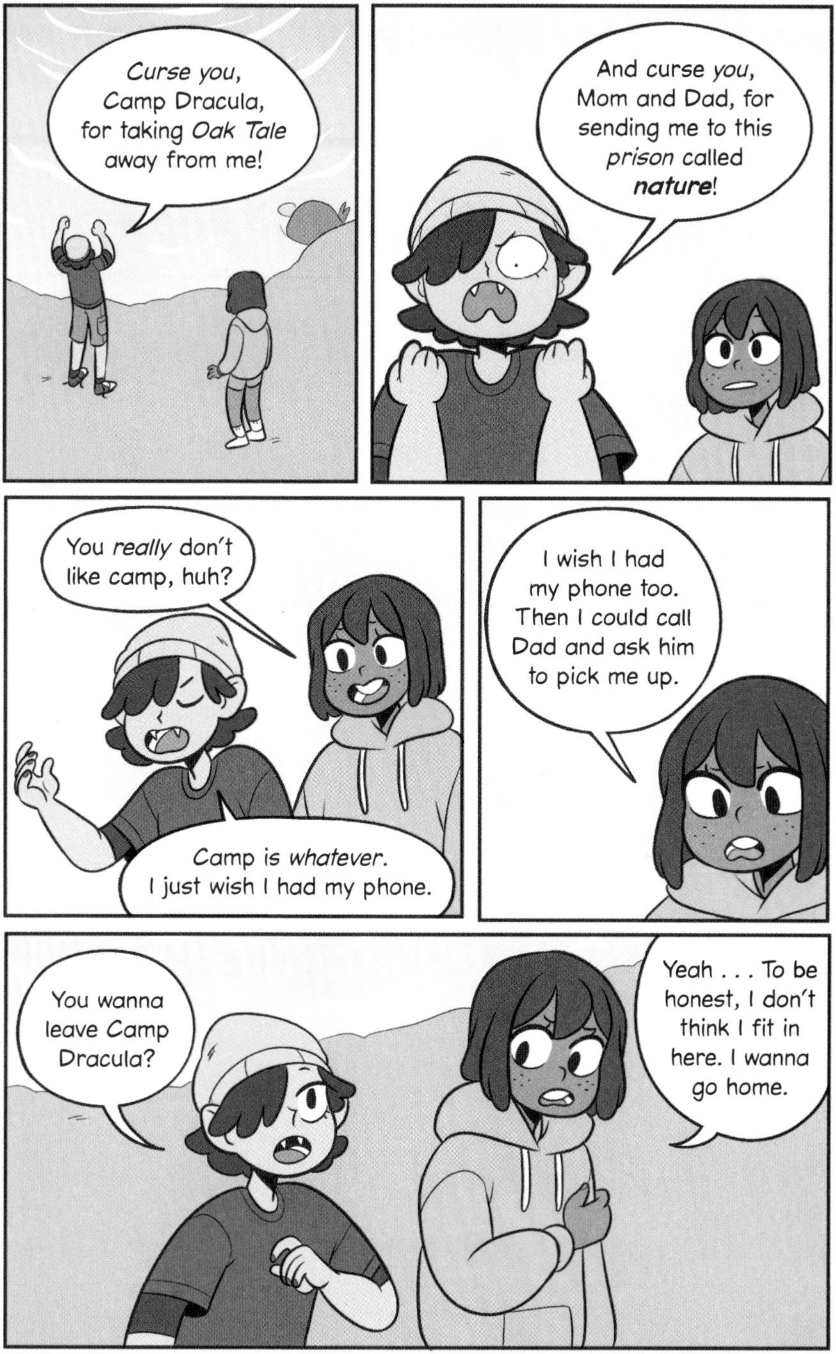
Curse you, Camp Dracula, for taking *Oak Tale* away from me!
And curse *you,* Mom and Dad, for sending me to this *prison* called ***nature***!
You *really* don't like camp, huh?
Camp is whatever. I just wish I had my phone.
I wish I had my phone too. Then I could call Dad and ask him to pick me up.
You wanna leave Camp Dracula?
Yeah . . . To be honest, I don't think I fit in here. I wanna go home.

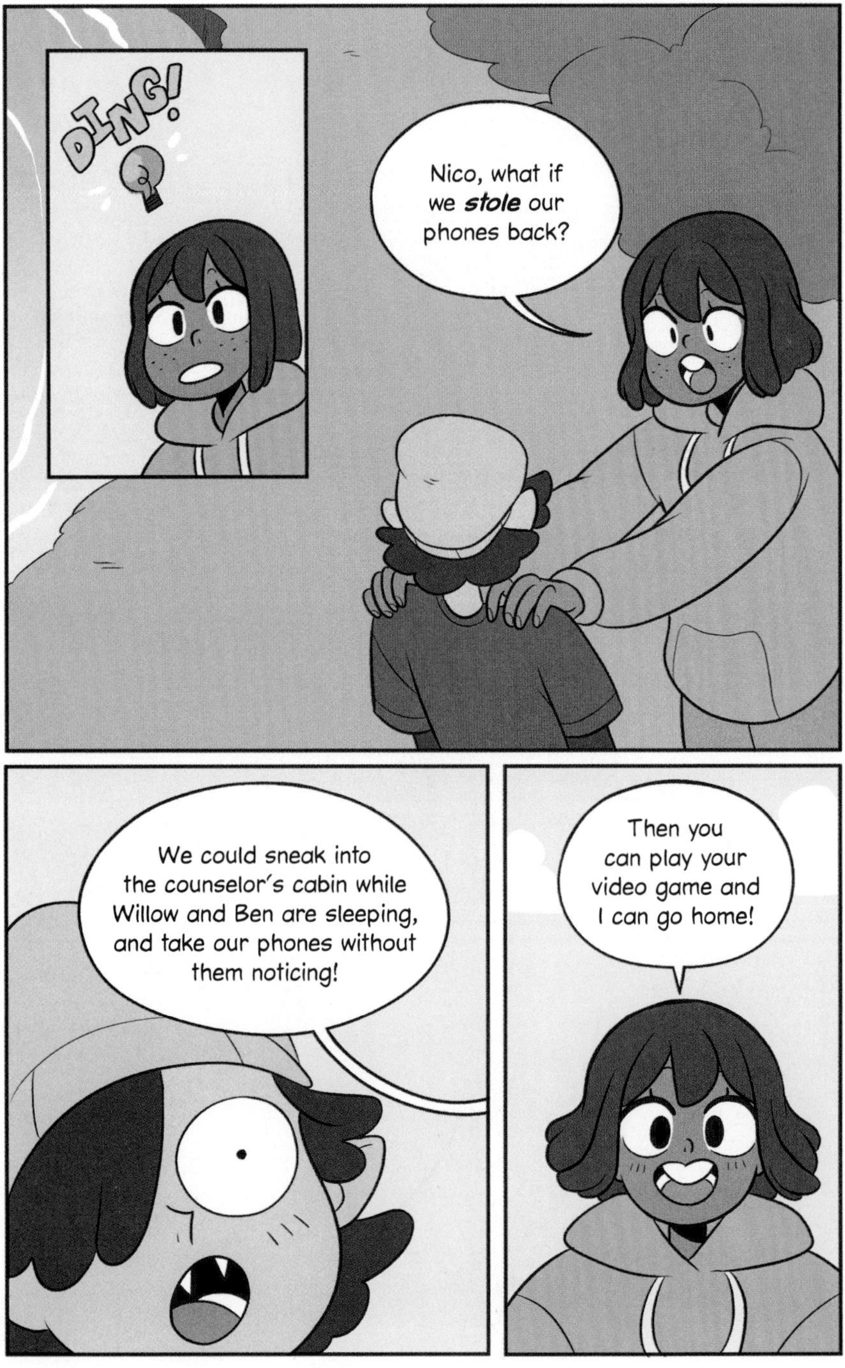
DING!
Nico, what if we *stole* our phones back?
We could sneak into the counselor's cabin while Willow and Ben are sleeping, and take our phones without them noticing!
Then you can play your video game and I can go home!

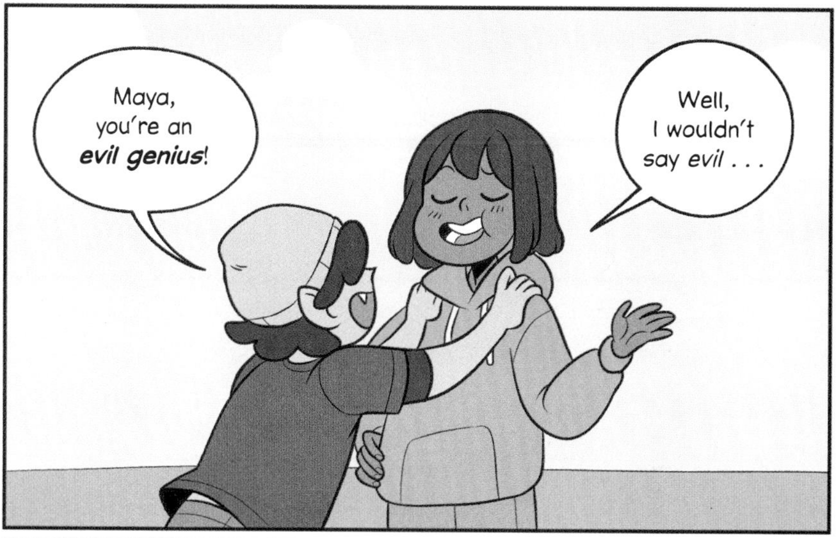
Maya, you're an ***evil genius***!
Well, I wouldn't say *evil* . . .

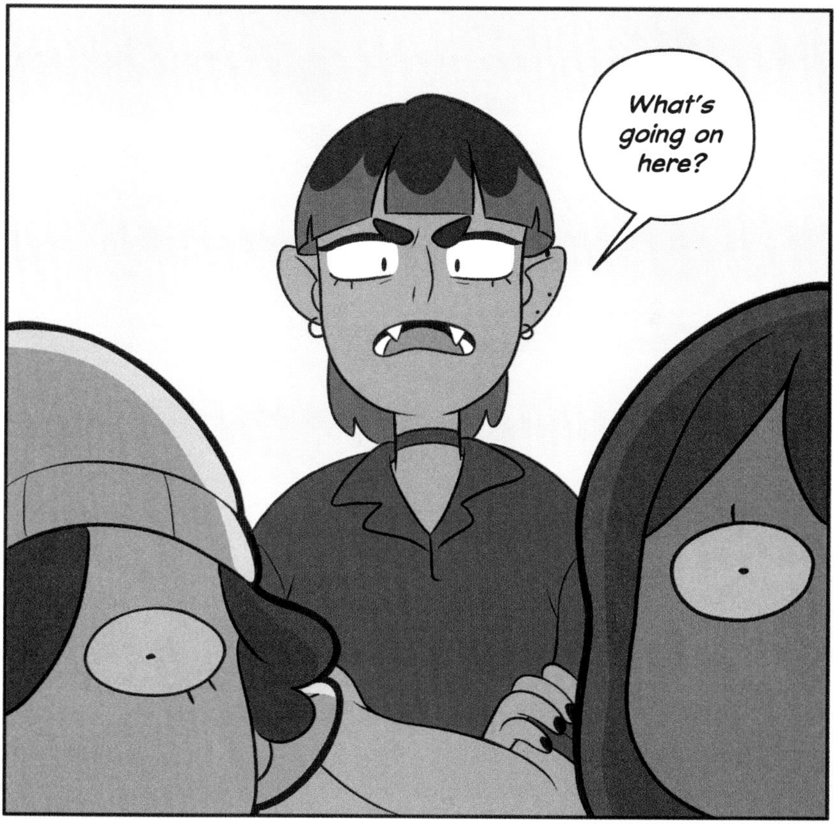
What's going on here?

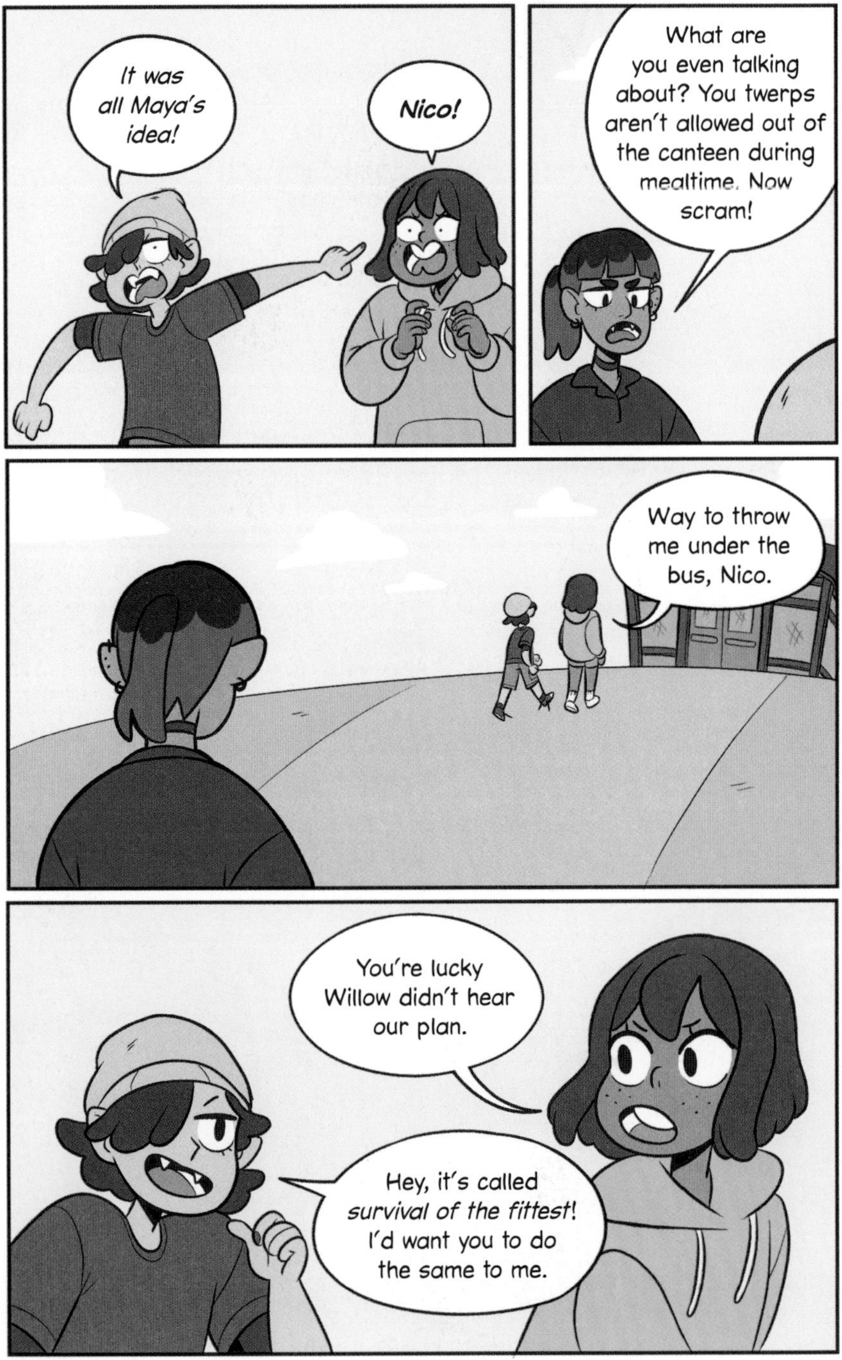
It was all Maya's idea!
Nico!
What are you even talking about? You twerps aren't allowed out of the canteen during mealtime. Now scram!
Way to throw me under the bus, Nico.
You're lucky Willow didn't hear our plan.
Hey, it's called *survival of the fittest*! I'd want you to do the same to me.

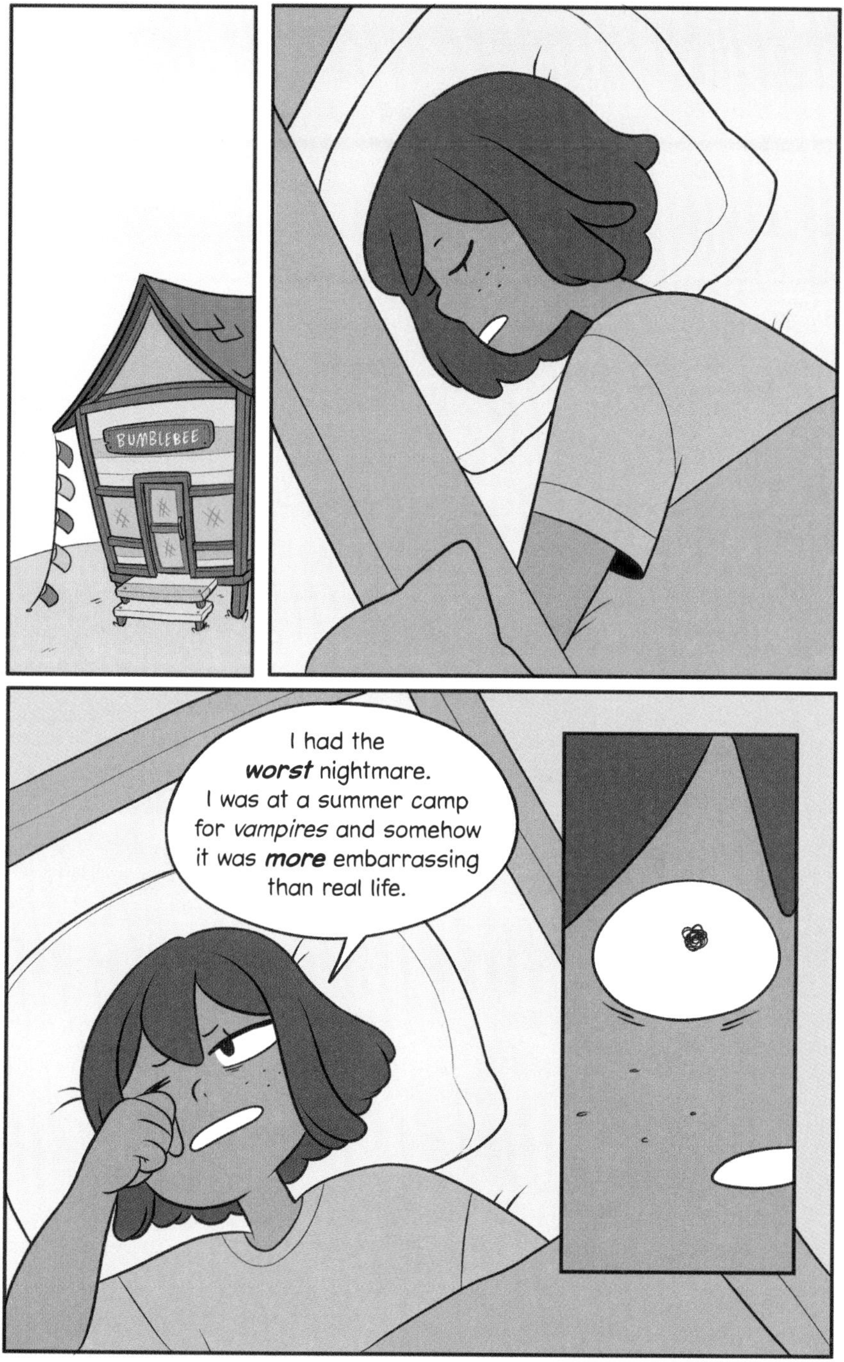
BUMBLEBEE
I had the **worst** nightmare. I was at a summer camp for *vampires* and somehow it was **more** embarrassing than real life.

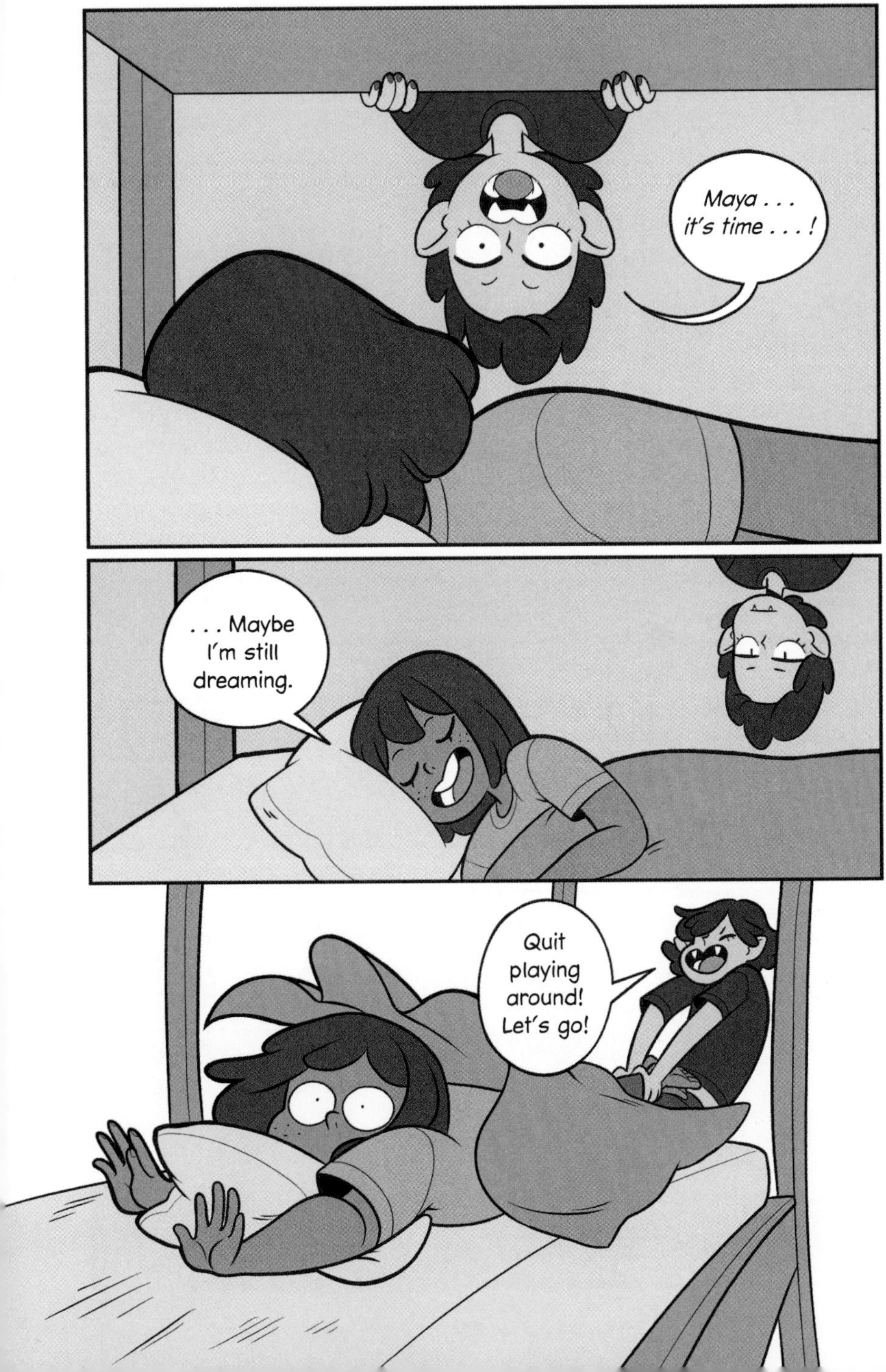
Maya . . . it's time . . . !
. . . Maybe I'm still dreaming.
Quit playing around! Let's go!

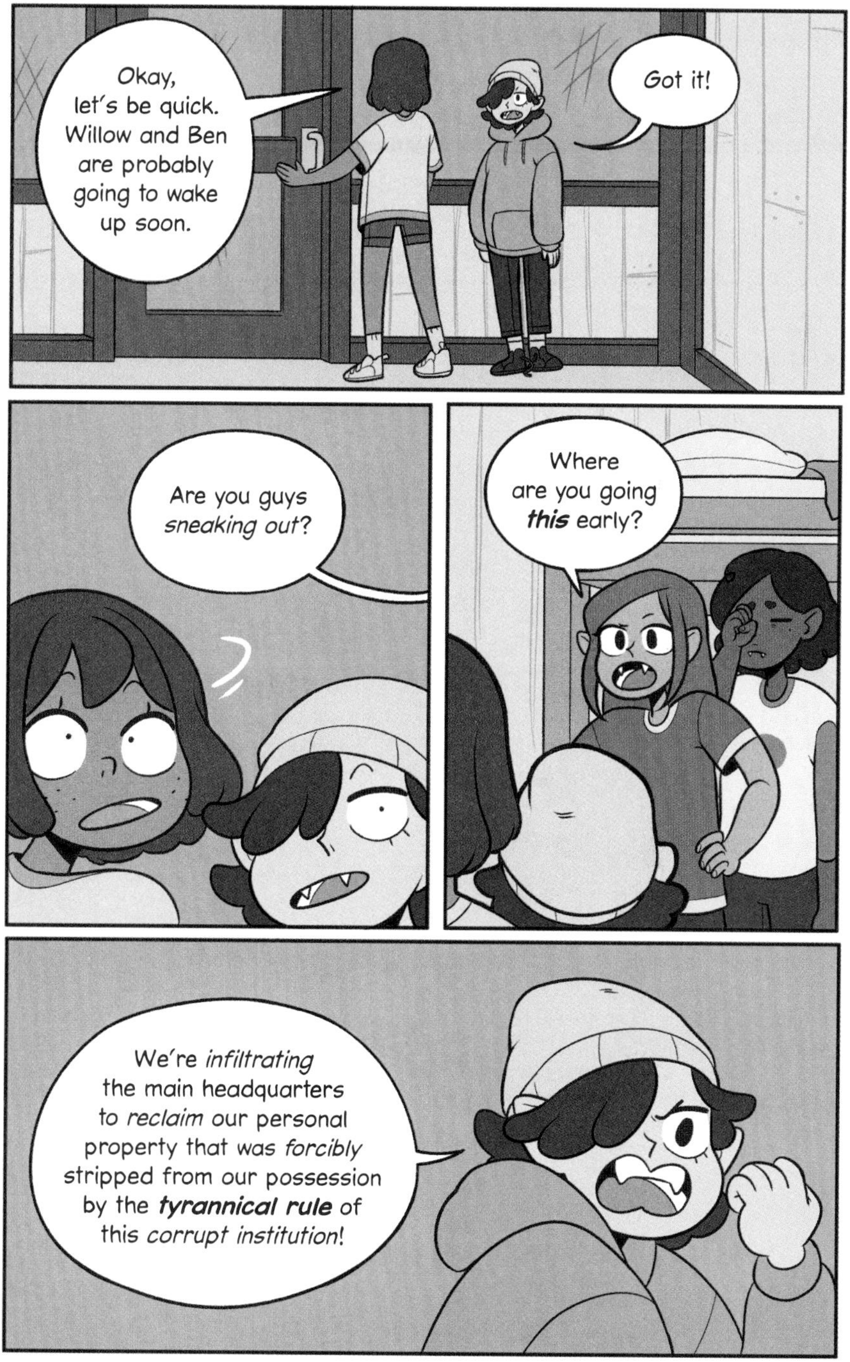
Okay, let's be quick. Willow and Ben are probably going to wake up soon.
Got it!
Are you guys *sneaking out*?
Where are you going ***this*** early?
We're *infiltrating* the main headquarters to *reclaim* our personal property that was *forcibly* stripped from our possession by the ***tyrannical rule*** of this *corrupt institution*!

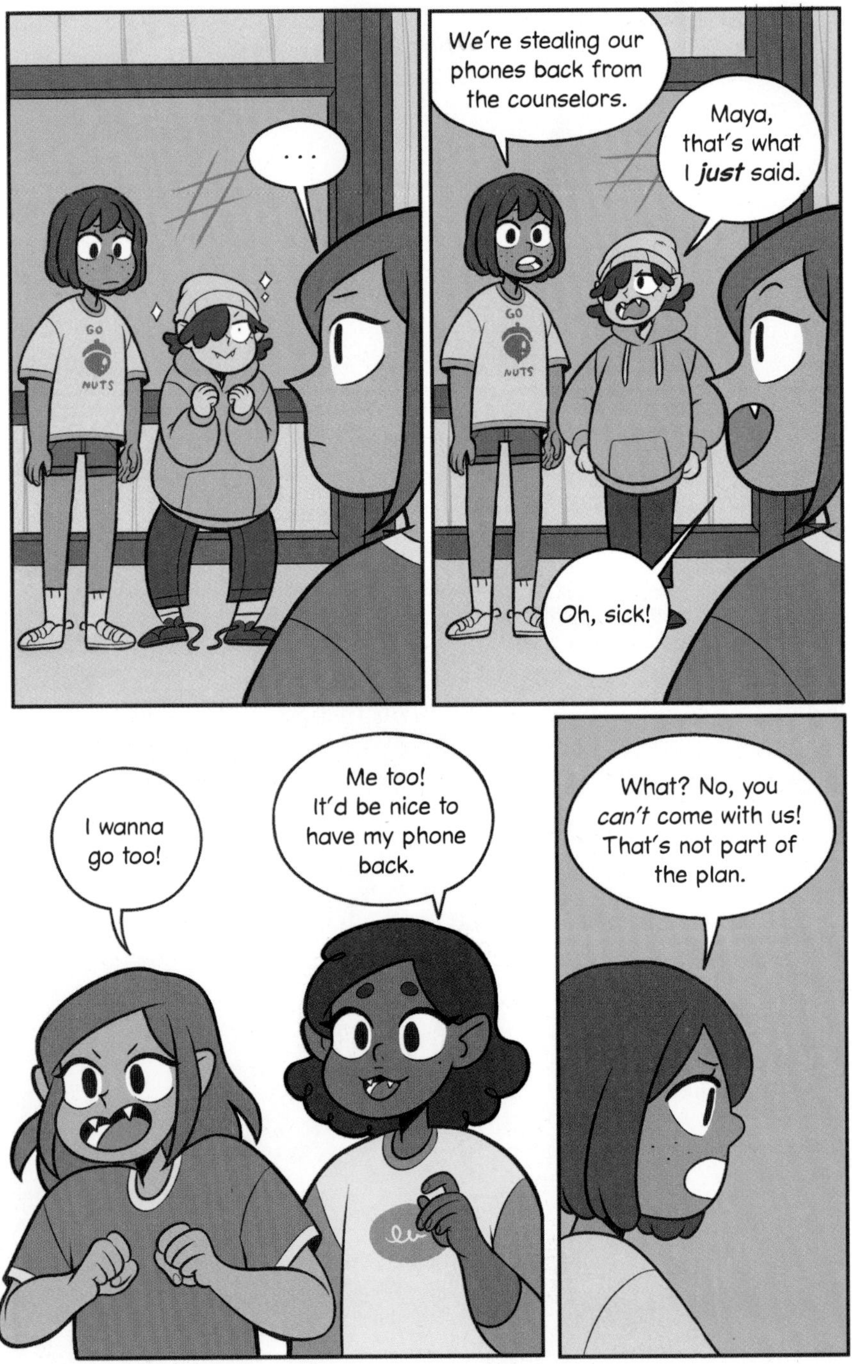
. . .
We're stealing our phones back from the counselors.
Maya, that's what I *just* said.
Oh, sick!
I wanna go too!
Me too! It'd be nice to have my phone back.
What? No, you *can't* come with us! That's not part of the plan.

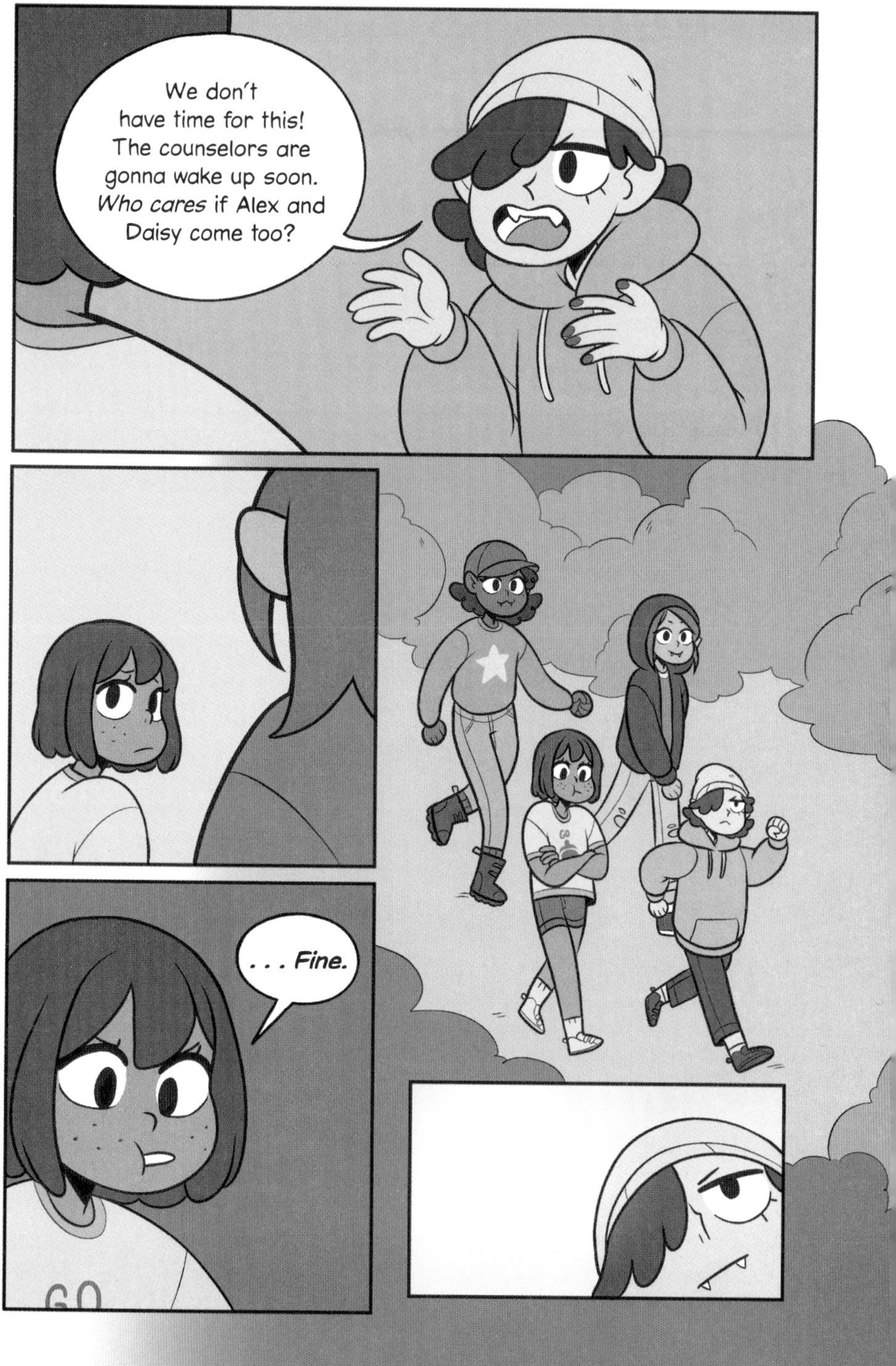
We don't have time for this! The counselors are gonna wake up soon. *Who cares* if Alex and Daisy come too?
GO
. . . Fine.
GO

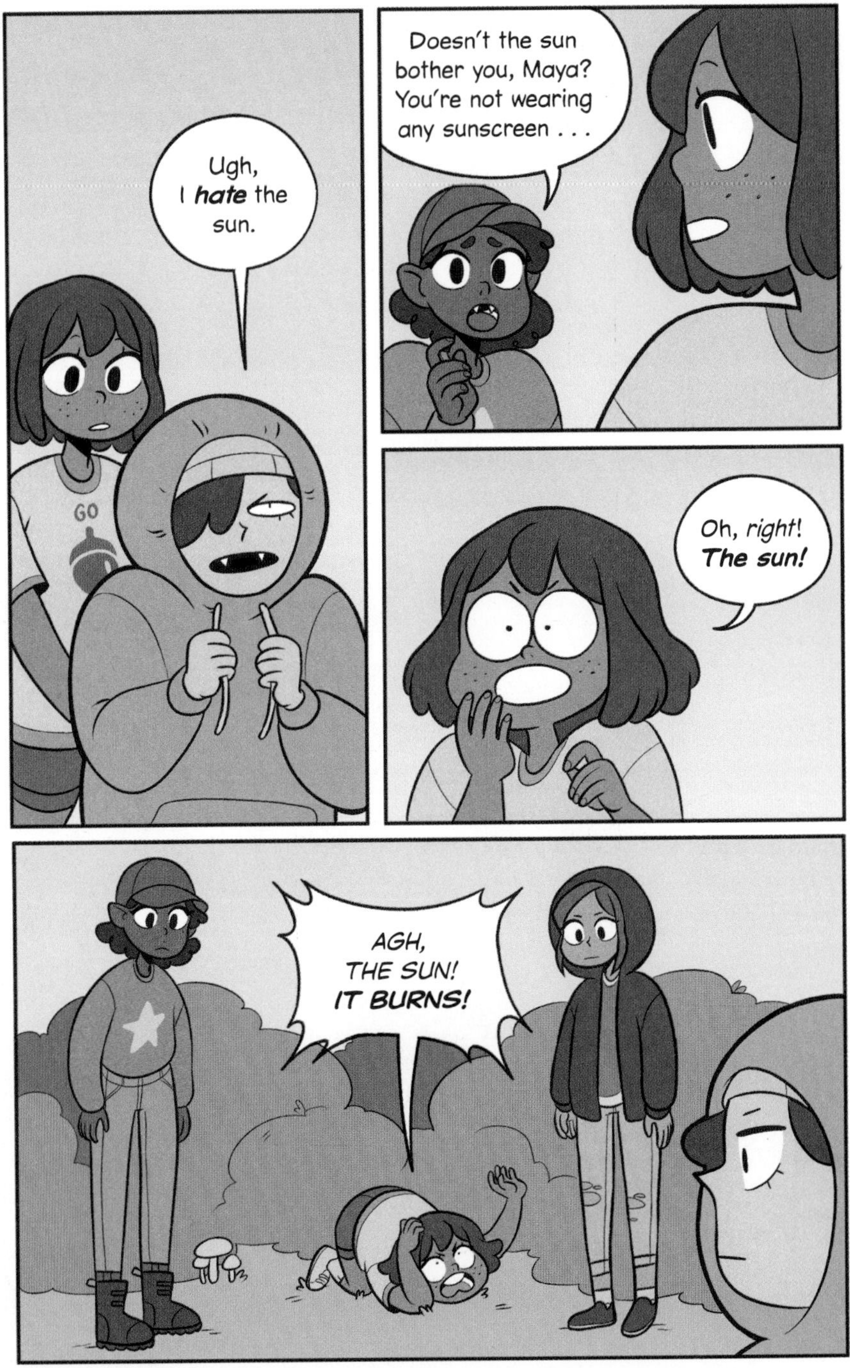
Ugh, I *hate* the sun.
Doesn't the sun bother you, Maya? You're not wearing any sunscreen . . .
Oh, right! **The sun!**
AGH, THE SUN! **IT BURNS!**
GO

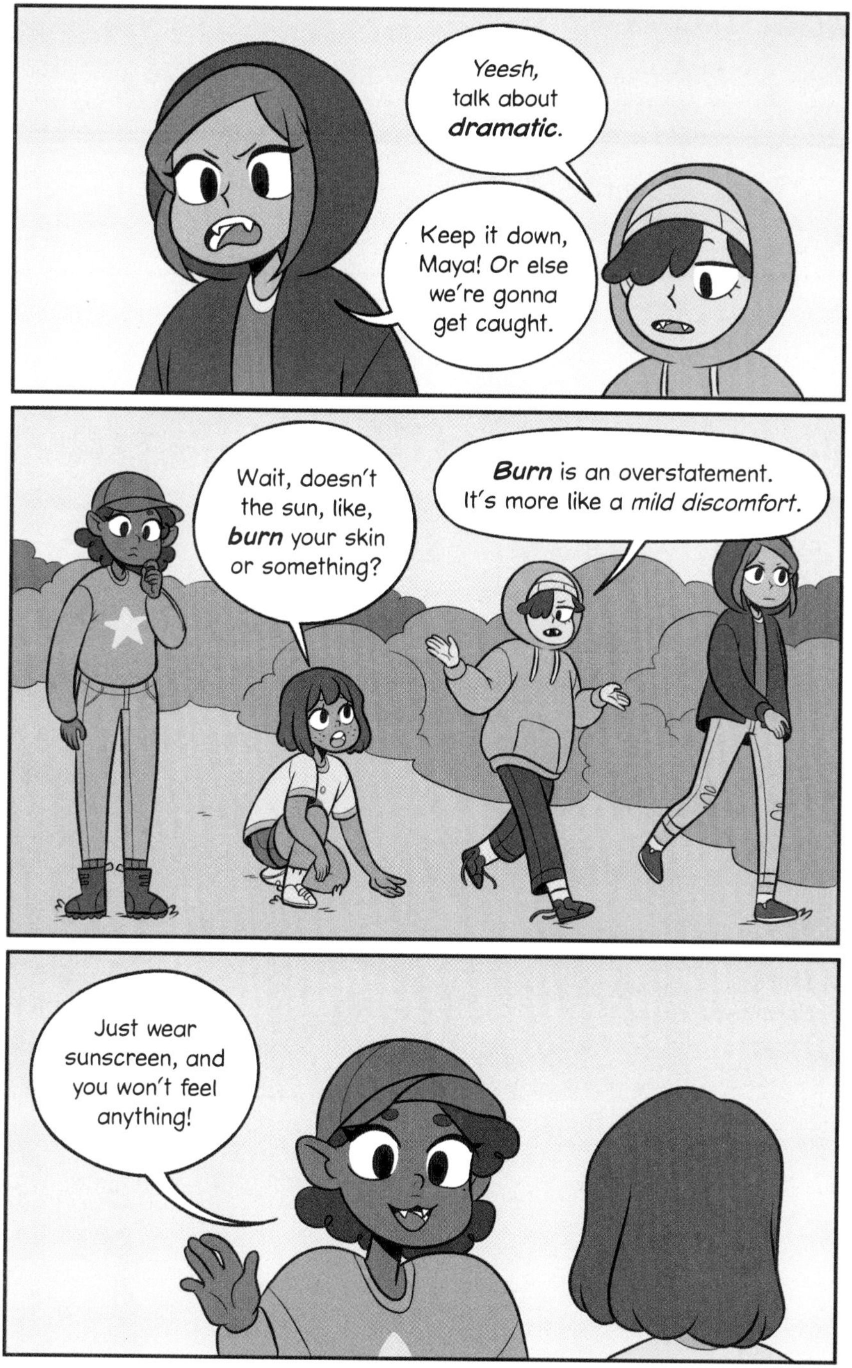
Yeesh, talk about **dramatic**.
Keep it down, Maya! Or else we're gonna get caught.
Wait, doesn't the sun, like, **burn** your skin or something?
Burn is an overstatement. It's more like a *mild discomfort*.
Just wear sunscreen, and you won't feel anything!

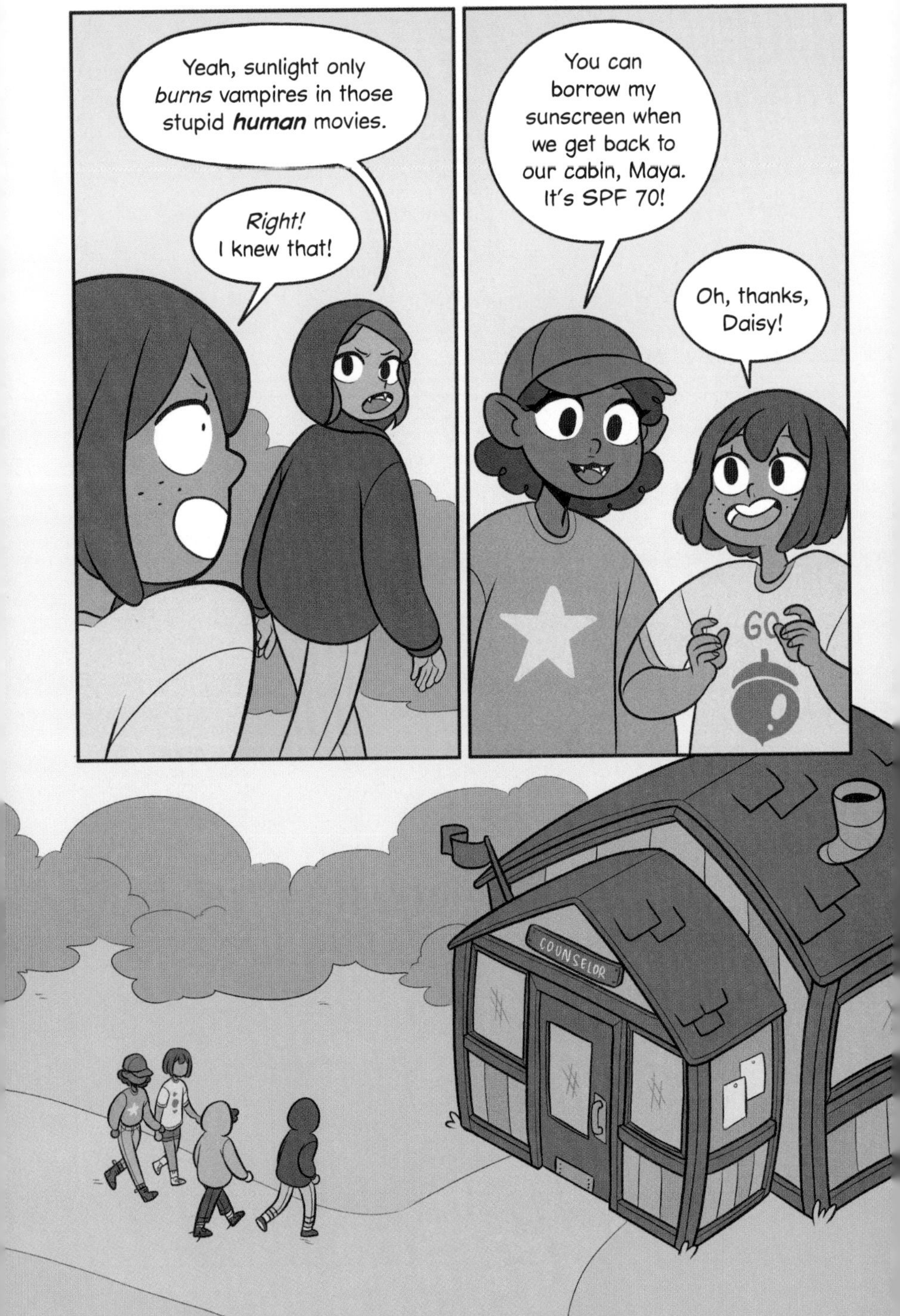
Yeah, sunlight only *burns* vampires in those stupid ***human*** movies.
Right! I knew that!
You can borrow my sunscreen when we get back to our cabin, Maya. It's SPF 70!
Oh, thanks, Daisy!
COUNSELOR

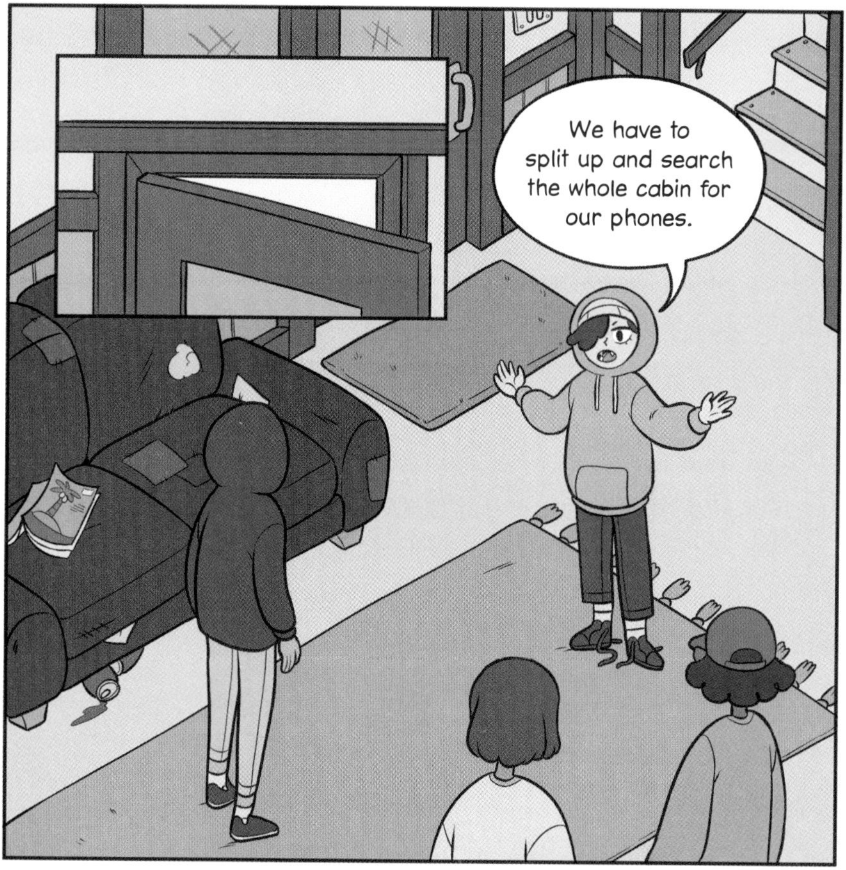
We have to split up and search the whole cabin for our phones.

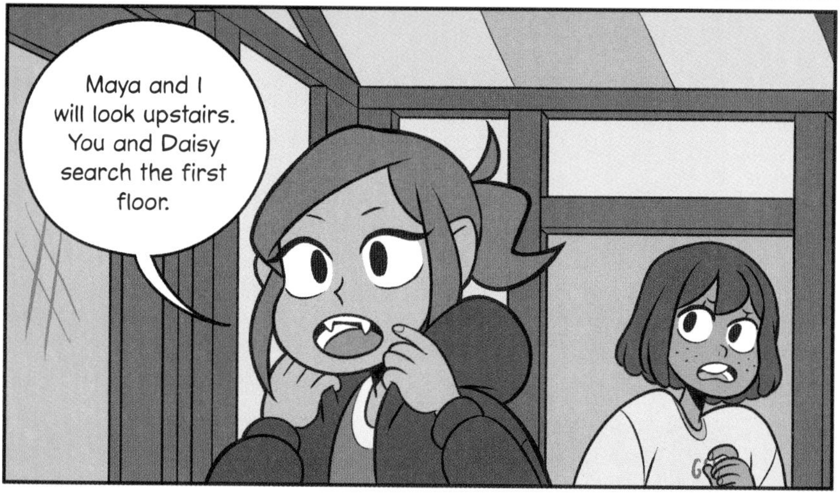
Maya and I will look upstairs. You and Daisy search the first floor.

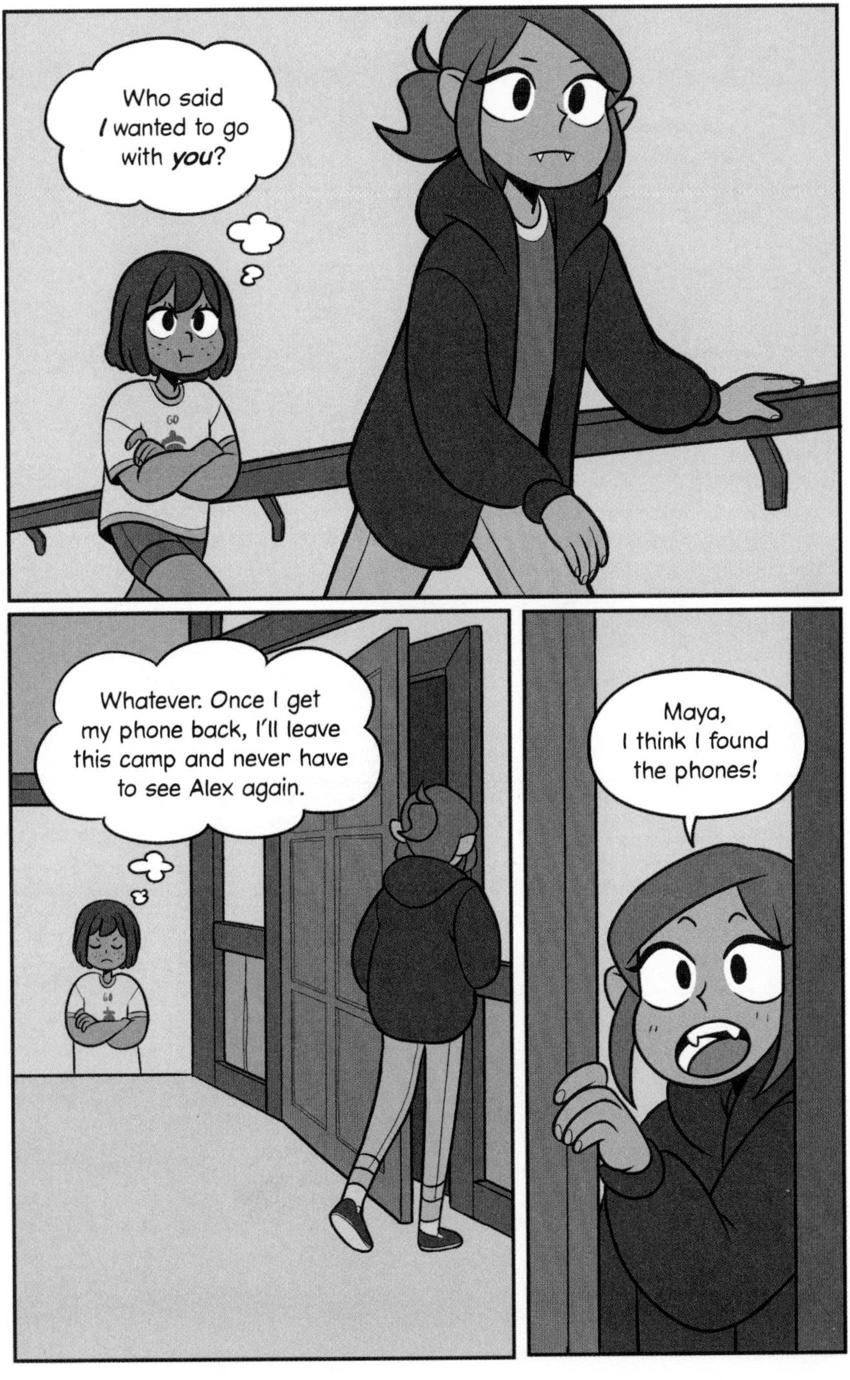
Who said *I* wanted to go with ***you***?
Whatever. Once I get my phone back, I'll leave this camp and never have to see Alex again.
Maya, I think I found the phones!

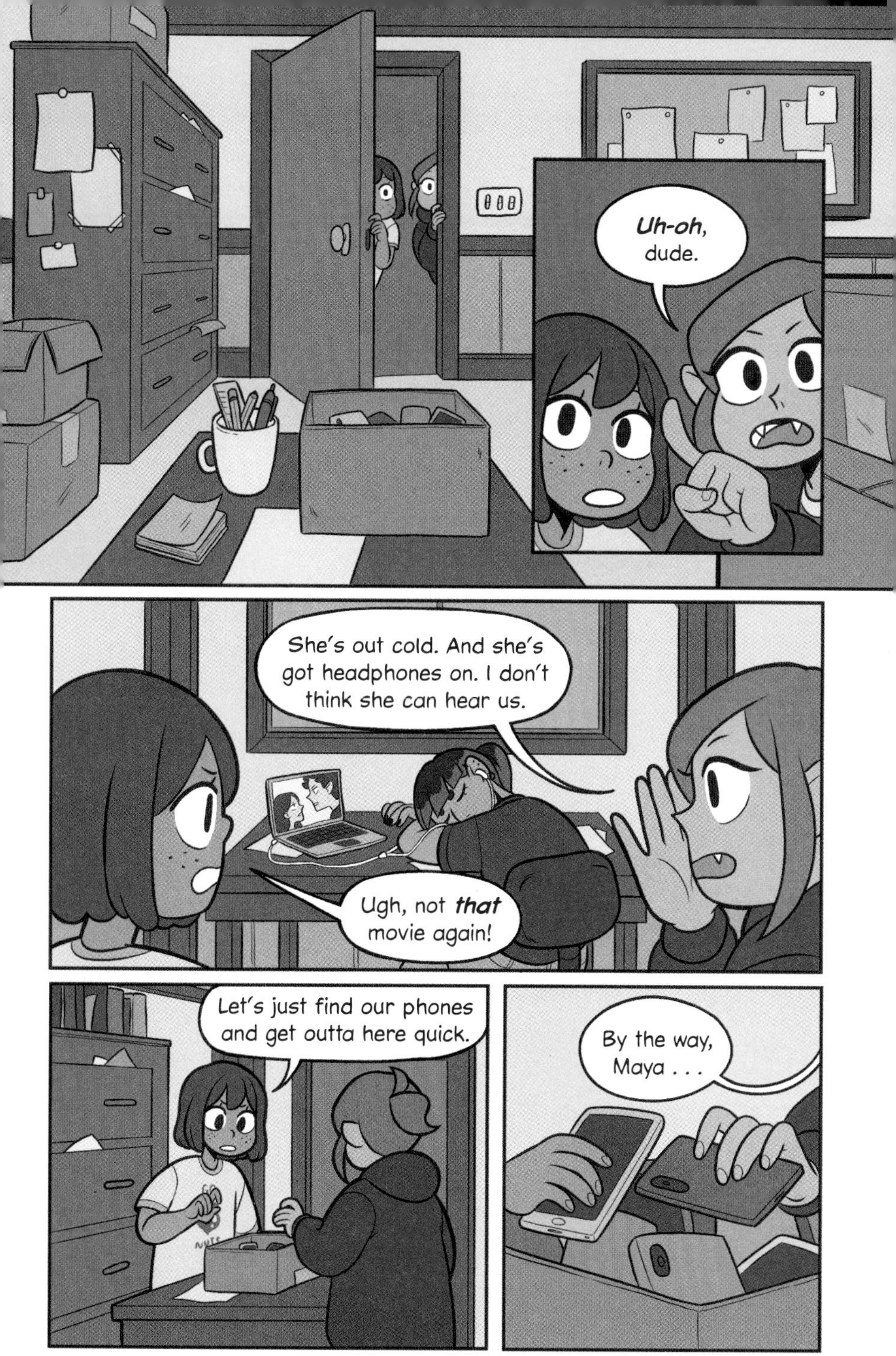
Uh-oh,
dude.
She's out cold. And she's got headphones on. I don't think she can hear us.
Ugh, not that movie again!
Let's just find our phones and get outta here quick.
By the way, Maya . . .

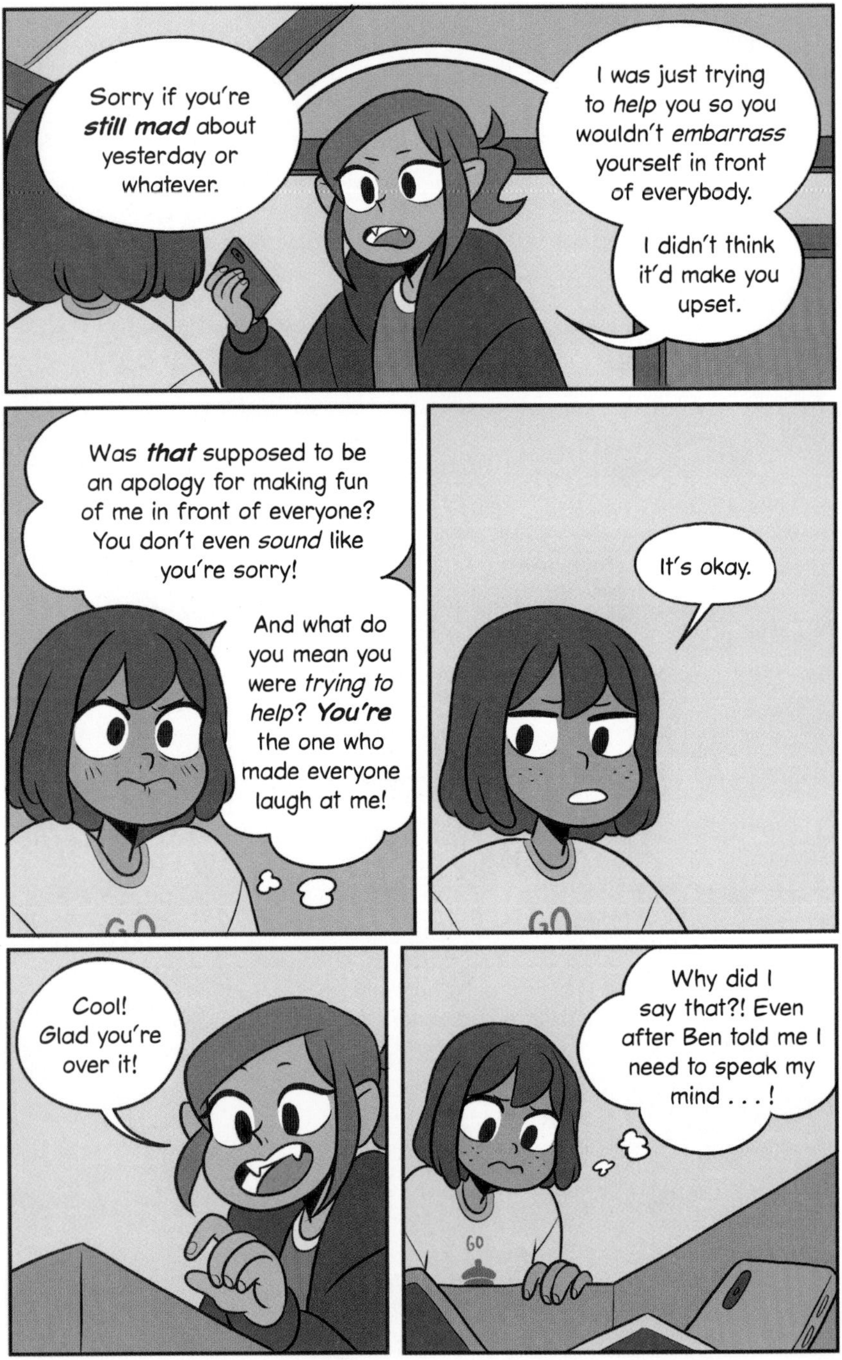
Sorry if you're ***still mad*** about yesterday or whatever.
I was just trying to *help* you so you wouldn't *embarrass* yourself in front of everybody.
I didn't think it'd make you upset.
Was ***that*** supposed to be an apology for making fun of me in front of everyone? You don't even *sound* like you're sorry!
And what do you mean you were *trying to help*? ***You're*** the one who made everyone laugh at me!
GO
It's okay.
GO
Cool! Glad you're over it!
Why did I say that?! Even after Ben told me I need to speak my mind . . . !
GO

This is just like when I couldn't tell Dad how I felt about Charlotte moving in.

SLIP!

THUNK!

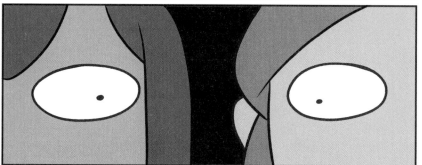

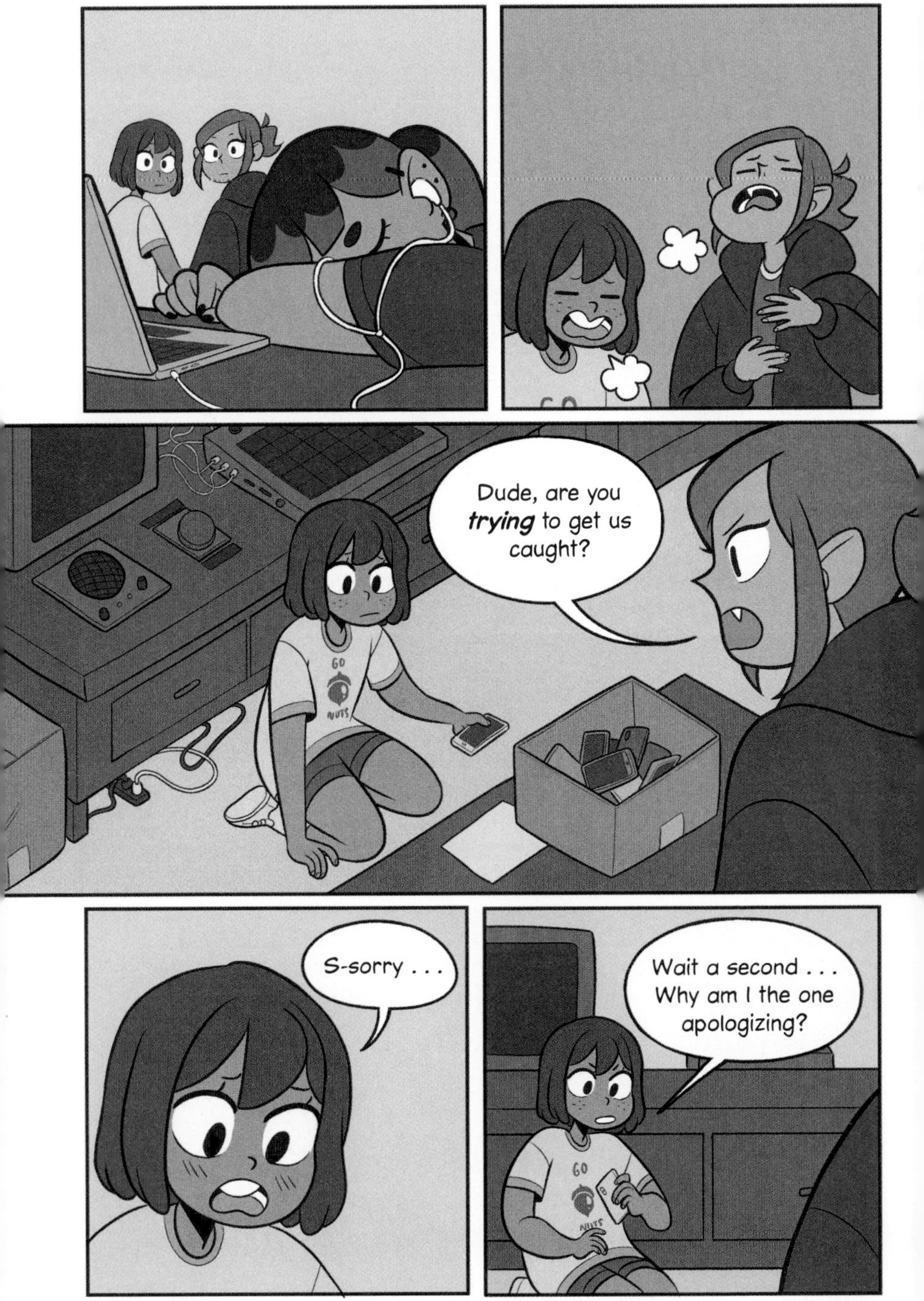

GO
Dude, are you *trying* to get us caught?
GO NUTS
S-sorry . . .
Wait a second . . . Why am I the one apologizing?
GO NUTS

You've been *picking on me* since the *bus ride* to camp!
I shouldn't have to say sorry to ***you***–
IN CASE OF
EMERGENCY
BEEP!
IN CASE OF
EMERGENCY
Uh-oh.

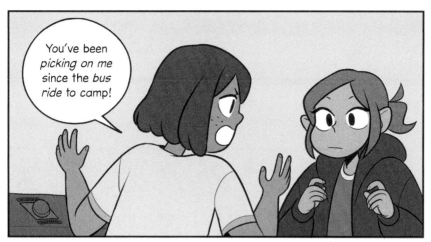

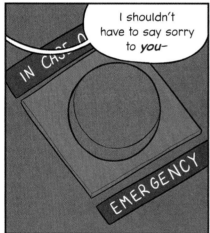

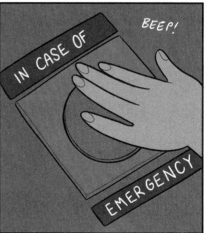

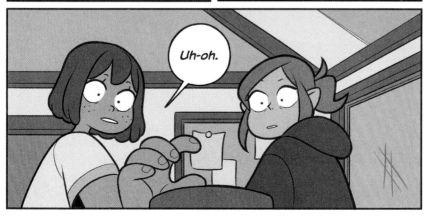

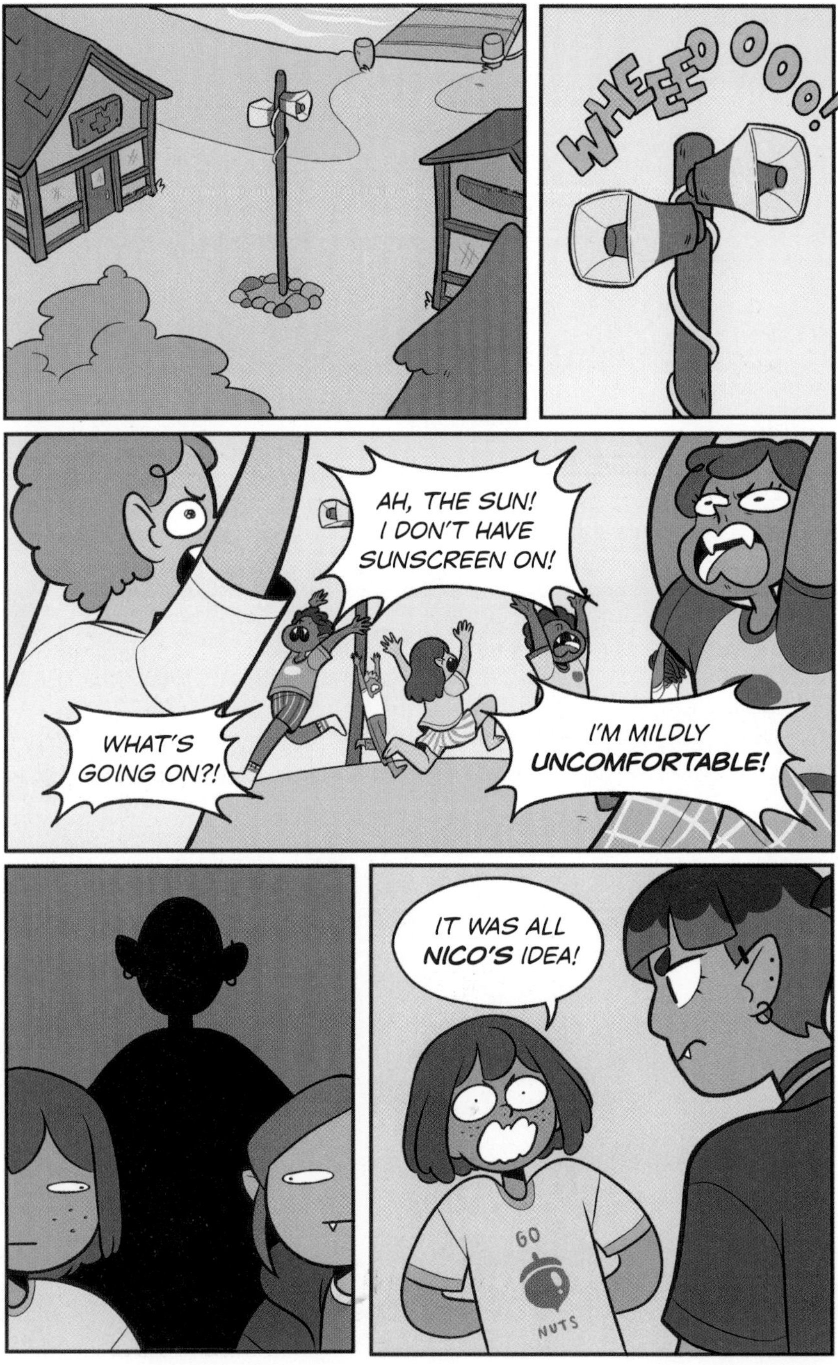
WHEEEOOOO!
AH, THE SUN!
I DON'T HAVE
SUNSCREEN ON!
WHAT'S
GOING ON?!
I'M MILDLY
UNCOMFORTABLE!
IT WAS ALL
NICO'S IDEA!
GO
NUTS

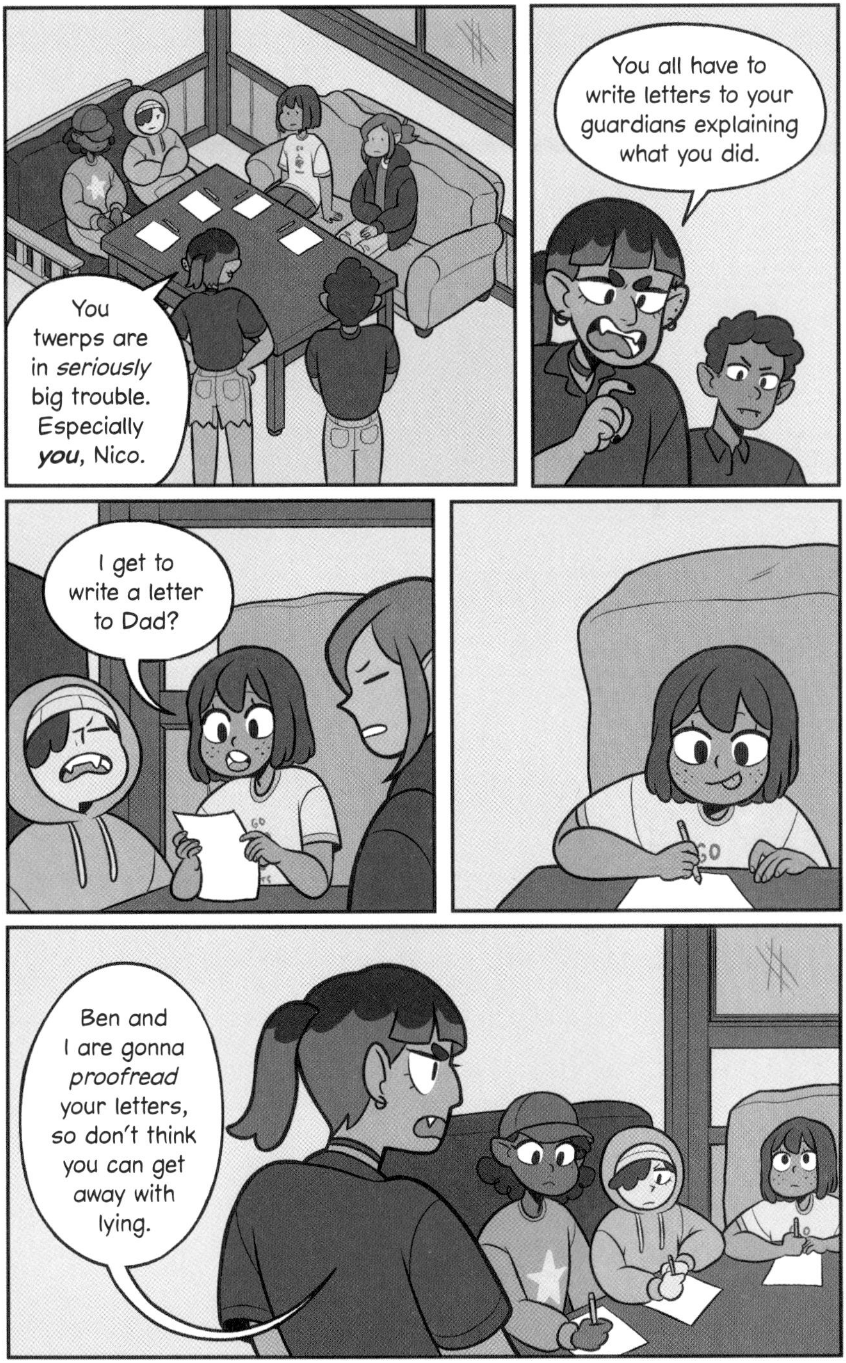
You twerps are in *seriously* big trouble. Especially ***you***, Nico.
You all have to write letters to your guardians explaining what you did.
I get to write a letter to Dad?
Ben and I are gonna *proofread* your letters, so don't think you can get away with lying.

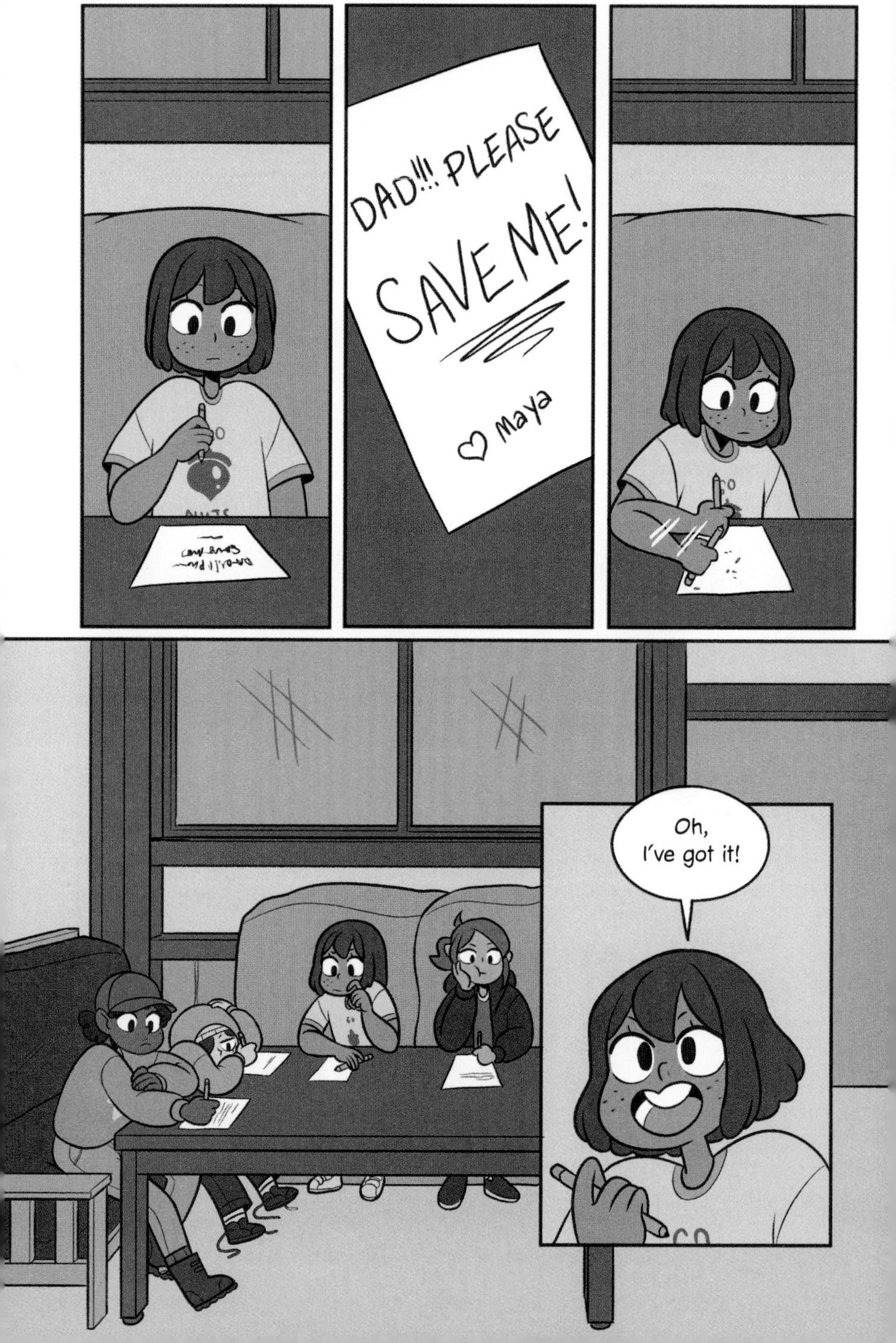
DAD!!! PLEASE
SAVE ME!
♡ maya
Oh,
I've got it!

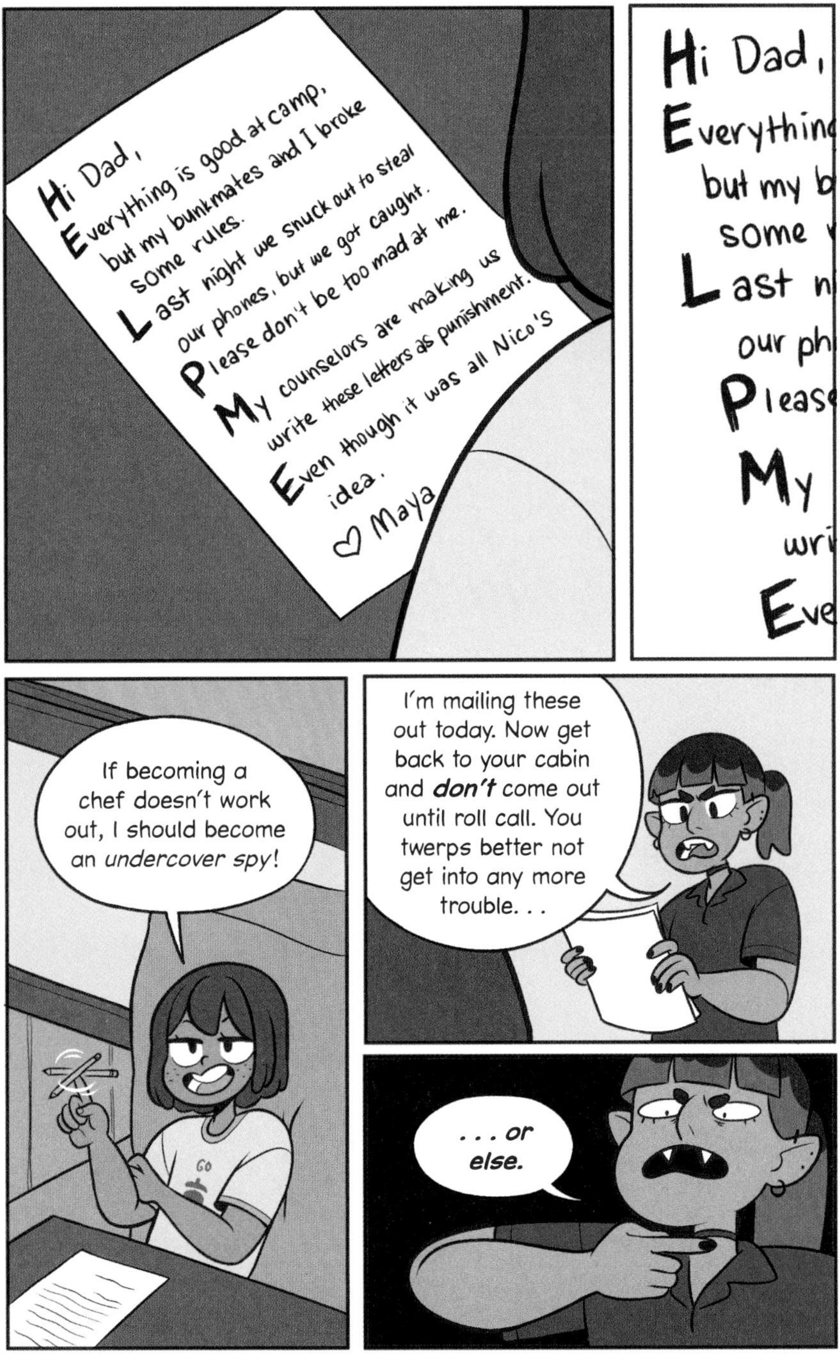
Hi Dad,
Everything is good at camp, but my bunkmates and I broke some rules.
Last night we snuck out to steal our phones, but we got caught.
Please don't be too mad at me.
My counselors are making us write these letters as punishment.
Even though it was all Nico's idea.
♡ Maya
Hi Dad,
Everythin
but my b
some
Last n
our ph
Pleas
My
wri
Eve
If becoming a chef doesn't work out, I should become an *undercover spy*!
GO
I'm mailing these out today. Now get back to your cabin and ***don't*** come out until roll call. You twerps better not get into any more trouble. . .
. . . or else.

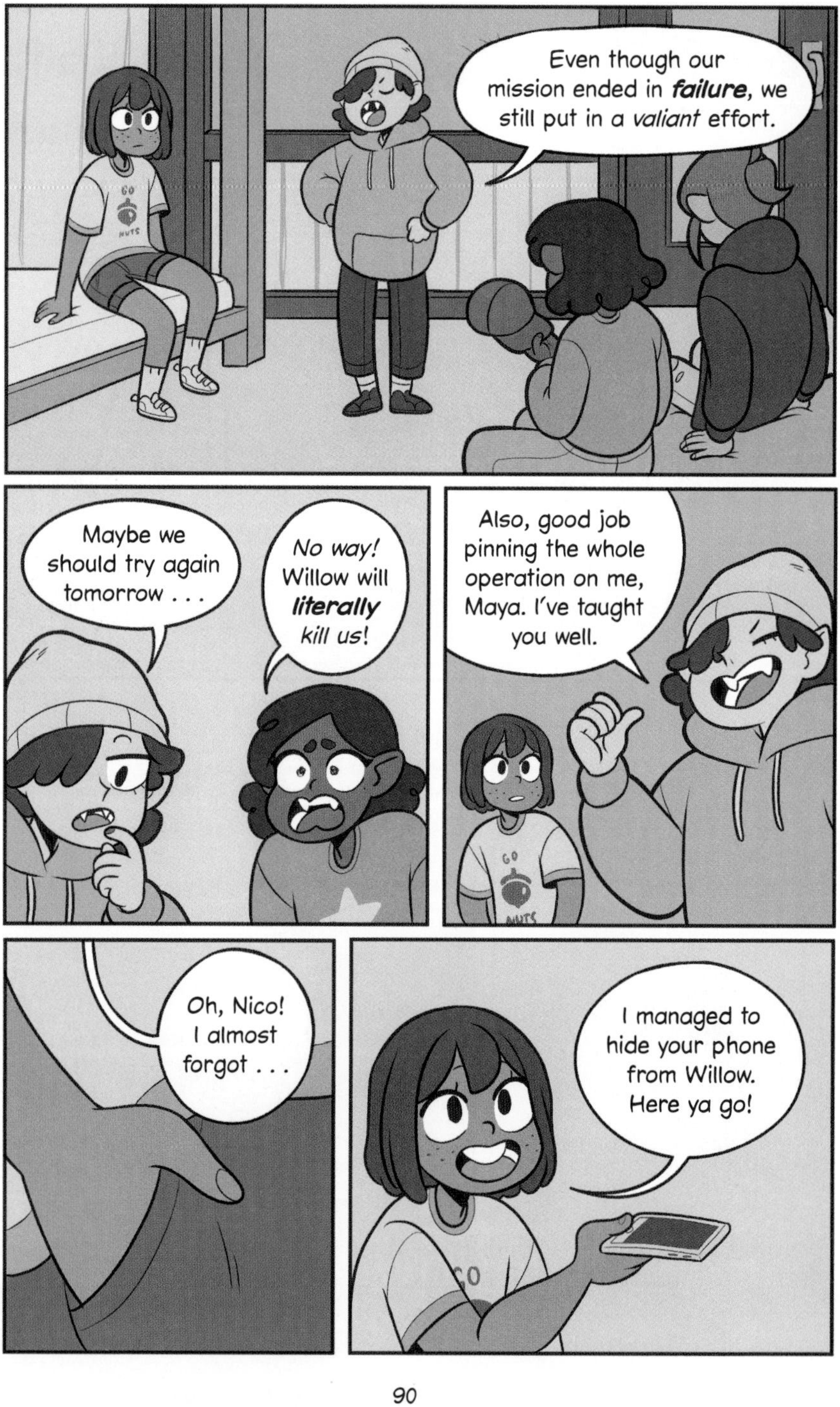
Even though our mission ended in ***failure***, we still put in a *valiant* effort.
Maybe we should try again tomorrow . . .
No way! Willow will ***literally*** *kill us*!
Also, good job pinning the whole operation on me, Maya. I've taught you well.
Oh, Nico! I almost forgot . . .
I managed to hide your phone from Willow. Here ya go!

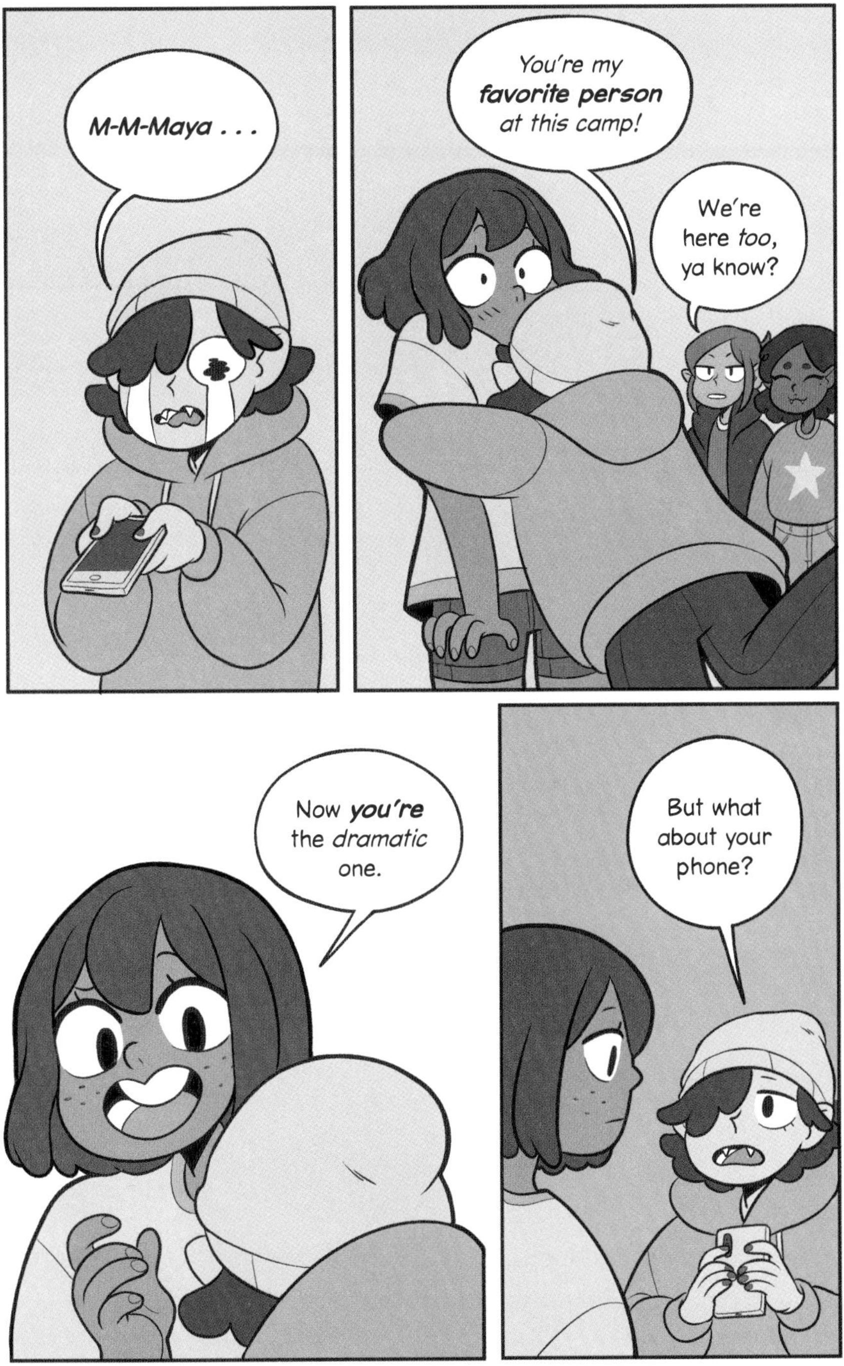
M-M-Maya . . .
You're my **favorite person** at this camp!
We're here *too*, ya know?
Now ***you're*** the *dramatic* one.
But what about your phone?

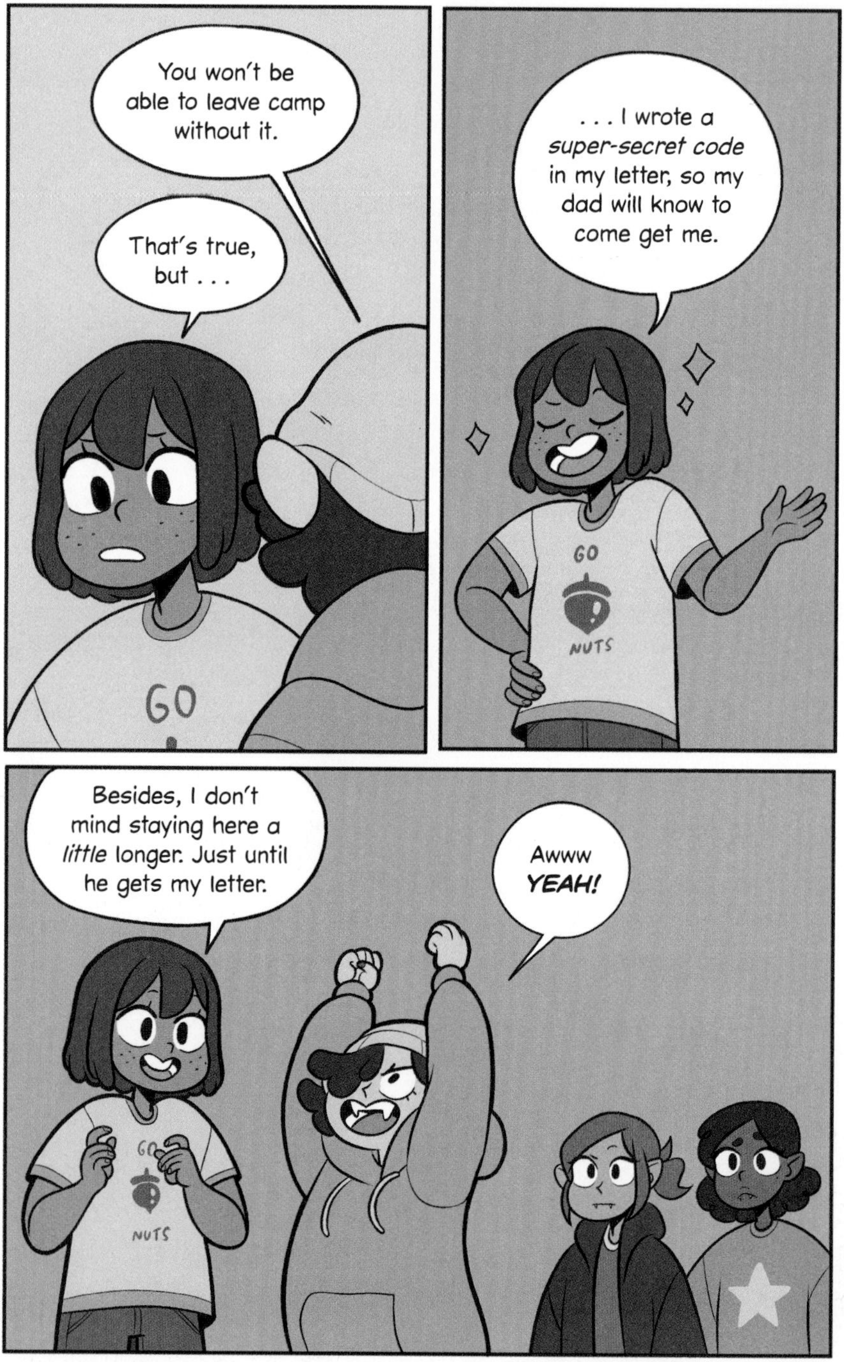
You won't be able to leave camp without it.
That's true, but . . .
. . . I wrote a *super-secret code* in my letter, so my dad will know to come get me.
GO NUTS
Besides, I don't mind staying here a *little* longer. Just until he gets my letter.
Awww **YEAH!**
GO NUTS

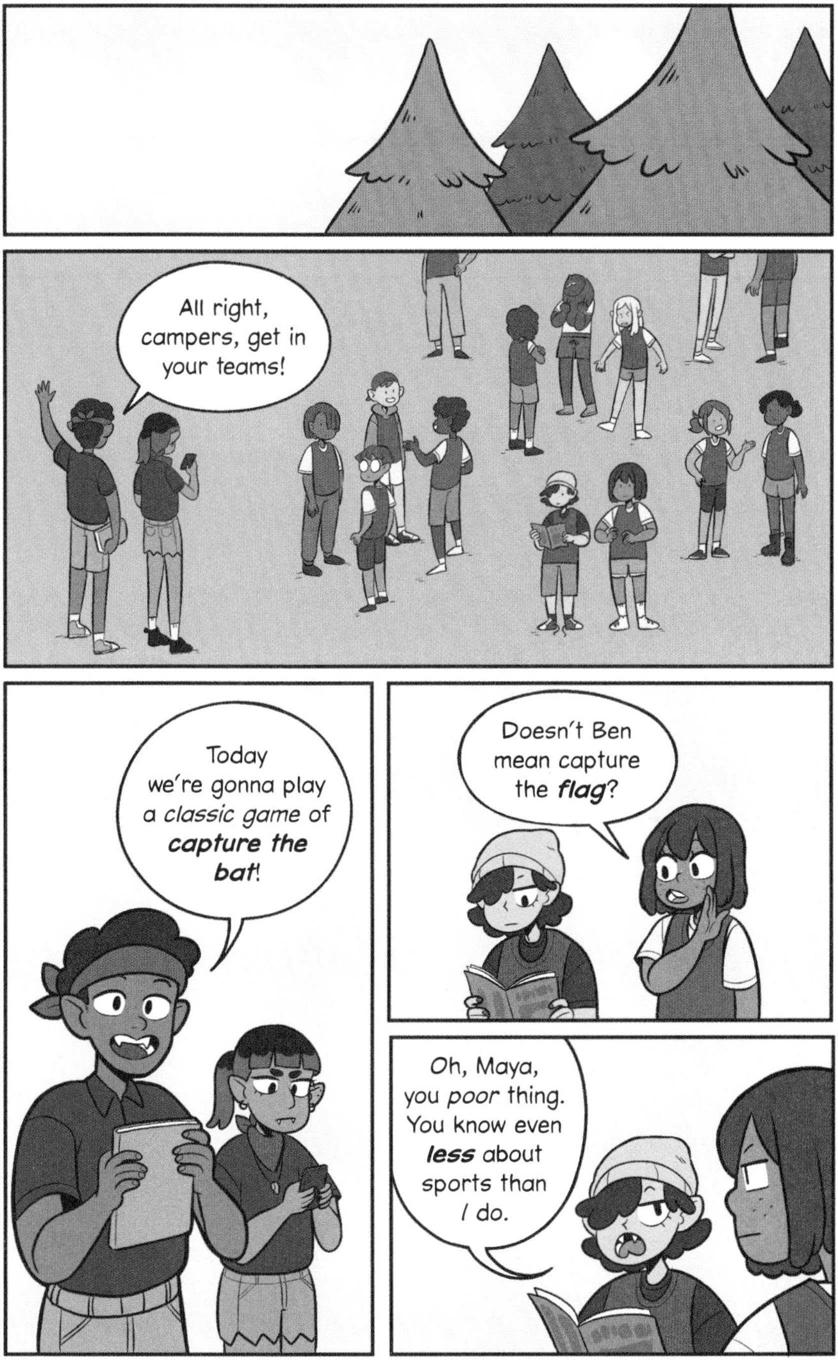
All right, campers, get in your teams!
Today we're gonna play a *classic game* of **capture the bat**!
Doesn't Ben mean capture the ***flag***?
Oh, Maya, you *poor* thing. You know even ***less*** about sports than *I* do.

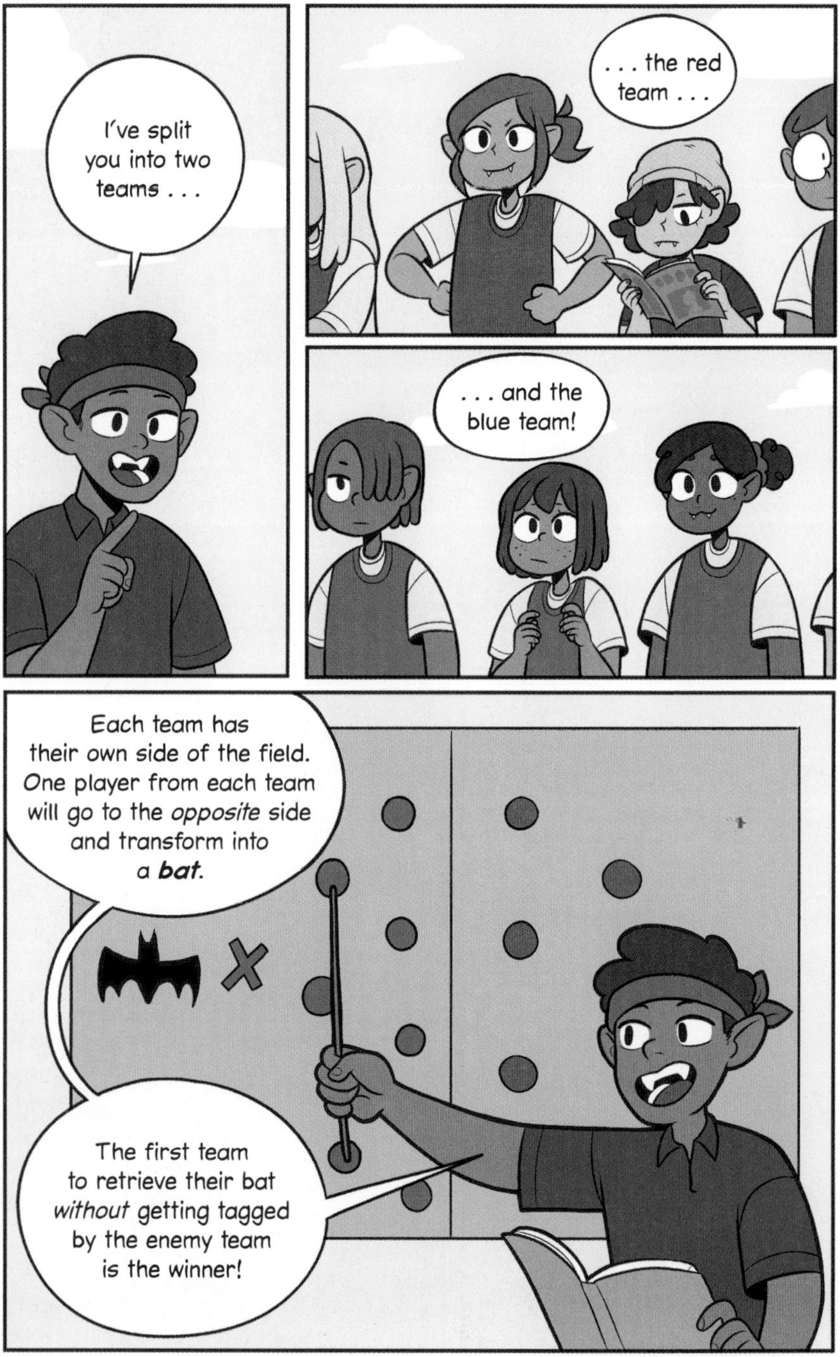

I've split you into two teams . . .
. . . the red team . . .
. . . and the blue team!
Each team has their own side of the field. One player from each team will go to the *opposite* side and transform into a ***bat***.
The first team to retrieve their bat *without* getting tagged by the enemy team is the winner!

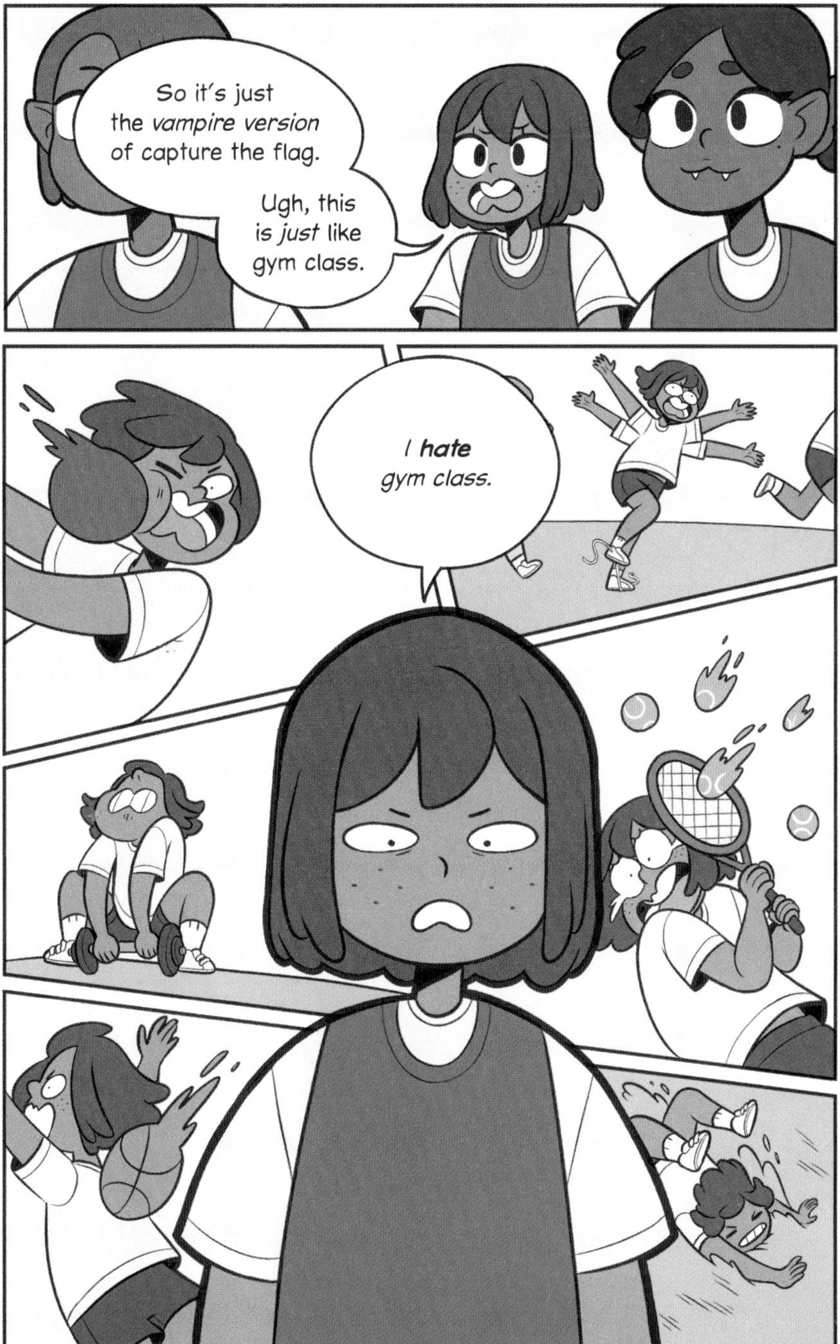
So it's just the *vampire version* of capture the flag.
Ugh, this is *just* like gym class.
I **hate** gym class.

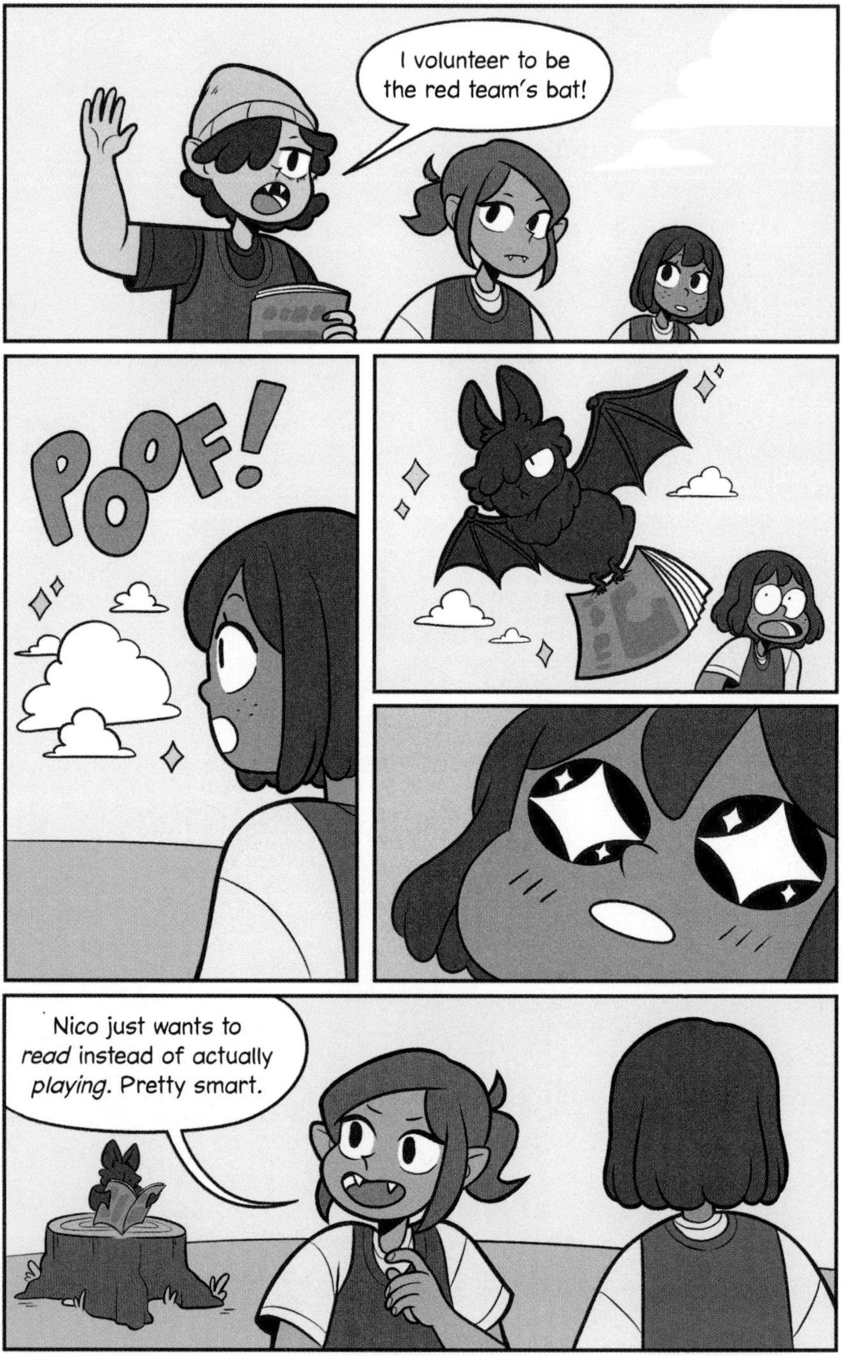
I volunteer to be the red team's bat!
POOF!
Nico just wants to *read* instead of actually *playing*. Pretty smart.

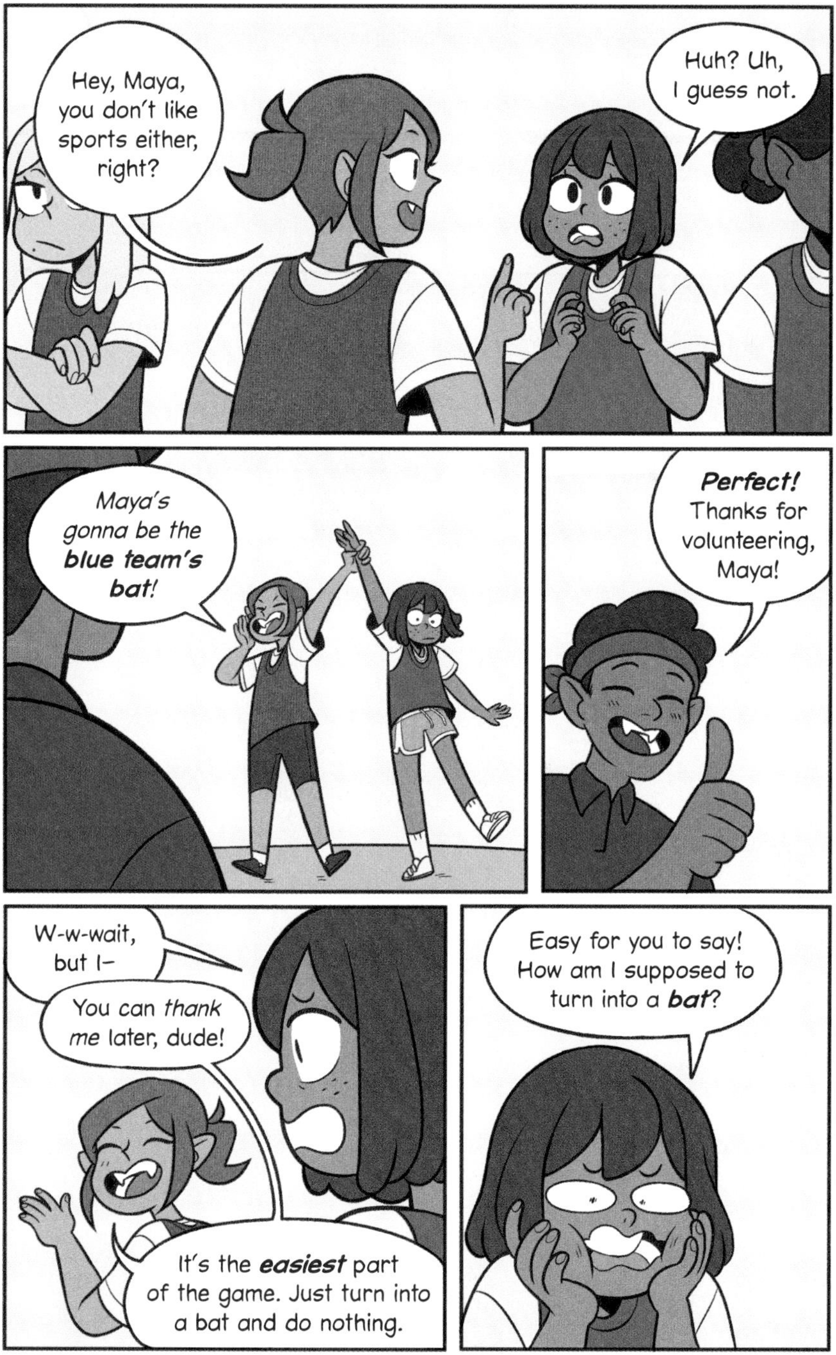
Hey, Maya, you don't like sports either, right?
Huh? Uh, I guess not.
Maya's gonna be the **blue team's bat**!
Perfect! Thanks for volunteering, Maya!
W-w-wait, but I–
You can *thank me* later, dude!
It's the ***easiest*** part of the game. Just turn into a bat and do nothing.
Easy for you to say! How am I supposed to turn into a ***bat***?

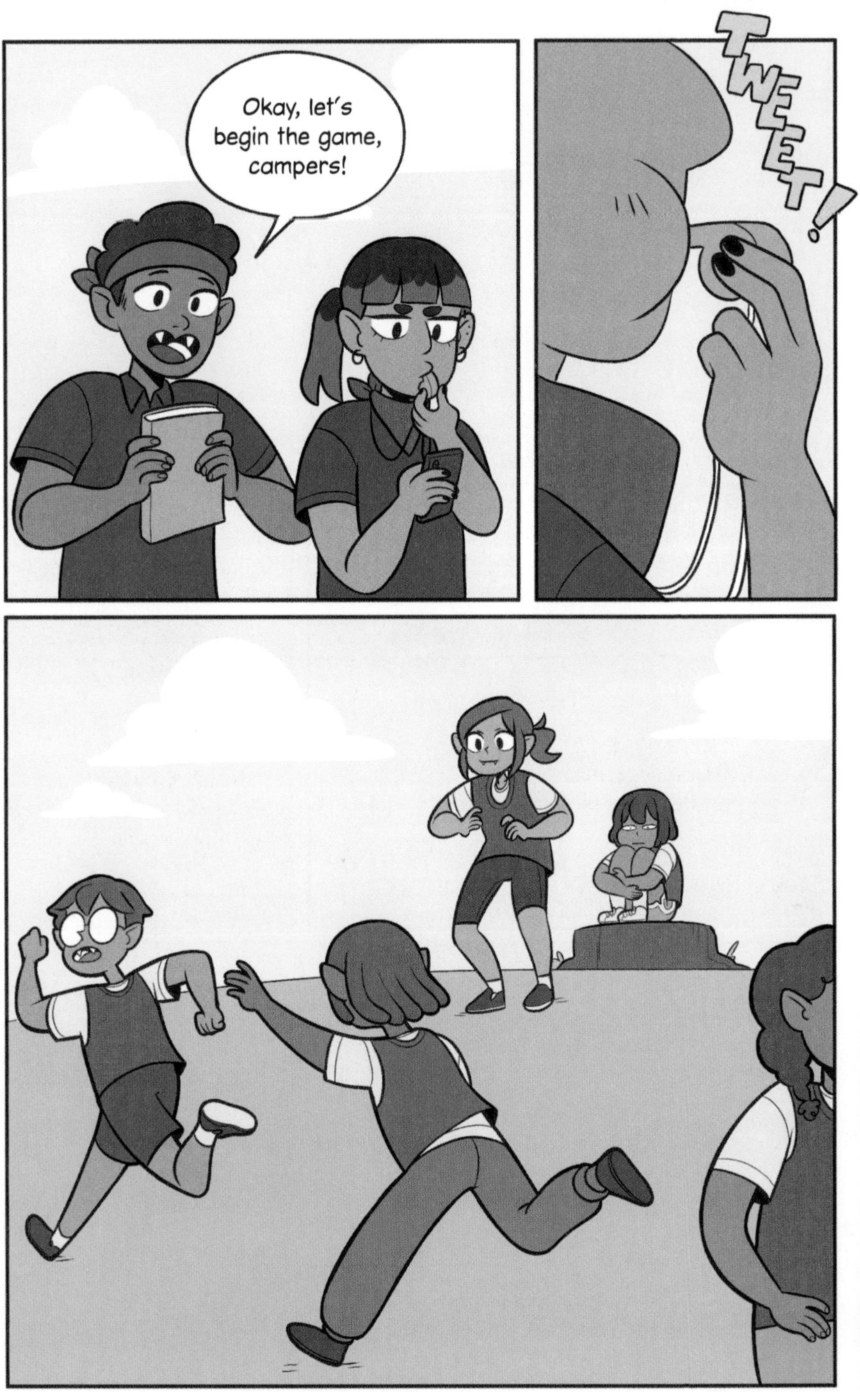
Okay, let's begin the game, campers!
TWEET!

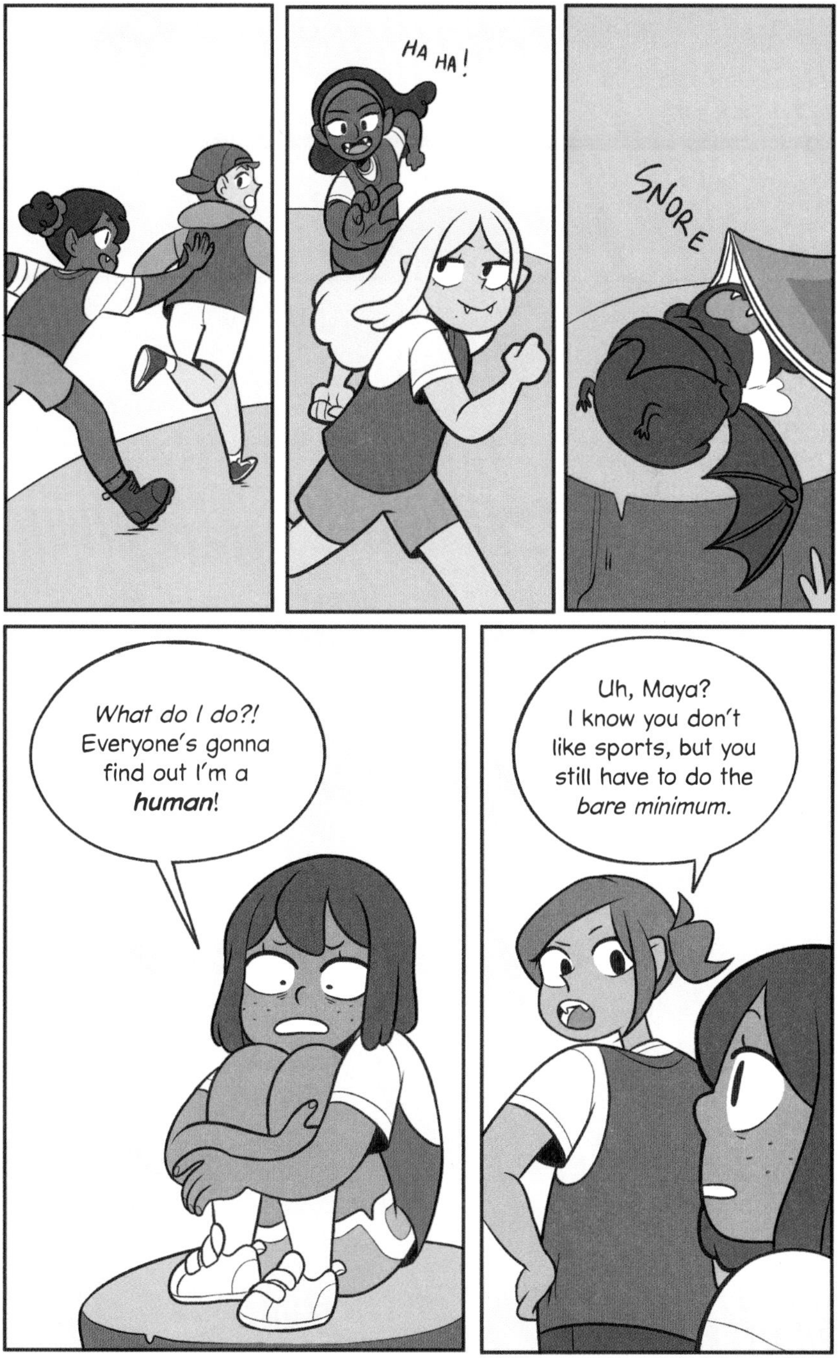
HA HA!
SNORE
What do I do?! Everyone's gonna find out I'm a **human**!
Uh, Maya? I know you don't like sports, but you still have to do the *bare minimum*.

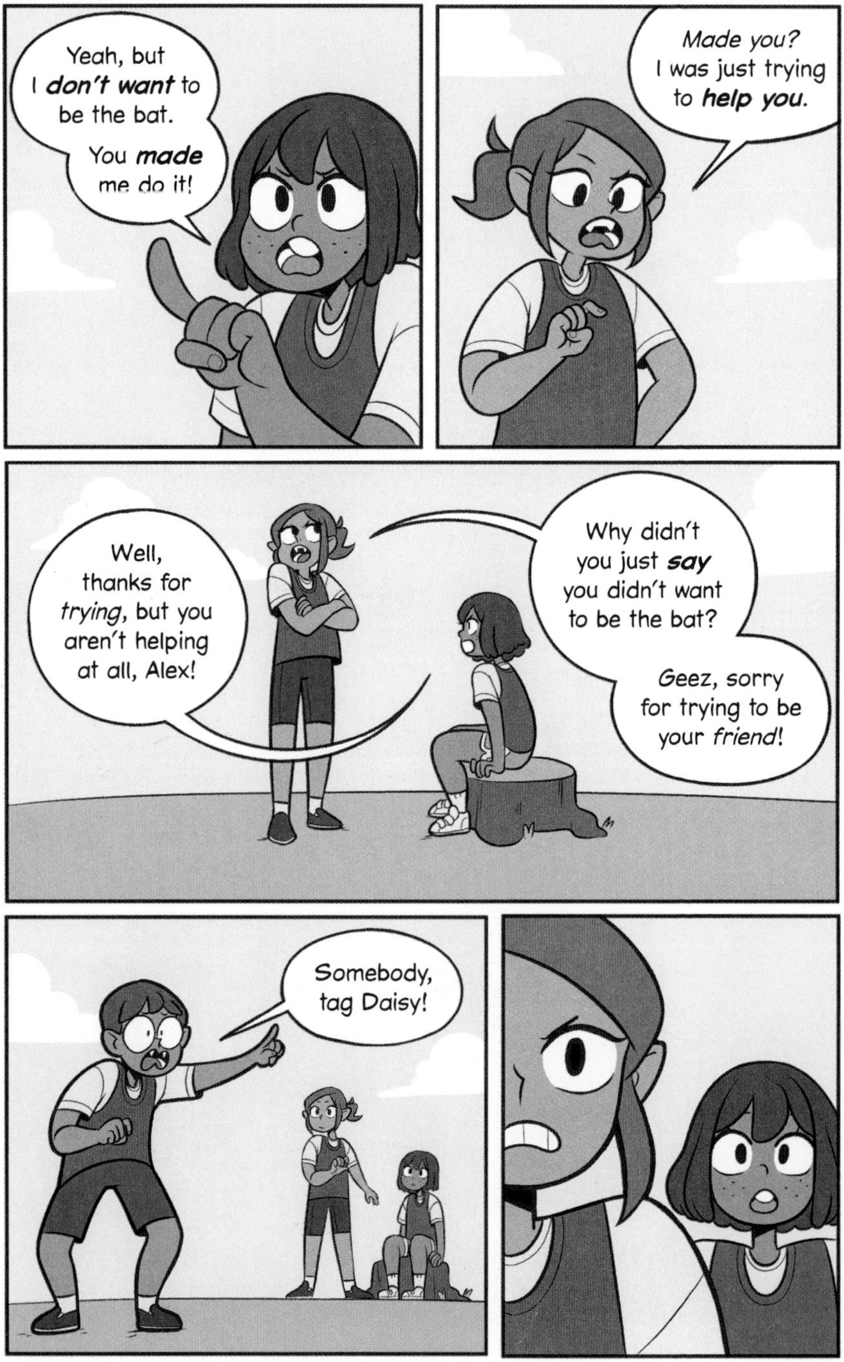

Yeah, but I **don't want** to be the bat.
You **made** me do it!
Made you? I was just trying to **help you.**
Why didn't you just ***say*** you didn't want to be the bat?
Geez, sorry for trying to be your *friend*!
Well, thanks for *trying*, but you aren't helping at all, Alex!
Somebody, tag Daisy!

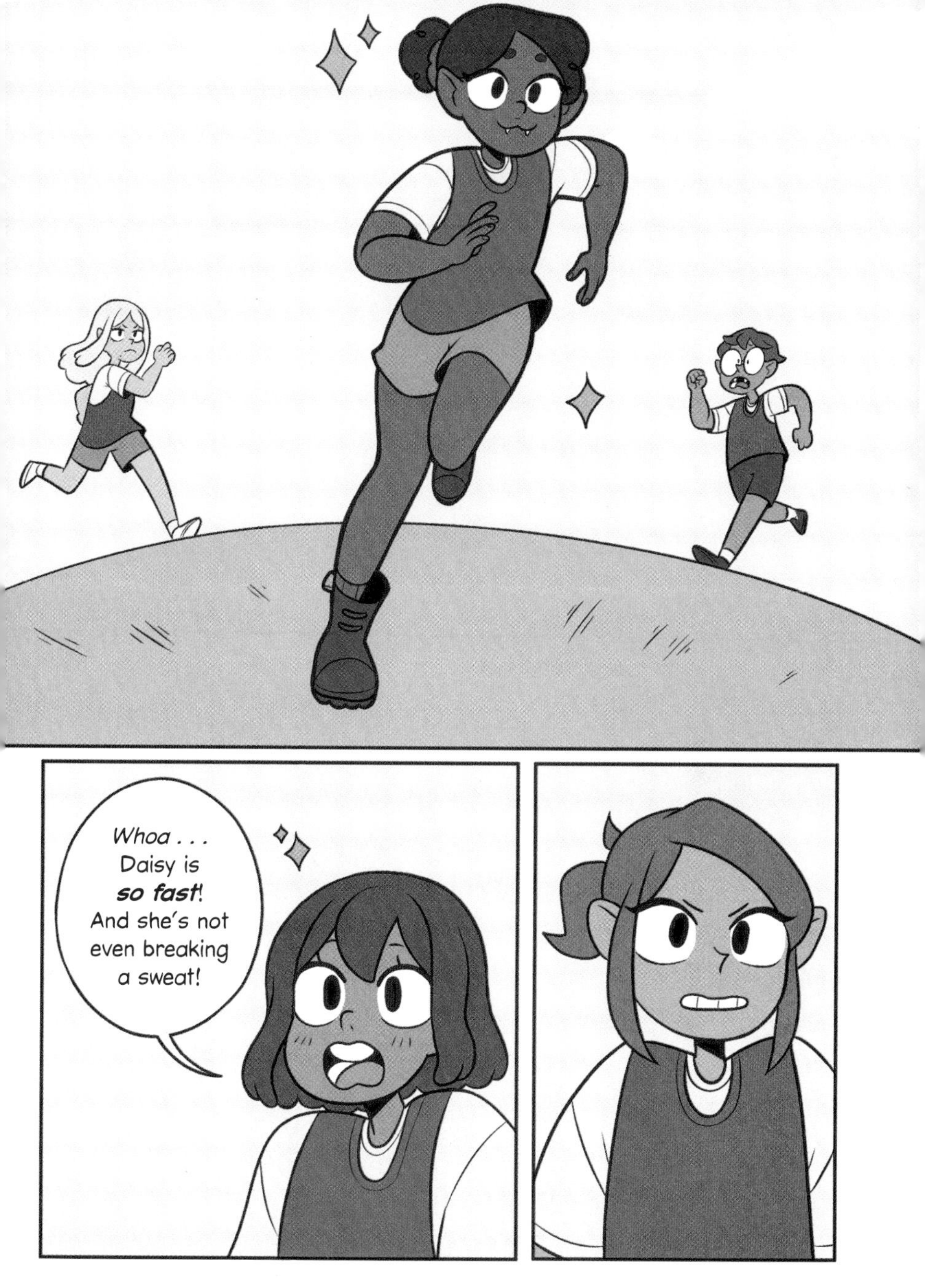
Whoa . . .
Daisy is
so fast!
And she's not
even breaking
a sweat!

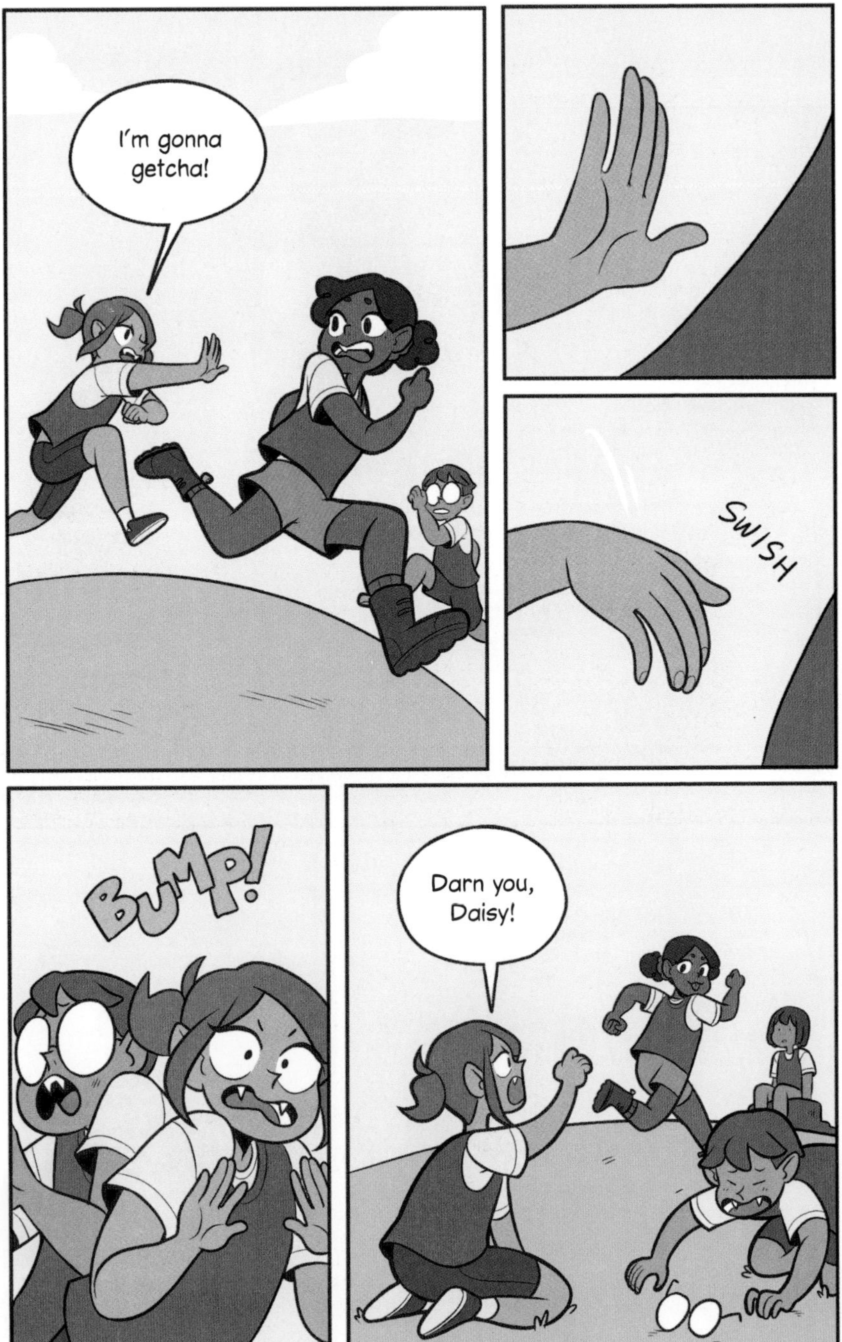
I'm gonna getcha!
SWISH
BUMP!
Darn you, Daisy!

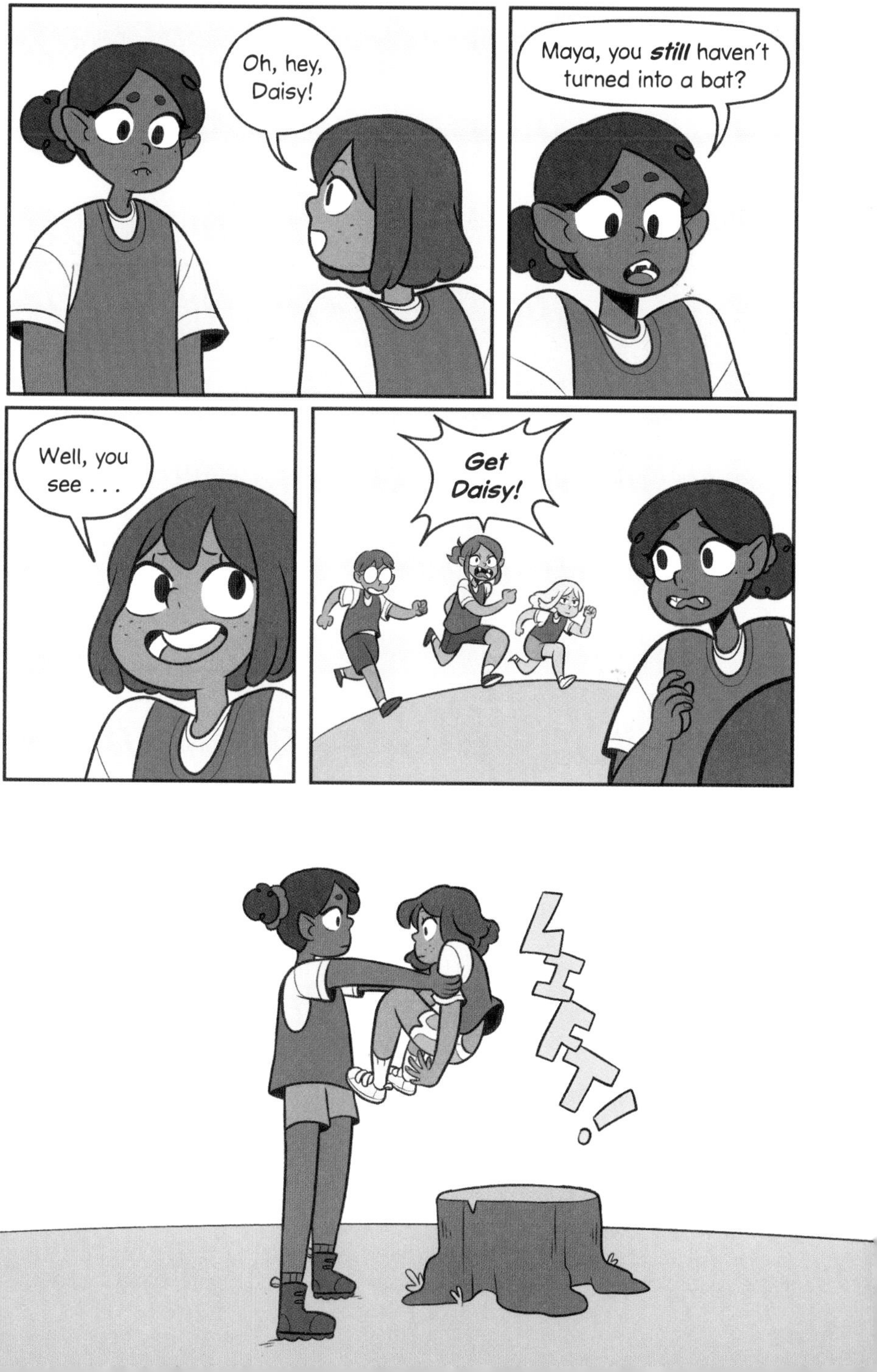
Oh, hey, Daisy!
Maya, you *still* haven't turned into a bat?
Well, you see . . .
Get Daisy!
LIFT!

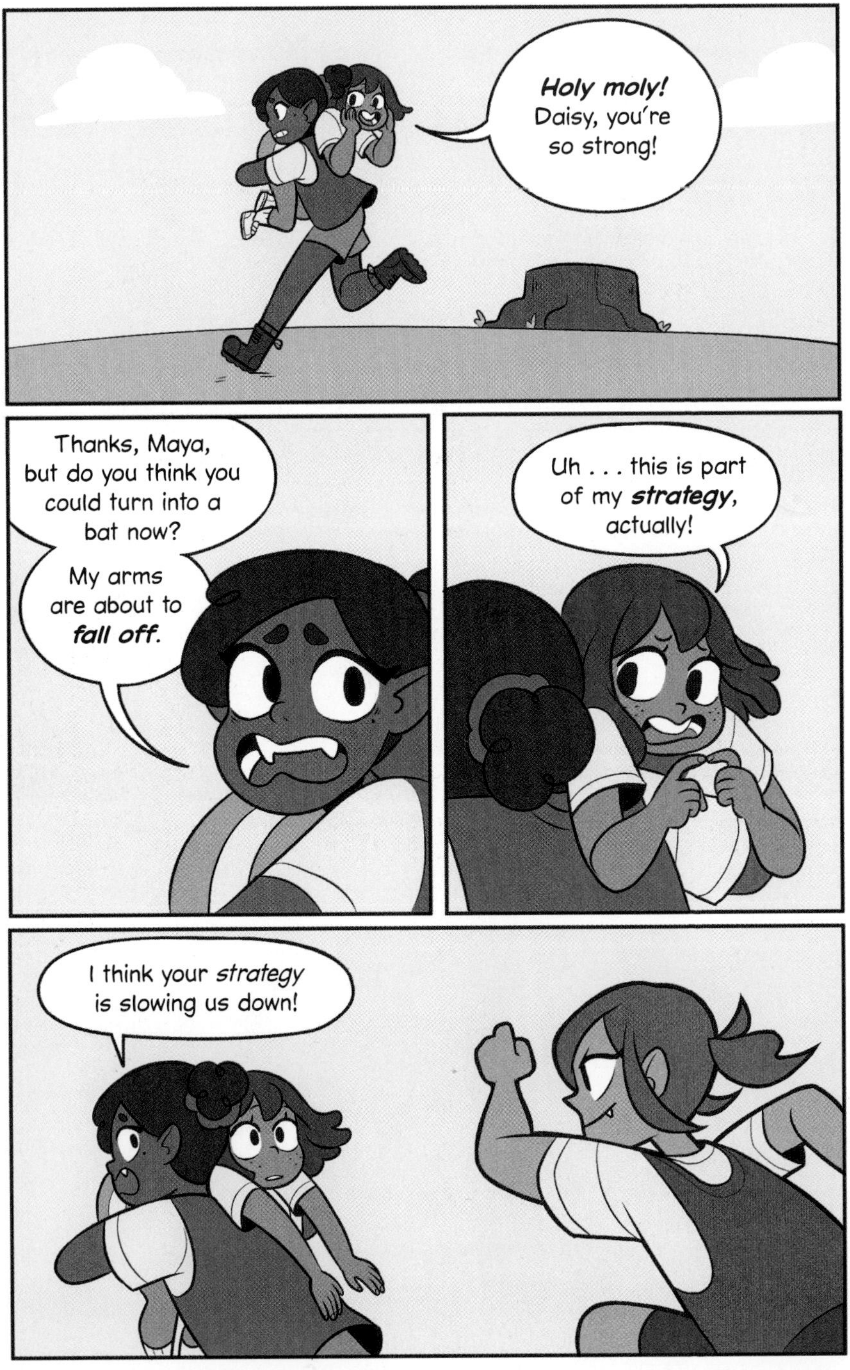

Holy moly! Daisy, you're so strong!
Thanks, Maya, but do you think you could turn into a bat now?
My arms are about to **fall off**.
Uh . . . this is part of my **strategy**, actually!
I think your *strategy* is slowing us down!

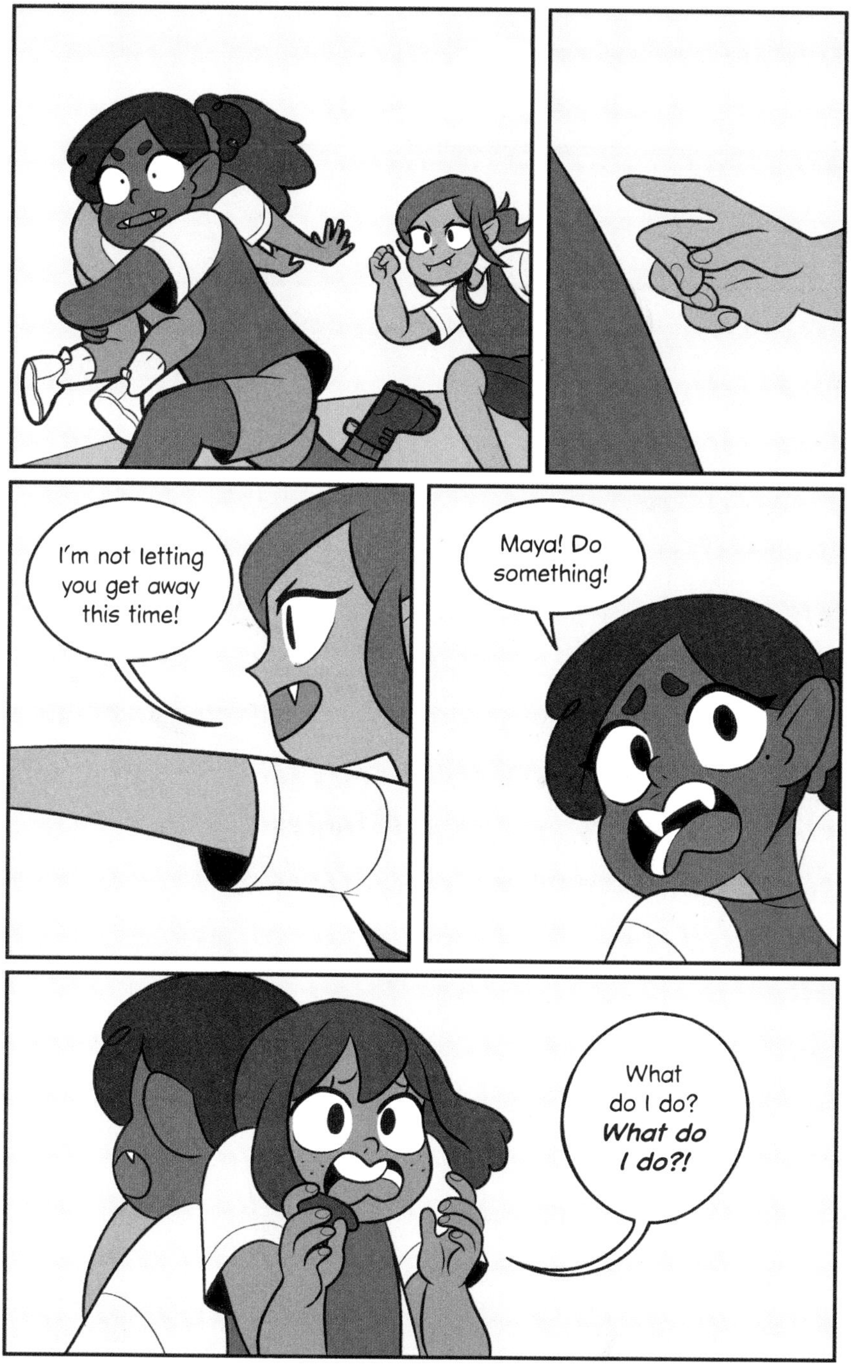
I'm not letting you get away this time!
Maya! Do something!
What do I do? ***What do I do?!***

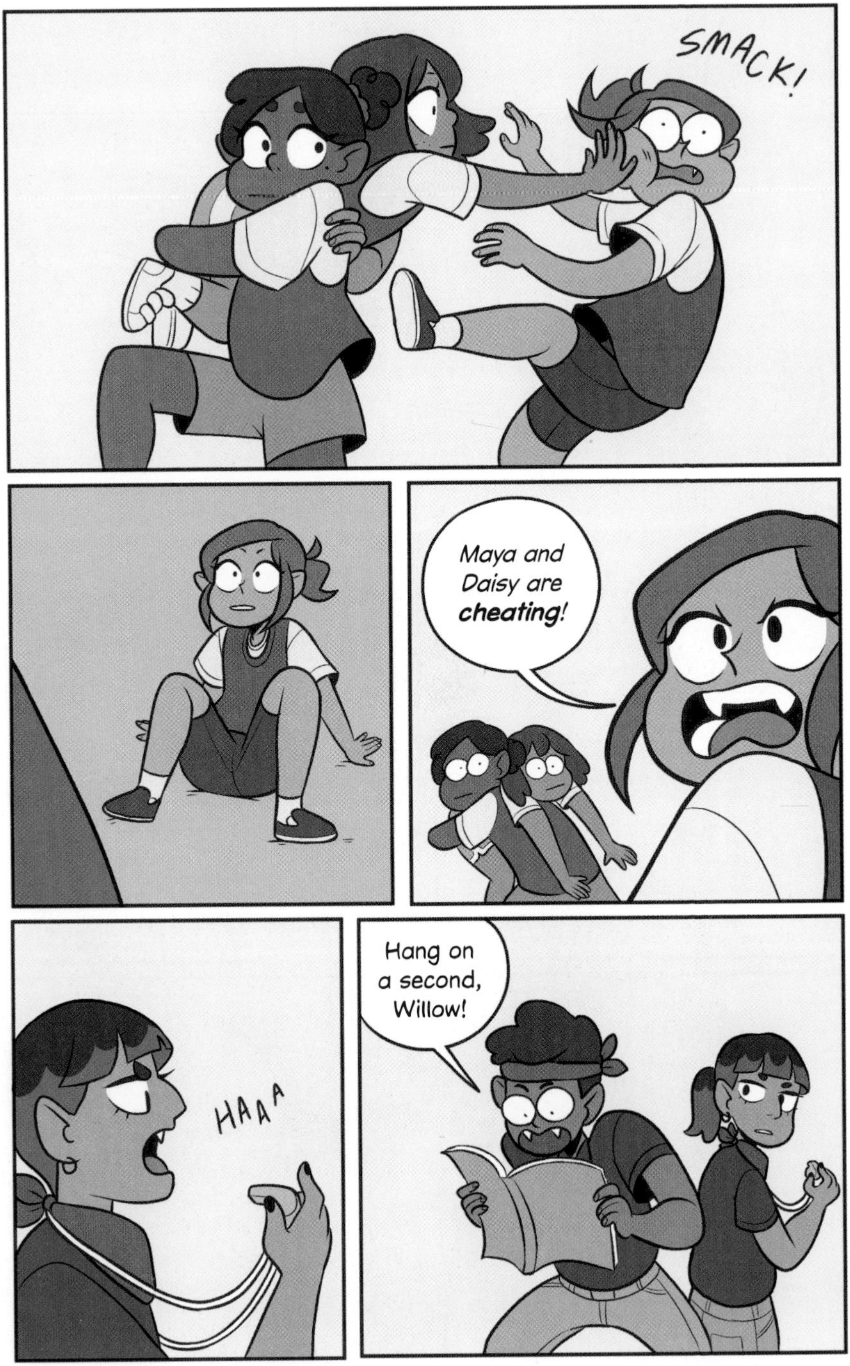
SMACK!
Maya and Daisy are cheating!
HAAA
Hang on a second, Willow!

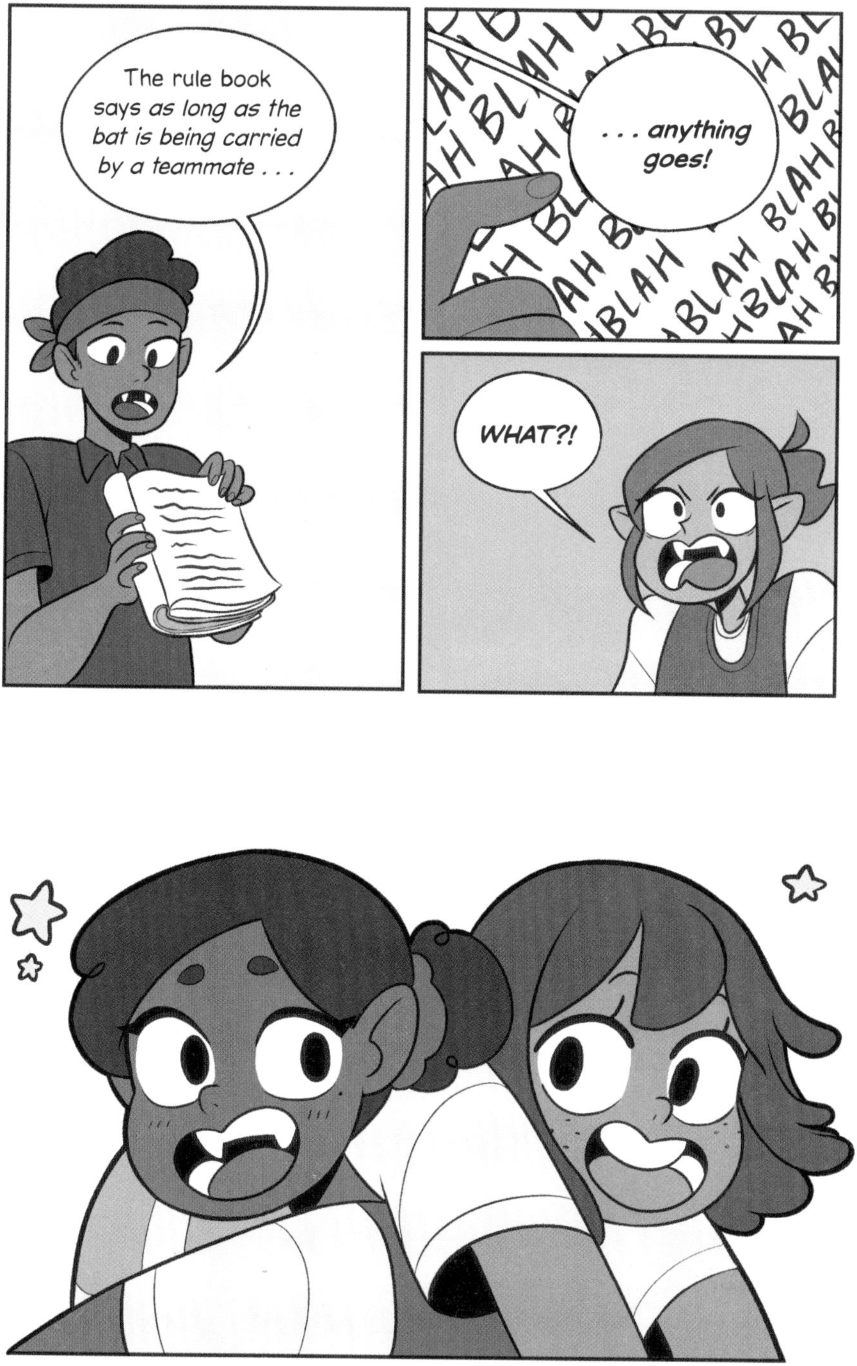
The rule book says as long as the bat is being carried by a teammate . . .
. . . anything goes!
WHAT?!

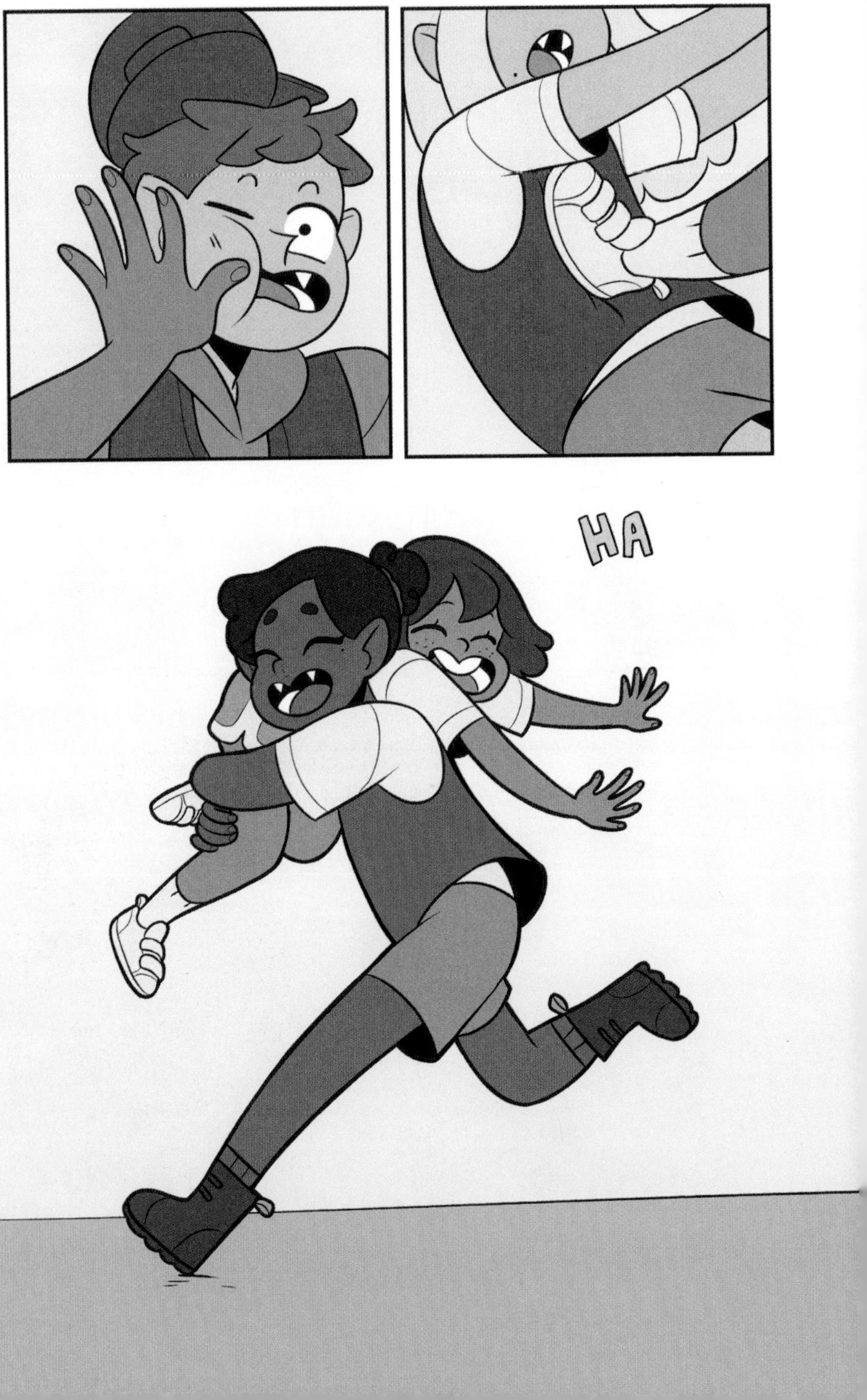
HA

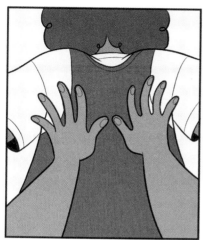

HA

HA

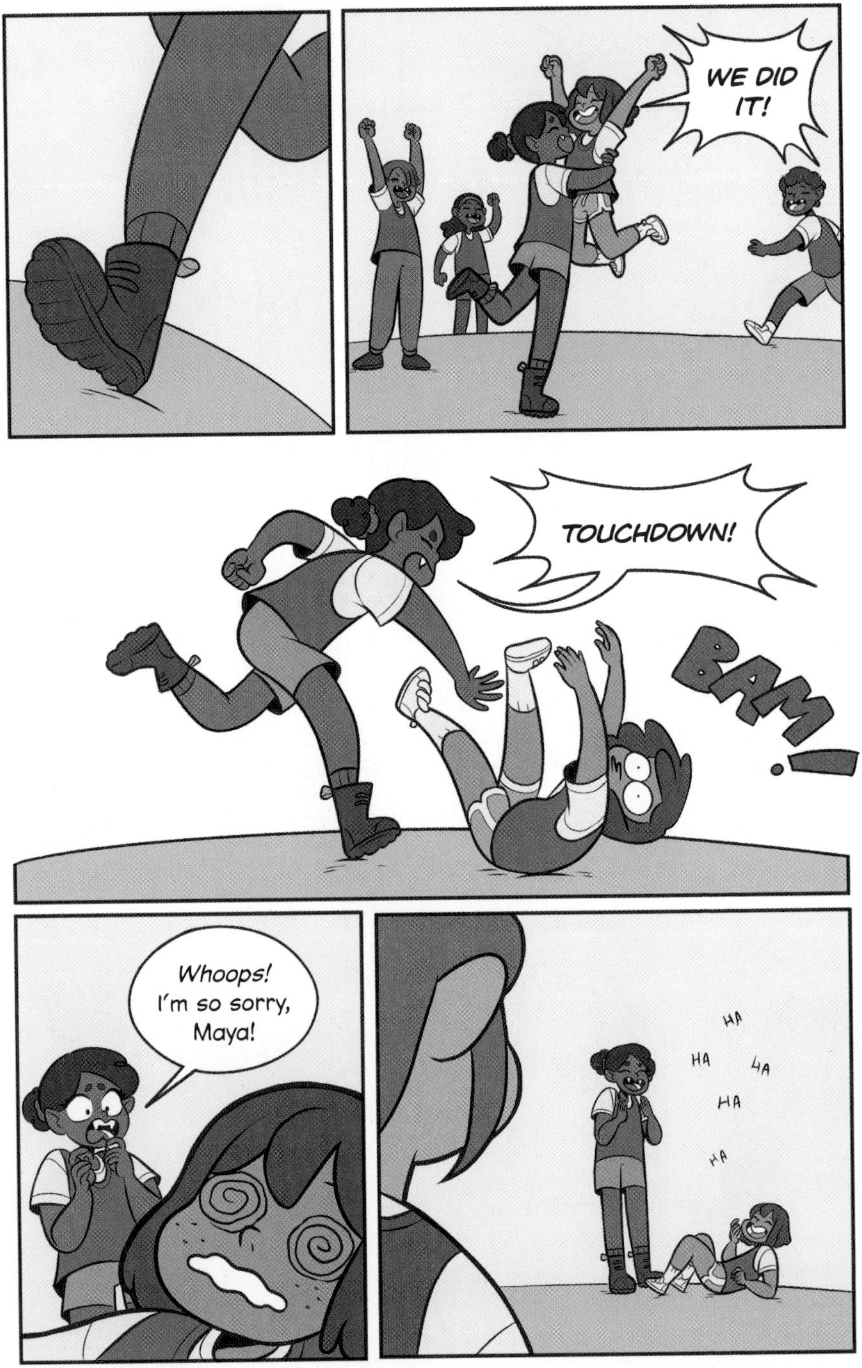
WE DID IT!
TOUCHDOWN!
BAM!
Whoops! I'm so sorry, Maya!
HA
HA
HA
HA
HA

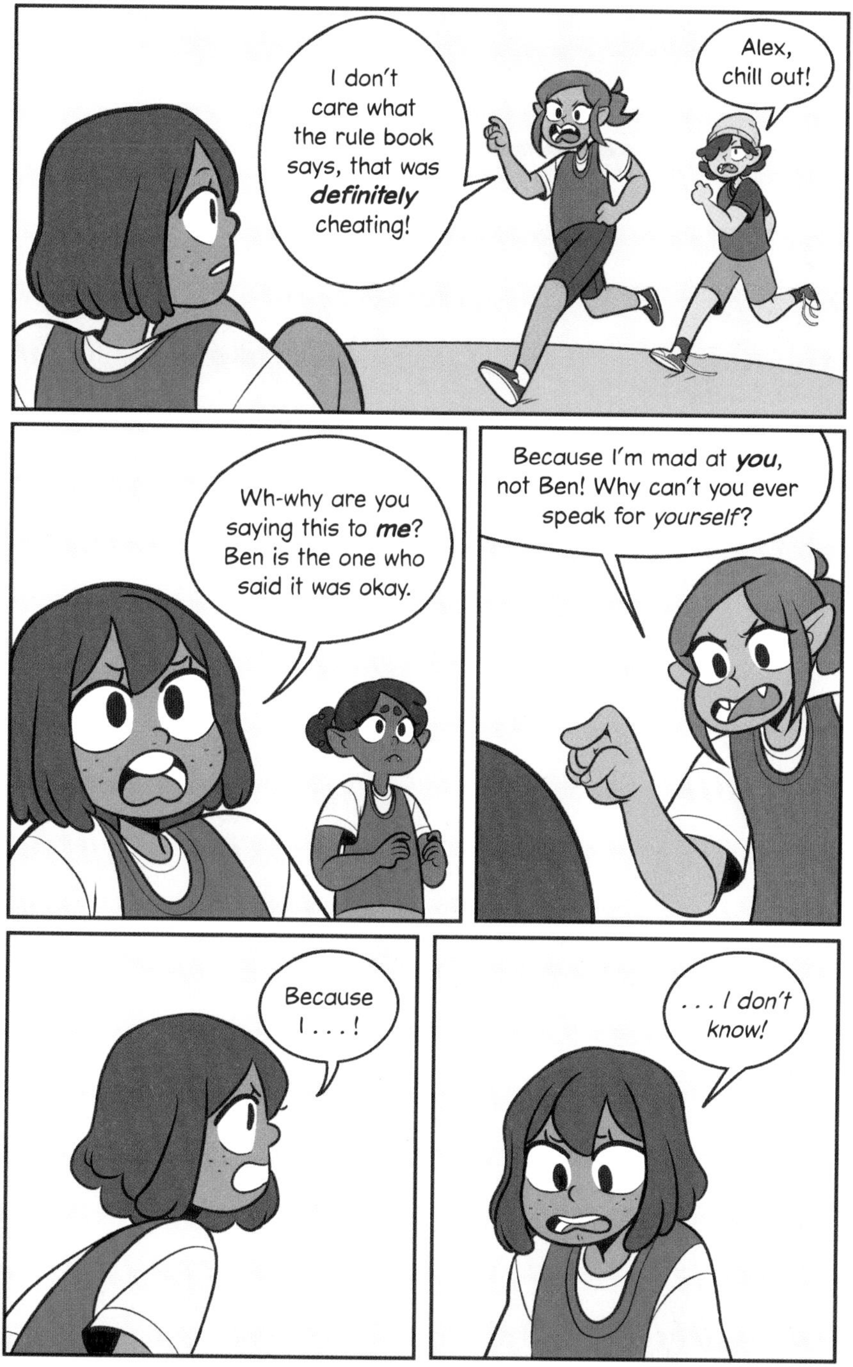
I don't care what the rule book says, that was *definitely* cheating!
Alex, chill out!
Wh-why are you saying this to *me*? Ben is the one who said it was okay.
Because I'm mad at *you*, not Ben! Why can't you ever speak for *yourself*?
Because I . . . !
. . . I don't know!

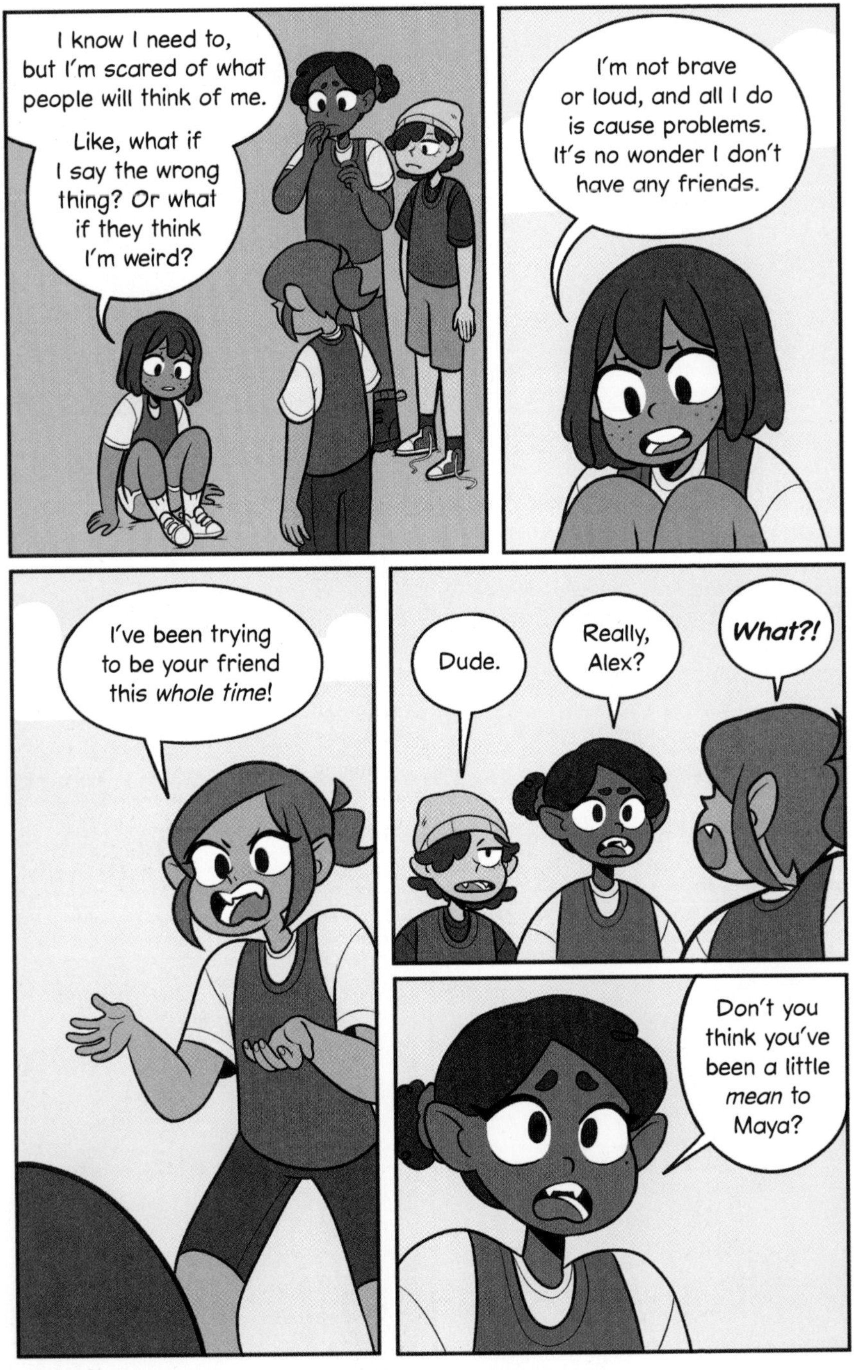

I know I need to, but I'm scared of what people will think of me.
Like, what if I say the wrong thing? Or what if they think I'm weird?
I'm not brave or loud, and all I do is cause problems. It's no wonder I don't have any friends.
I've been trying to be your friend this *whole time*!
Dude.
Really, Alex?
What?!
Don't you think you've been a little *mean* to Maya?

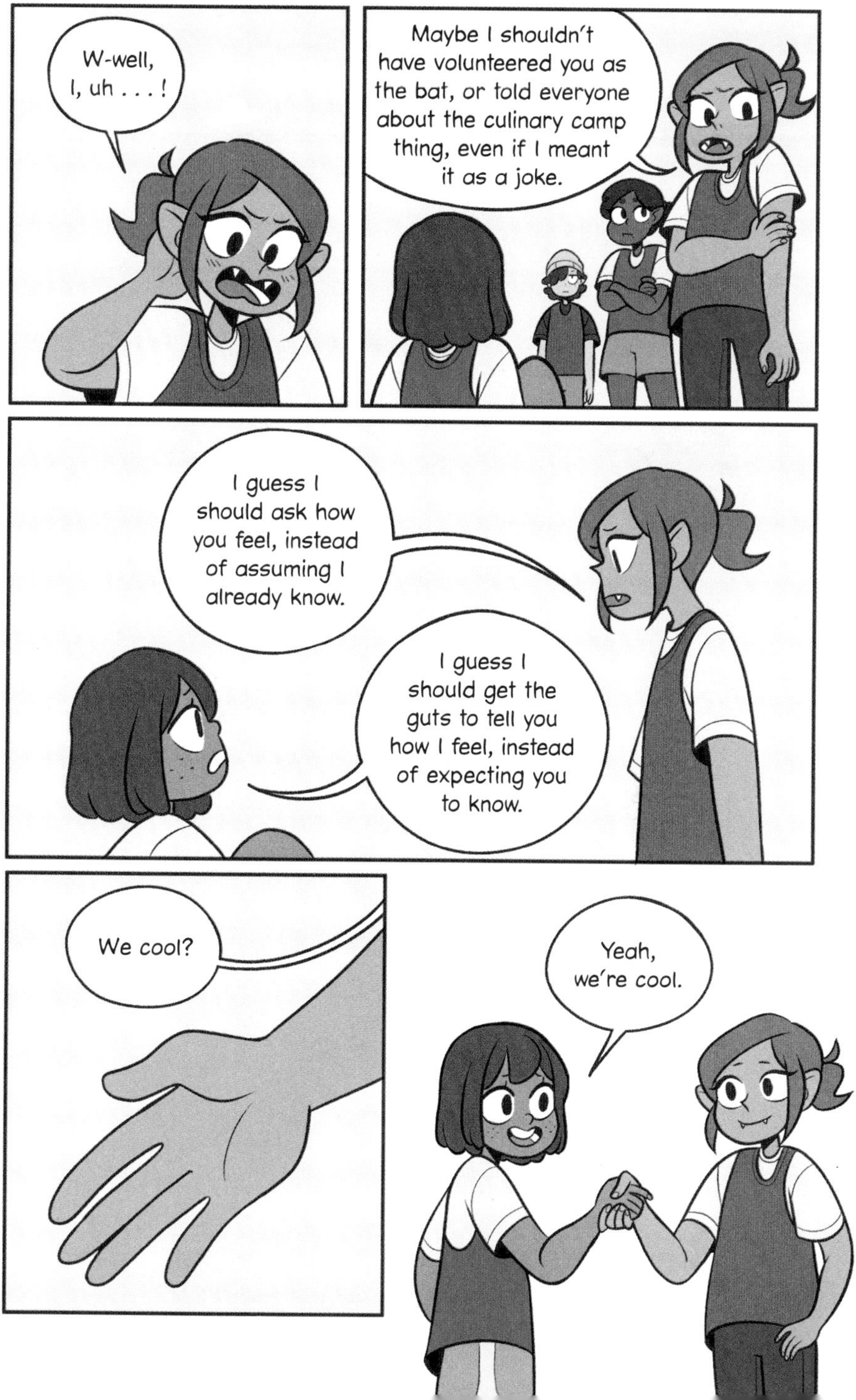
W-well, I, uh . . . !
Maybe I shouldn't have volunteered you as the bat, or told everyone about the culinary camp thing, even if I meant it as a joke.
I guess I should ask how you feel, instead of assuming I already know.
I guess I should get the guts to tell you how I feel, instead of expecting you to know.
We cool?
Yeah, we're cool.

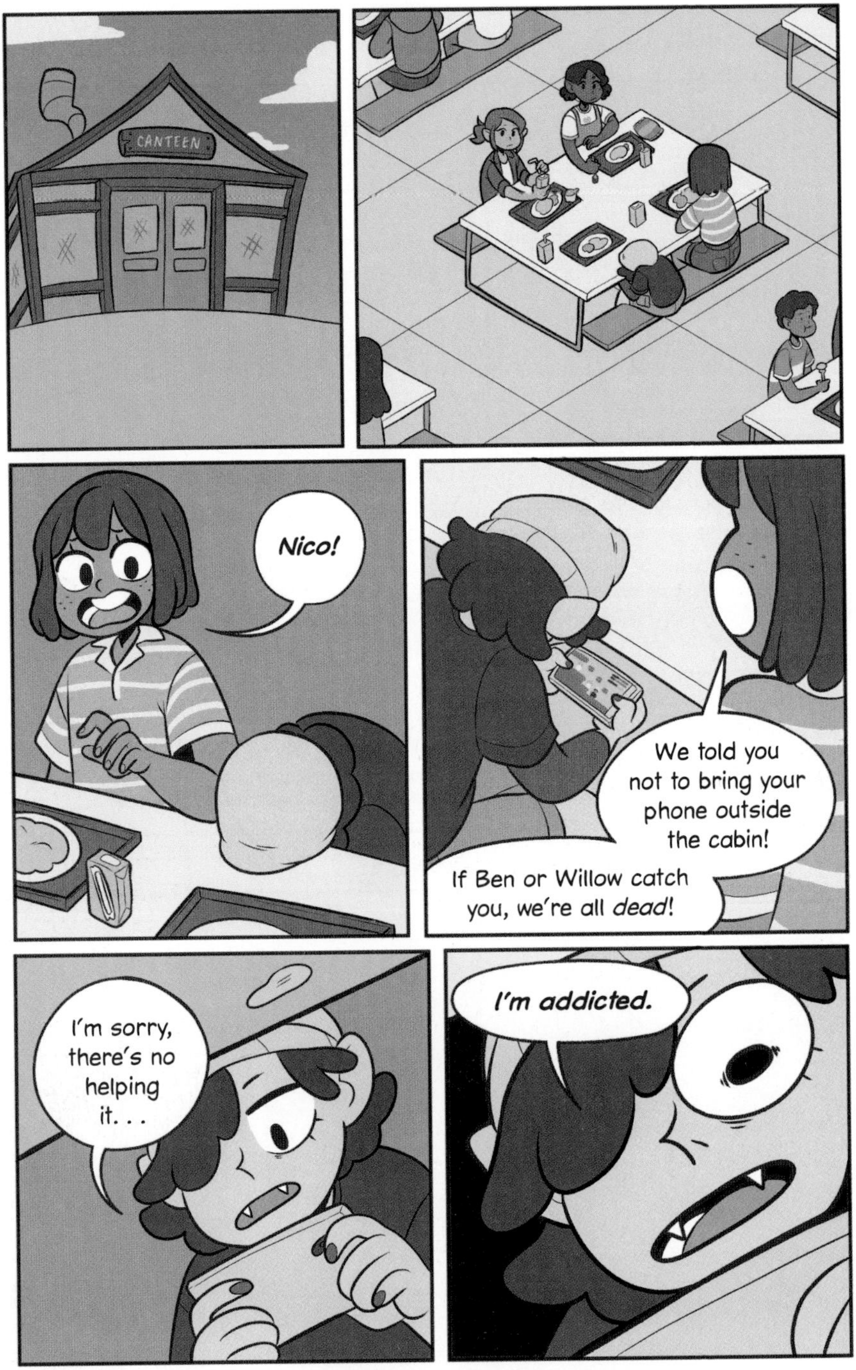
CANTEEN
Nico!
We told you not to bring your phone outside the cabin!
If Ben or Willow catch you, we're all *dead*!
I'm sorry, there's no helping it. . .
I'm addicted.

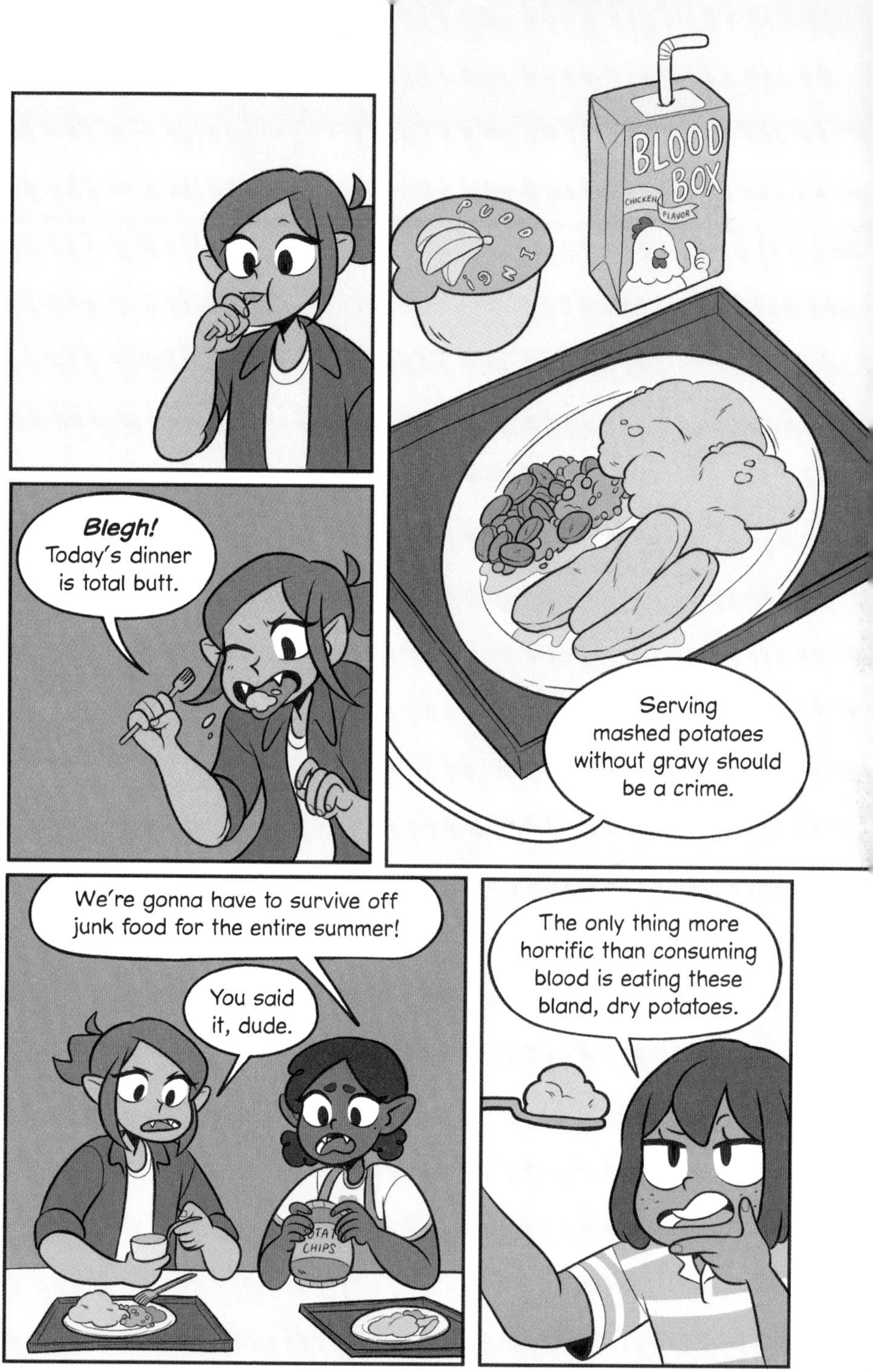
PUDDING
BLOOD BOX
CHICKEN FLAVOR
Blegh! Today's dinner is total butt.
Serving mashed potatoes without gravy should be a crime.
We're gonna have to survive off junk food for the entire summer!
You said it, dude.
CHIPS
The only thing more horrific than consuming blood is eating these bland, dry potatoes.

I've got an idea!
SO
Hmm . . .
CREAM CHEESE
I'll need this . . .
. . . some of these . . .
BUTTER
. . . and *this*!
POTATO CHIPS

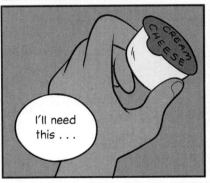

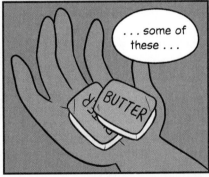

My chips!

Don't worry, Daisy! I promise this is for the greater good.

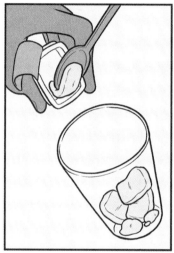

Now, I just need a way to melt all this butter.

What about this microwave?

That's perfect!

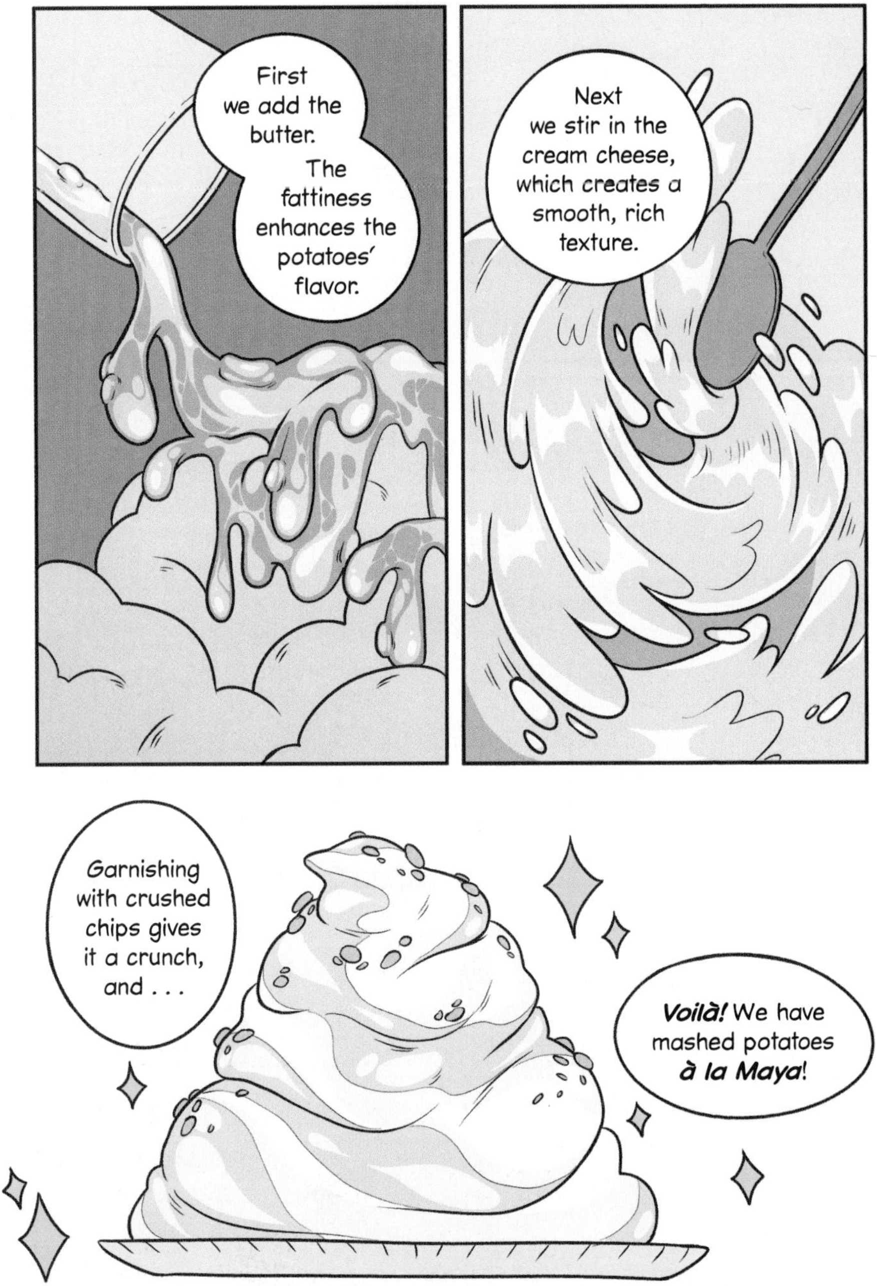
First we add the butter.
The fattiness enhances the potatoes' flavor.
Next we stir in the cream cheese, which creates a smooth, rich texture.
Garnishing with crushed chips gives it a crunch, and . . .
Voilà! We have mashed potatoes ***à la Maya***!

WHAT THE HECK, DUDE?! How did you do that?!

These are the **greatest** mashed potatoes I've ever had!

Not bad, Maya, not bad.

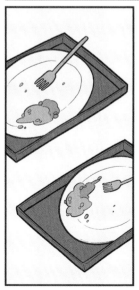

Where'd you learn how to cook, Maya?

Well, my dad taught me the basics when I was a kid, but now I just watch Kiki Cooks online.

She's, like, the coolest person **ever**.

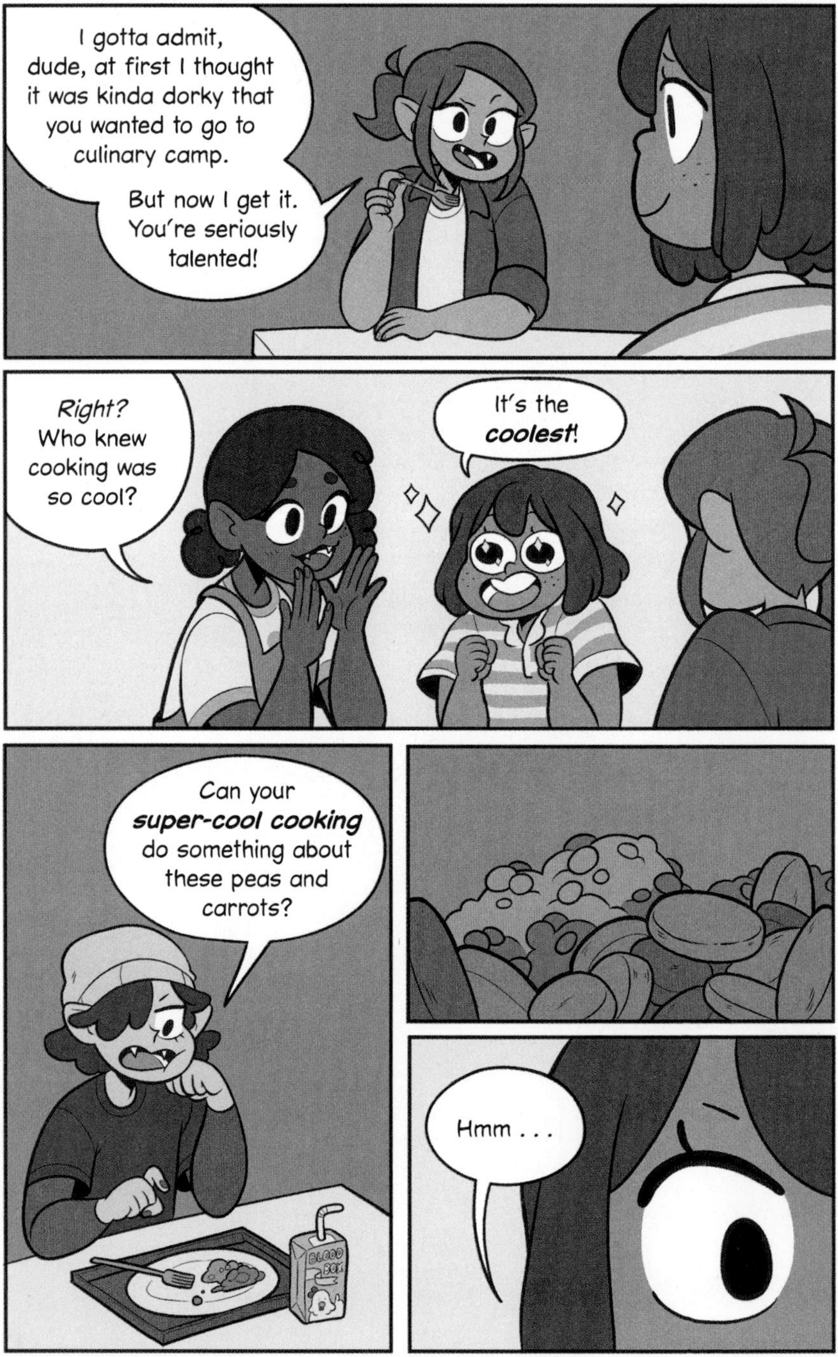
I gotta admit, dude, at first I thought it was kinda dorky that you wanted to go to culinary camp.
But now I get it. You're seriously talented!
Right? Who knew cooking was so cool?
It's the ***coolest***!
Can your ***super-cool cooking*** do something about these peas and carrots?
Hmm . . .
BLOOD BOX

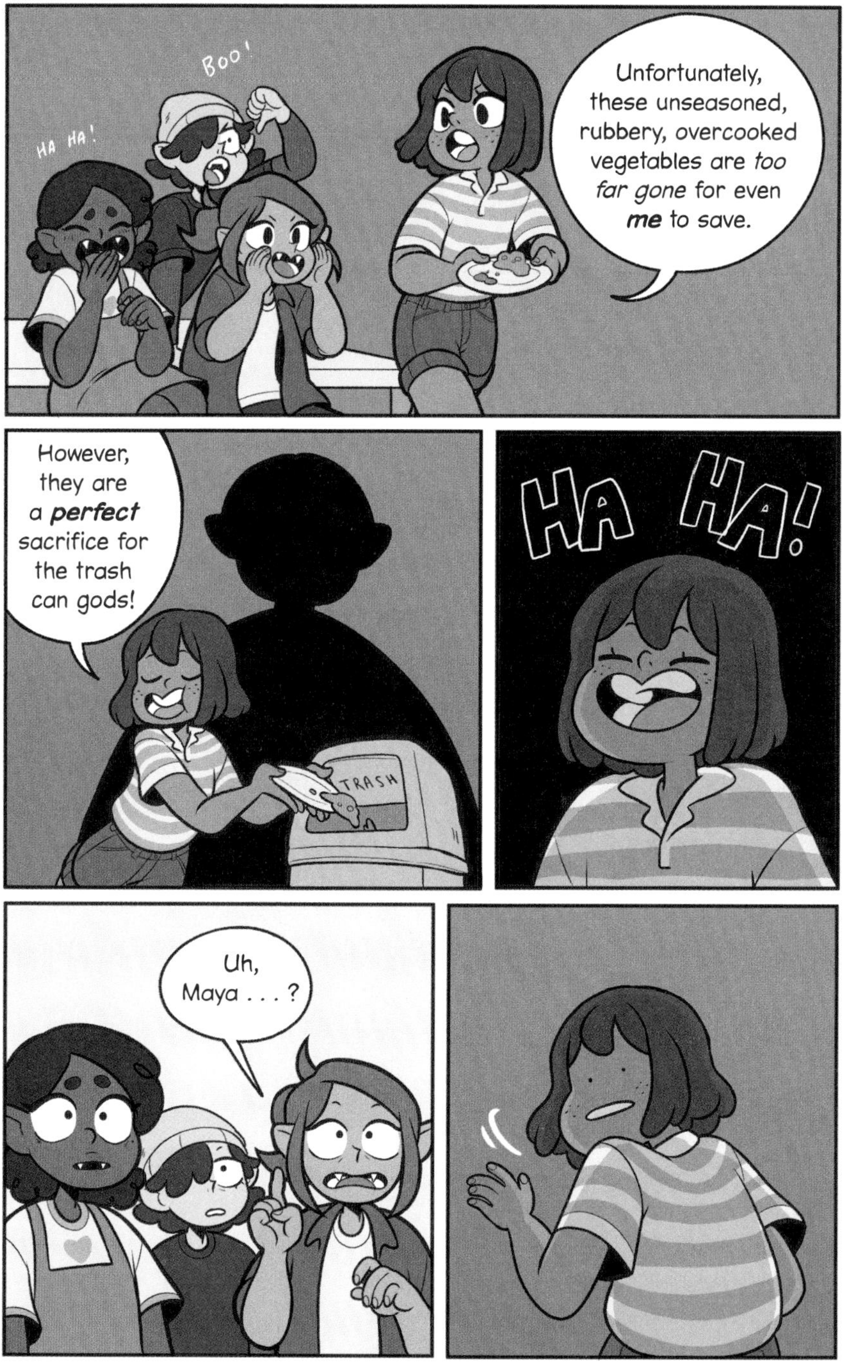
HA HA!
BOO!
Unfortunately, these unseasoned, rubbery, overcooked vegetables are *too far gone* for even **me** to save.
However, they are a ***perfect*** sacrifice for the trash can gods!
TRASH
HA HA!
Uh, Maya . . . ?

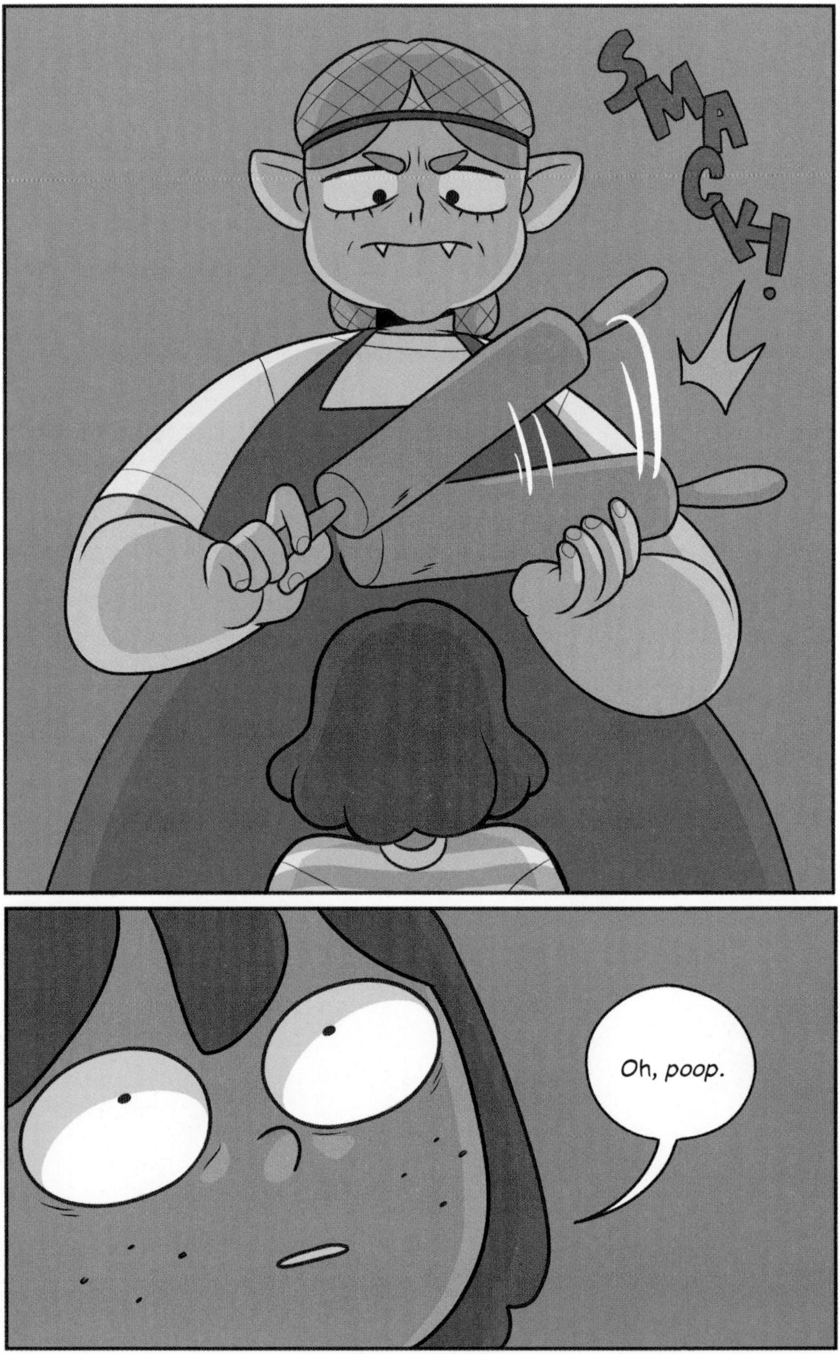
SMACK!
Oh, poop.

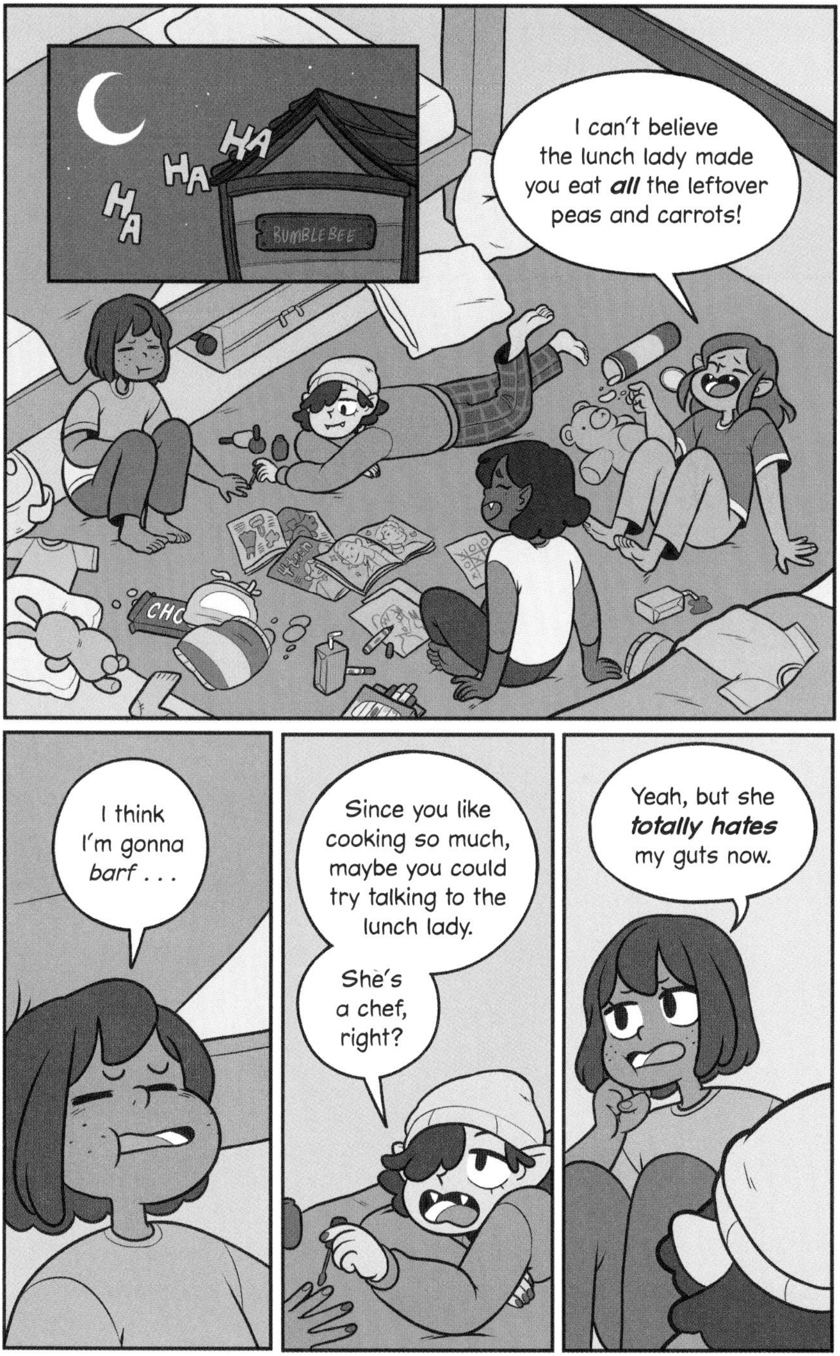
HA
HA
HA
BUMBLEBEE
I can't believe the lunch lady made you eat *all* the leftover peas and carrots!
CHO
I think I'm gonna *barf* . . .
Since you like cooking so much, maybe you could try talking to the lunch lady.
She's a chef, right?
Yeah, but she ***totally hates*** my guts now.

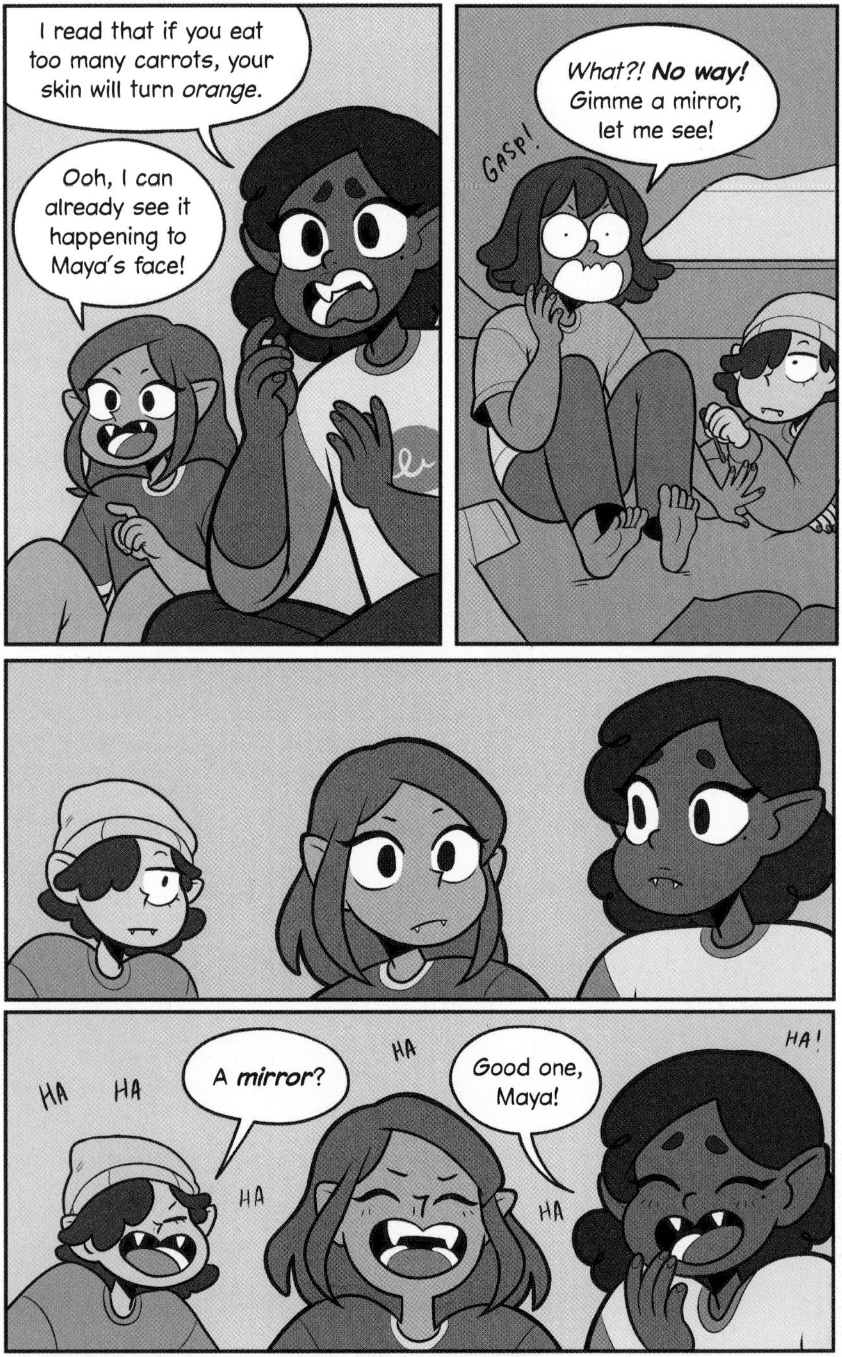
I read that if you eat too many carrots, your skin will turn *orange*.
Ooh, I can already see it happening to Maya's face!
GASP!
*What?! **No way!*** Gimme a mirror, let me see!
HA
HA
A ***mirror***?
HA
HA
Good one, Maya!
HA!
HA

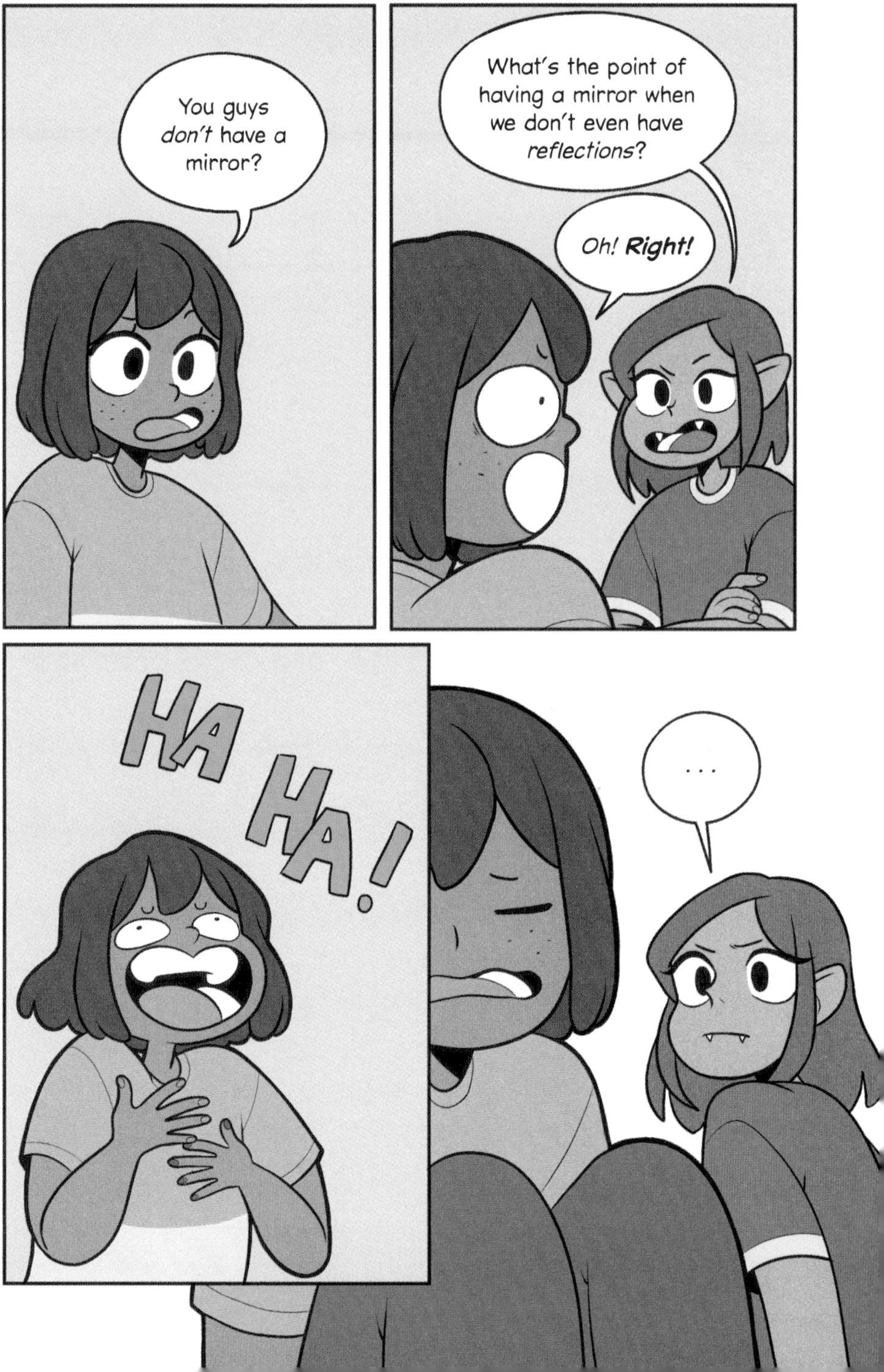
You guys *don't* have a mirror?
What's the point of having a mirror when we don't even have *reflections*?
Oh! **Right!**
HA HA HA!
. . .

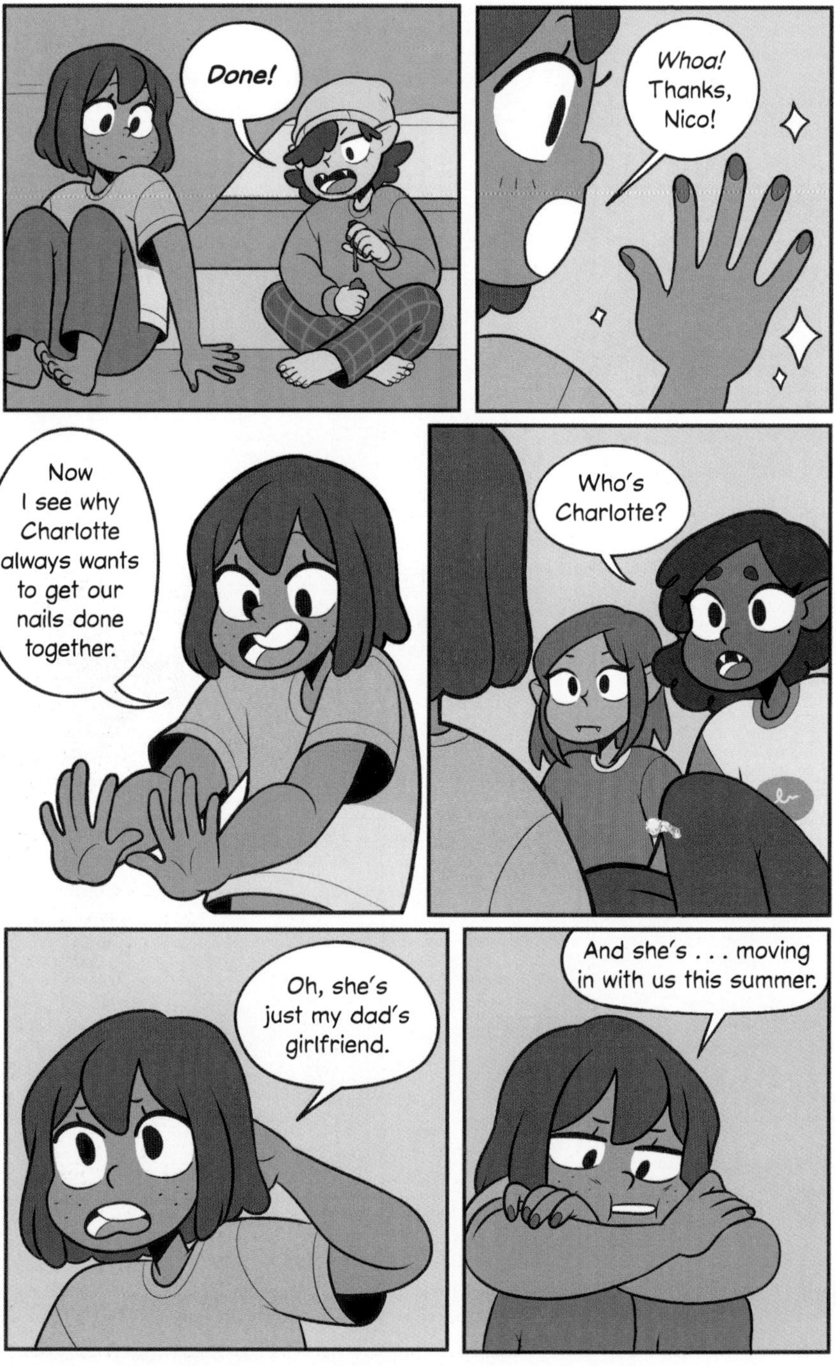
Done!
Whoa! Thanks, Nico!
Now I see why Charlotte always wants to get our nails done together.
Who's Charlotte?
Oh, she's just my dad's girlfriend.
And she's . . . moving in with us this summer.

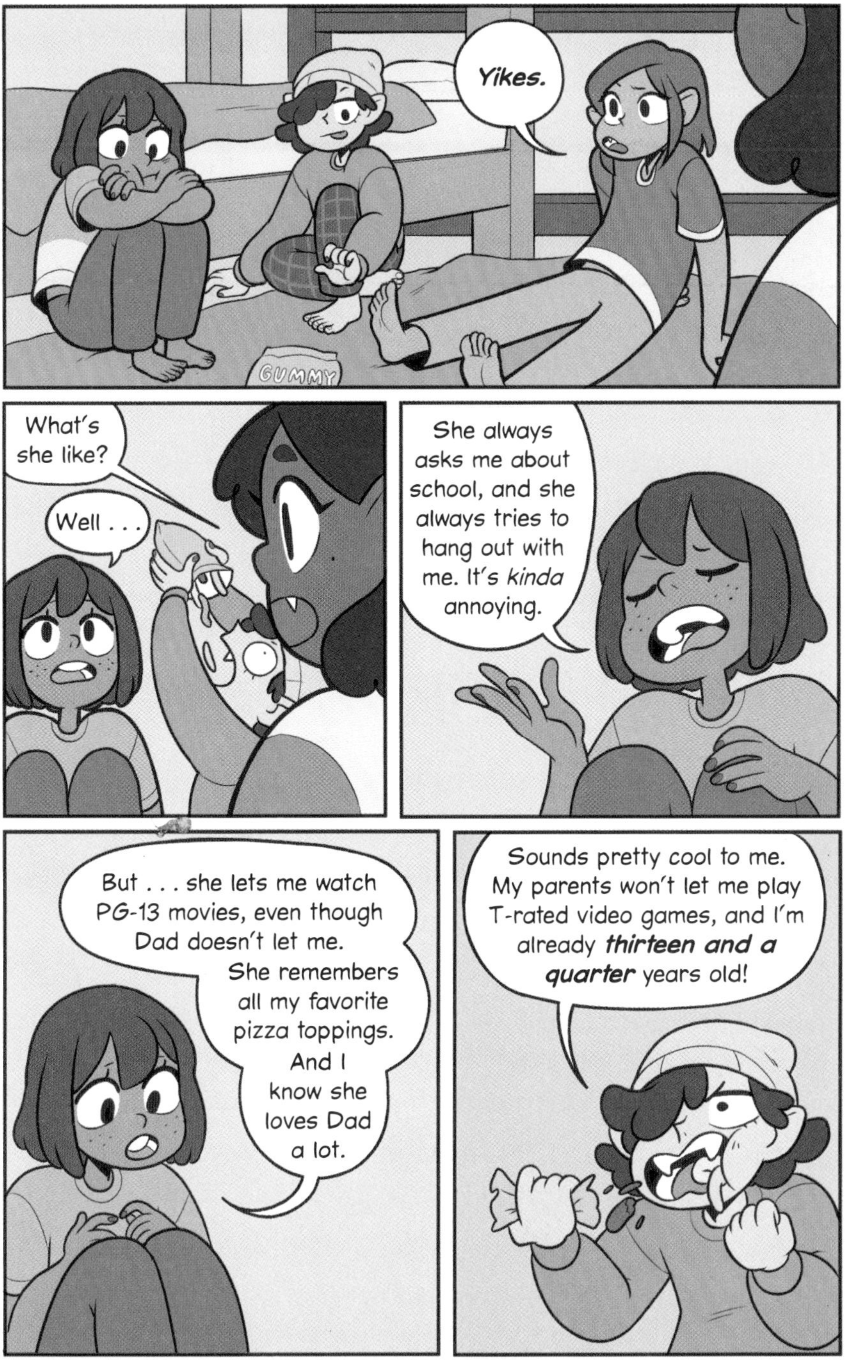
Yikes.
GUMMY
What's she like?
Well . . .
She always asks me about school, and she always tries to hang out with me. It's *kinda* annoying.
But . . . she lets me watch PG-13 movies, even though Dad doesn't let me.
She remembers all my favorite pizza toppings.
And I know she loves Dad a lot.
Sounds pretty cool to me. My parents won't let me play T-rated video games, and I'm already ***thirteen and a quarter*** years old!

Yeah, I guess Charlotte isn't *that* bad. But . . .

It's always been just my dad and me.

It's weird thinking that things are gonna be *different* now.

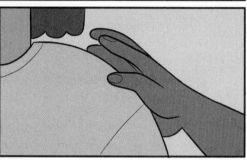

Change is always *pretty* scary, but that doesn't mean it's *bad*.

I mean, you changed those nasty mashed potatoes into something delicious!

You sound like my dad, Daisy.

What can I say? I'm wise beyond my years.

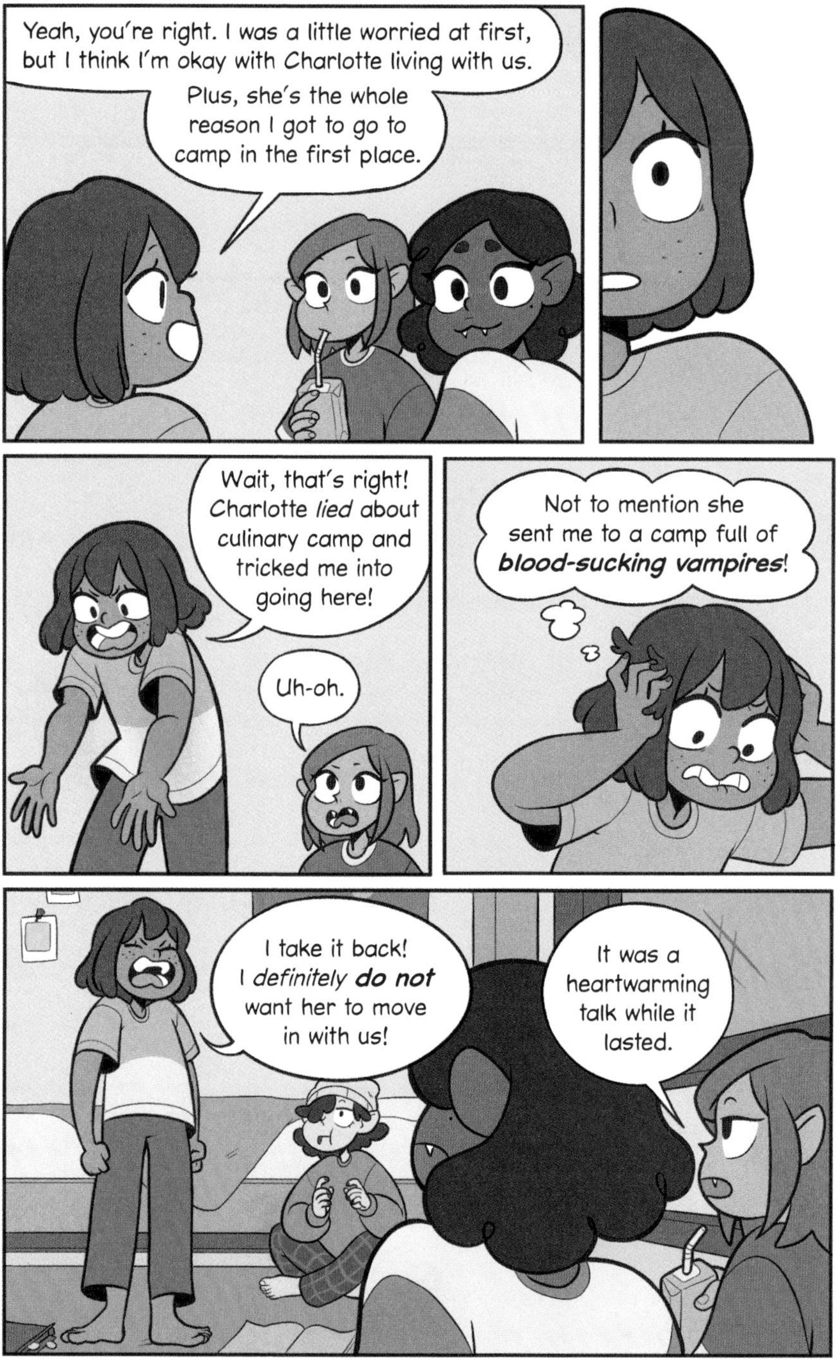

Yeah, you're right. I was a little worried at first, but I think I'm okay with Charlotte living with us.
Plus, she's the whole reason I got to go to camp in the first place.
Wait, that's right! Charlotte *lied* about culinary camp and tricked me into going here!
Uh-oh.
Not to mention she sent me to a camp full of ***blood-sucking vampires***!
I take it back! I *definitely* **do not** want her to move in with us!
It was a heartwarming talk while it lasted.

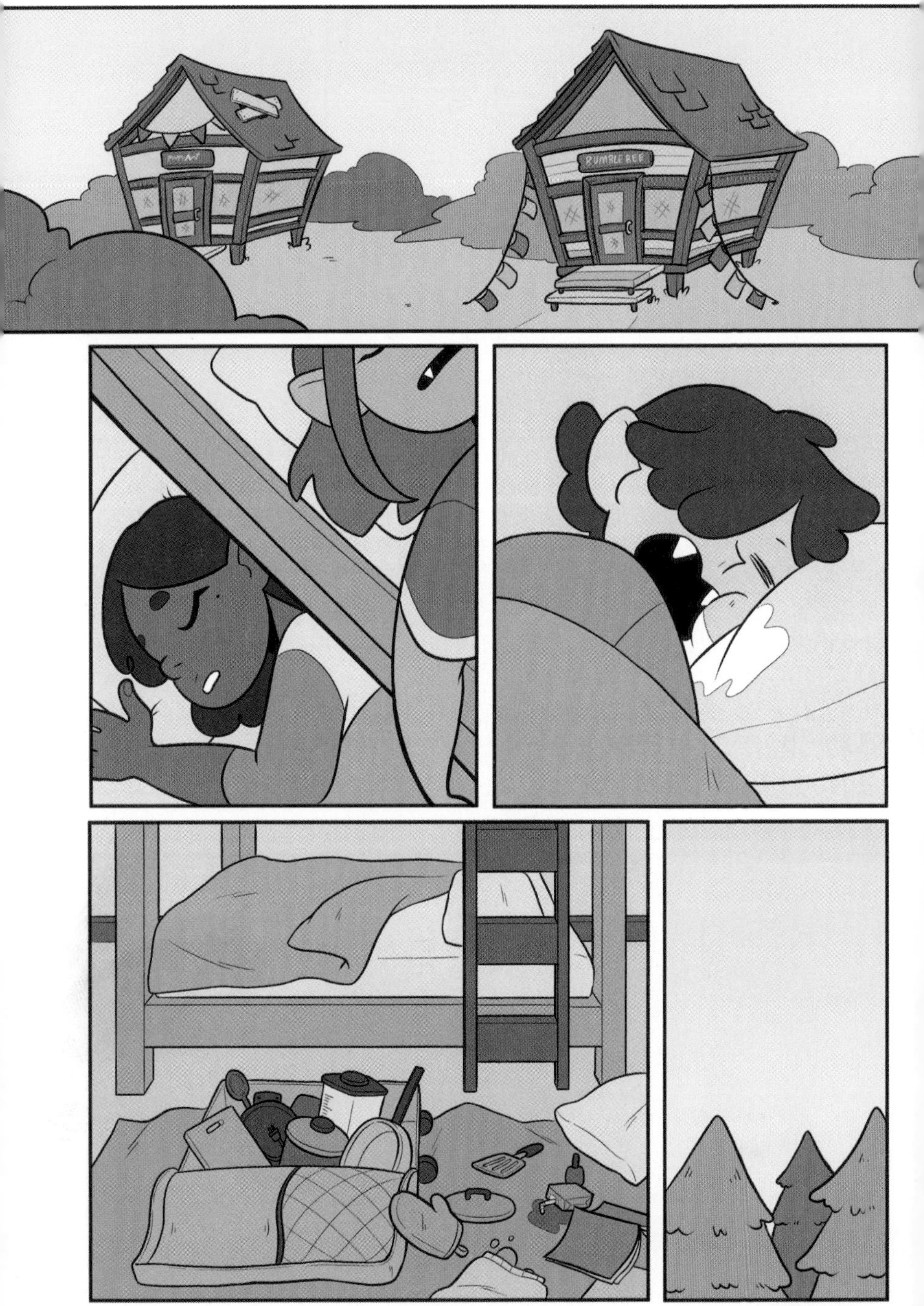
RUMBLE BEE

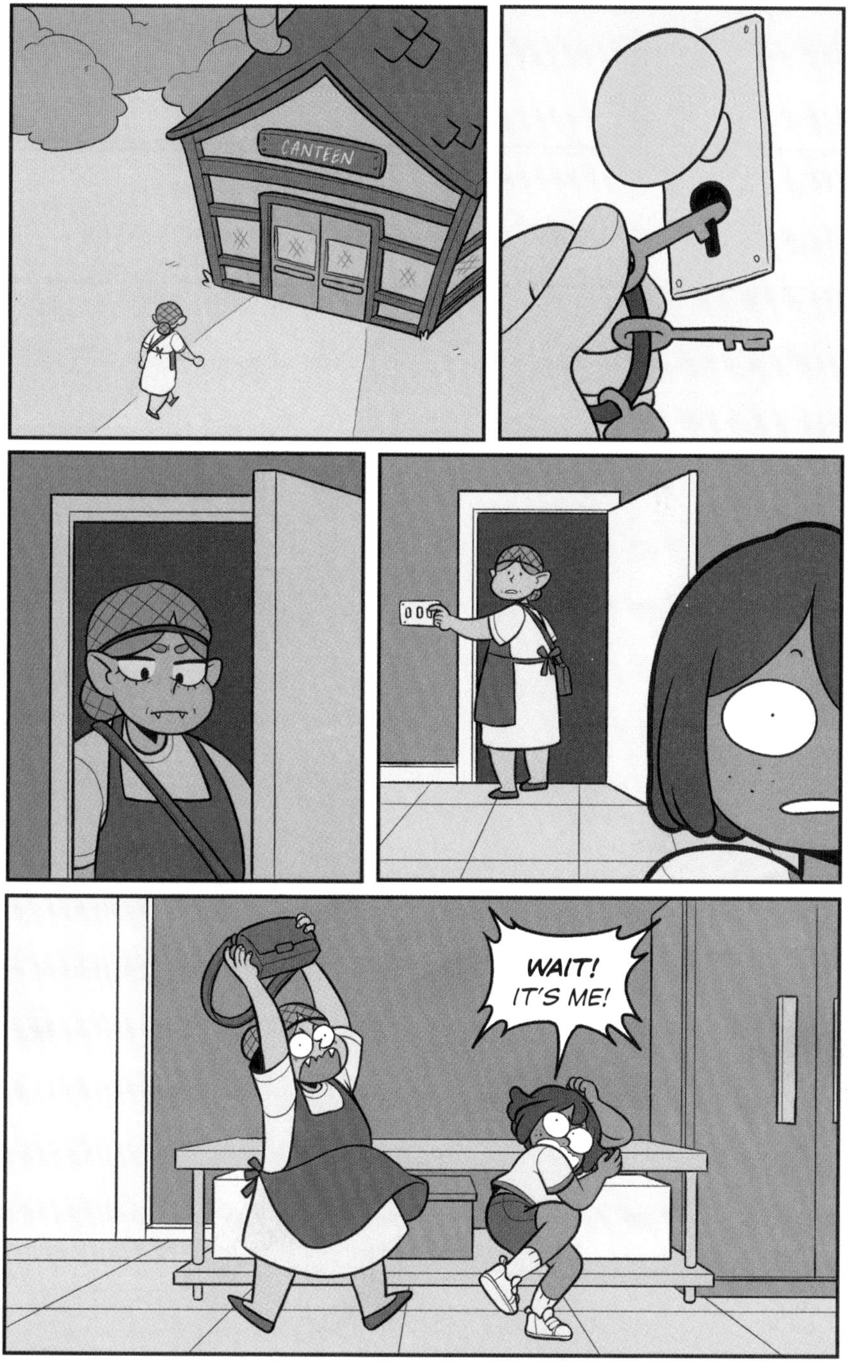
CANTEEN
WAIT!
IT'S ME!

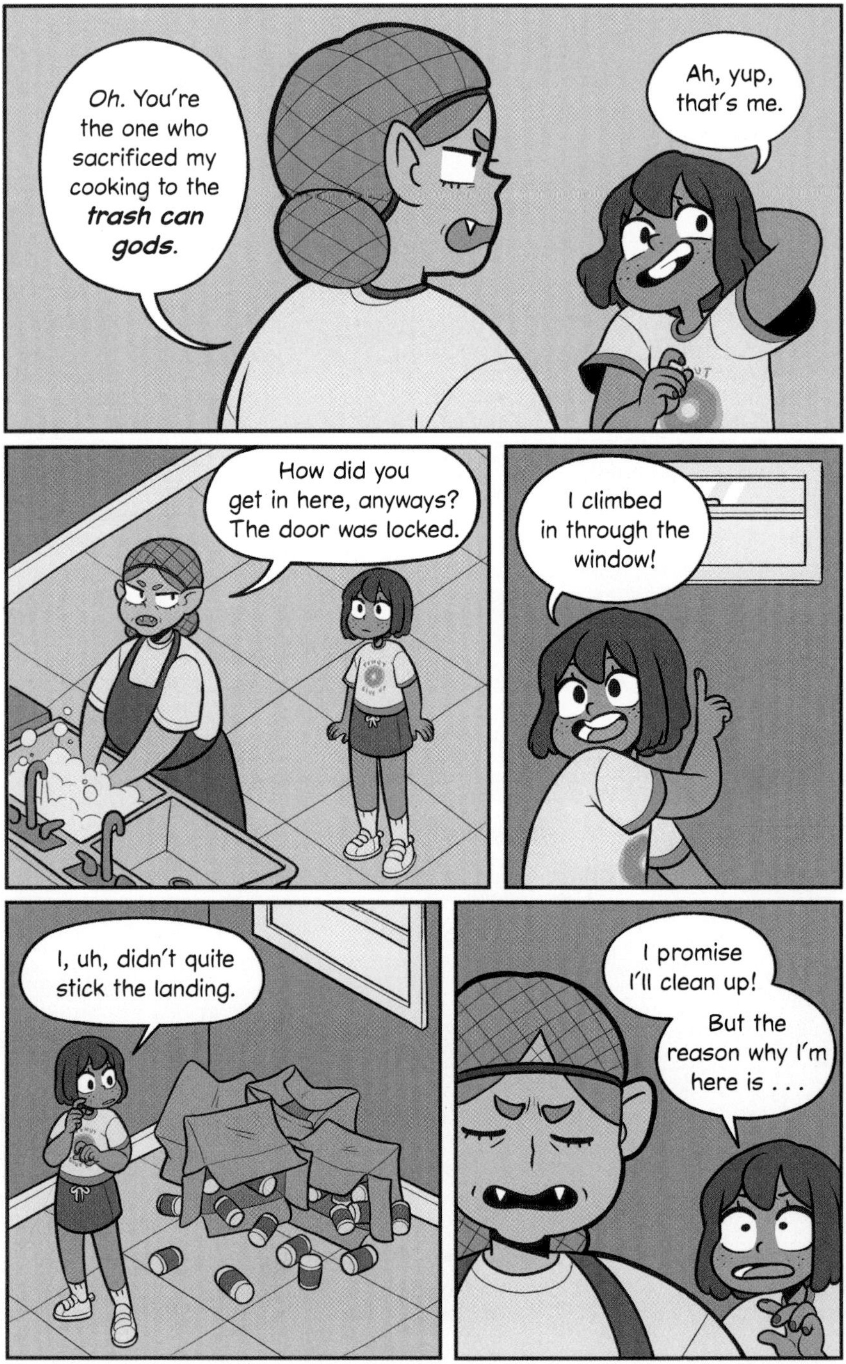
Oh. You're the one who sacrificed my cooking to the ***trash can gods***.
Ah, yup, that's me.
How did you get in here, anyways? The door was locked.
I climbed in through the window!
I, uh, didn't quite stick the landing.
I promise I'll clean up!
But the reason why I'm here is . . .

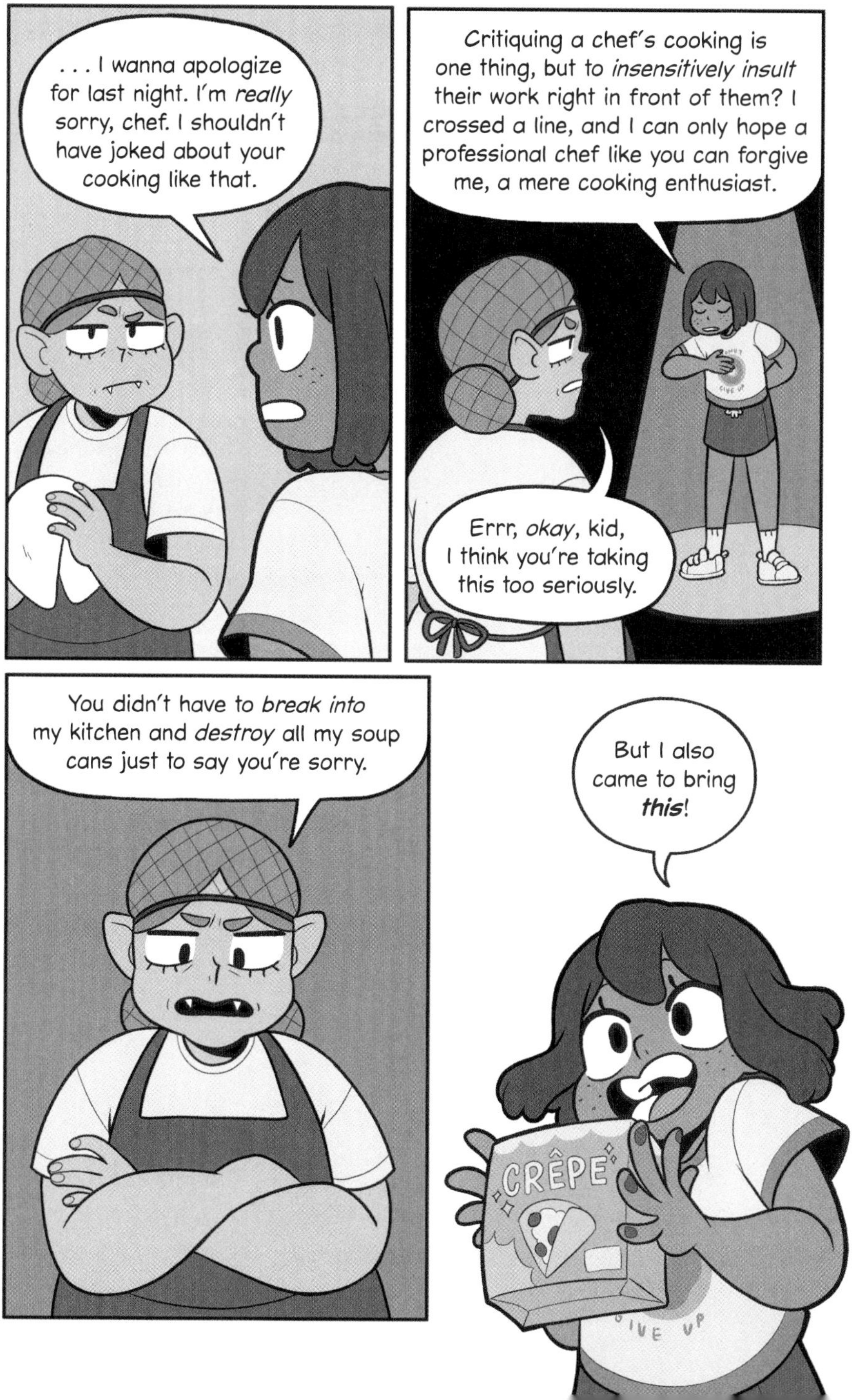
. . . I wanna apologize for last night. I'm *really* sorry, chef. I shouldn't have joked about your cooking like that.
Critiquing a chef's cooking is one thing, but to *insensitively insult* their work right in front of them? I crossed a line, and I can only hope a professional chef like you can forgive me, a mere cooking enthusiast.
Errr, *okay*, kid, I think you're taking this too seriously.
You didn't have to *break into* my kitchen and *destroy* all my soup cans just to say you're sorry.
But I also came to bring ***this***!
CRÊPE
GIVE UP

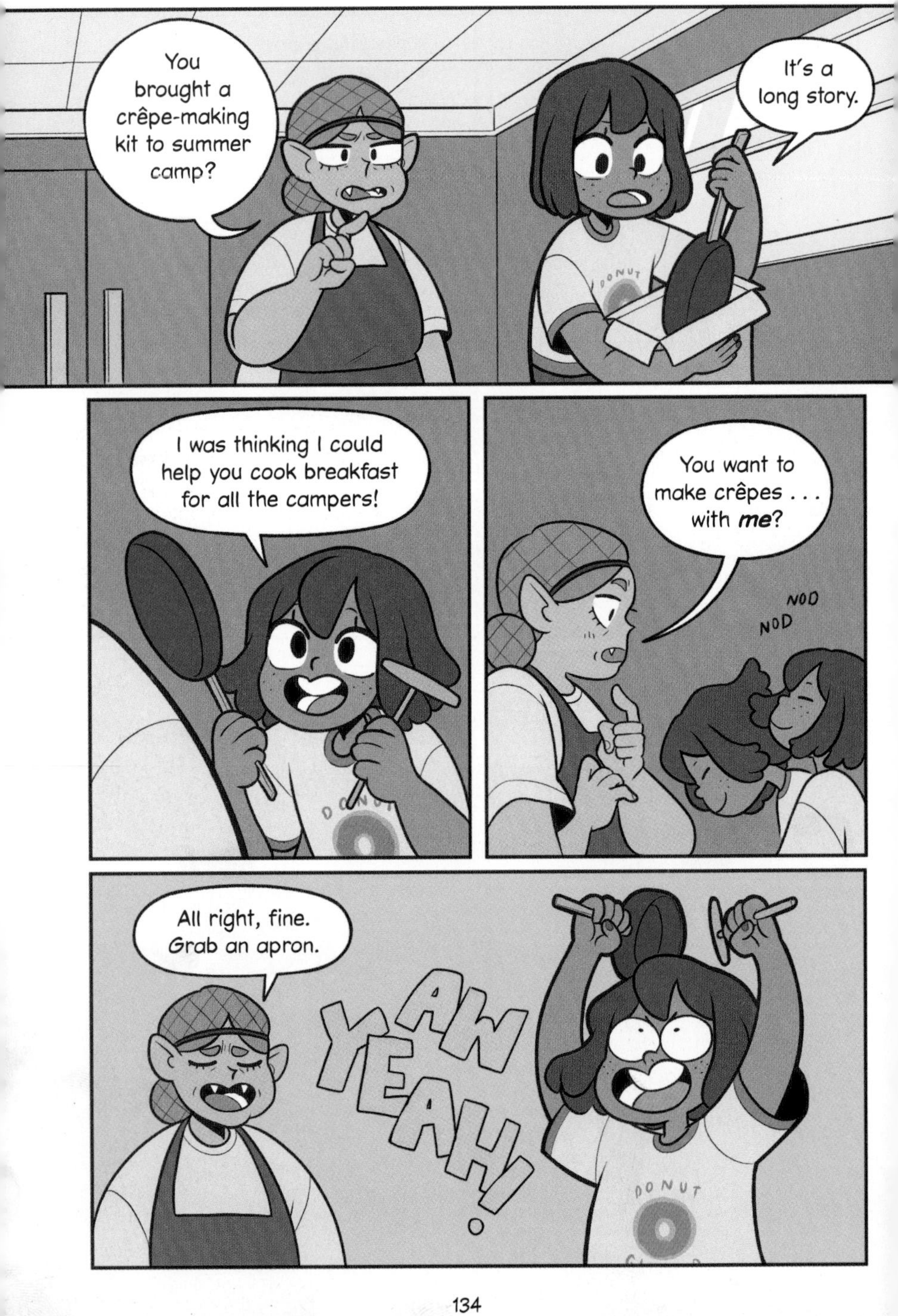

You brought a crêpe-making kit to summer camp?
It's a long story.
I was thinking I could help you cook breakfast for all the campers!
You want to make crêpes . . . with **me**?
NOD NOD
All right, fine. Grab an apron.
AW YEAH!

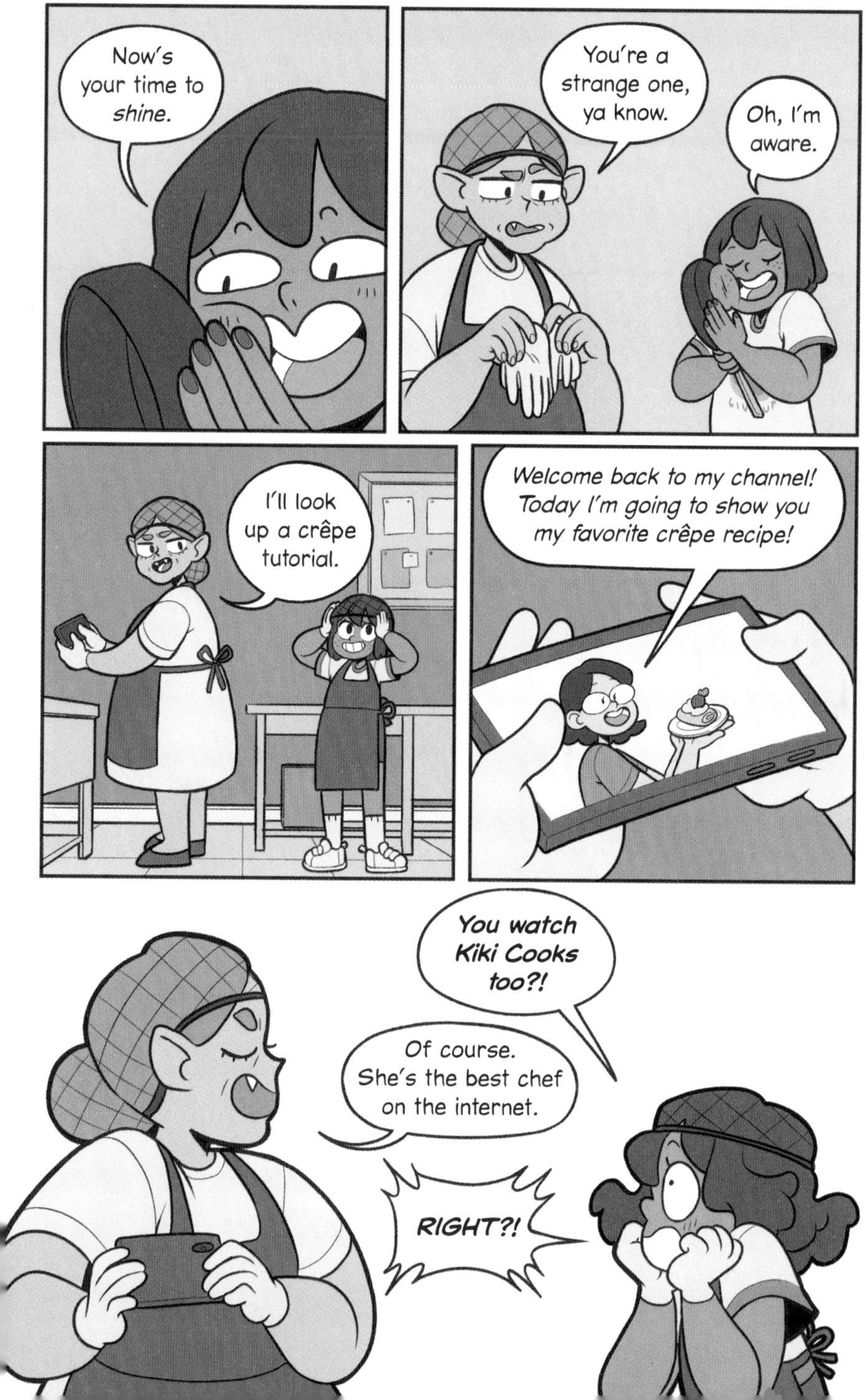

Now's your time to *shine.*
You're a strange one, ya know.
Oh, I'm aware.
I'll look up a crêpe tutorial.
Welcome back to my channel! Today I'm going to show you my favorite crêpe recipe!
You watch Kiki Cooks too?!
Of course. She's the best chef on the internet.
RIGHT?!

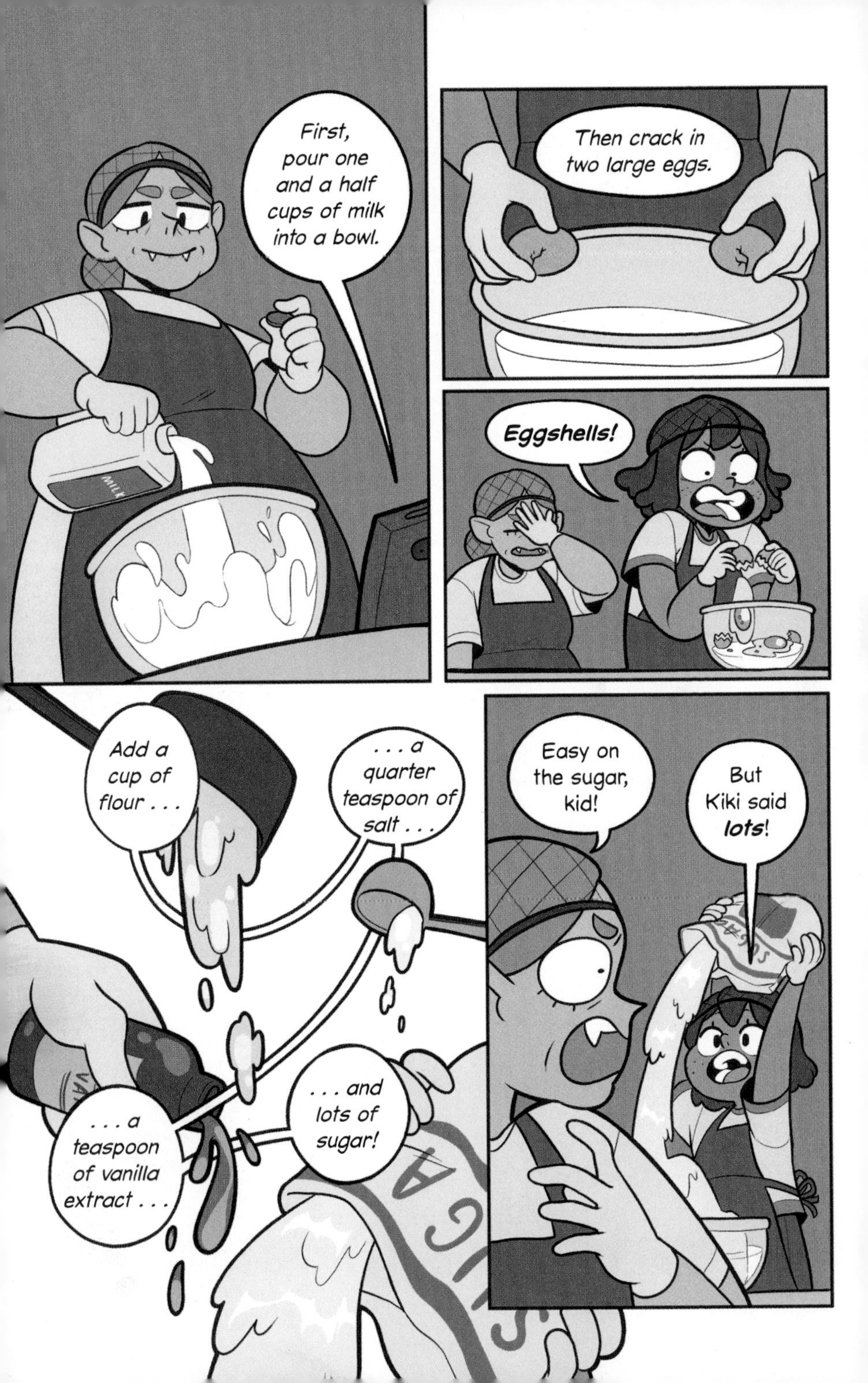
First, pour one and a half cups of milk into a bowl.
MILK
Then crack in two large eggs.
Eggshells!
Add a cup of flour . . .
. . . a quarter teaspoon of salt . . .
. . . a teaspoon of vanilla extract . . .
. . . and lots of sugar!
Easy on the sugar, kid!
But Kiki said **lots**!

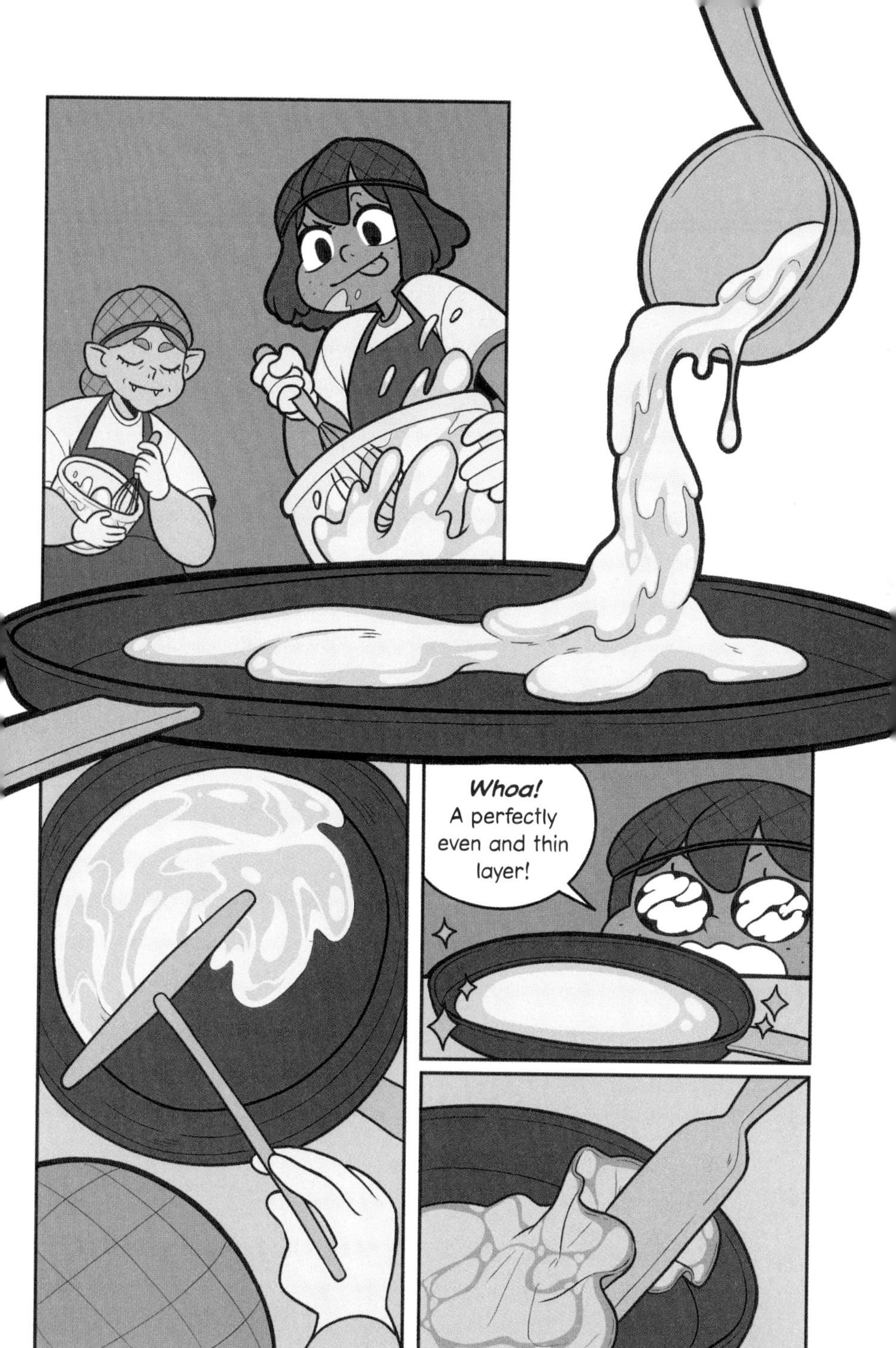
Whoa! A perfectly even and thin layer!

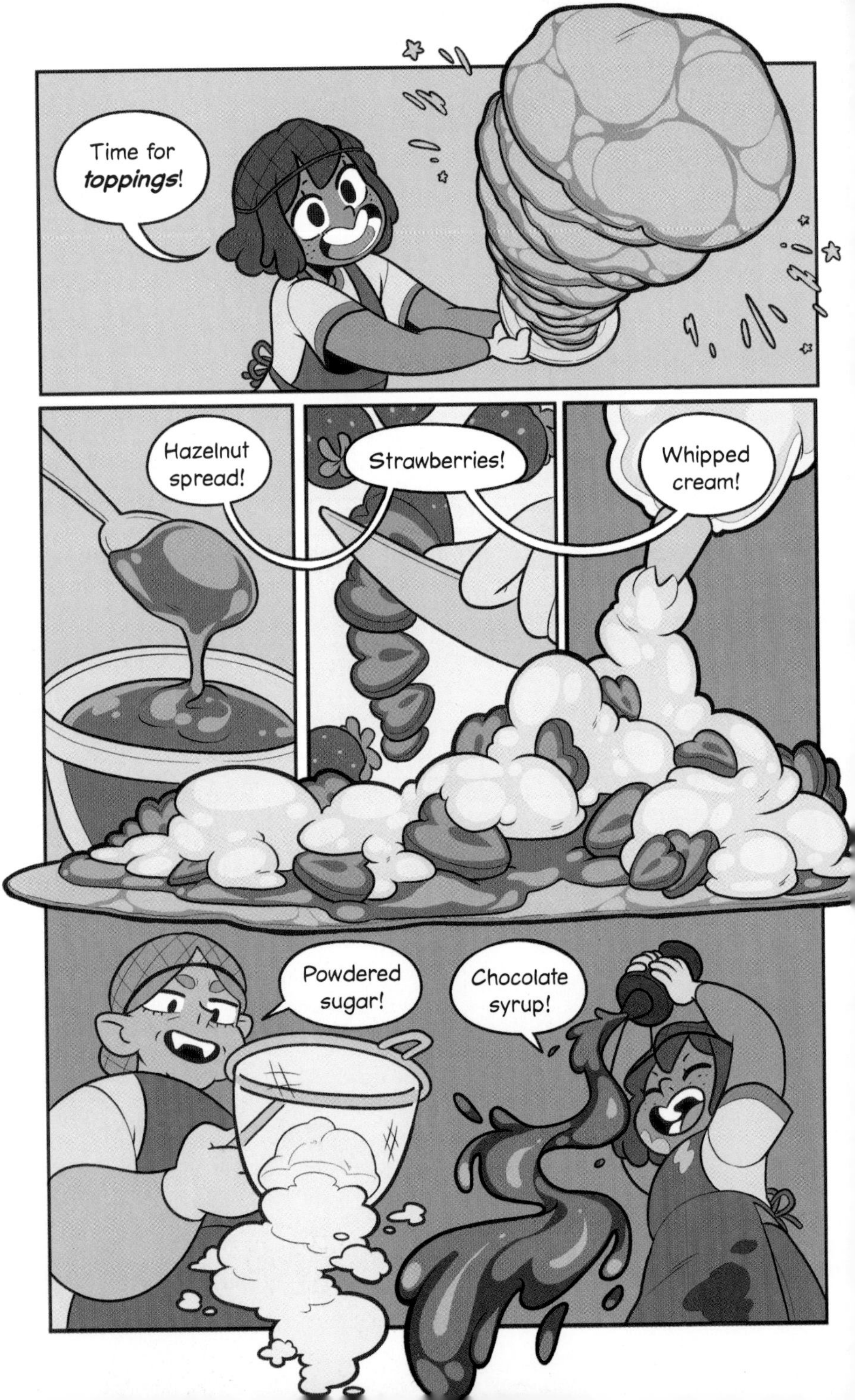
Time for *toppings*!
Hazelnut spread!
Strawberries!
Whipped cream!
Powdered sugar!
Chocolate syrup!

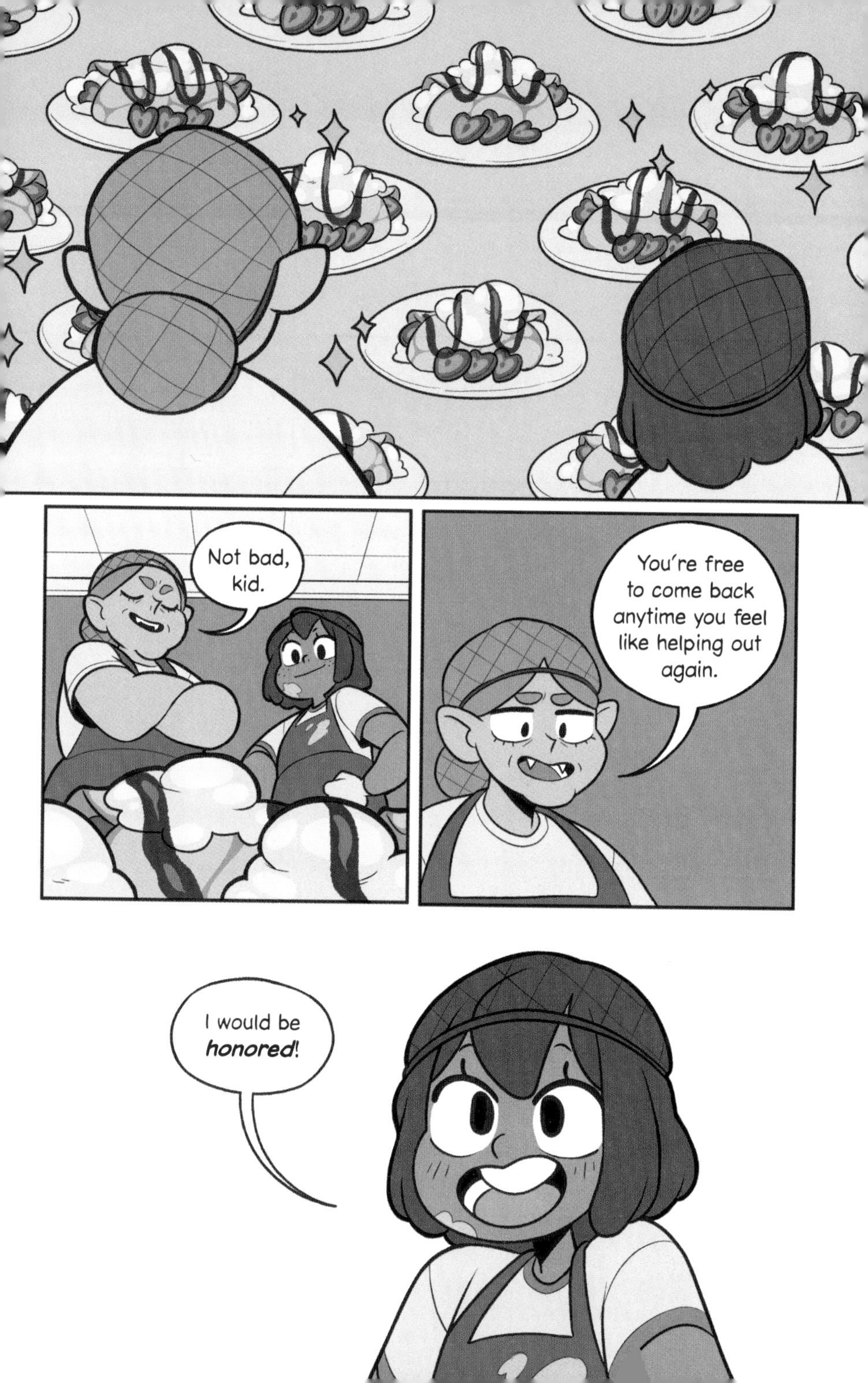

Not bad, kid.
You're free to come back anytime you feel like helping out again.
I would be ***honored***!

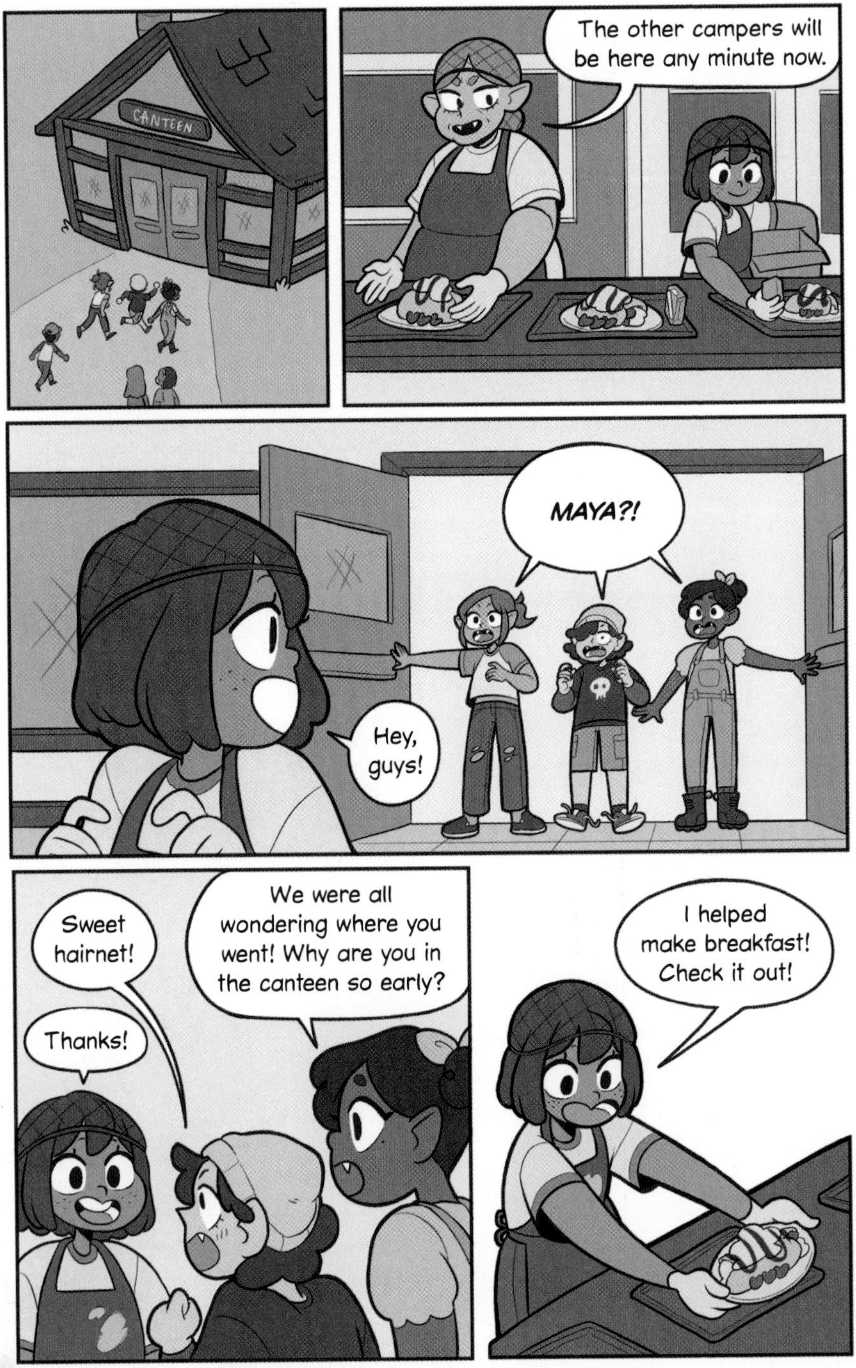

CANTEEN
The other campers will be here any minute now.
MAYA?!
Hey, guys!
Sweet hairnet!
Thanks!
We were all wondering where you went! Why are you in the canteen so early?
I helped make breakfast! Check it out!

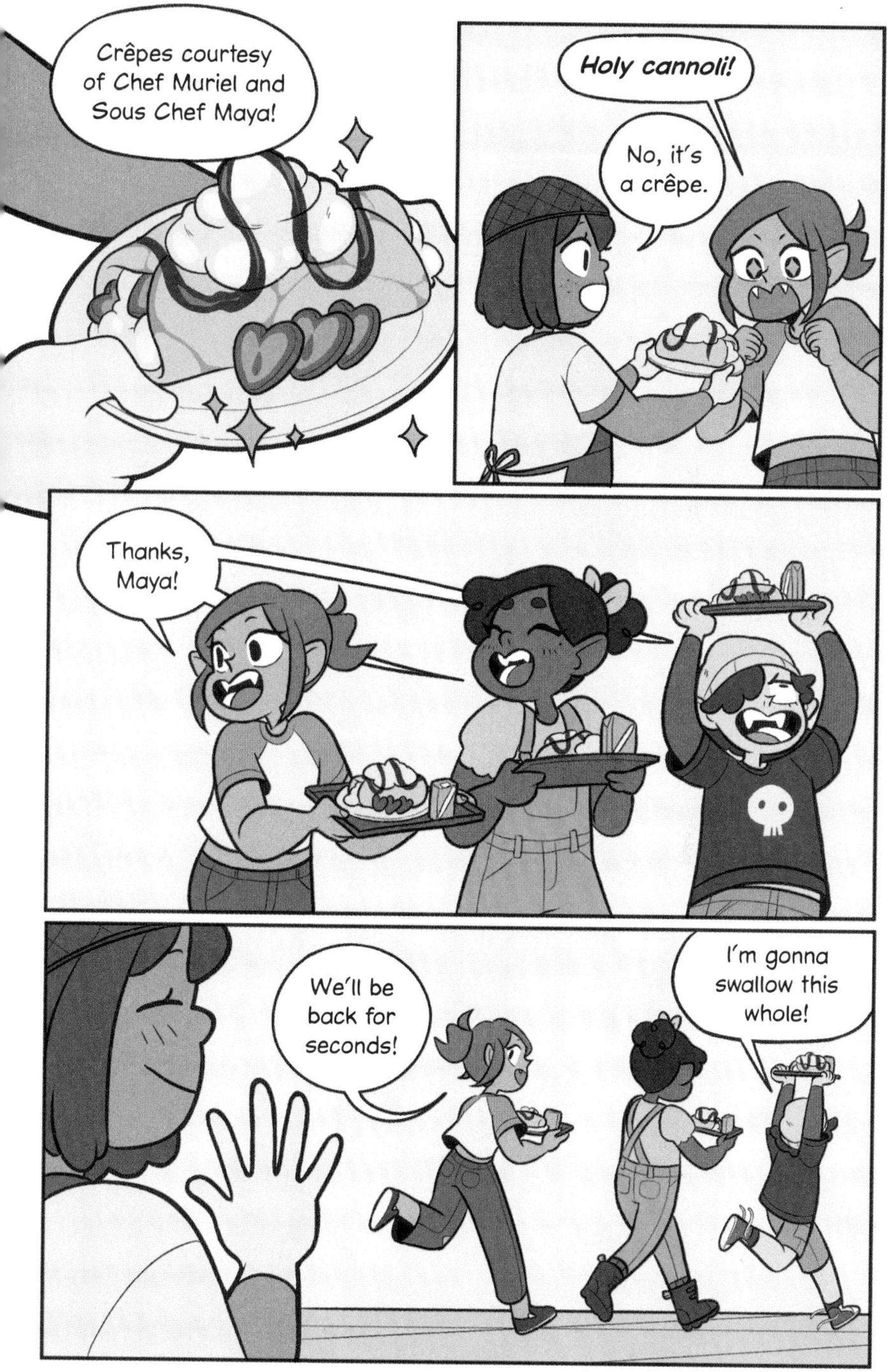
Crêpes courtesy of Chef Muriel and Sous Chef Maya!
Holy cannoli!
No, it's a crêpe.
Thanks, Maya!
We'll be back for seconds!
I'm gonna swallow this whole!

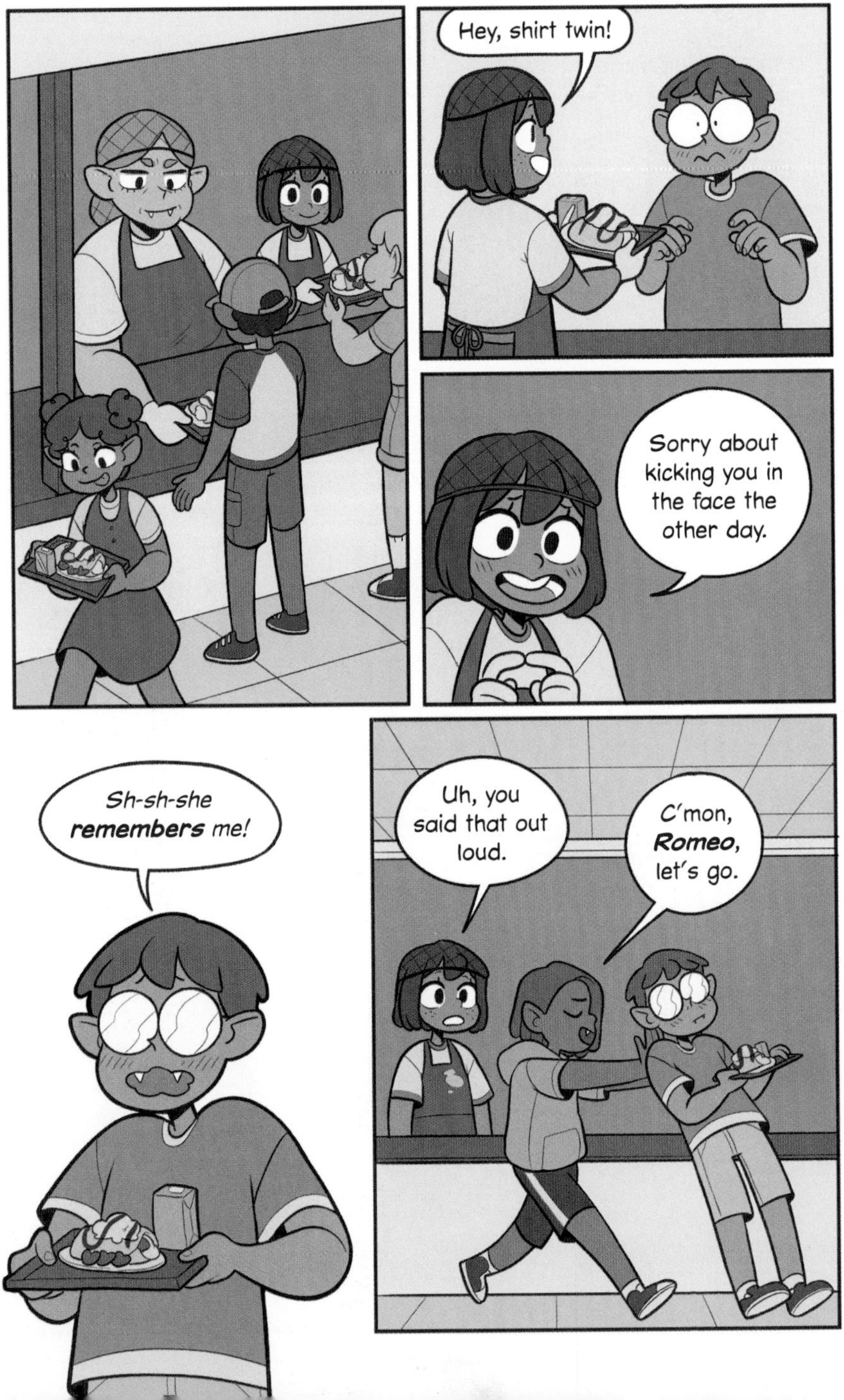
Hey, shirt twin!
Sorry about kicking you in the face the other day.
Sh-sh-she **remembers** me!
Uh, you said that out loud.
C'mon, ***Romeo***, let's go.

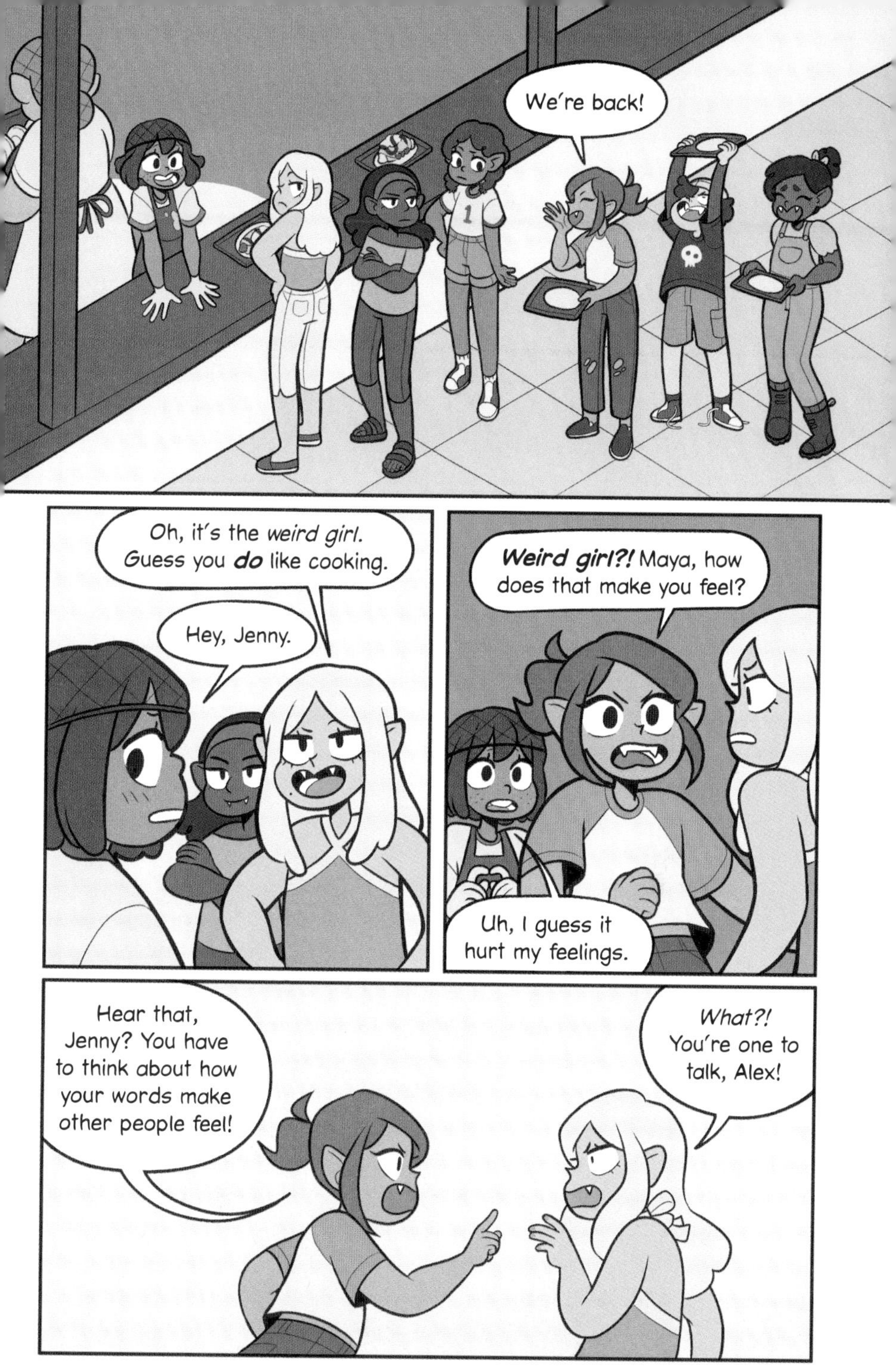
We're back!
Oh, it's the *weird girl*. Guess you **do** like cooking.
Hey, Jenny.
Weird girl?! Maya, how does that make you feel?
Uh, I guess it hurt my feelings.
Hear that, Jenny? You have to think about how your words make other people feel!
What?! You're one to talk, Alex!

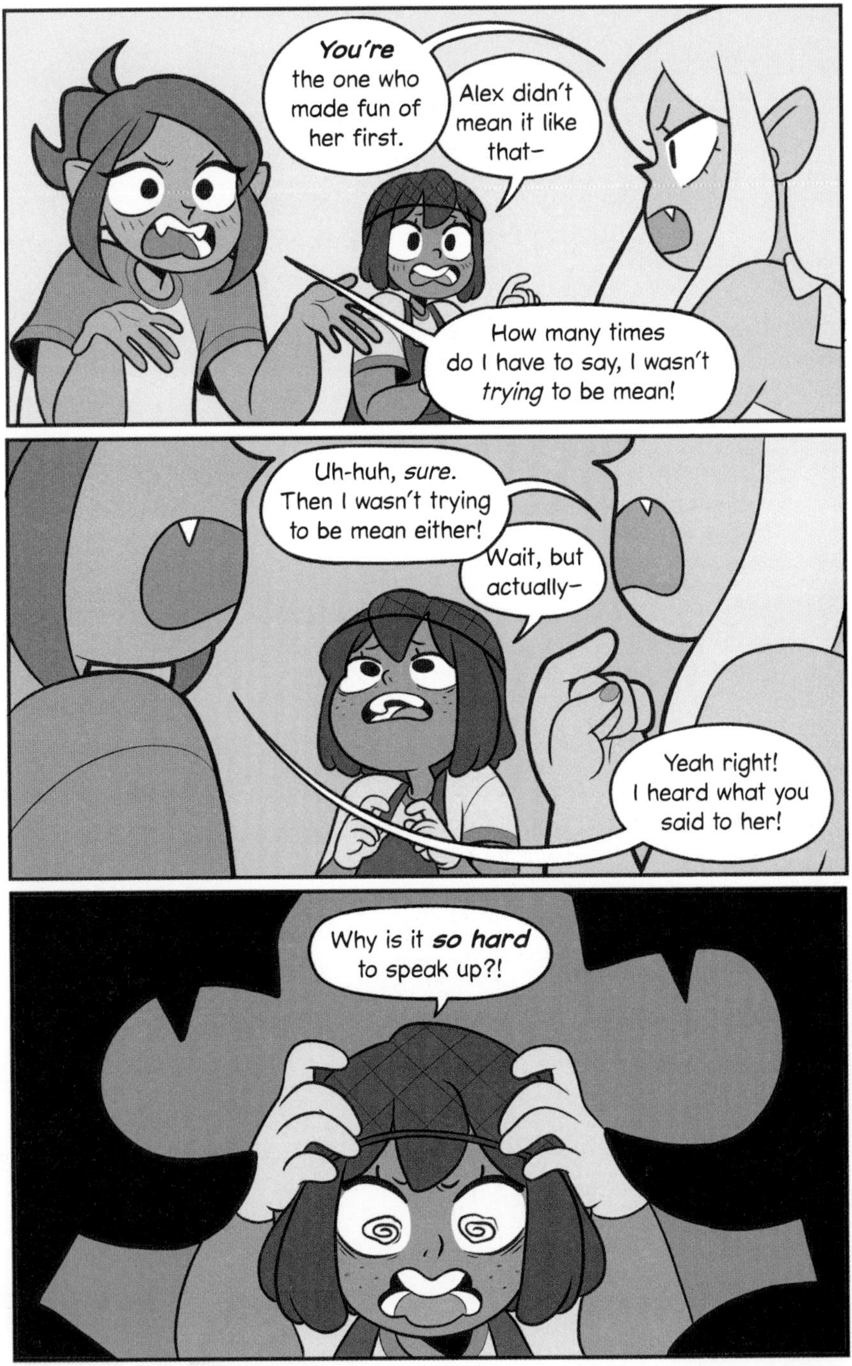
You're the one who made fun of her first.
Alex didn't mean it like that–
How many times do I have to say, I wasn't trying to be mean!
Uh-huh, sure. Then I wasn't trying to be mean either!
Wait, but actually–
Yeah right! I heard what you said to her!
Why is it so hard to speak up?!

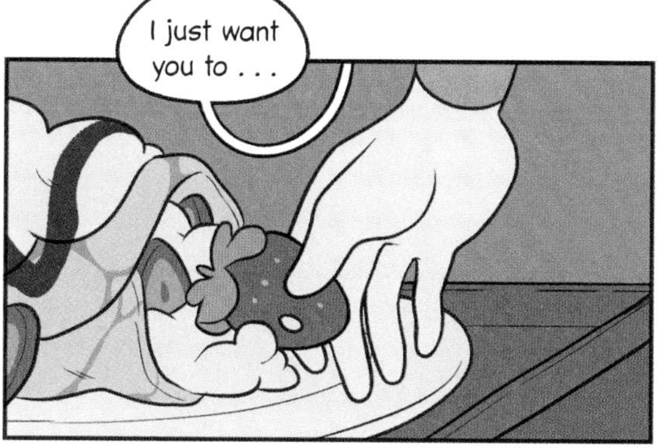
I just want you to . . .

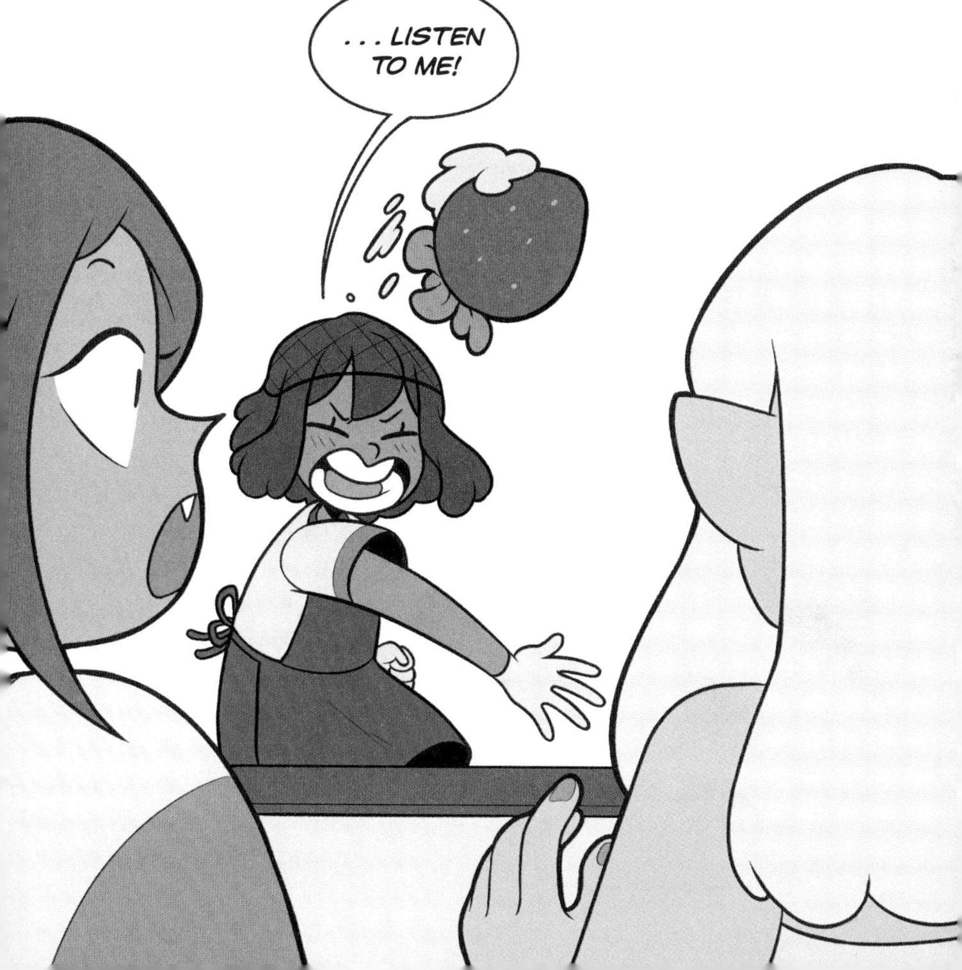
. . . LISTEN TO ME!

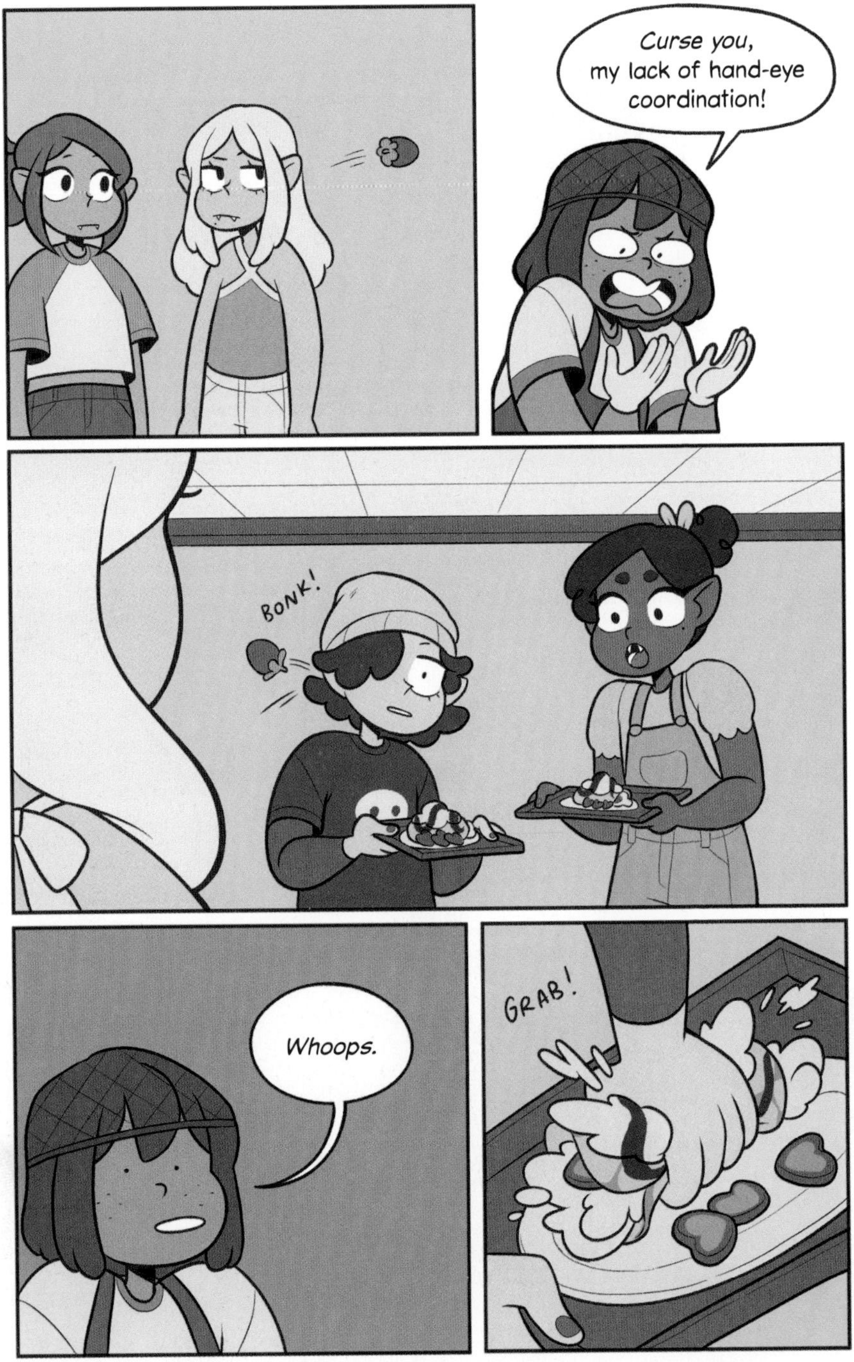
Curse you, my lack of hand-eye coordination!
BONK!
Whoops.
GRAB!

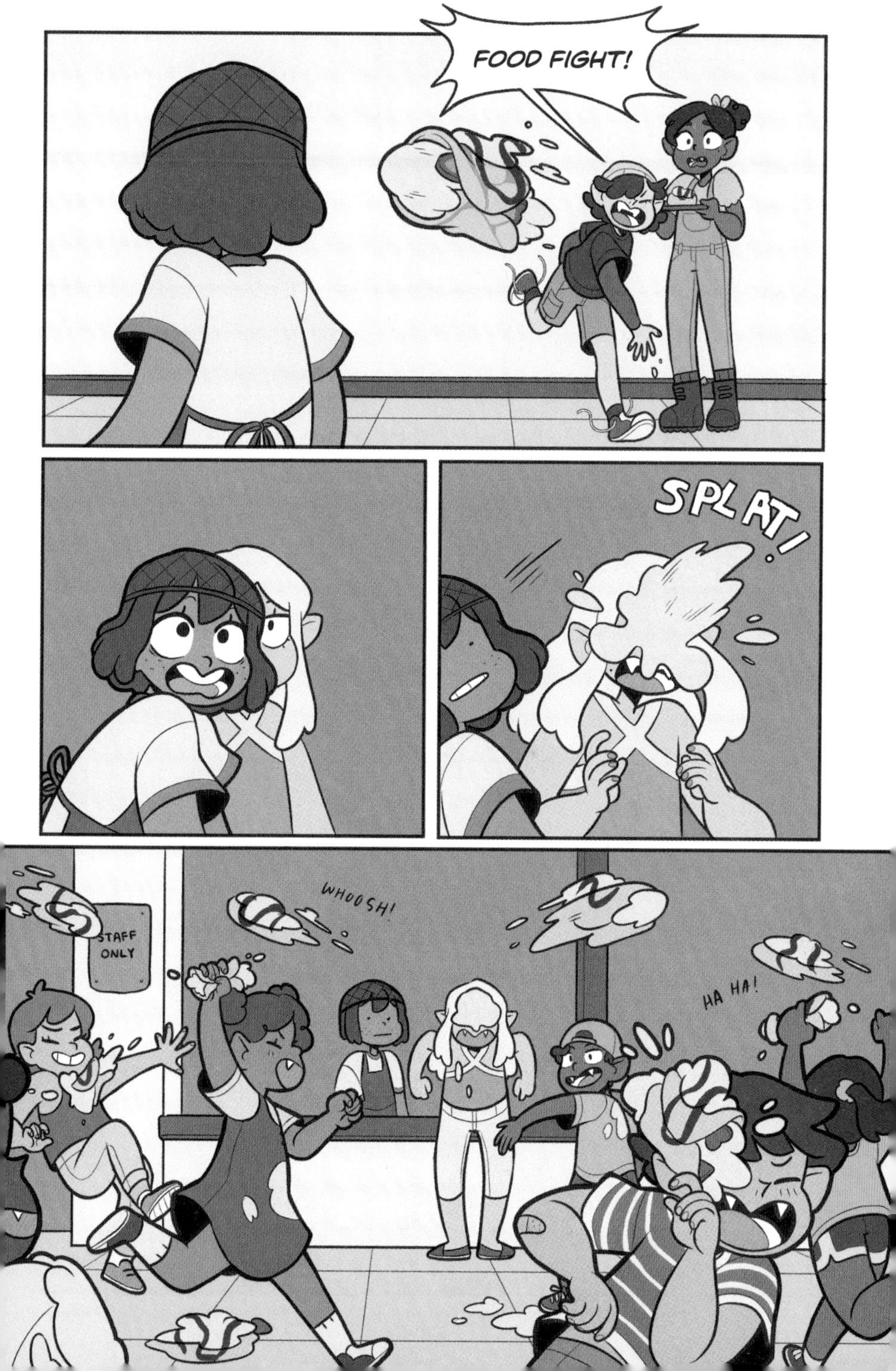
FOOD FIGHT!
SPLAT!
WHOOSH!
STAFF ONLY
HA HA!

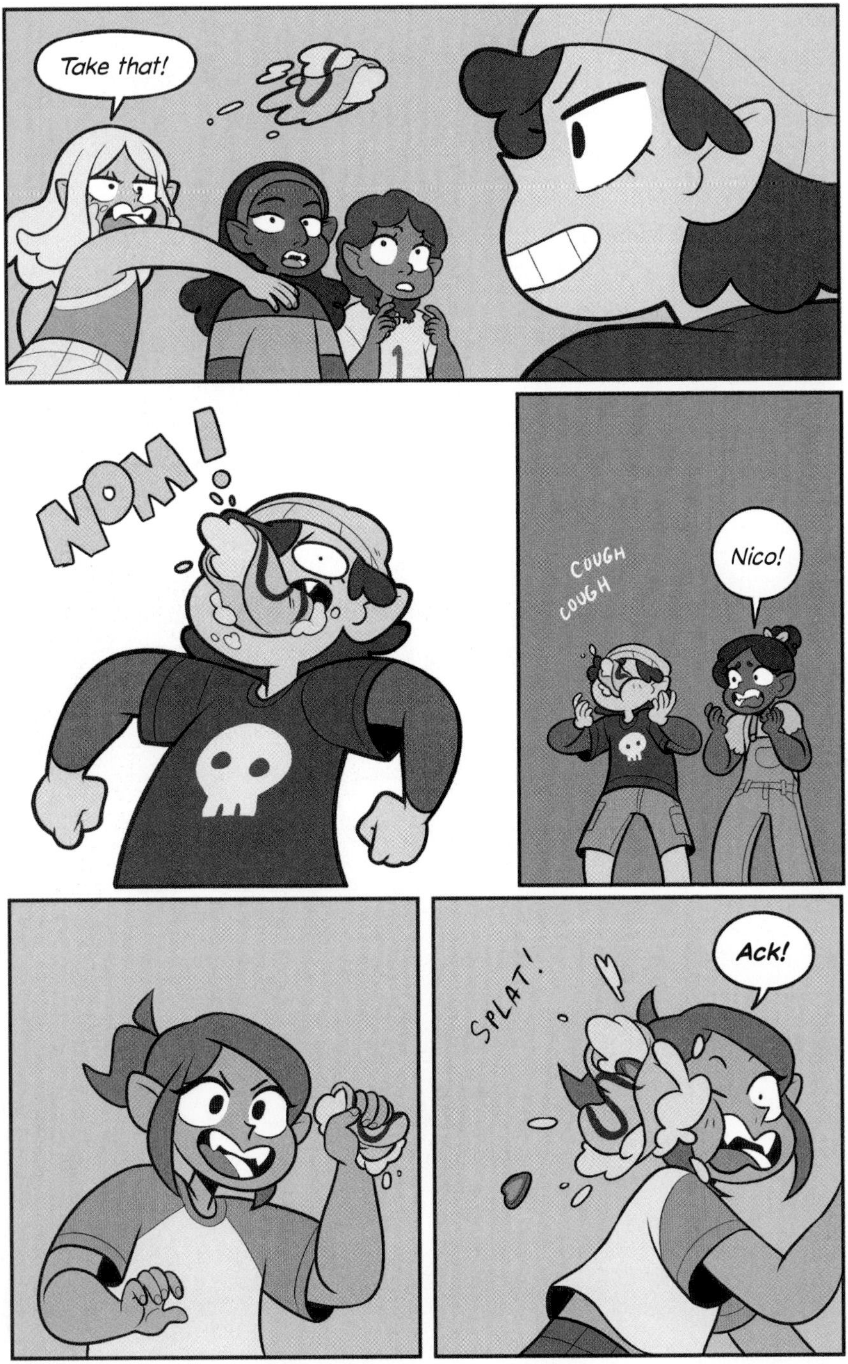
Take that!
NOM!
COUGH
COUGH
Nico!
SPLAT!
Ack!

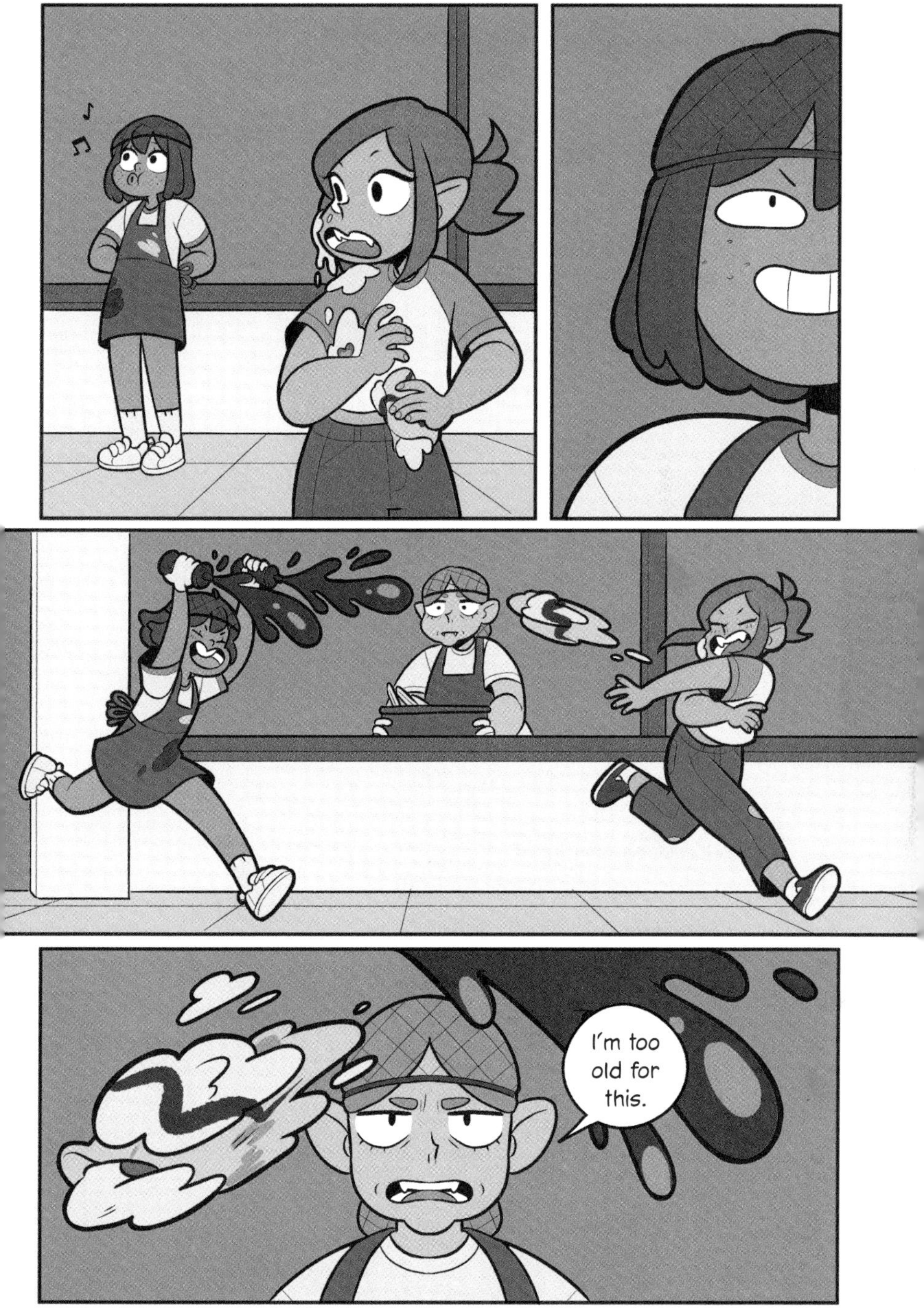
I'm too
old for
this.

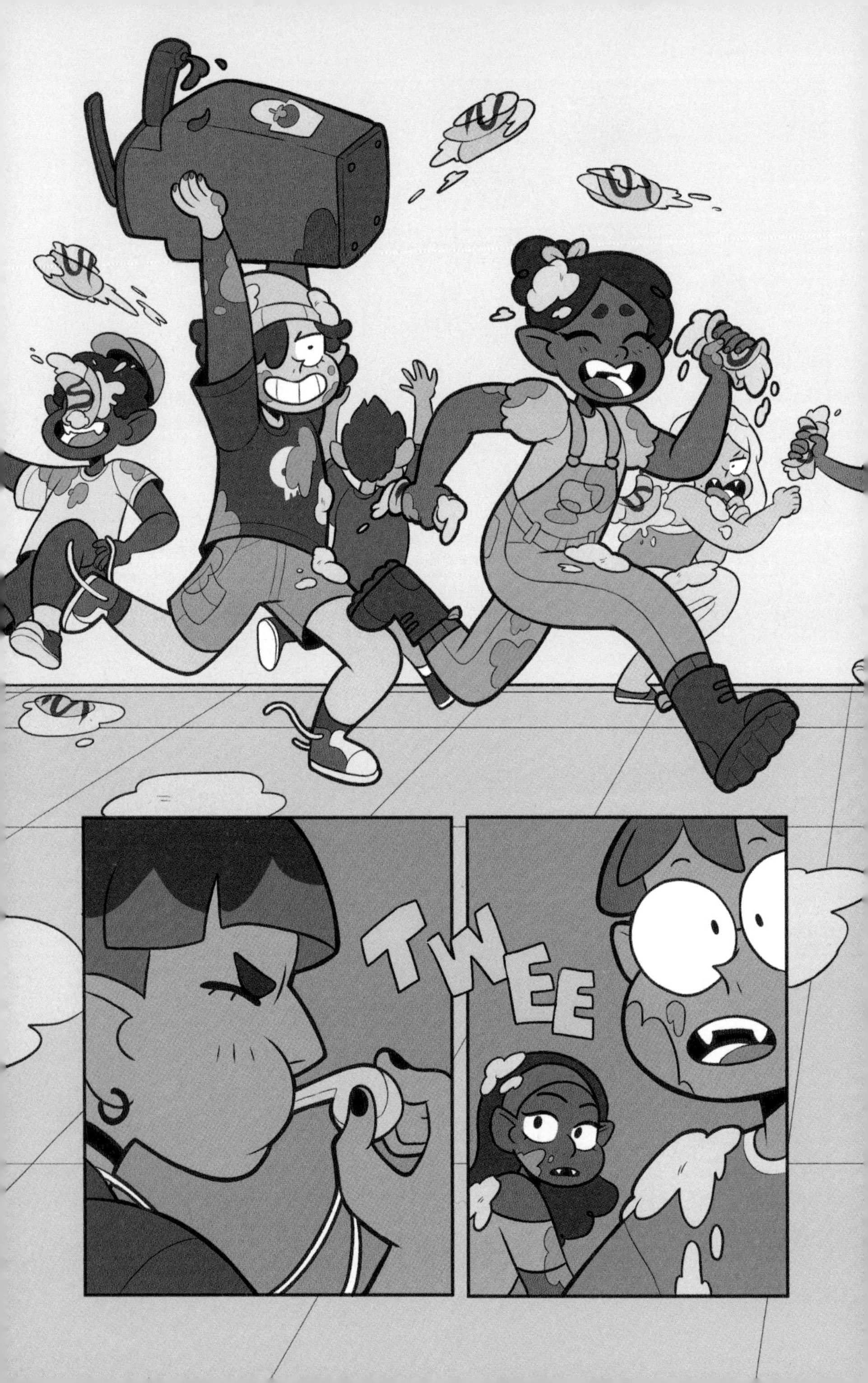
TWEE

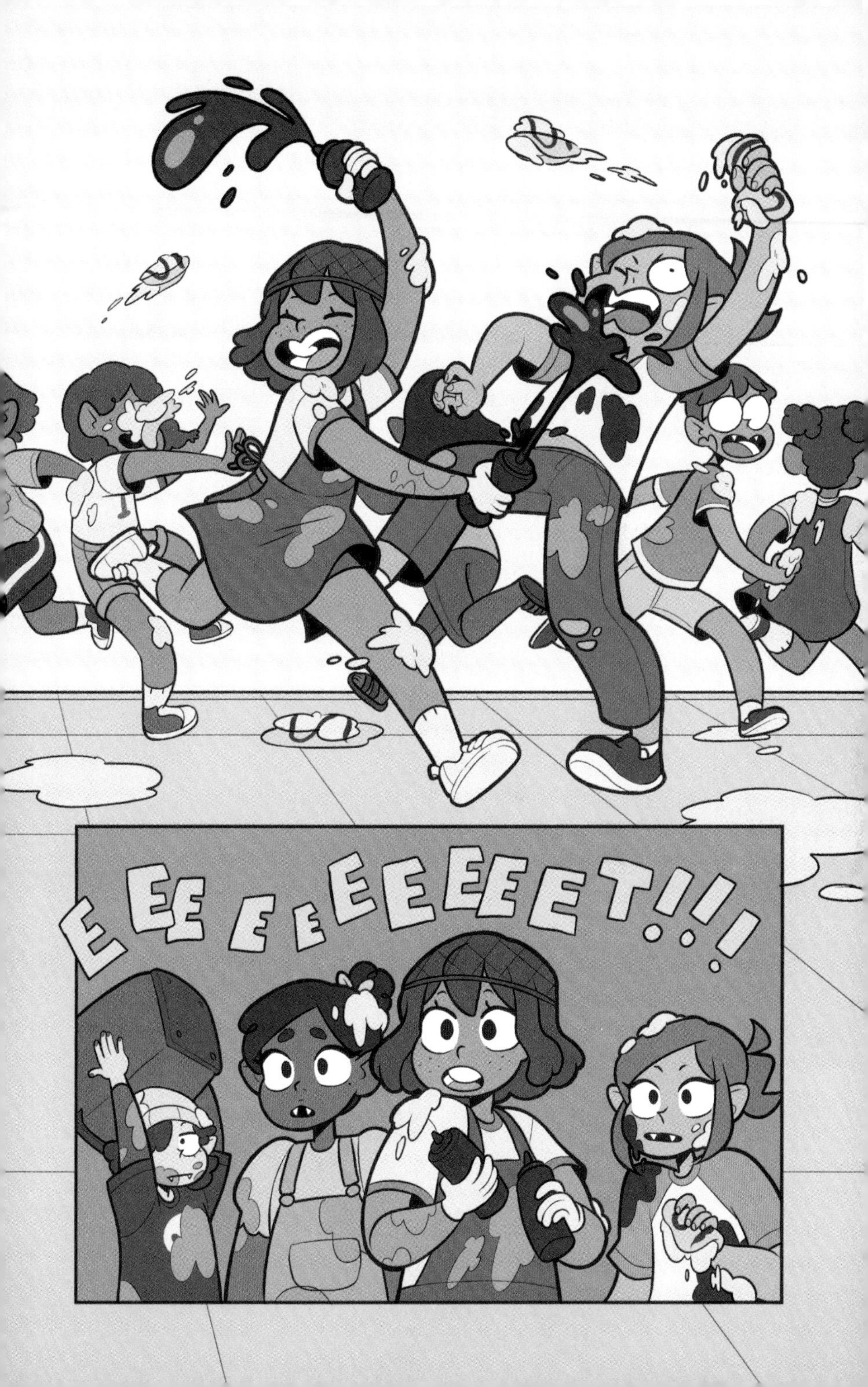
EEEEEEEEEET!!!!

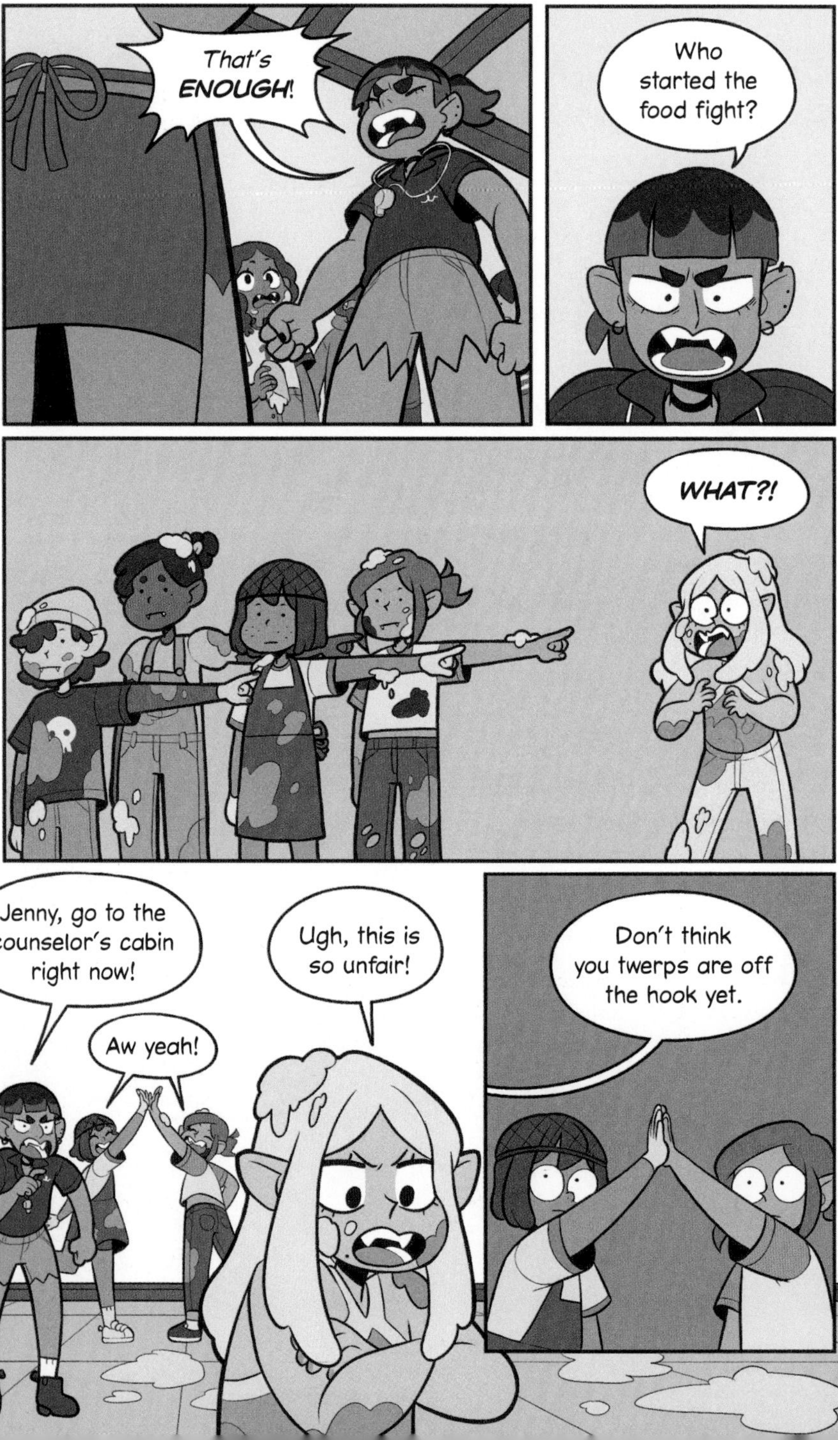
That's
ENOUGH!
Who started the food fight?
WHAT?!
Jenny, go to the counselor's cabin right now!
Aw yeah!
Ugh, this is so unfair!
Don't think you twerps are off the hook yet.

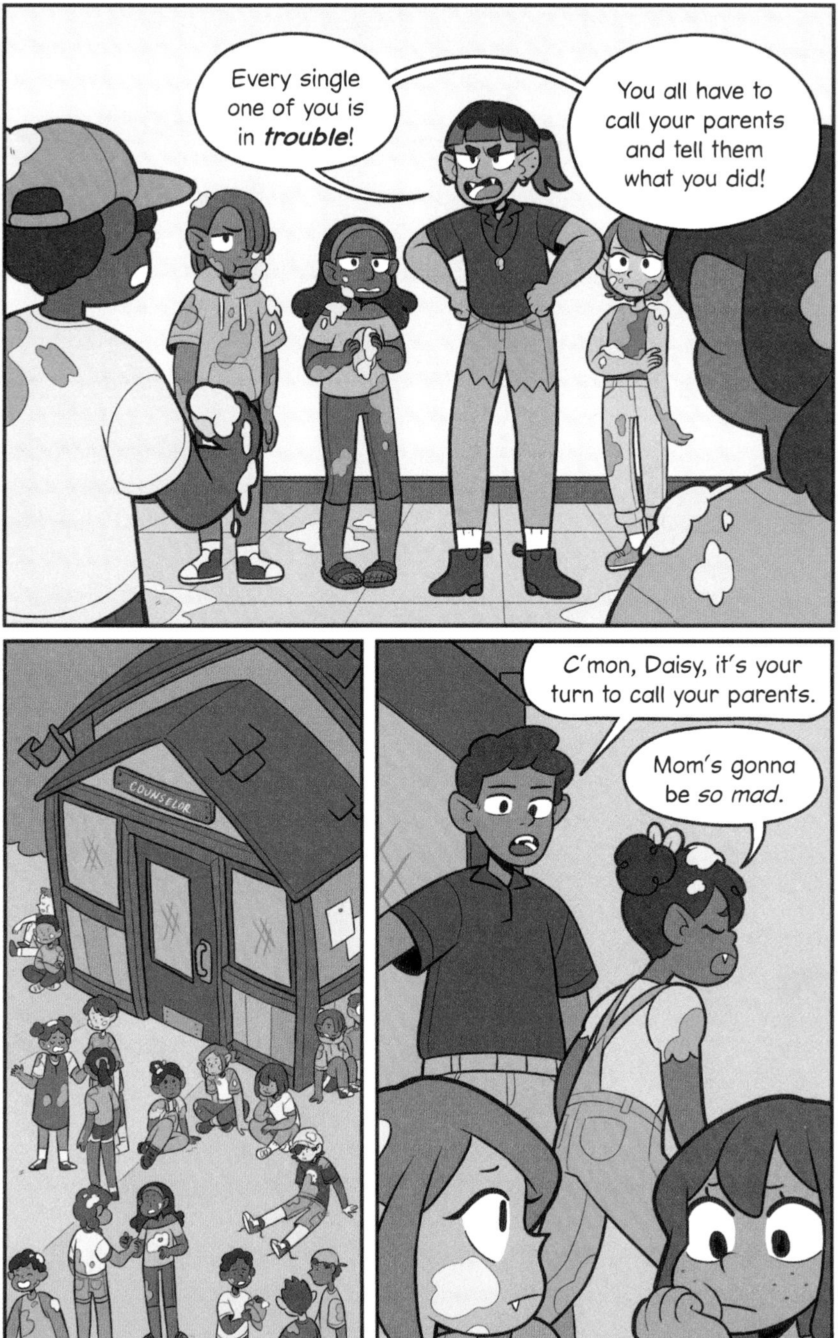
Every single one of you is in ***trouble***!
You all have to call your parents and tell them what you did!
COUNSELOR
C'mon, Daisy, it's your turn to call your parents.
Mom's gonna be *so mad*.

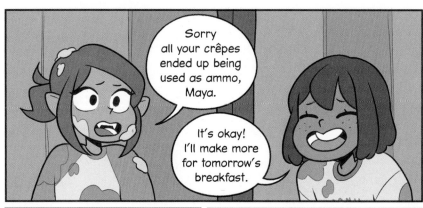

Sorry all your crêpes ended up being used as ammo, Maya.

It's okay! I'll make more for tomorrow's breakfast.

If Muriel lets me back into the kitchen, that is.

By the way, thanks for sticking up for me earlier. I wish I could be tough like you.

I dunno, dude, it was *pretty tough* how you **almost** hit Jenny with that strawberry.

Ugh, don't remind me.

Maybe *sometimes* it's good to be tough. But other times it makes it hard to make friends.

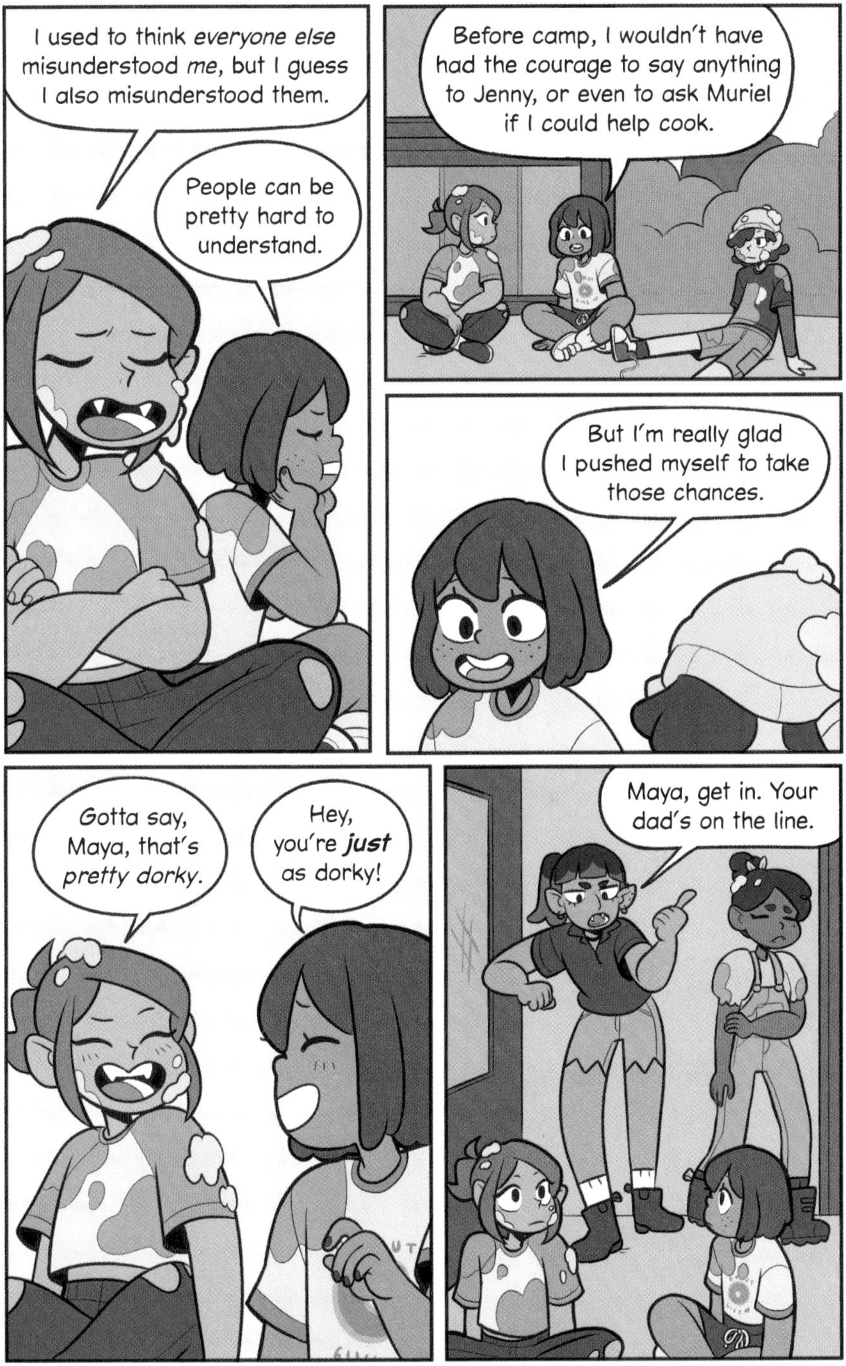
I used to think *everyone else* misunderstood *me*, but I guess I also misunderstood them.
People can be pretty hard to understand.
Before camp, I wouldn't have had the courage to say anything to Jenny, or even to ask Muriel if I could help cook.
But I'm really glad I pushed myself to take those chances.
Gotta say, Maya, that's *pretty dorky.*
Hey, you're ***just*** as dorky!
Maya, get in. Your dad's on the line.

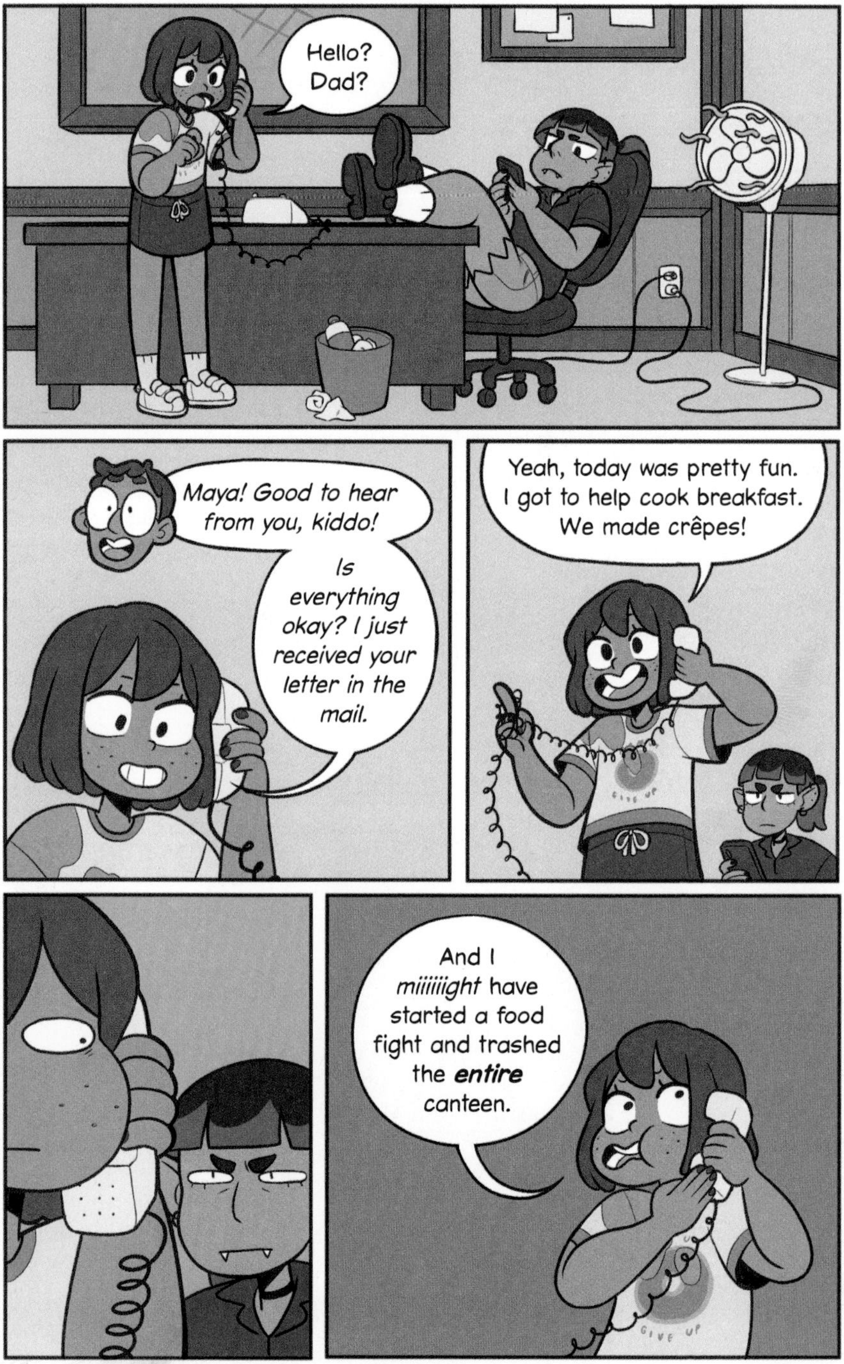
Hello? Dad?
Maya! Good to hear from you, kiddo!
Is everything okay? I just received your letter in the mail.
Yeah, today was pretty fun. I got to help cook breakfast. We made crêpes!
GIVE UP
And I *miiiiiight* have started a food fight and trashed the ***entire*** canteen.
GIVE UP

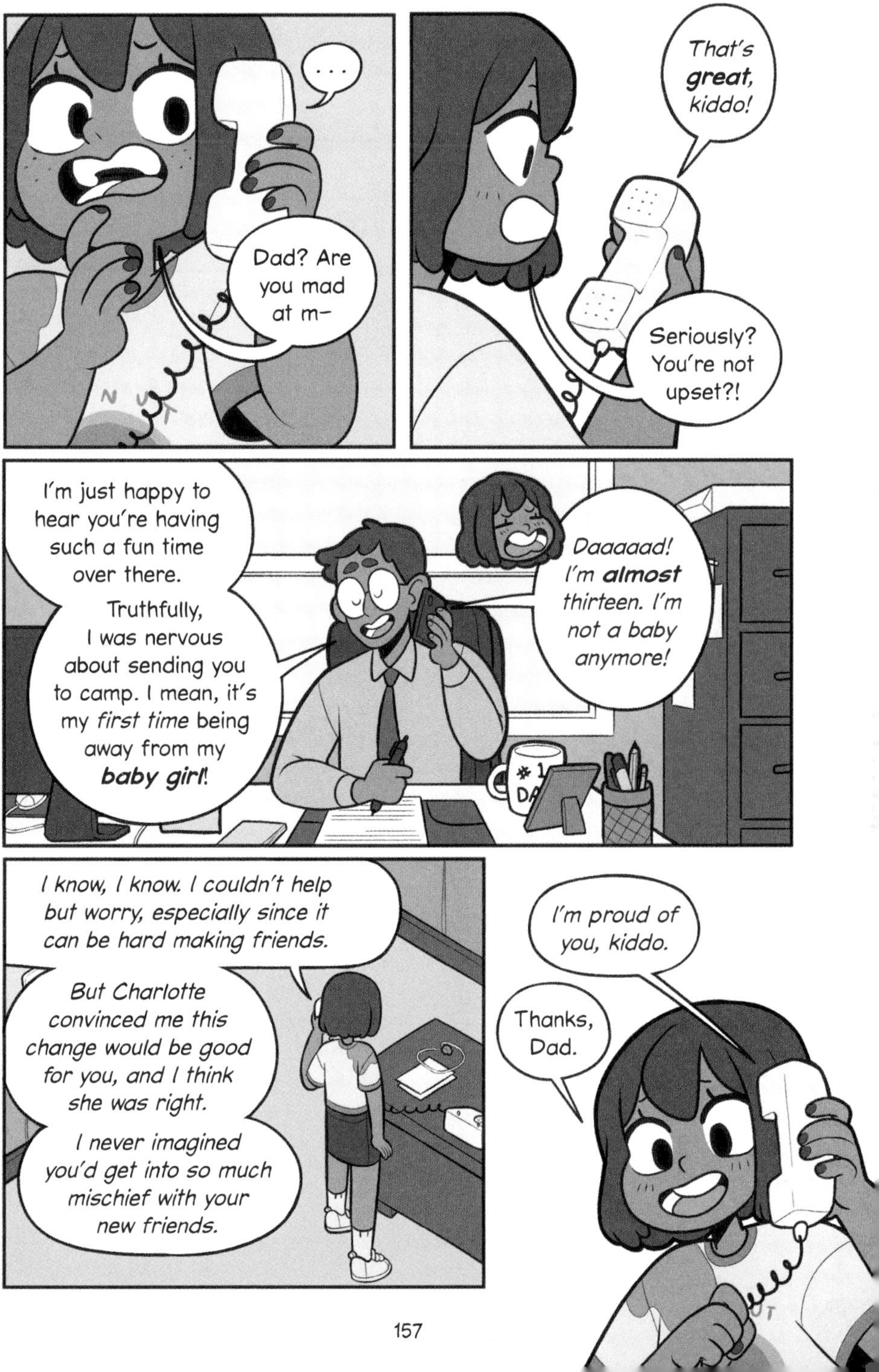
...
Dad? Are you mad at m–
That's **great,** kiddo!
Seriously? You're not upset?!
I'm just happy to hear you're having such a fun time over there.
Truthfully, I was nervous about sending you to camp. I mean, it's my *first time* being away from my ***baby girl***!
*Daaaaad! I'm **almost** thirteen. I'm not a baby anymore!*
#1 DAD
I know, I know. I couldn't help but worry, especially since it can be hard making friends.
But Charlotte convinced me this change would be good for you, and I think she was right.
I never imagined you'd get into so much mischief with your new friends.
I'm proud of you, kiddo.
Thanks, Dad.

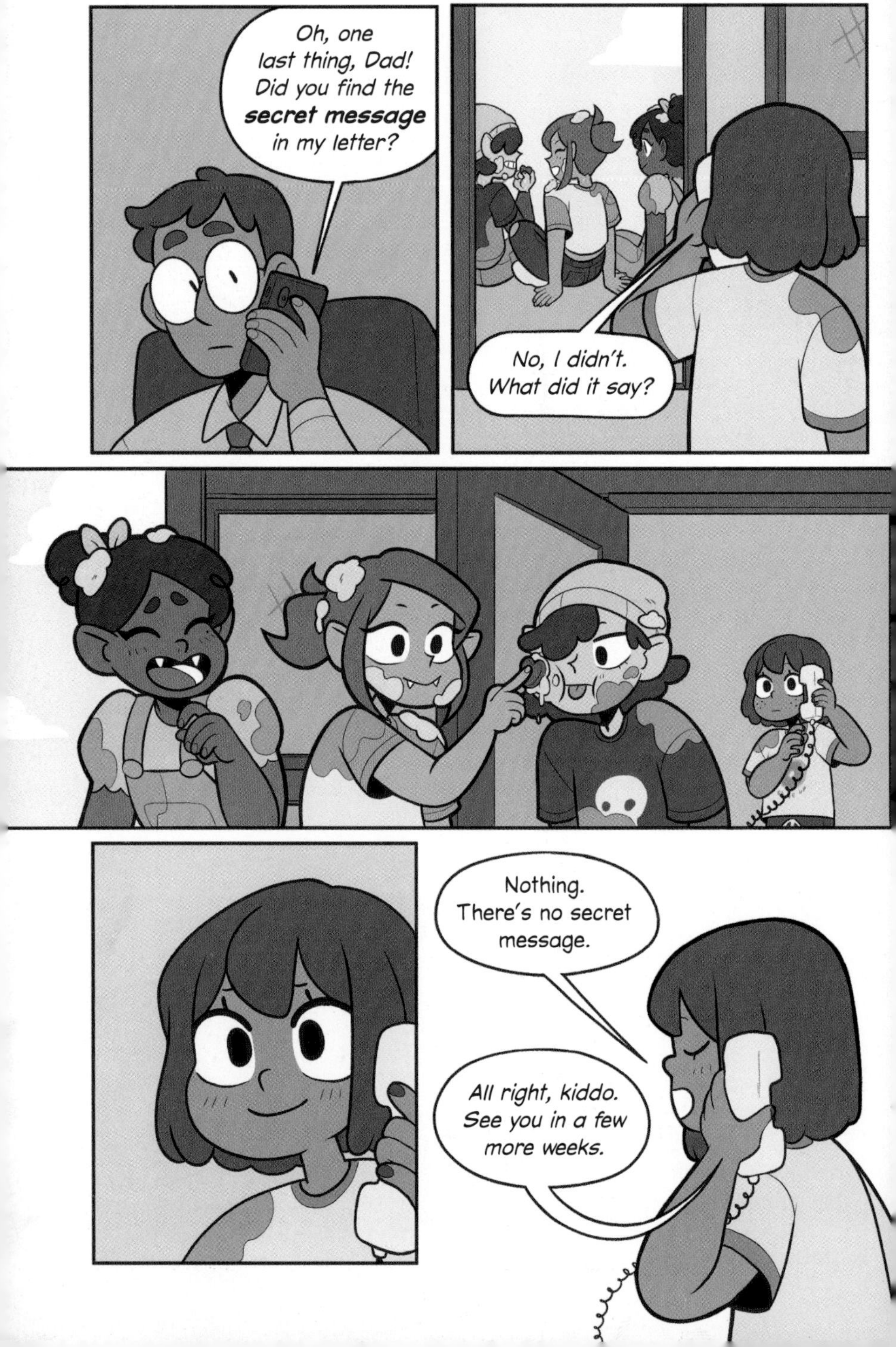
Oh, one last thing, Dad! Did you find the **secret message** in my letter?
No, I didn't. What did it say?
Nothing. There's no secret message.
All right, kiddo. See you in a few more weeks.

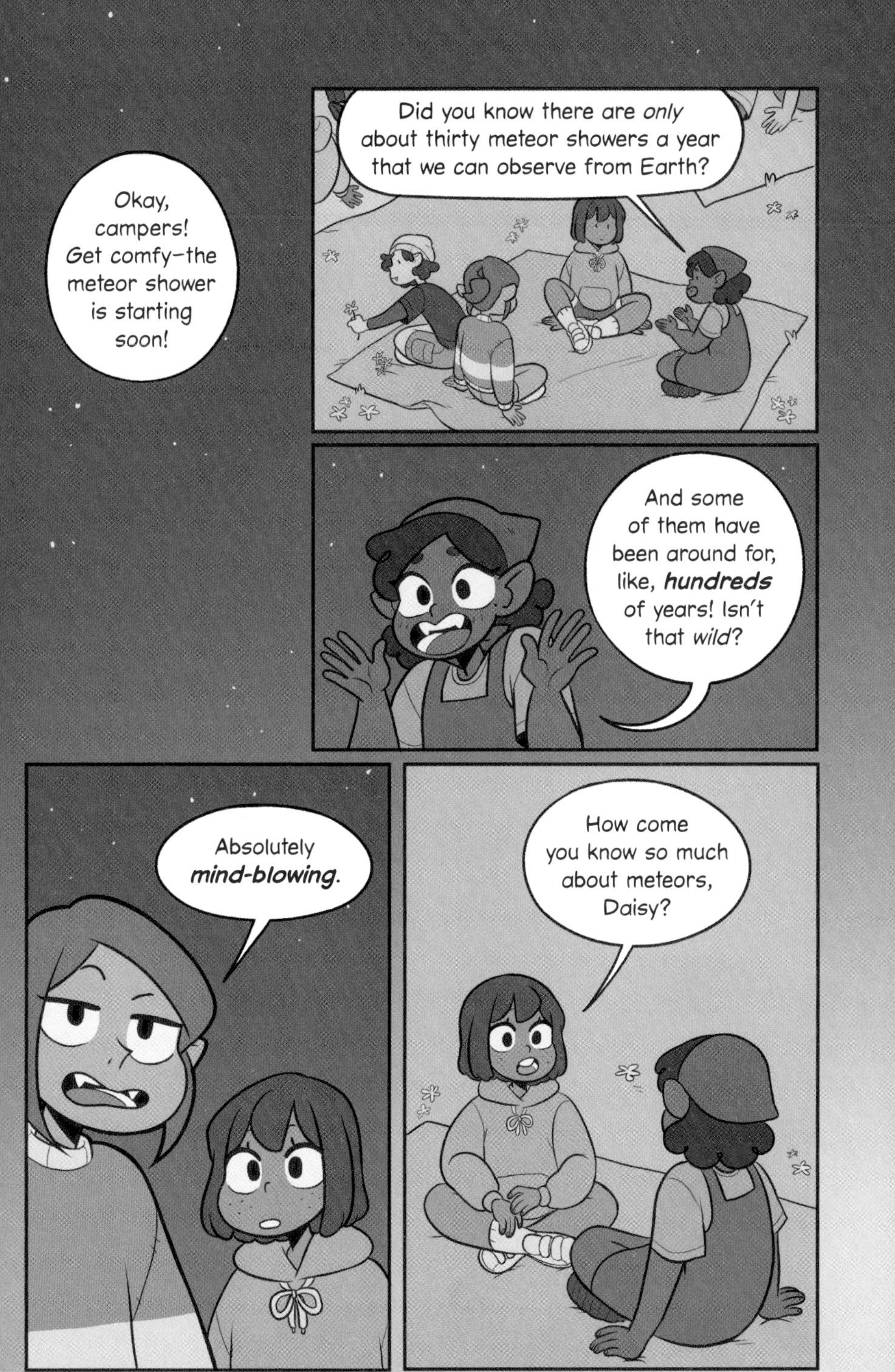
Okay, campers! Get comfy—the meteor shower is starting soon!
Did you know there are *only* about thirty meteor showers a year that we can observe from Earth?
And some of them have been around for, like, ***hundreds*** of years! Isn't that *wild*?
Absolutely ***mind-blowing***.
How come you know so much about meteors, Daisy?

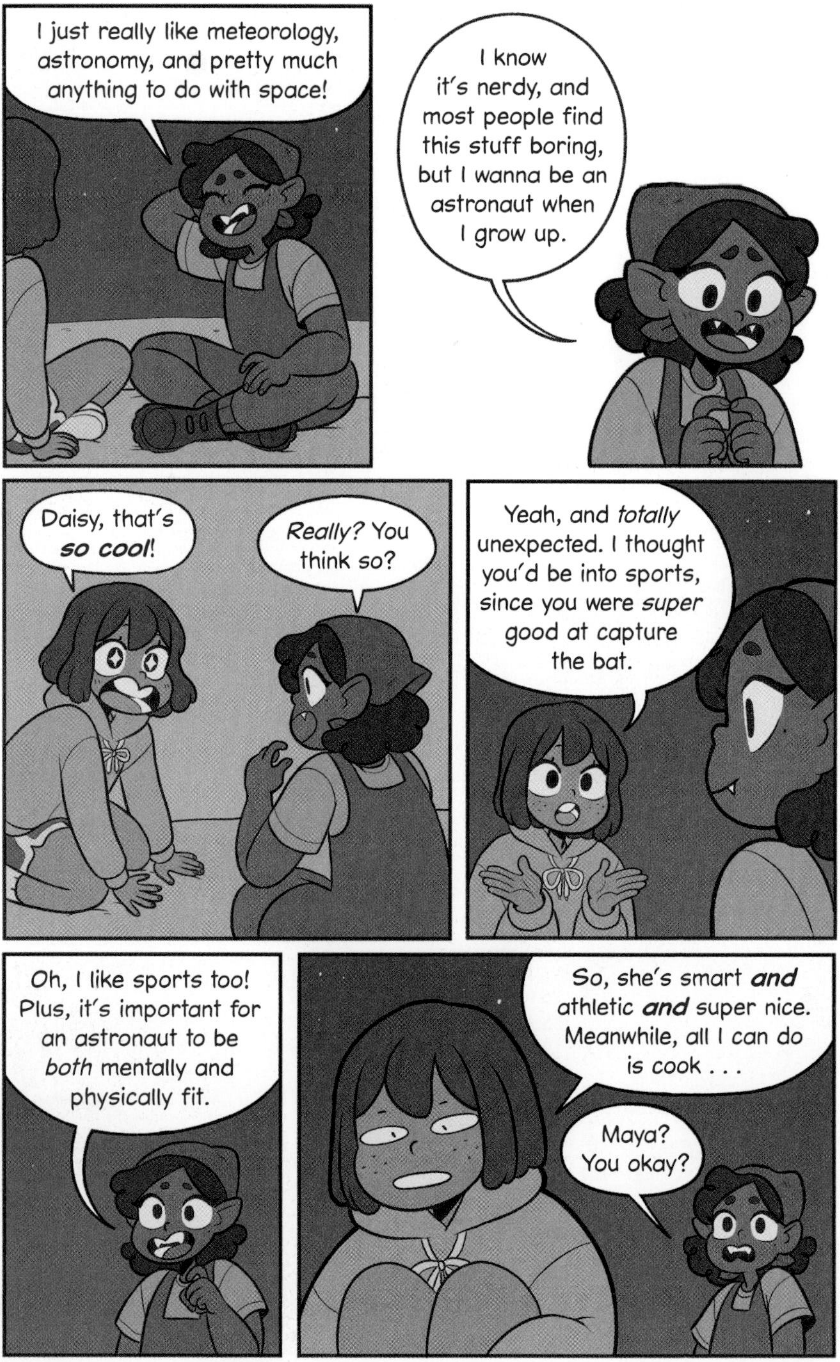
I just really like meteorology, astronomy, and pretty much anything to do with space!
I know it's nerdy, and most people find this stuff boring, but I wanna be an astronaut when I grow up.
Daisy, that's ***so cool***!
Really? You think so?
Yeah, and *totally* unexpected. I thought you'd be into sports, since you were *super* good at capture the bat.
Oh, I like sports too! Plus, it's important for an astronaut to be *both* mentally and physically fit.
So, she's smart ***and*** athletic ***and*** super nice. Meanwhile, all I can do is cook . . .
Maya? You okay?

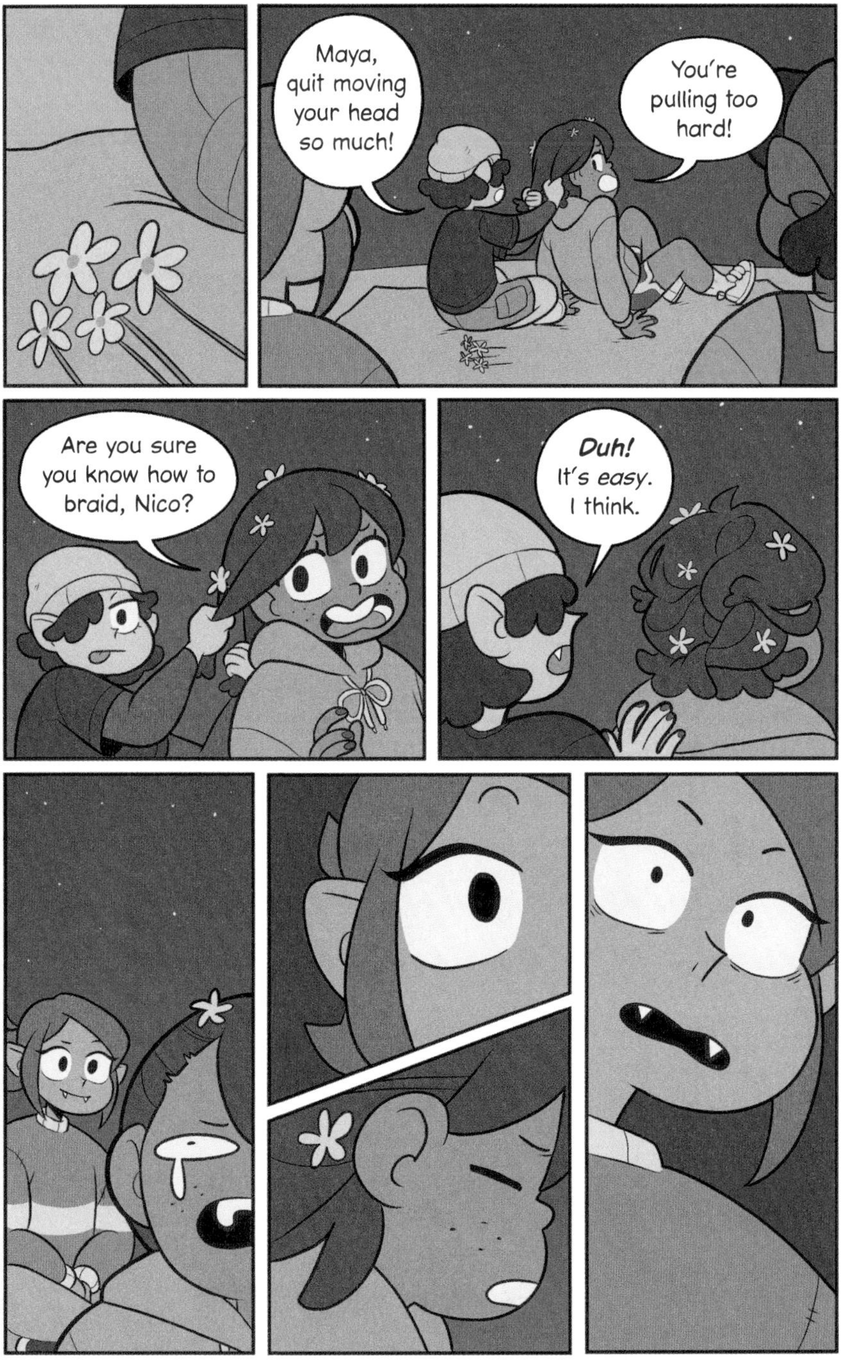
Maya, quit moving your head so much!
You're pulling too hard!
Are you sure you know how to braid, Nico?
Duh! It's *easy*. I think.

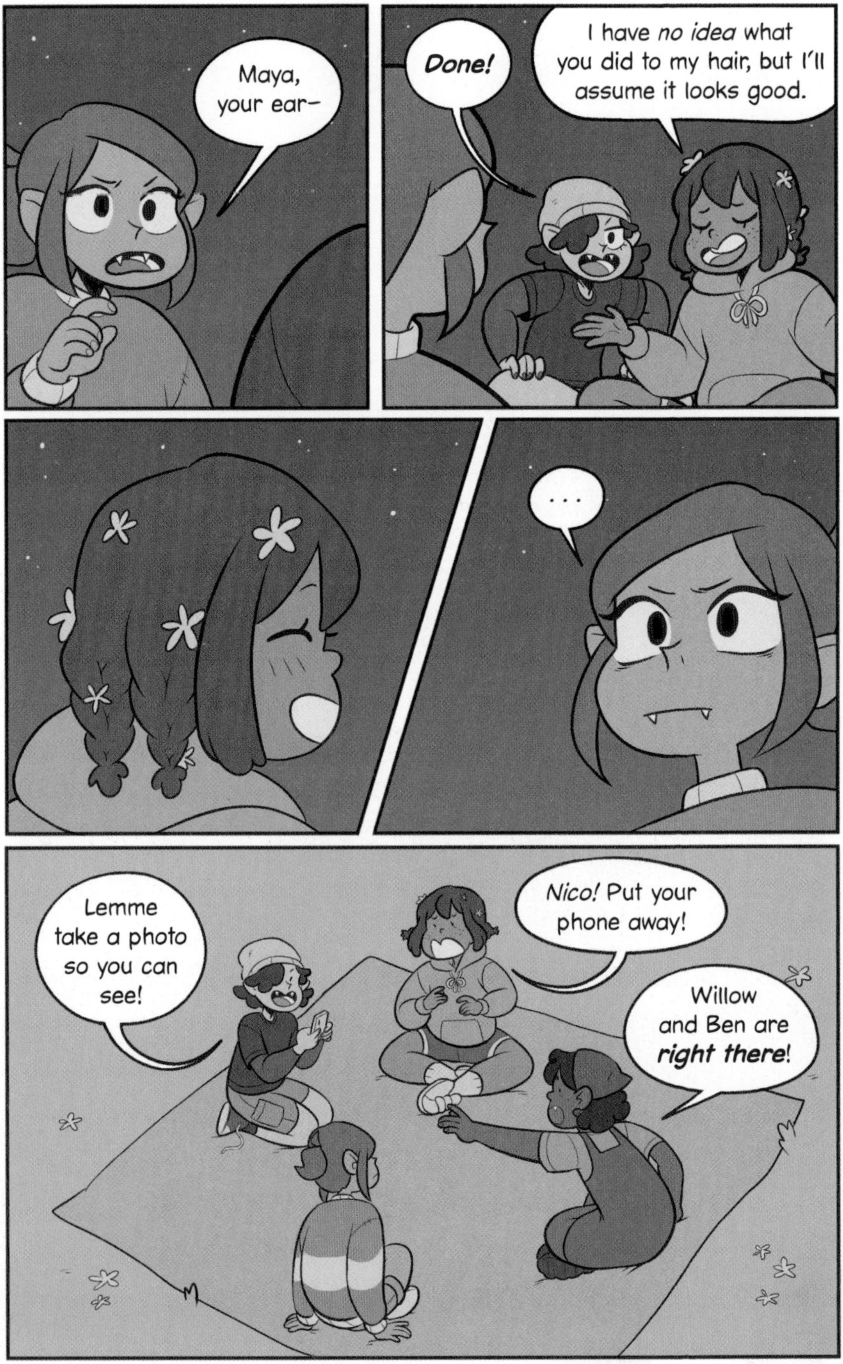

Maya, your ear–
Done!
I have *no idea* what you did to my hair, but I'll assume it looks good.
. . .
Lemme take a photo so you can see!
Nico! Put your phone away!
Willow and Ben are ***right there***!

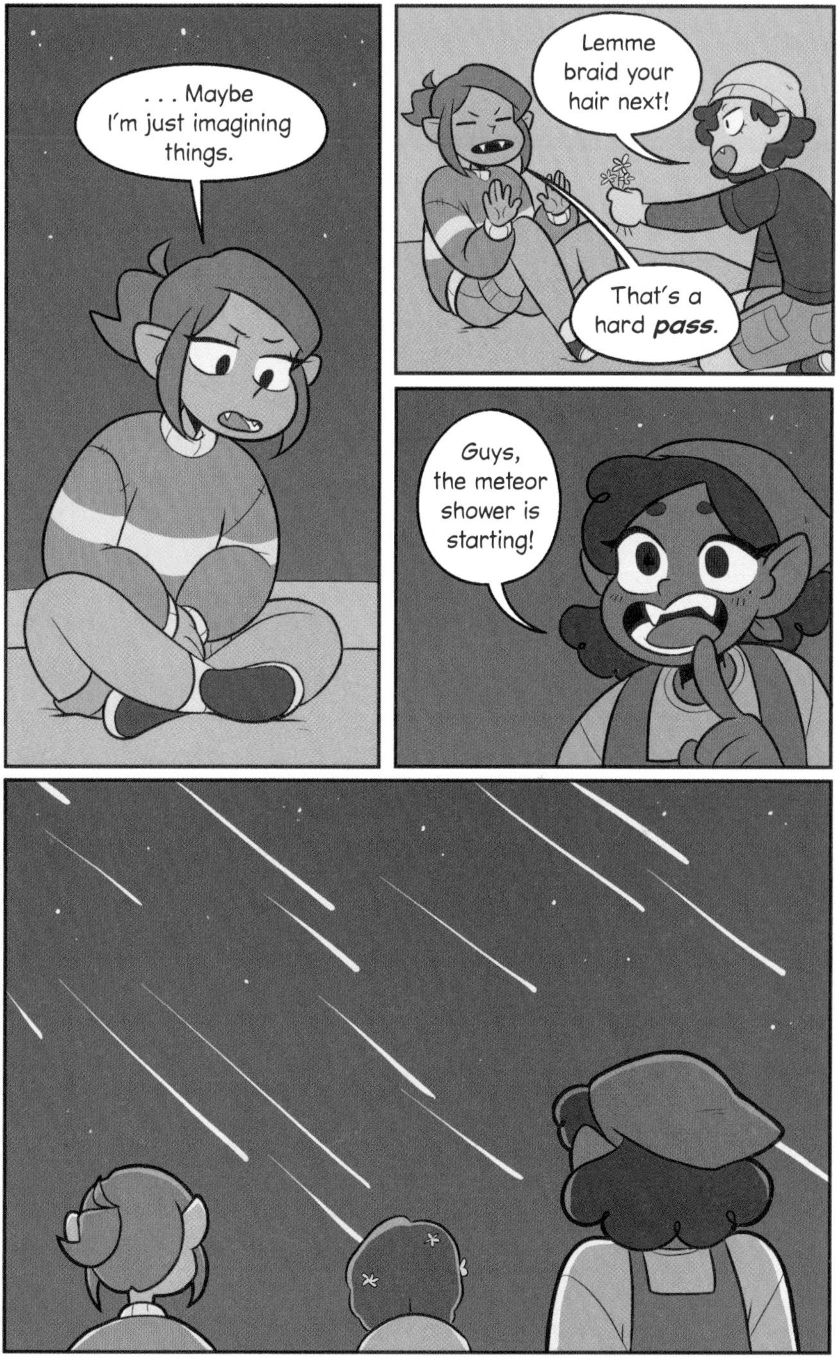
. . . Maybe I'm just imagining things.
Lemme braid your hair next!
That's a hard **pass**.
Guys, the meteor shower is starting!

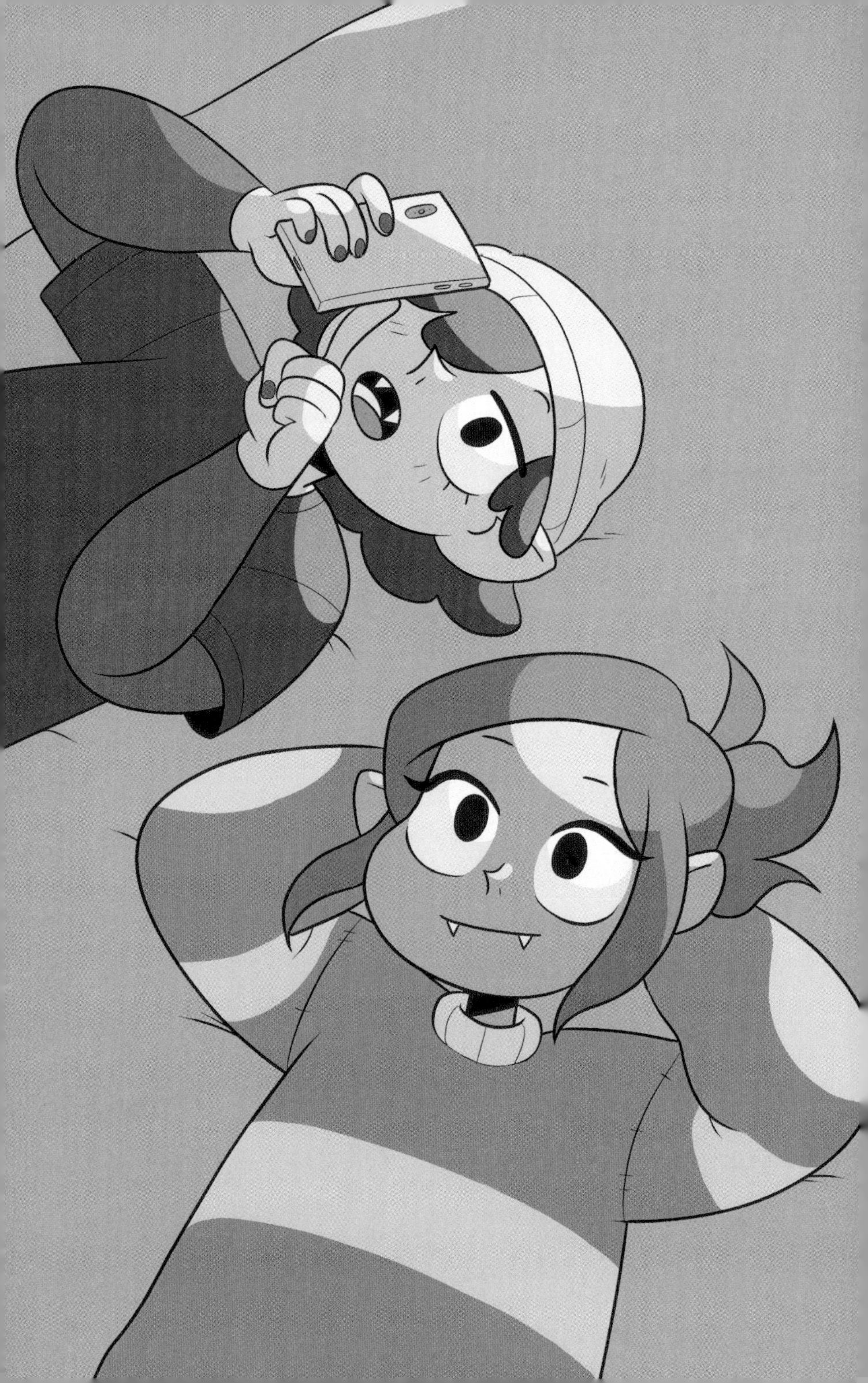

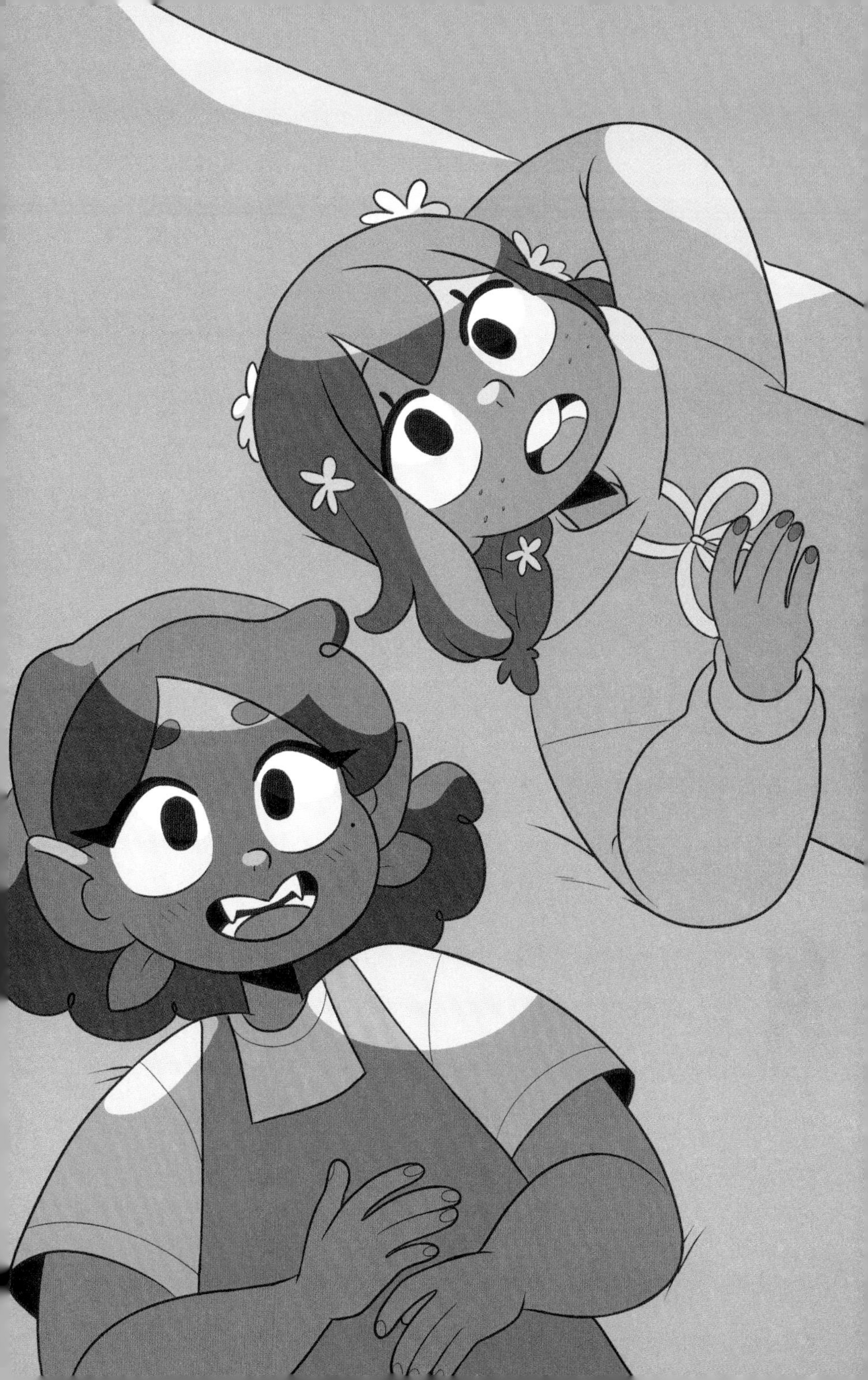

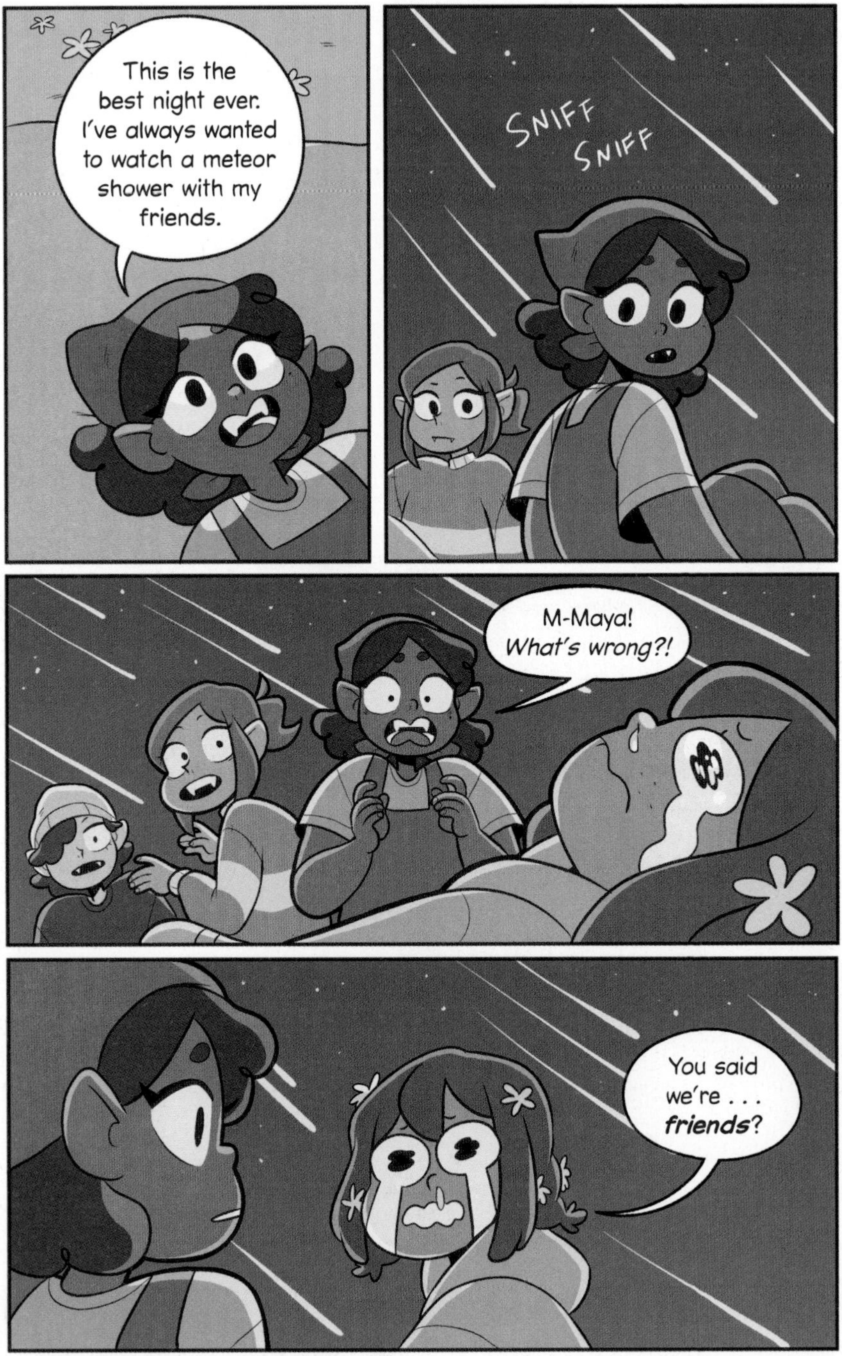
This is the best night ever. I've always wanted to watch a meteor shower with my friends.
SNIFF SNIFF
M-Maya! What's wrong?!
You said we're . . . **friends**?

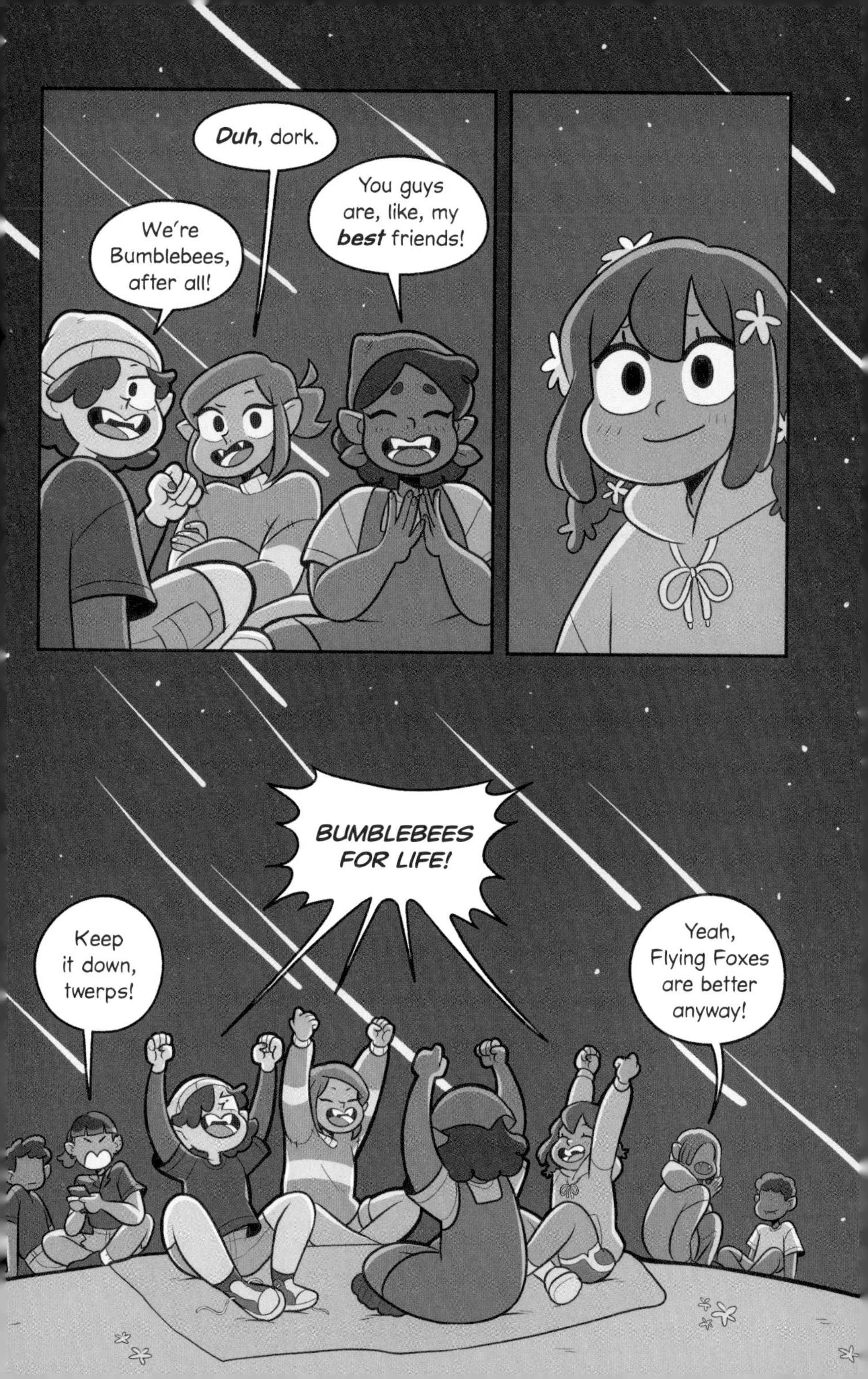

We're Bumblebees, after all!
Duh, dork.
You guys are, like, my ***best*** friends!
BUMBLEBEES FOR LIFE!
Keep it down, twerps!
Yeah, Flying Foxes are better anyway!

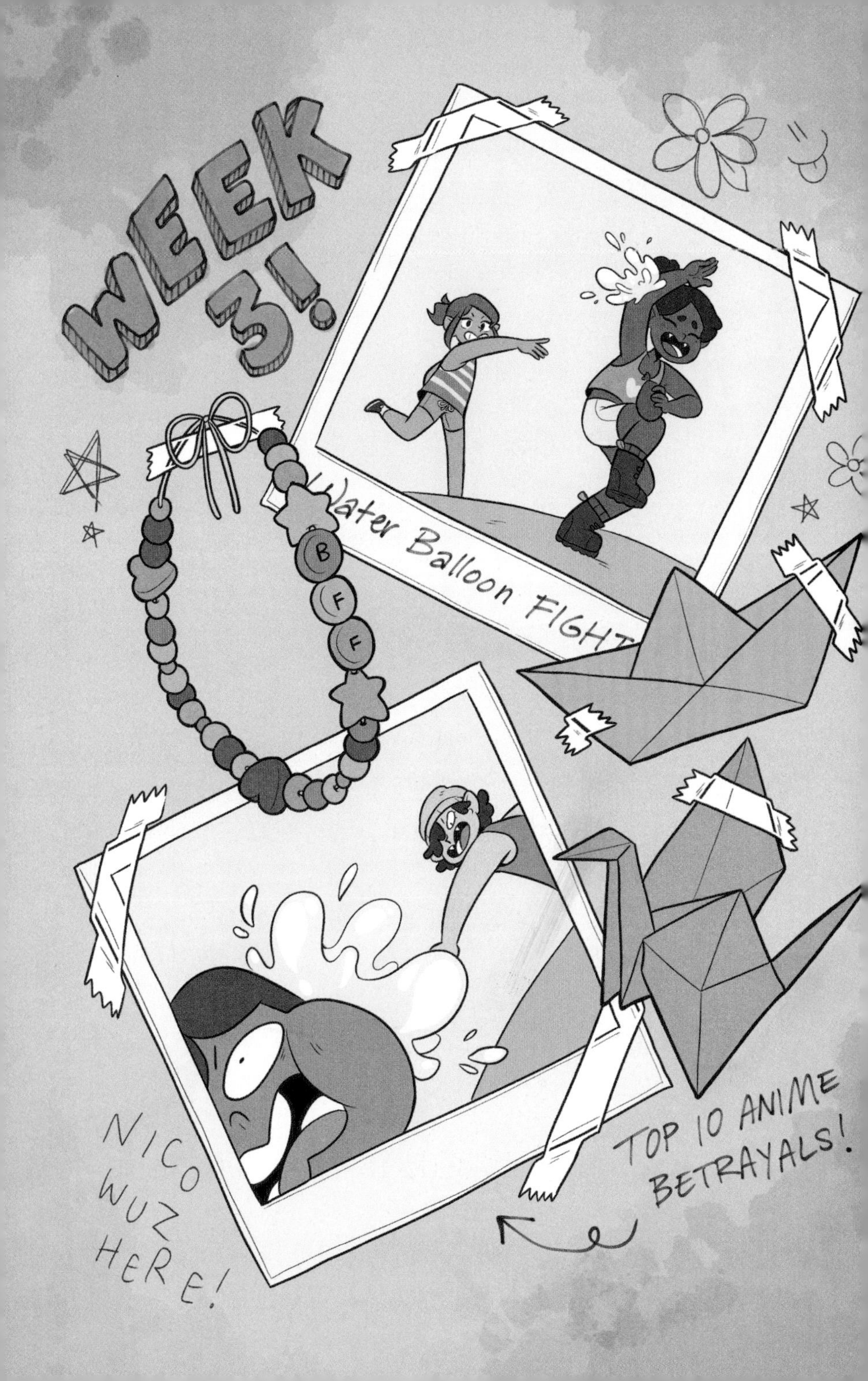
WEEK 3!
Water Balloon FIGHT
BFF
NICO WUZ HERE!
TOP 10 ANIME BETRAYALS!

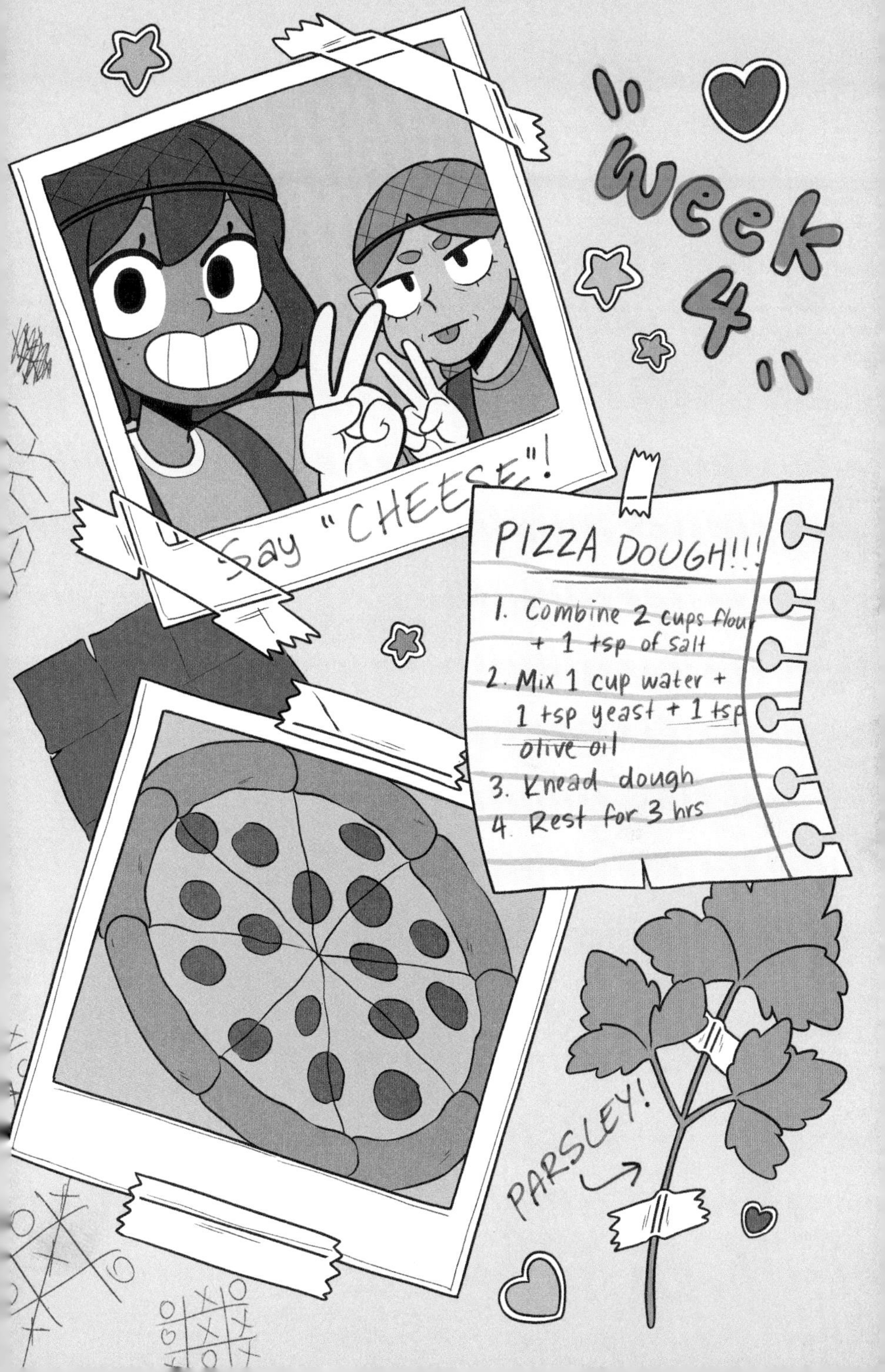
"Week 4"
Say "CHEESE"!
PIZZA DOUGH!!!
1. Combine 2 cups flour + 1 tsp of salt
2. Mix 1 cup water + 1 tsp yeast + 1 tsp olive oil
3. Knead dough
4. Rest for 3 hrs
PARSLEY!

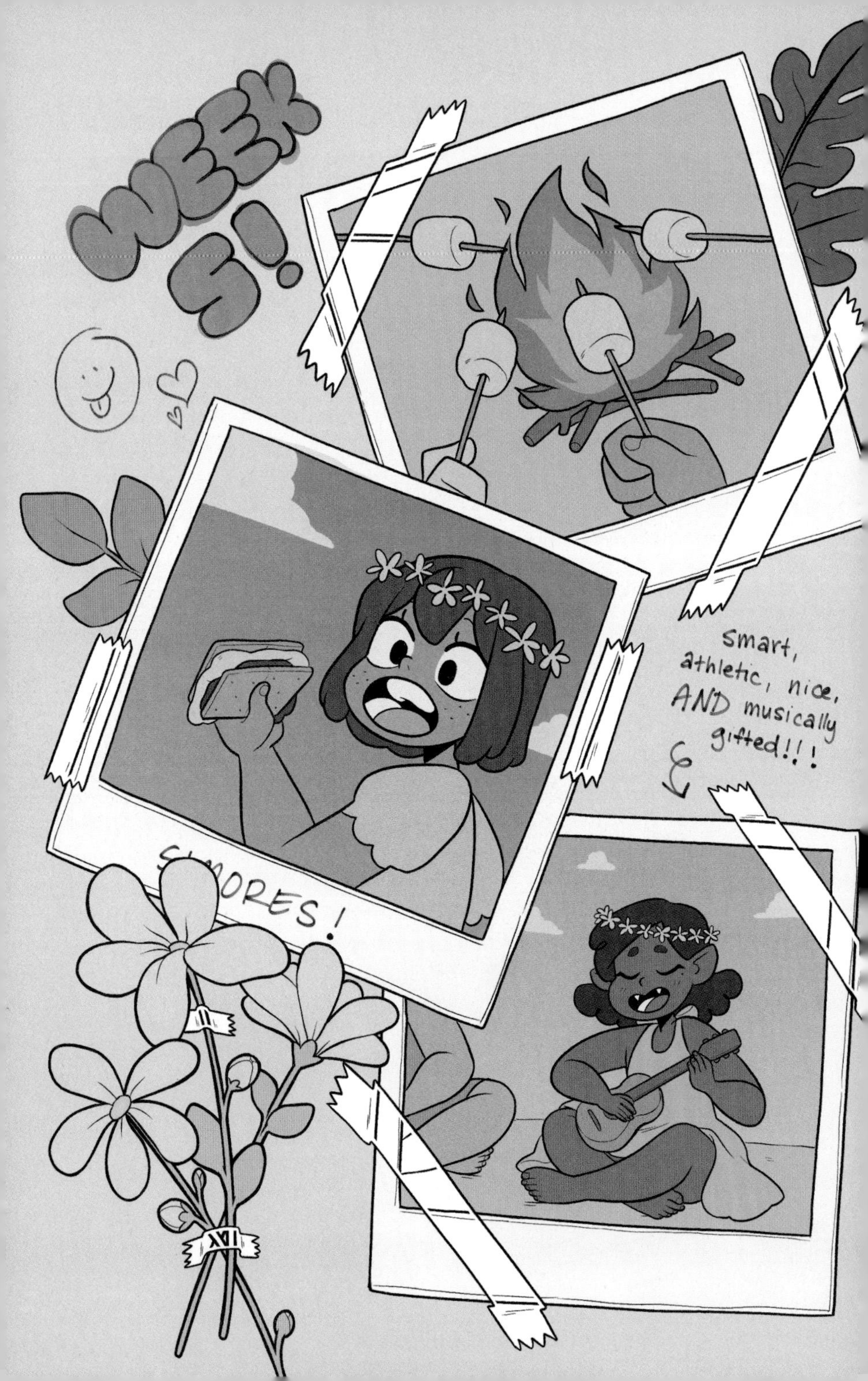
WEEK 5!
smart, athletic, nice, AND musically gifted!!!
S'MORES!

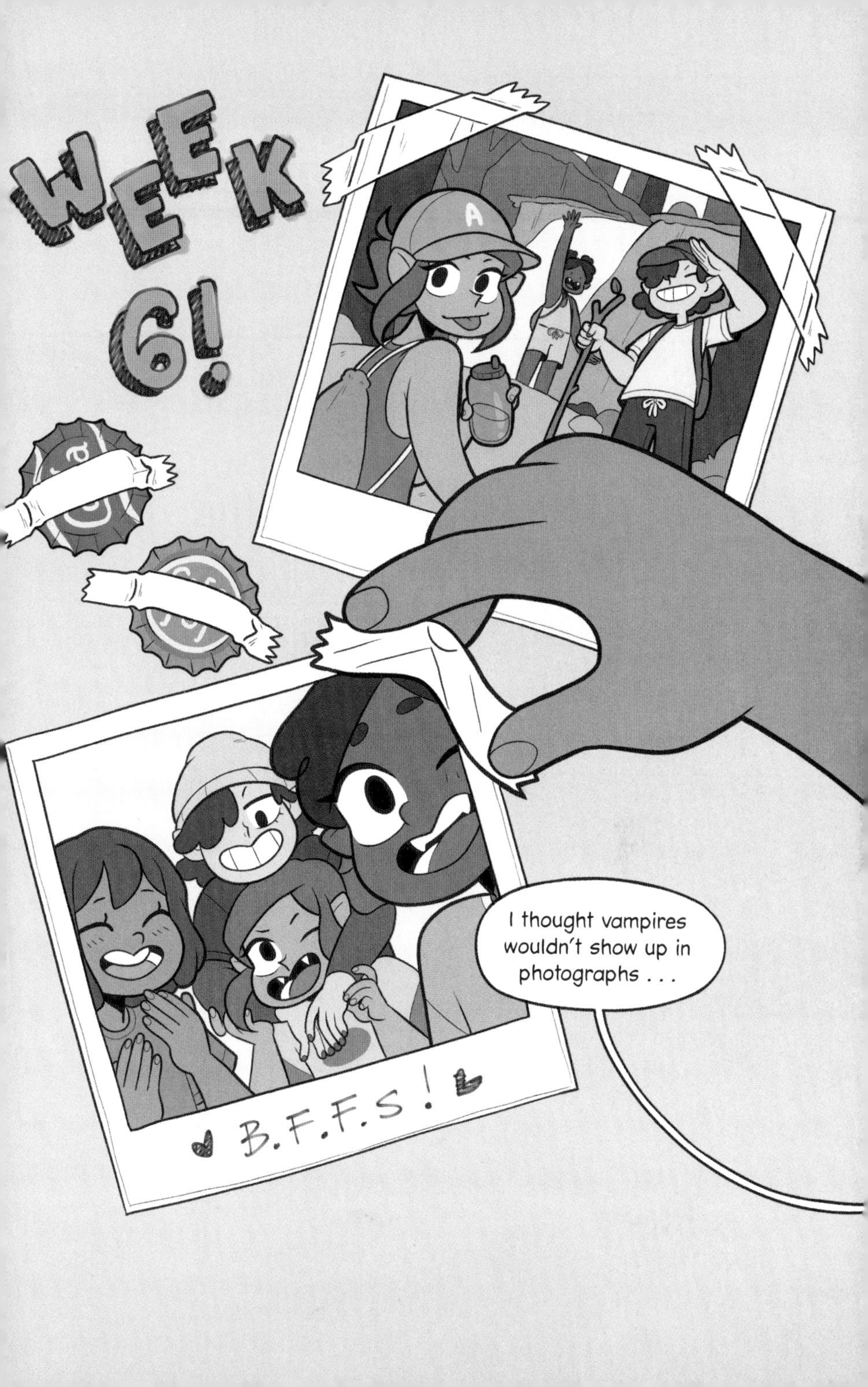
WEEK 6!
B.F.F.S!
I thought vampires wouldn't show up in photographs . . .

. . . but I guess that's just *another* myth that humans made up.

Maya, *let's go!* Willow's gonna kick our butts if we're late!

Coming!

Here ya go, Maya!

Grab a partner and complete this nature scavenger hunt.

The first pair to find everything on the list will win a prize!

PARTNER SCAVENGER HUNT

1. ☐ MUSHROOM
☐ FOUR-LEAF CLOVER
☐ PINE CONE
☐ ACORN
☐ BIRD FEATHER
☐ LILY PAD

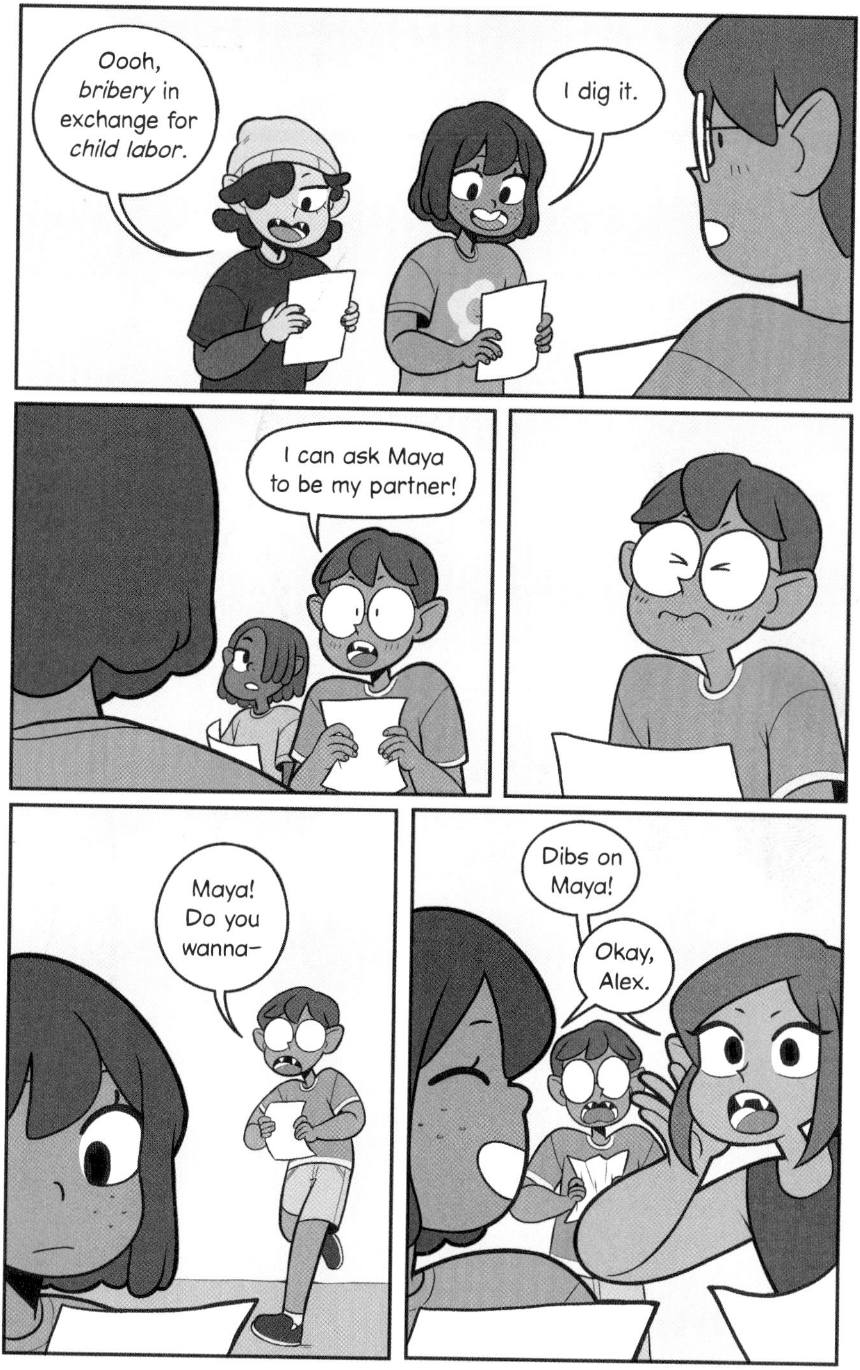
Oooh, *bribery* in exchange for *child labor.*
I dig it.
I can ask Maya to be my partner!
Maya! Do you wanna–
Dibs on Maya!
Okay, Alex.

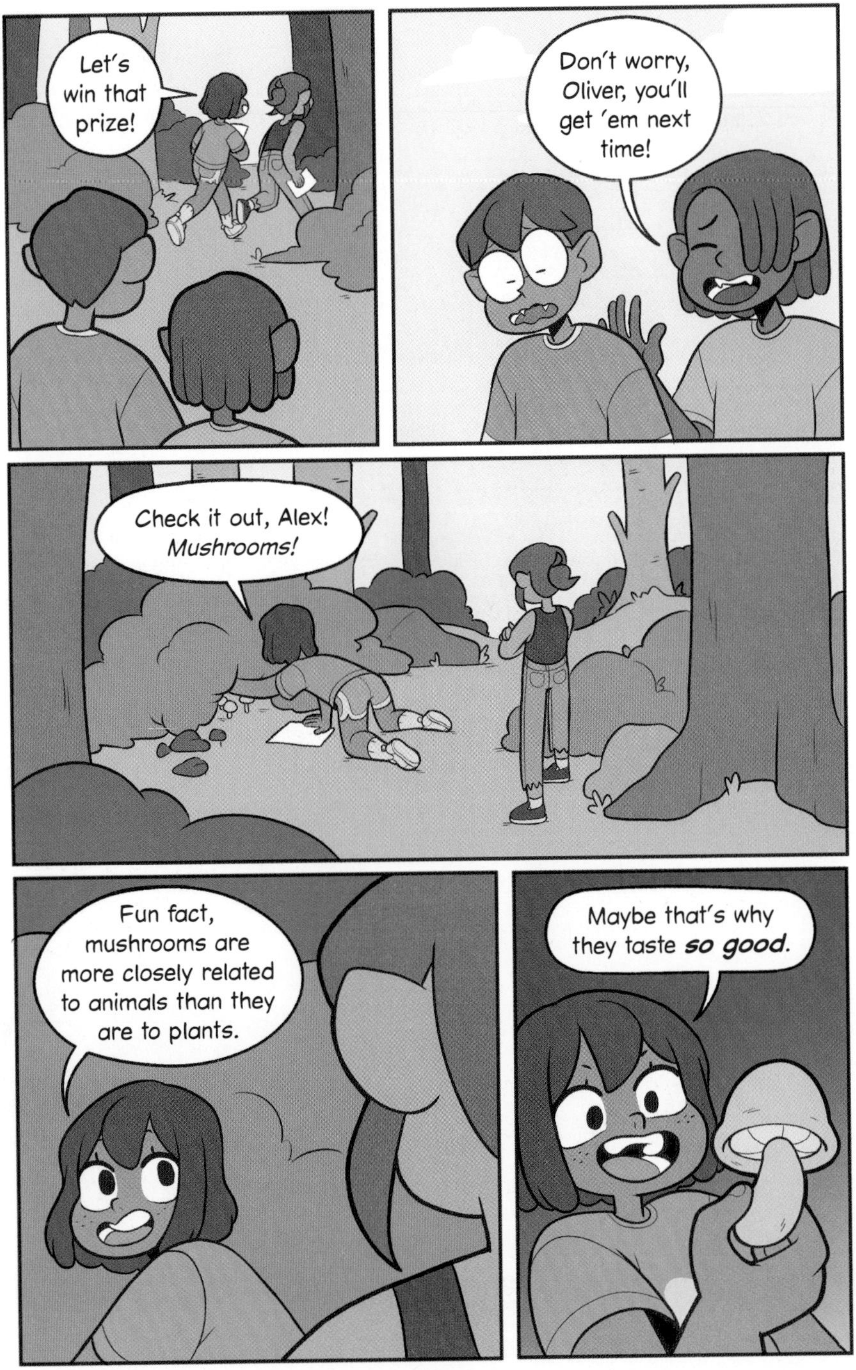
Let's win that prize!
Don't worry, Oliver, you'll get 'em next time!
Check it out, Alex! *Mushrooms!*
Fun fact, mushrooms are more closely related to animals than they are to plants.
Maybe that's why they taste ***so good***.

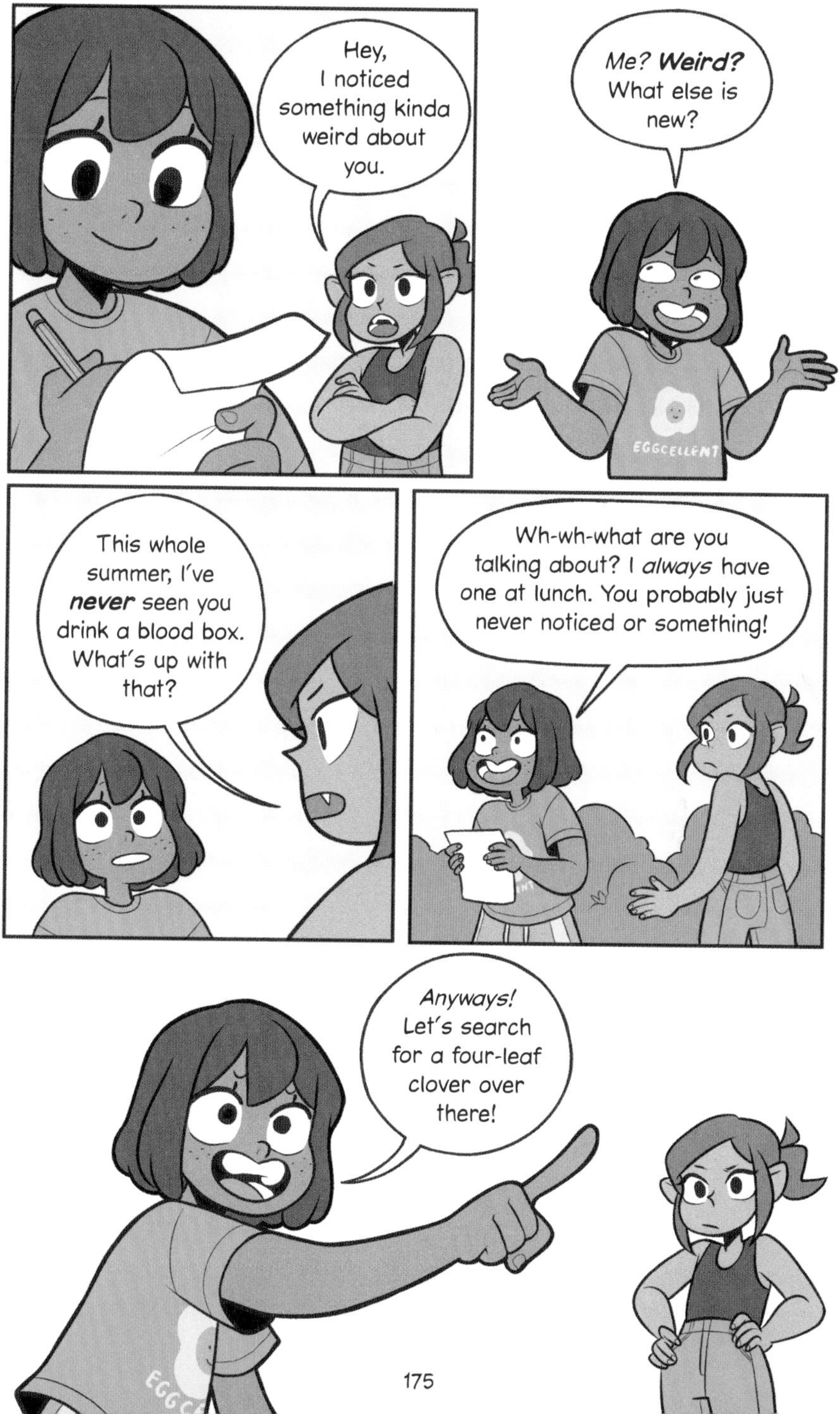

Hey, I noticed something kinda weird about you.
Me? *Weird?* What else is new?
EGGCELLENT
This whole summer, I've *never* seen you drink a blood box. What's up with that?
Wh-wh-what are you talking about? I *always* have one at lunch. You probably just never noticed or something!
Anyways! Let's search for a four-leaf clover over there!

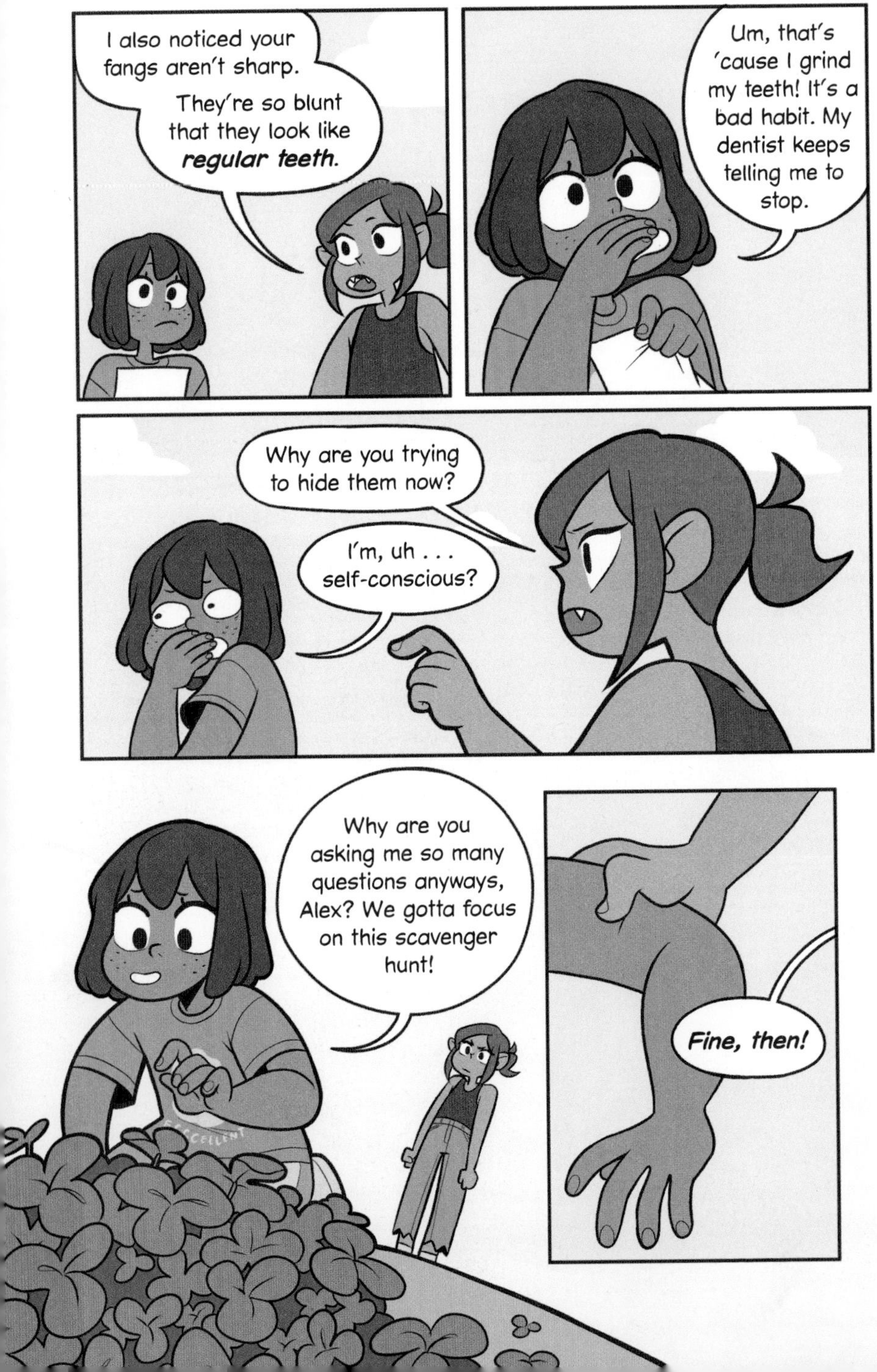
I also noticed your fangs aren't sharp.
They're so blunt that they look like ***regular teeth***.
Um, that's 'cause I grind my teeth! It's a bad habit. My dentist keeps telling me to stop.
Why are you trying to hide them now?
I'm, uh . . . self-conscious?
Why are you asking me so many questions anyways, Alex? We gotta focus on this scavenger hunt!
Fine, then!

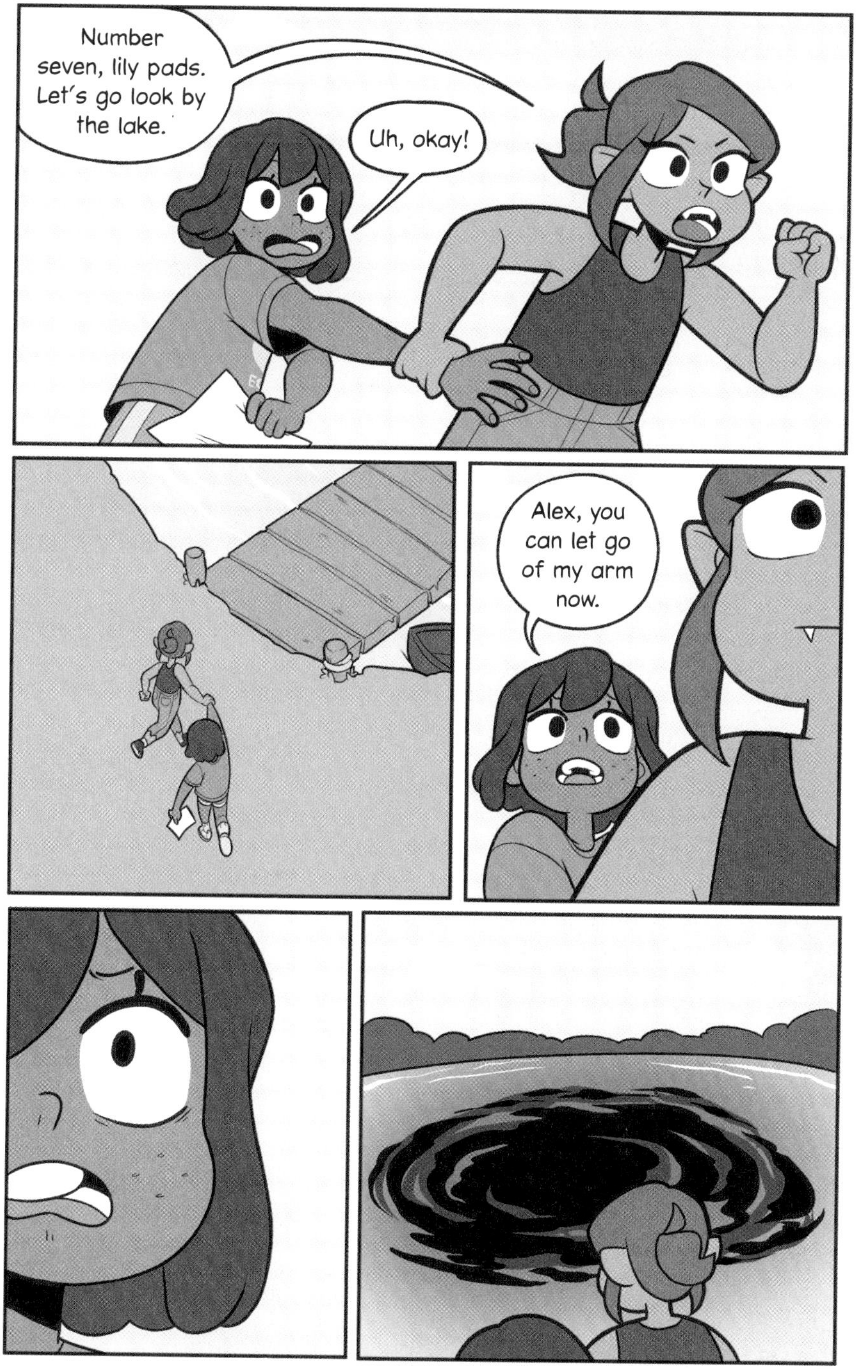
Number seven, lily pads. Let's go look by the lake.
Uh, okay!
Alex, you can let go of my arm now.

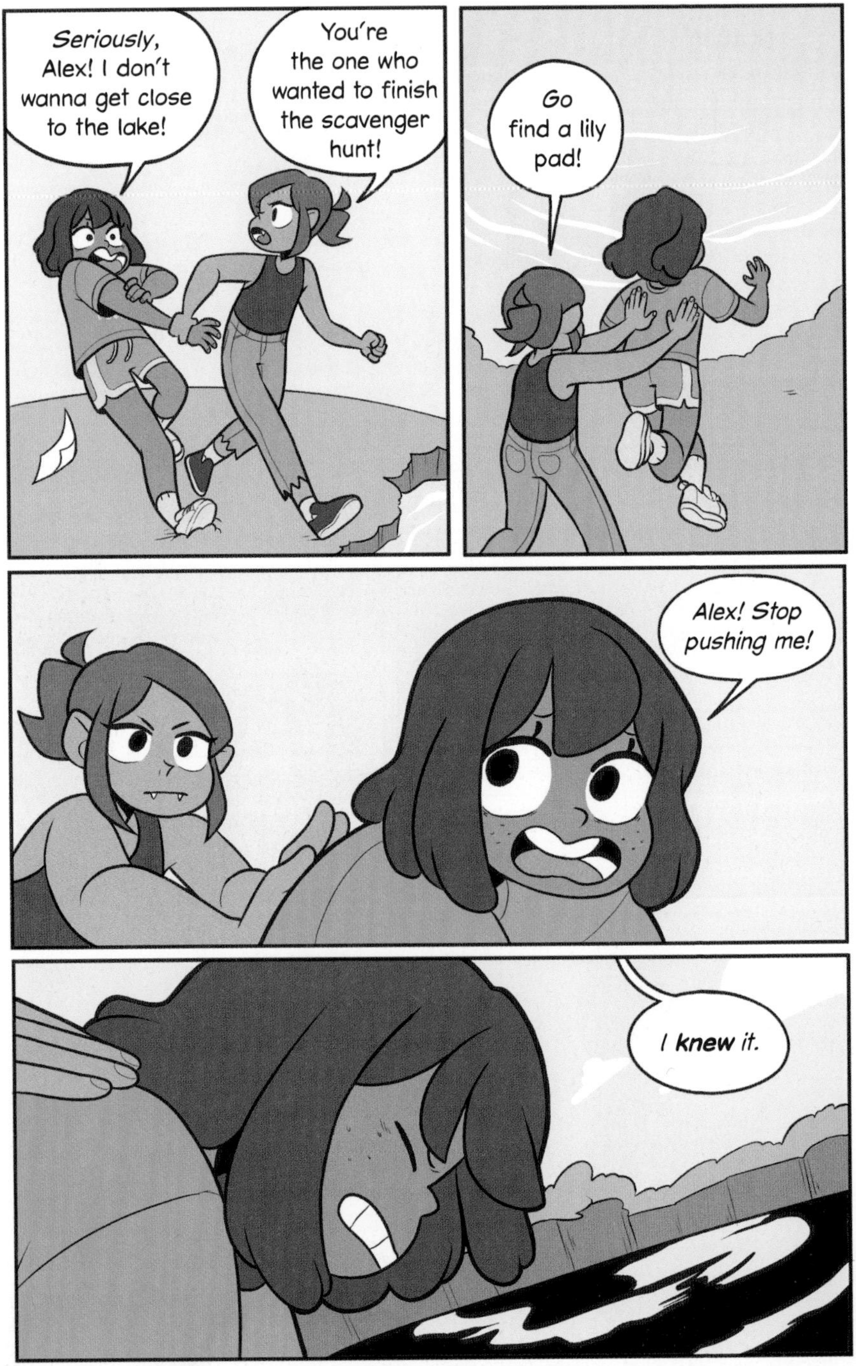
Seriously, Alex! I don't wanna get close to the lake!
You're the one who wanted to finish the scavenger hunt!
Go find a lily pad!
Alex! Stop pushing me!
I **knew** it.

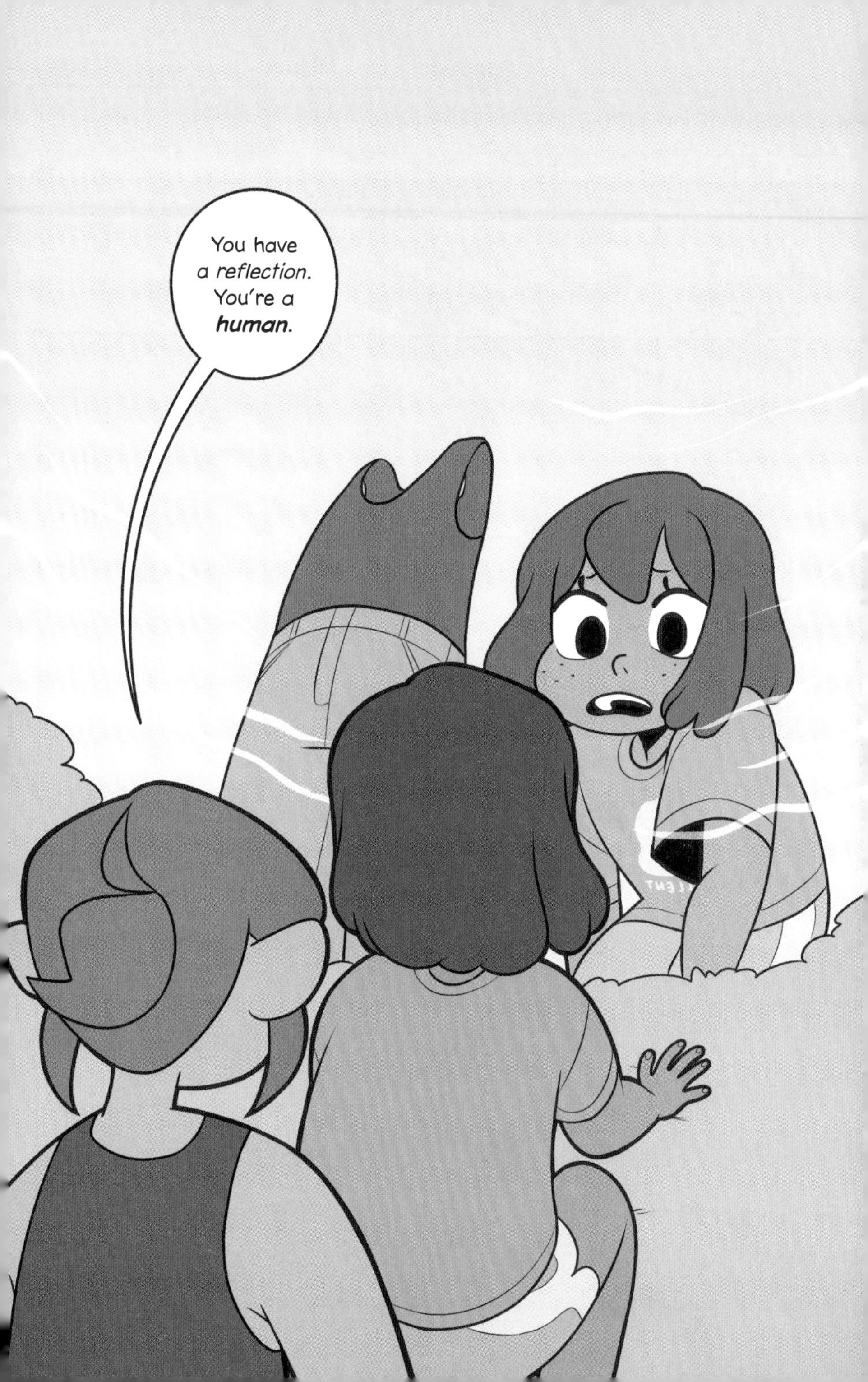
You have a *reflection*. You're a ***human***.

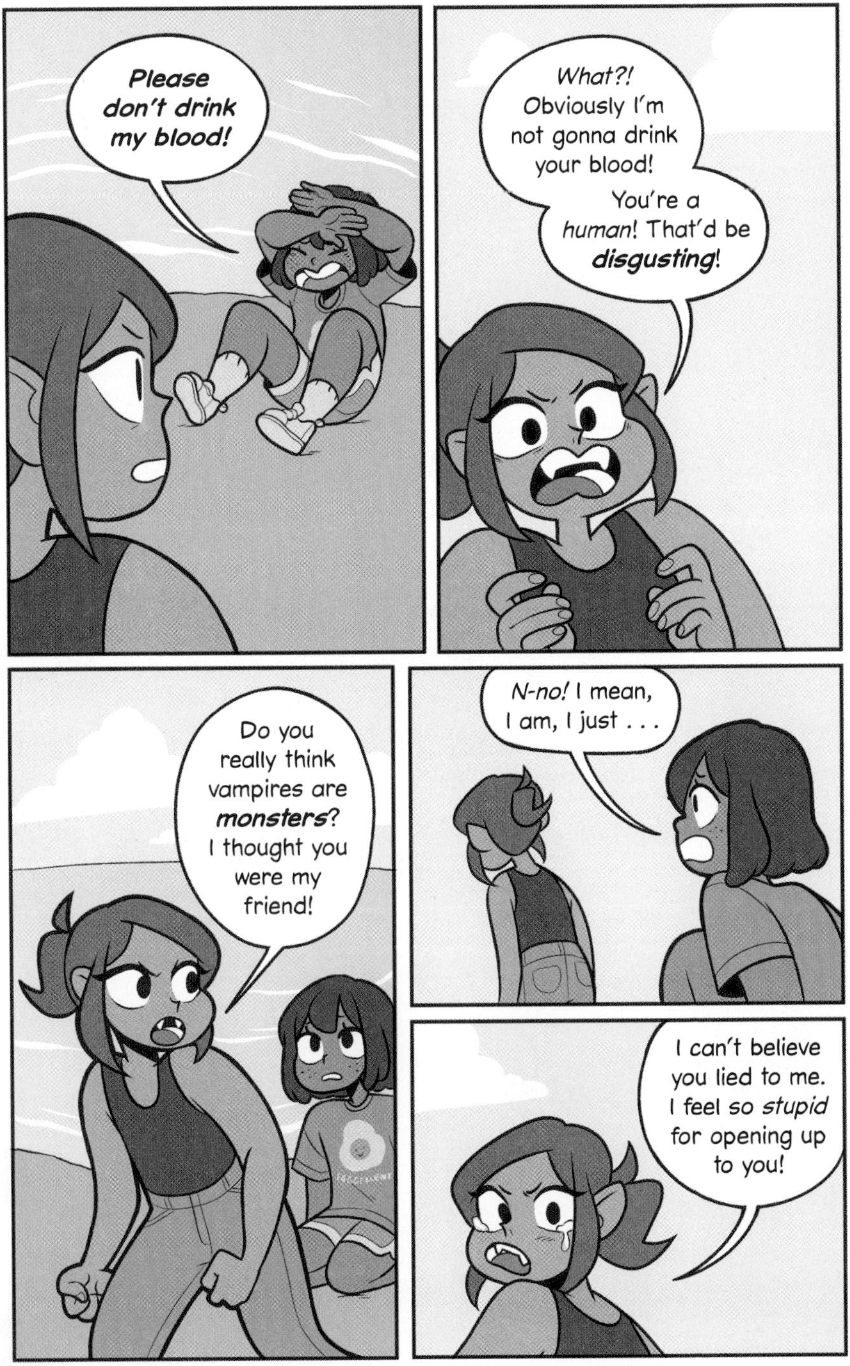
Please don't drink my blood!
What?! Obviously I'm not gonna drink your blood!
You're a human! That'd be disgusting!
Do you really think vampires are monsters? I thought you were my friend!
N-no! I mean, I am, I just . . .
I can't believe you lied to me. I feel so stupid for opening up to you!

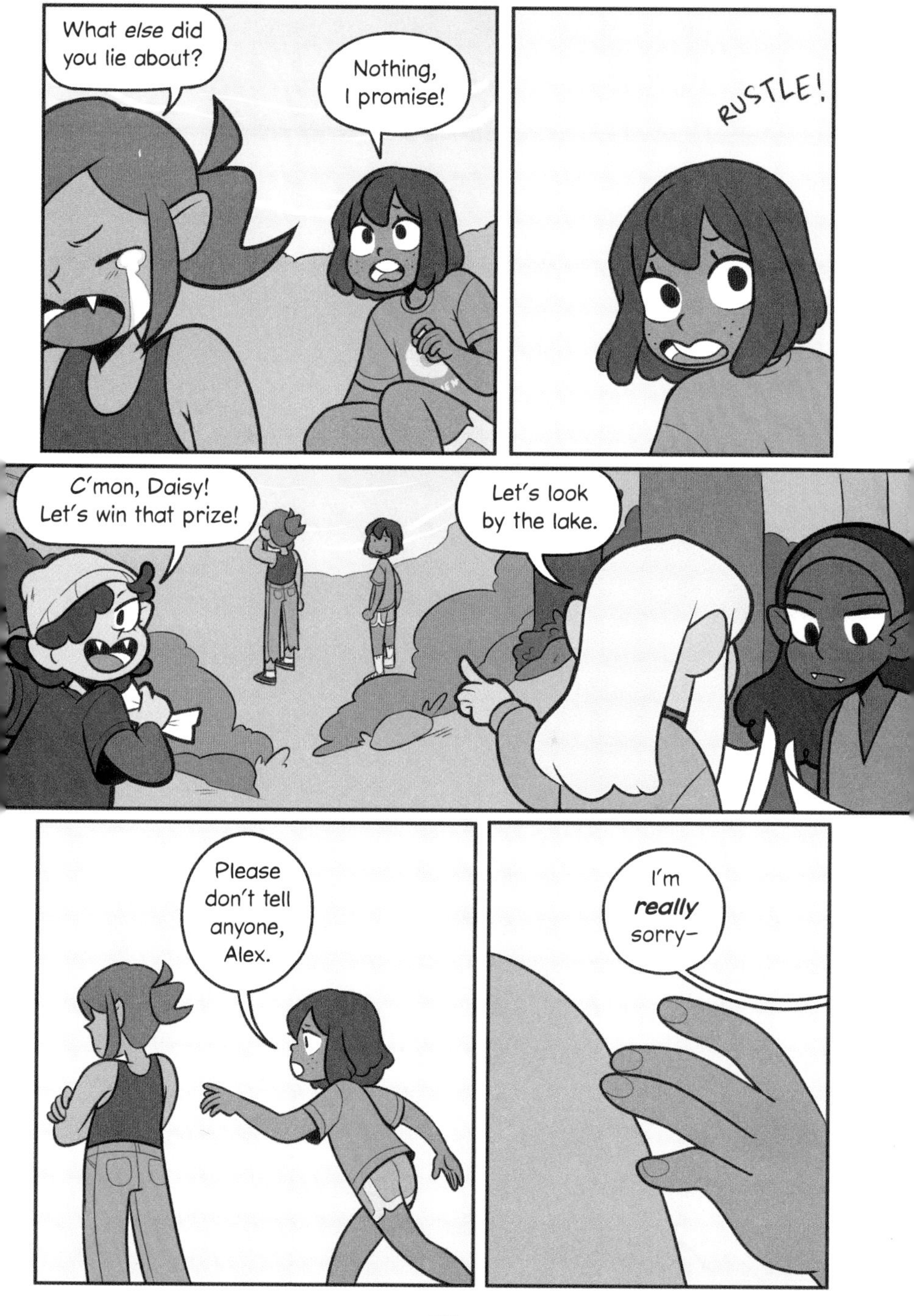
What *else* did you lie about?
Nothing, I promise!
RUSTLE!
C'mon, Daisy! Let's win that prize!
Let's look by the lake.
Please don't tell anyone, Alex.
I'm ***really*** sorry–

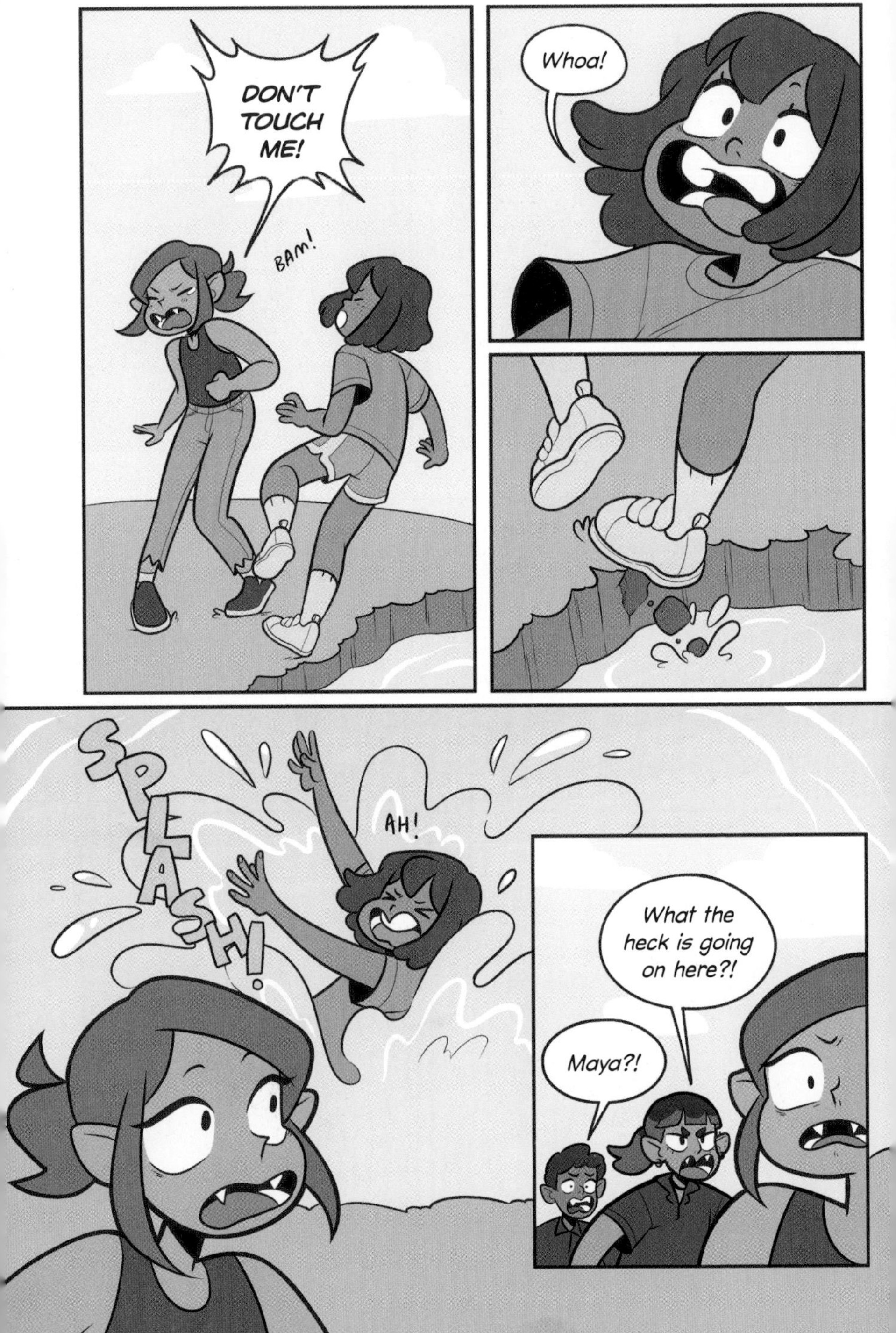
DON'T TOUCH ME!
BAM!
Whoa!
SPLASH!
AH!
What the heck is going on here?!
Maya?!

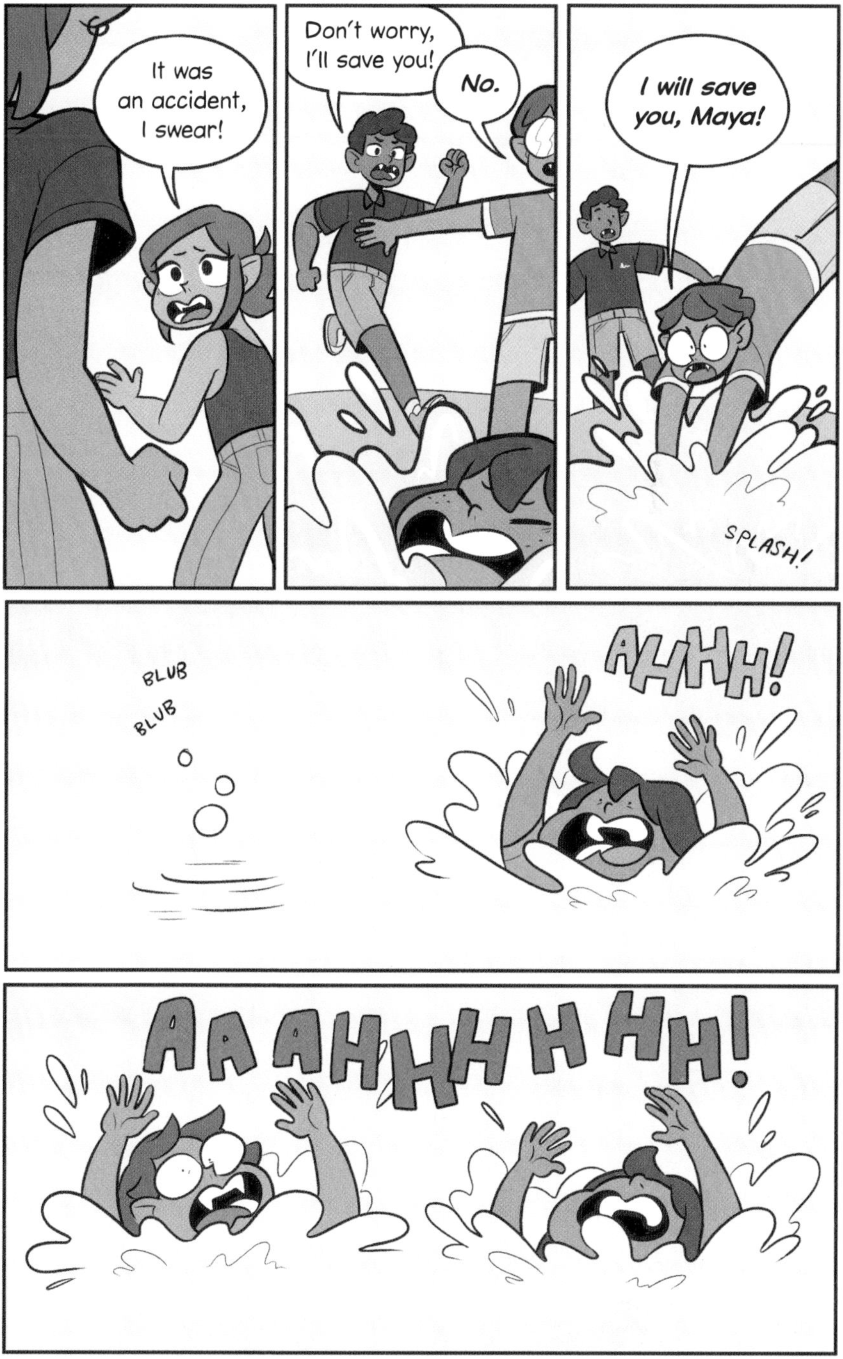
It was an accident, I swear!
Don't worry, I'll save you!
No.
I will save you, Maya!
SPLASH!
BLUB
BLUB
AHHH!
AAAHHHHHHH!

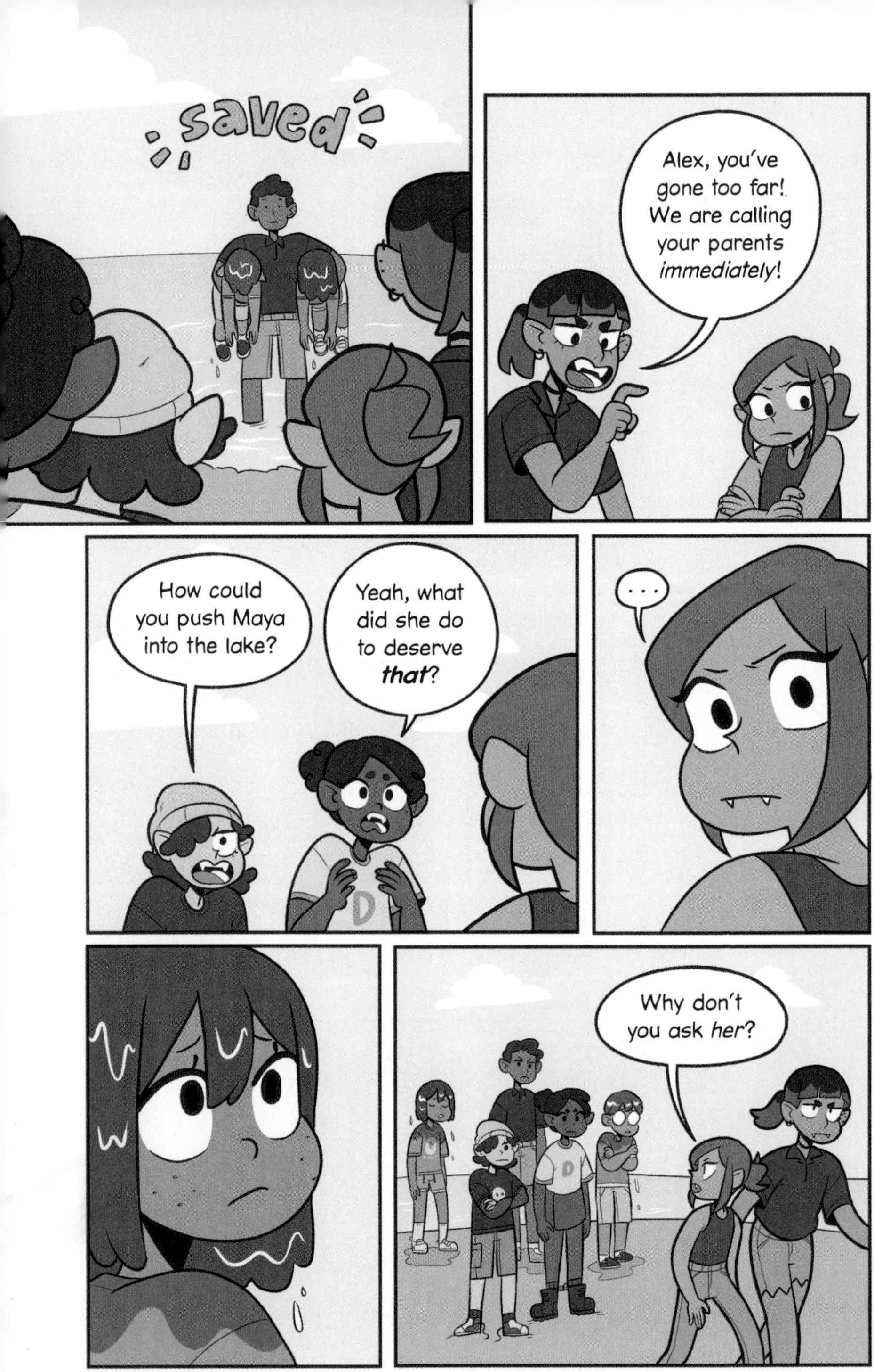
saved
Alex, you've gone too far! We are calling your parents *immediately*!
How could you push Maya into the lake?
Yeah, what did she do to deserve ***that***?
. . .
Why don't you ask *her*?

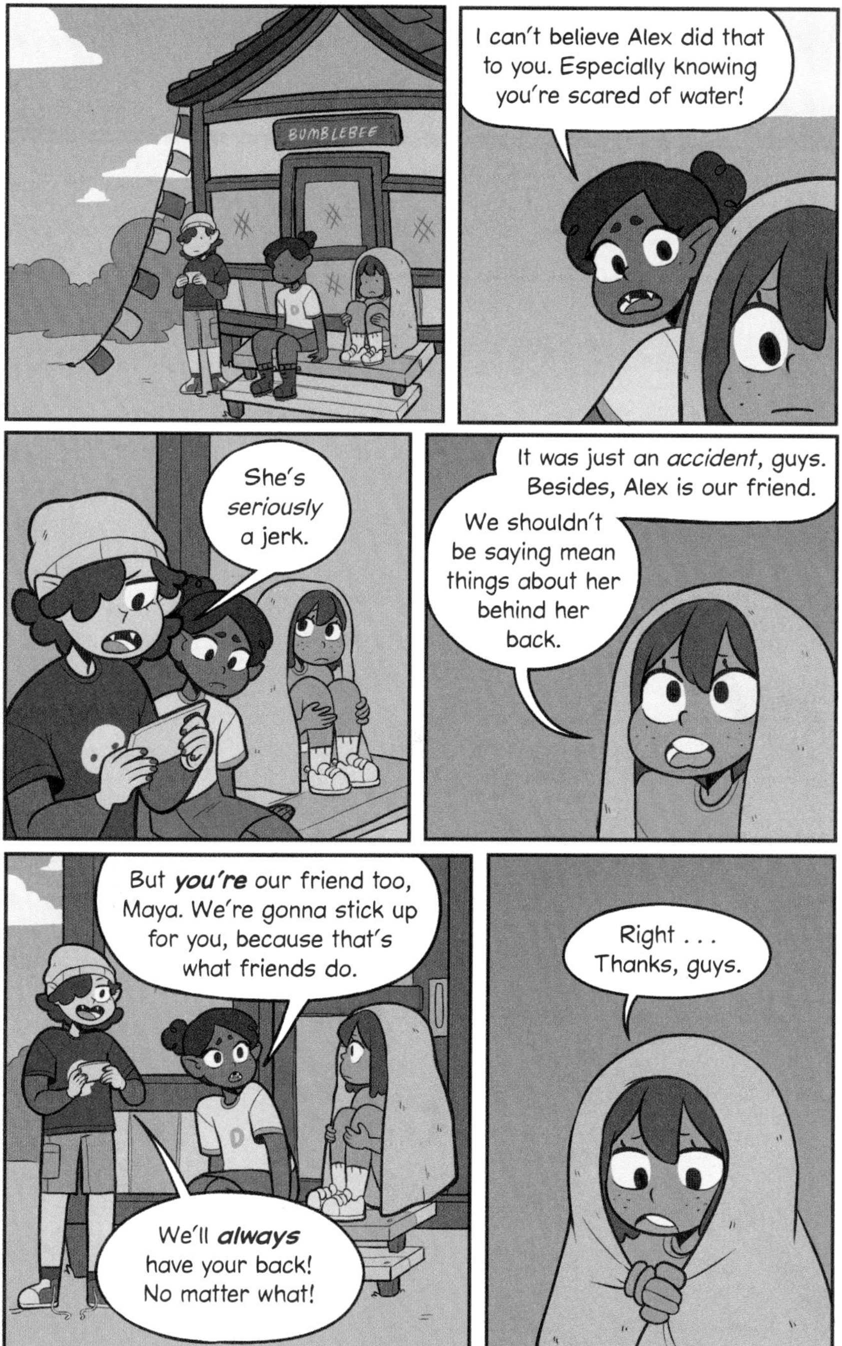
BUMBLEBEE
I can't believe Alex did that to you. Especially knowing you're scared of water!
She's *seriously* a jerk.
It was just an *accident*, guys. Besides, Alex is our friend.
We shouldn't be saying mean things about her behind her back.
But ***you're*** our friend too, Maya. We're gonna stick up for you, because that's what friends do.
We'll ***always*** have your back! No matter what!
Right . . . Thanks, guys.

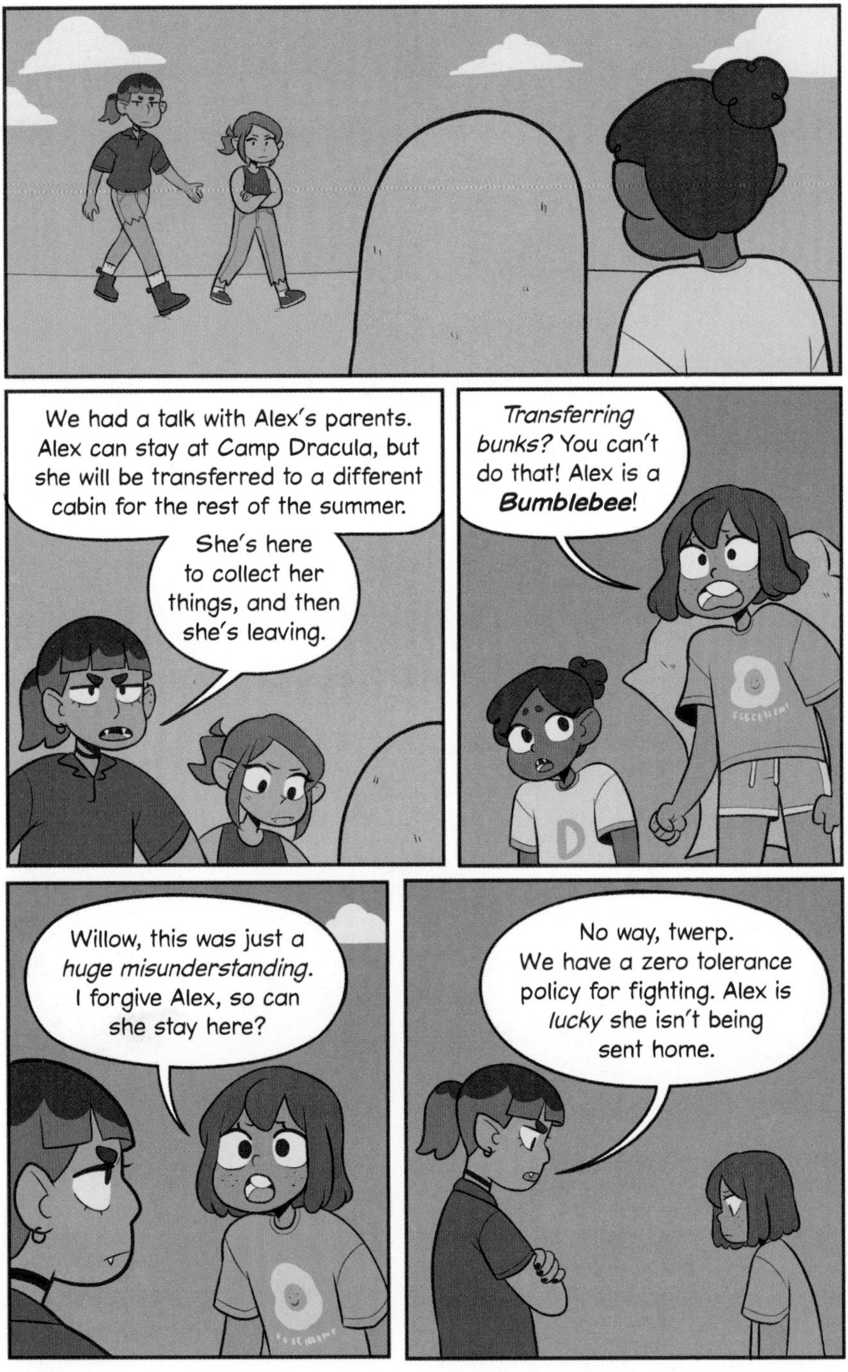
We had a talk with Alex's parents. Alex can stay at Camp Dracula, but she will be transferred to a different cabin for the rest of the summer.
She's here to collect her things, and then she's leaving.
Transferring bunks? You can't do that! Alex is a ***Bumblebee***!
Willow, this was just a *huge misunderstanding*. I forgive Alex, so can she stay here?
No way, twerp. We have a zero tolerance policy for fighting. Alex is *lucky* she isn't being sent home.

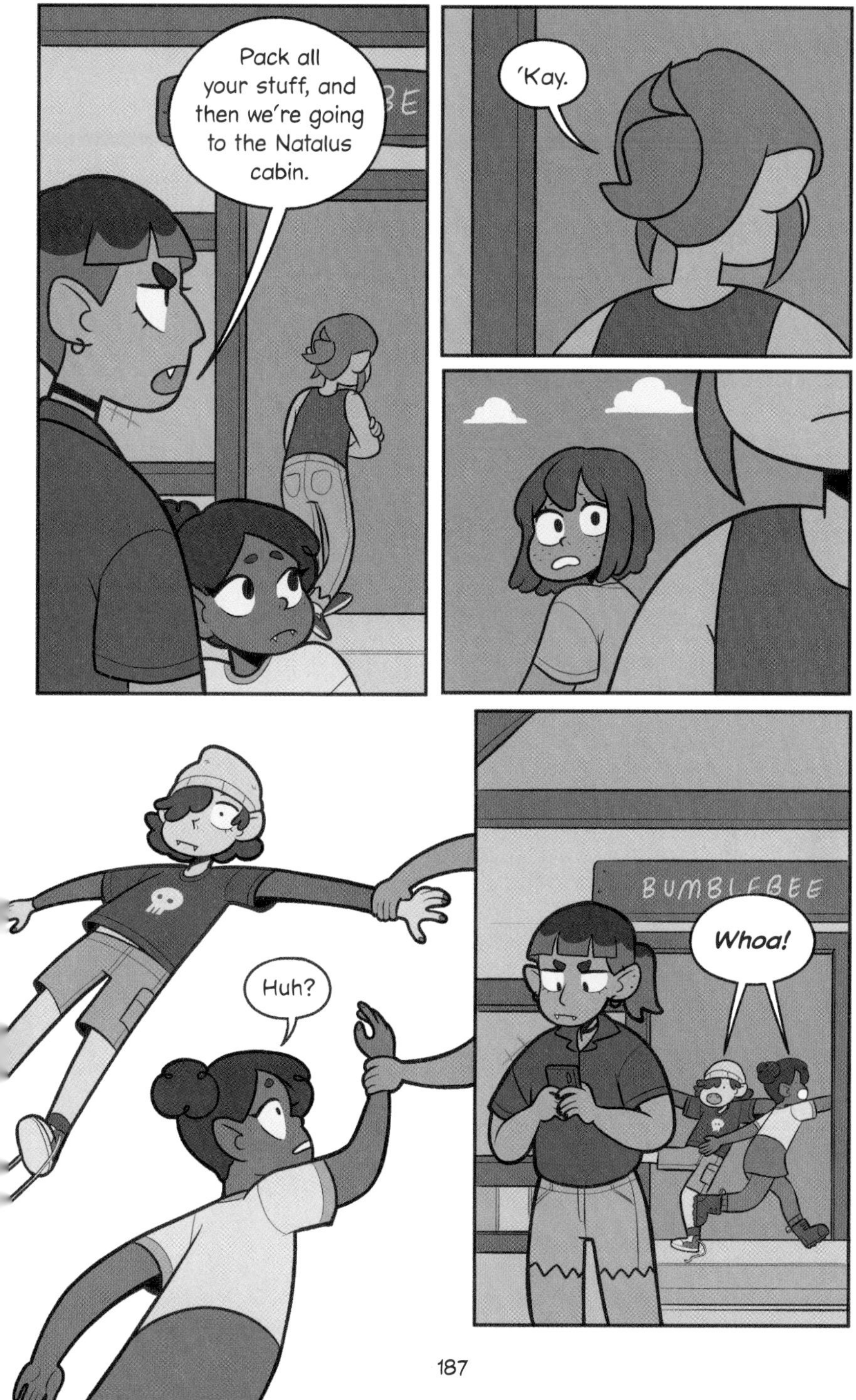
Pack all your stuff, and then we're going to the Natalus cabin.
'Kay.
Huh?
BUMBLEBEE
Whoa!

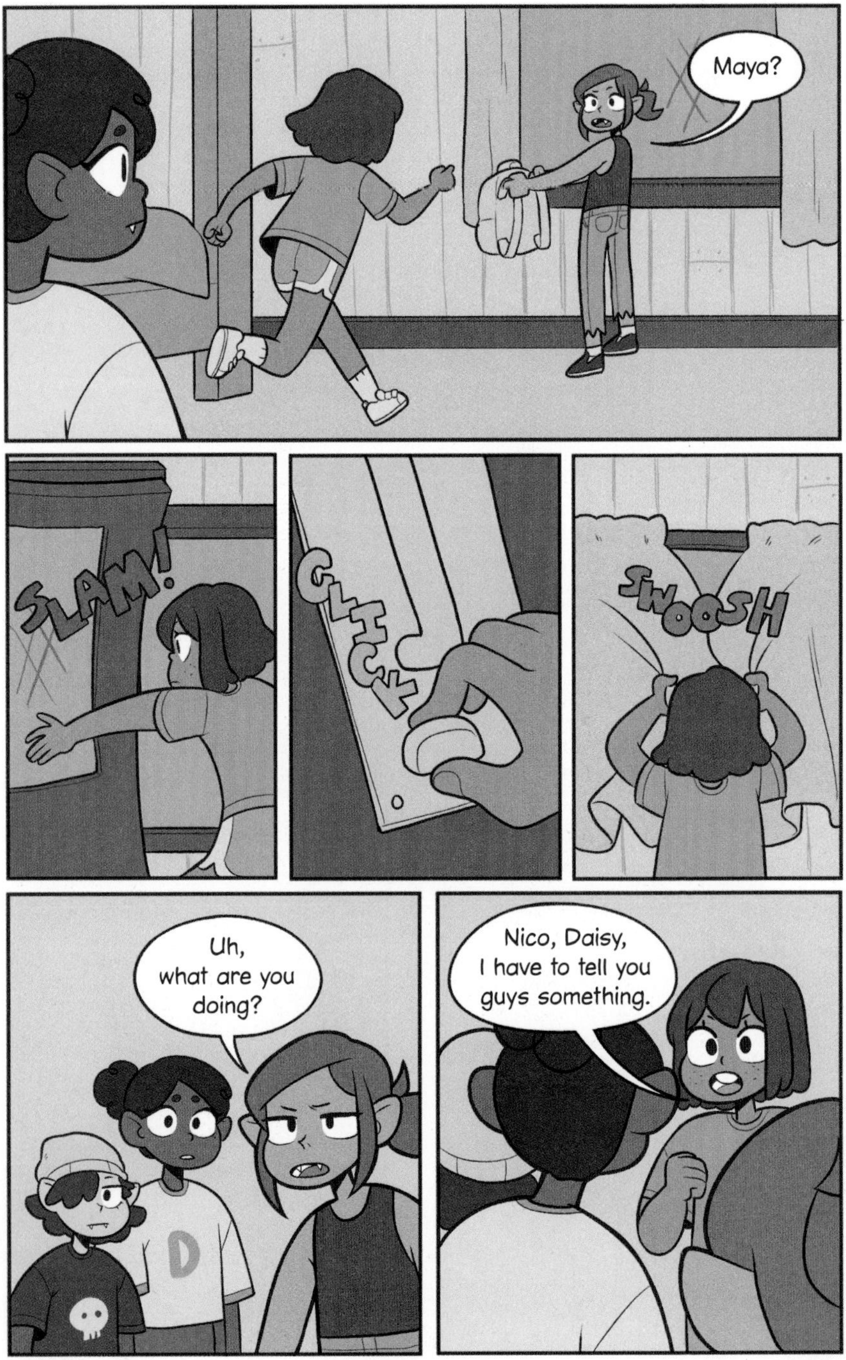
Maya?
SLAM!
CLICK
SWOOSH
Uh, what are you doing?
Nico, Daisy, I have to tell you guys something.

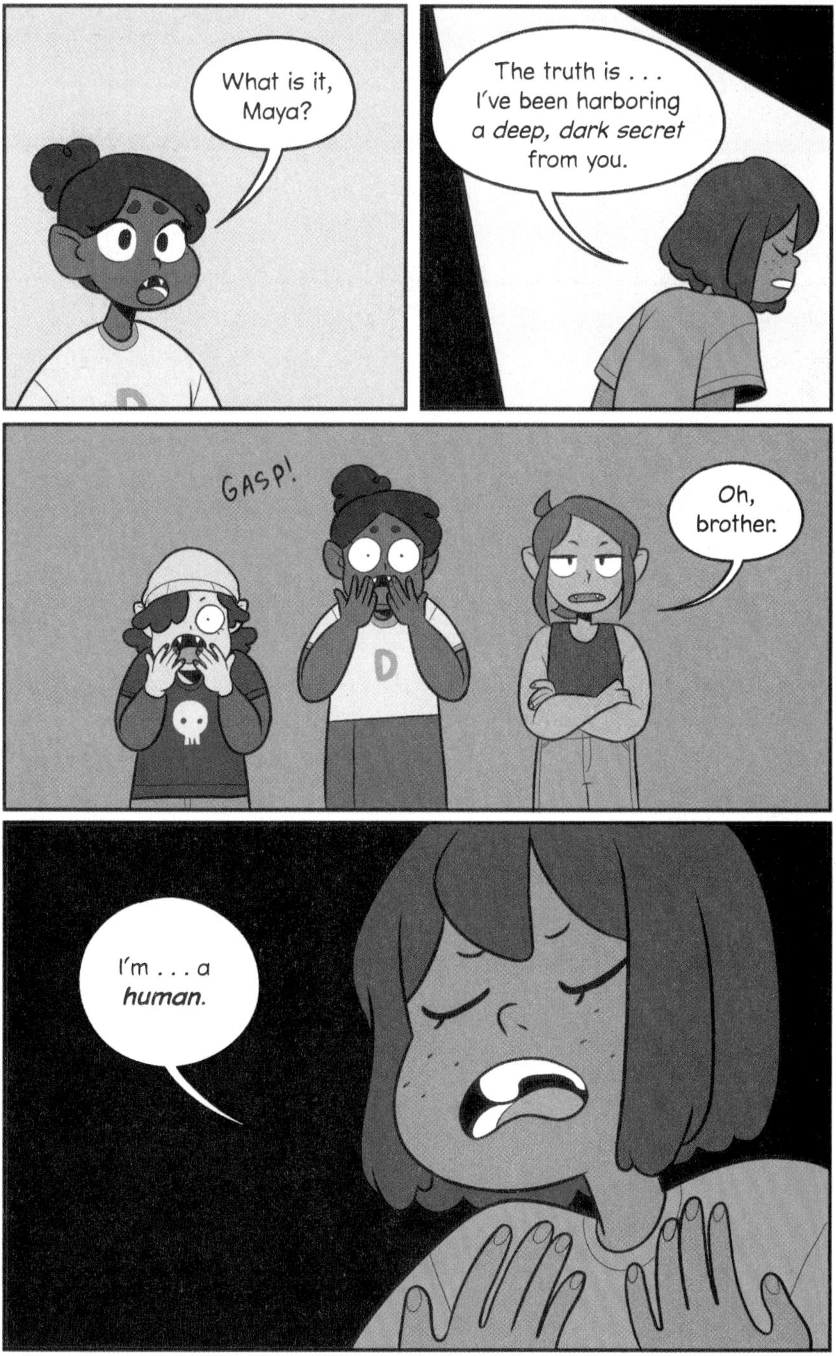
What is it, Maya?
The truth is . . . I've been harboring a *deep, dark secret* from you.
GASP!
Oh, brother.
I'm . . . a **human**.

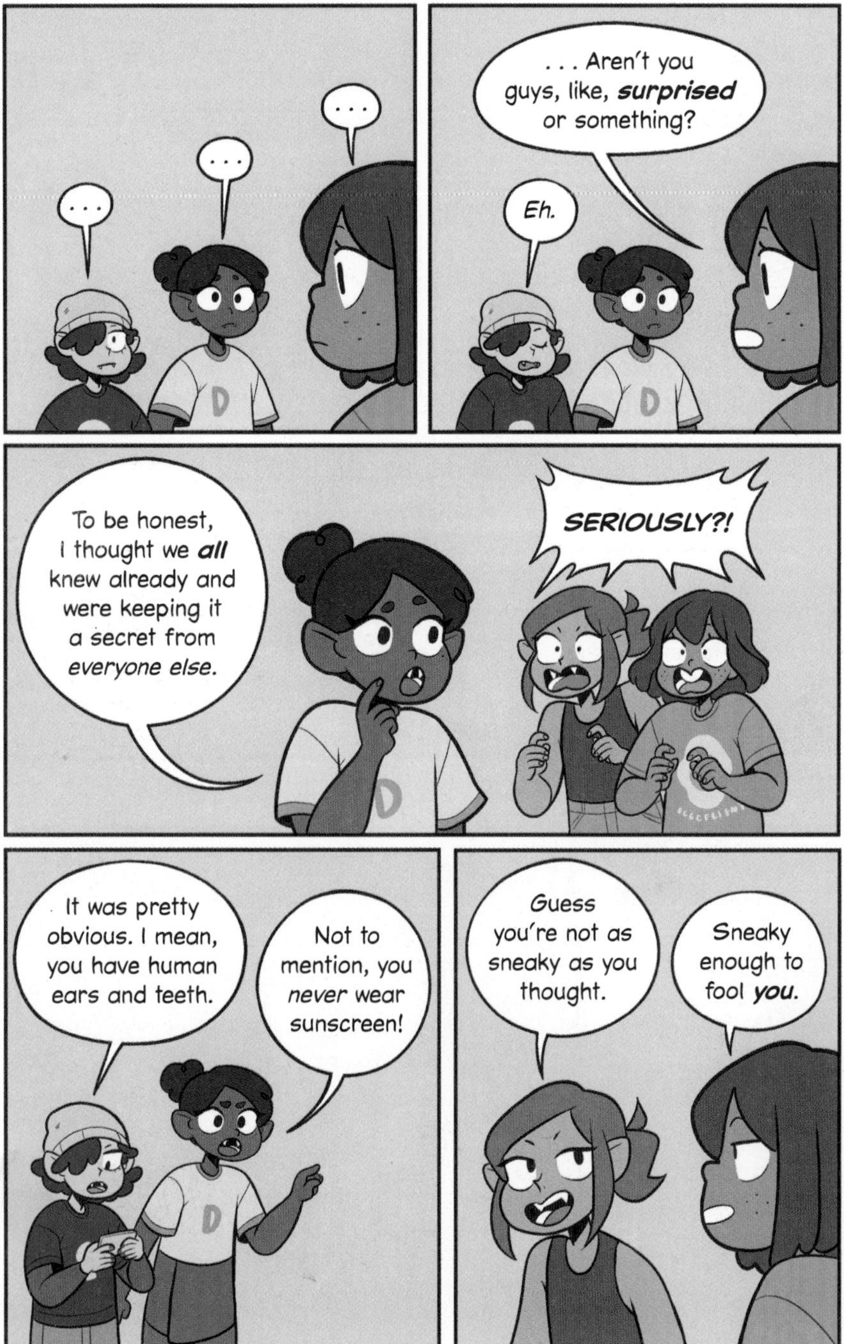
. . .
. . .
. . .
. . . Aren't you guys, like, **surprised** or something?
Eh.
To be honest, I thought we **all** knew already and were keeping it a secret from *everyone else.*
SERIOUSLY?!
It was pretty obvious. I mean, you have human ears and teeth.
Not to mention, you *never* wear sunscreen!
Guess you're not as sneaky as you thought.
Sneaky enough to fool **you**.

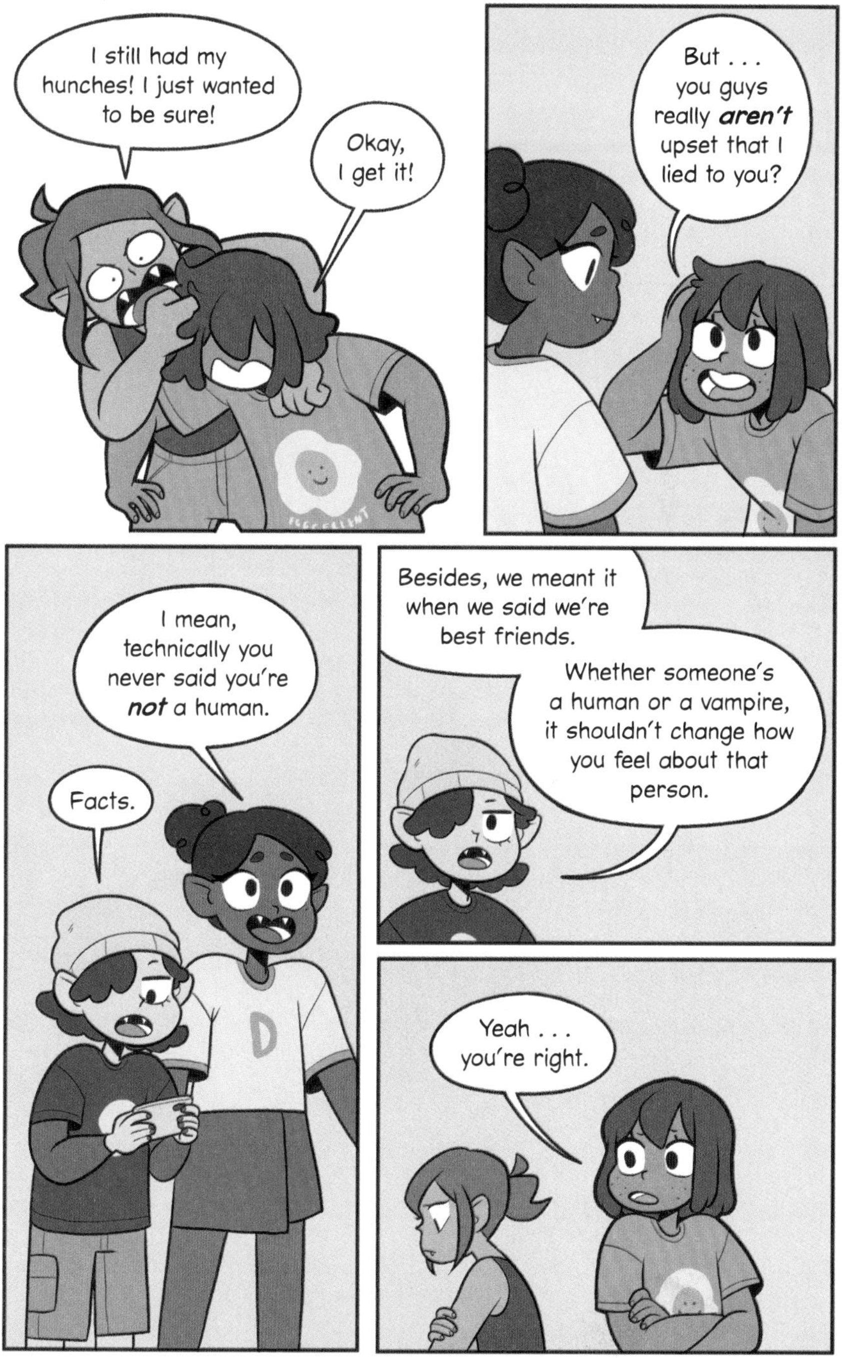
I still had my hunches! I just wanted to be sure!
Okay, I get it!
But . . . you guys really **aren't** upset that I lied to you?
I mean, technically you never said you're **not** a human.
Facts.
Besides, we meant it when we said we're best friends.
Whether someone's a human or a vampire, it shouldn't change how you feel about that person.
Yeah . . . you're right.

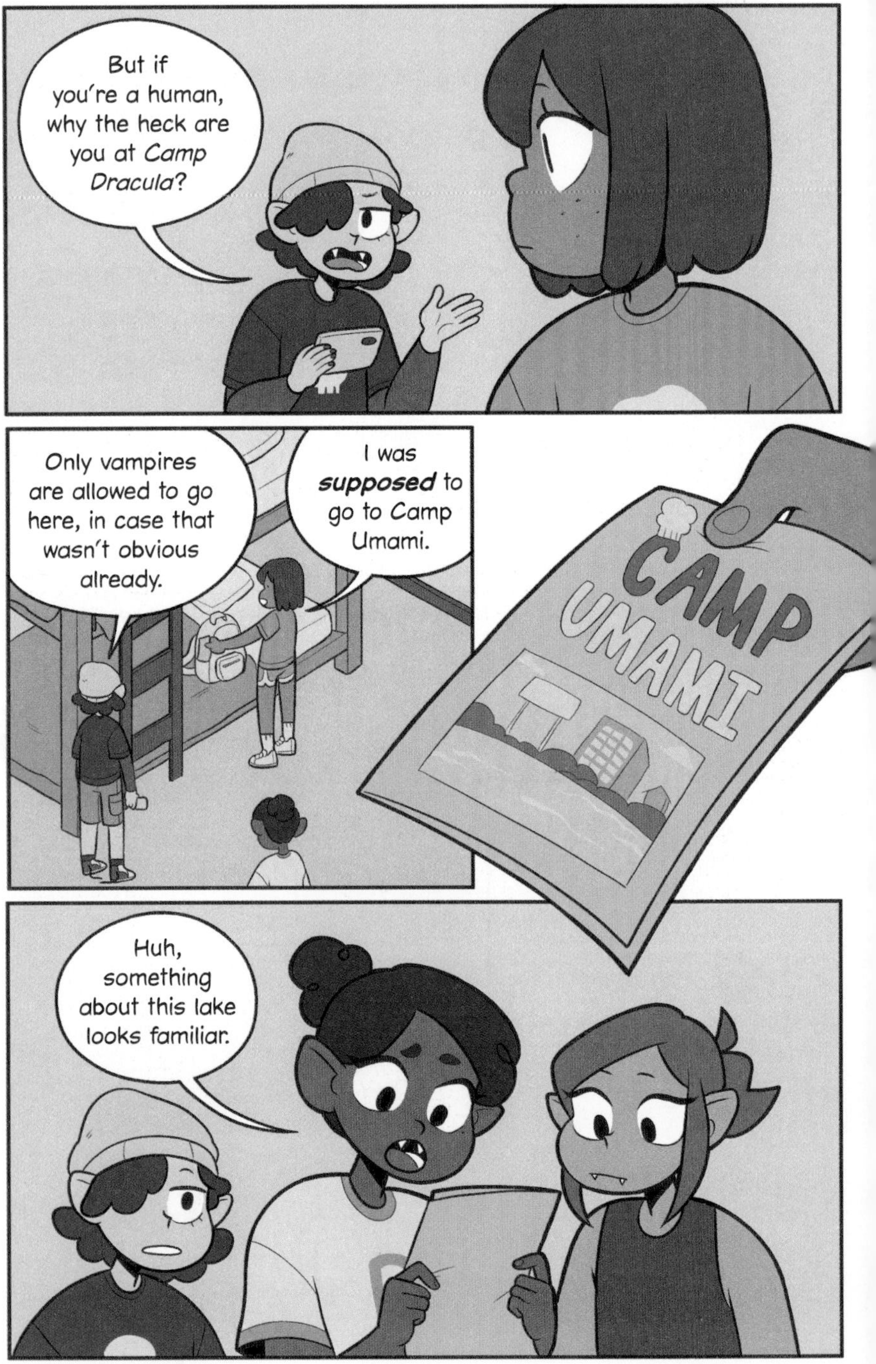
But if you're a human, why the heck are you at *Camp Dracula*?
Only vampires are allowed to go here, in case that wasn't obvious already.
I was ***supposed*** to go to Camp Umami.
CAMP UMAMI
Huh, something about this lake looks familiar.

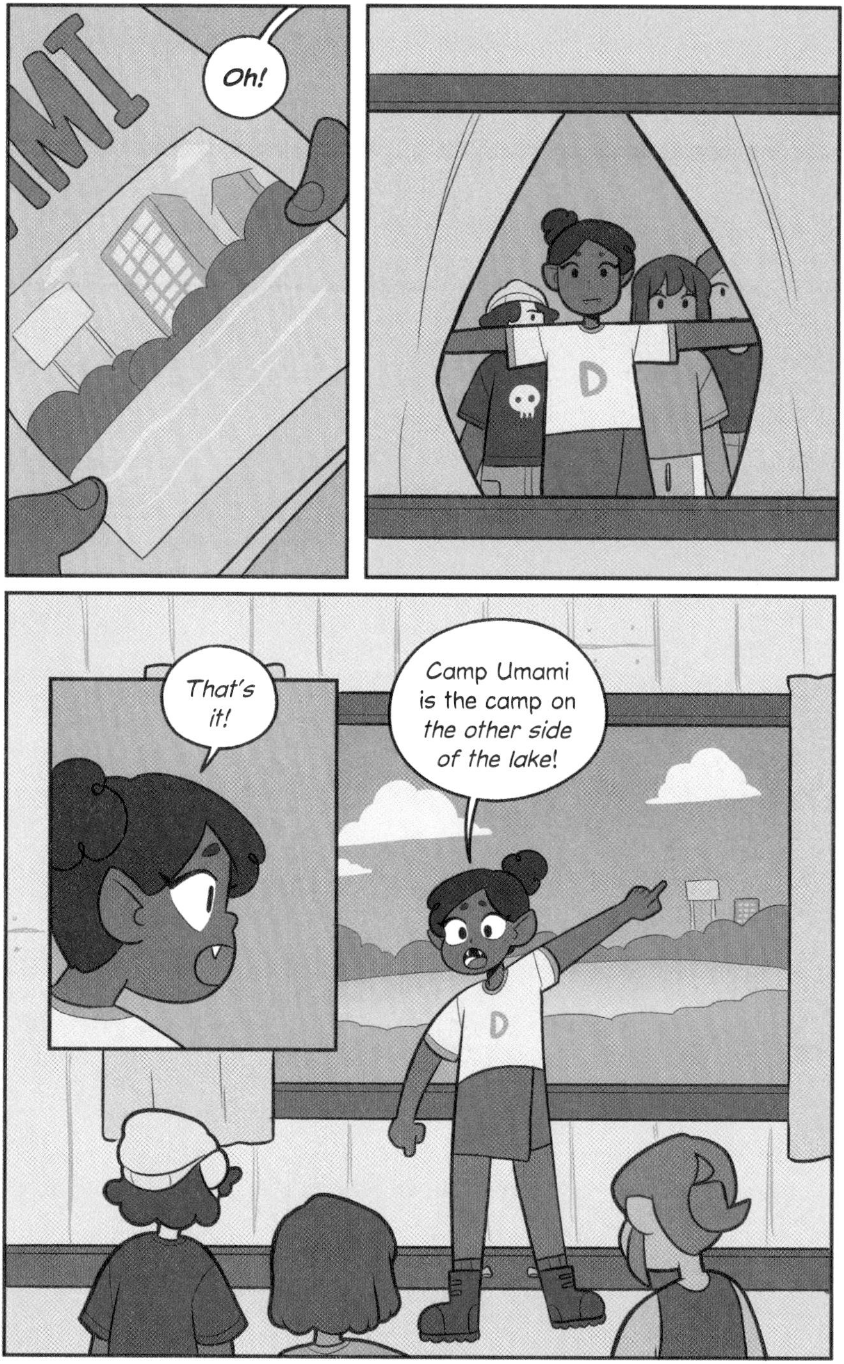
Oh!
That's it!
Camp Umami is the camp on the other side of the lake!

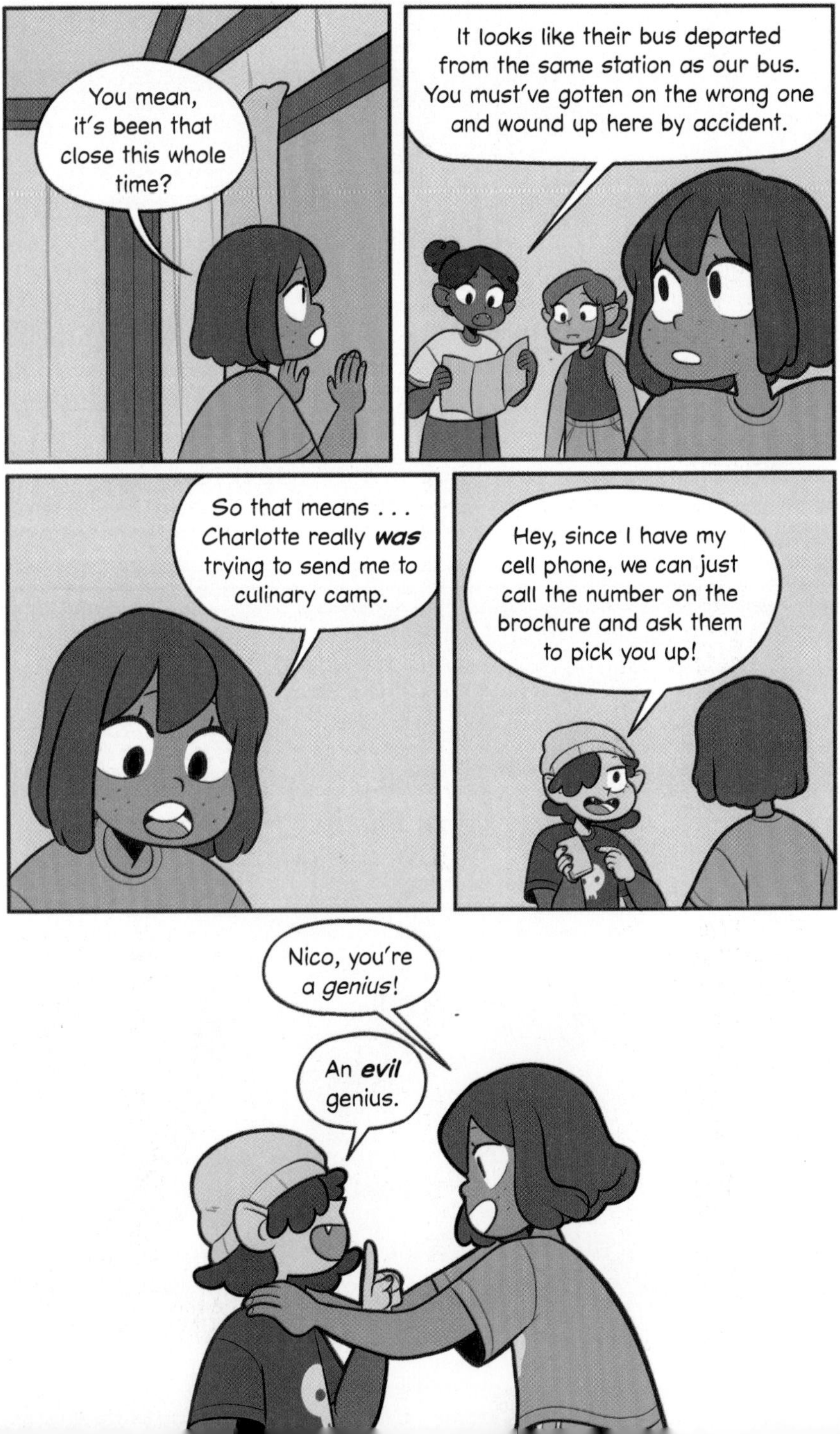
You mean, it's been that close this whole time?
It looks like their bus departed from the same station as our bus. You must've gotten on the wrong one and wound up here by accident.
So that means . . . Charlotte really ***was*** trying to send me to culinary camp.
Hey, since I have my cell phone, we can just call the number on the brochure and ask them to pick you up!
Nico, you're a *genius*!
An ***evil*** genius.

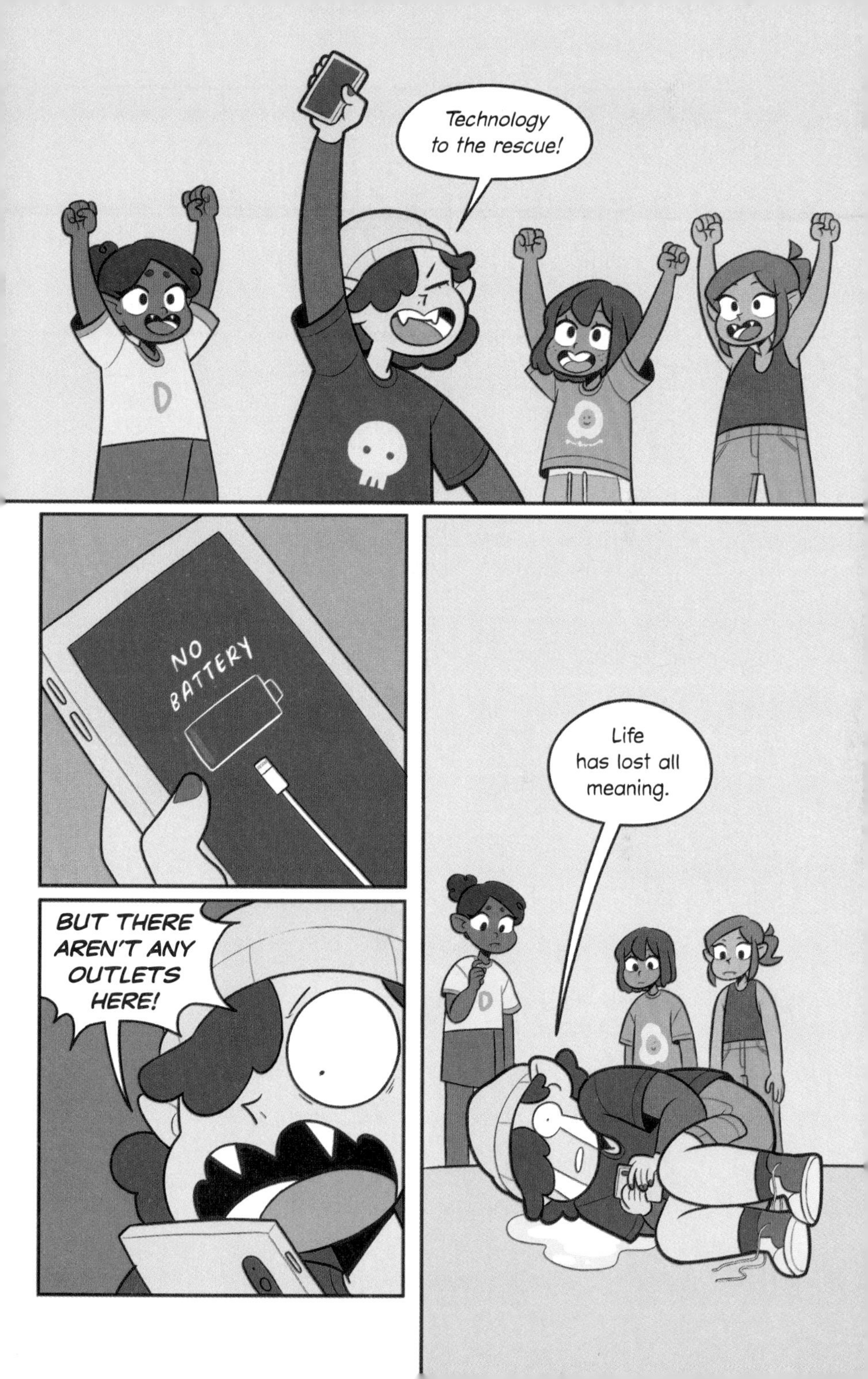
Technology to the rescue!
NO BATTERY
BUT THERE AREN'T ANY OUTLETS HERE!
Life has lost all meaning.

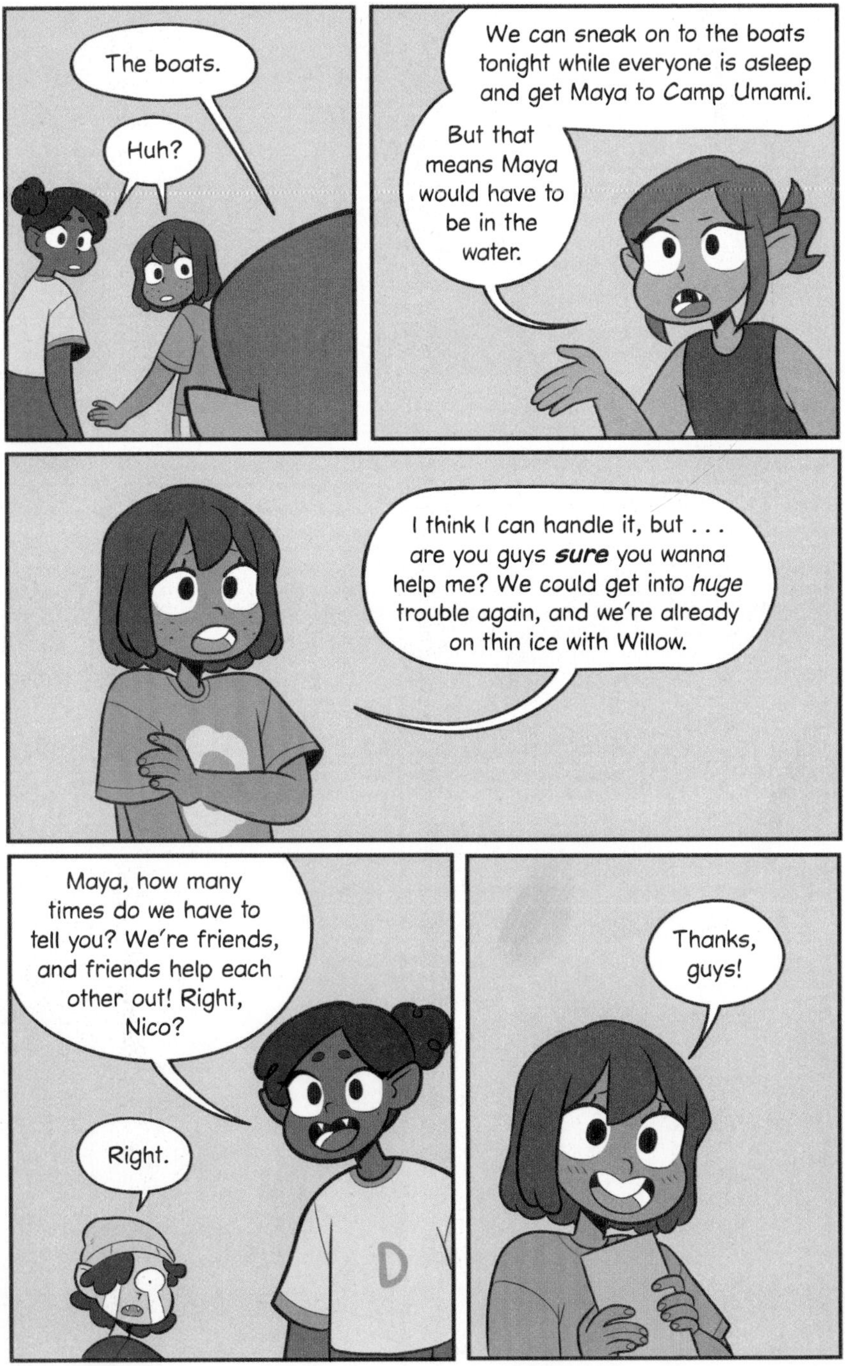
The boats.
Huh?
We can sneak on to the boats tonight while everyone is asleep and get Maya to Camp Umami.
But that means Maya would have to be in the water.
I think I can handle it, but . . . are you guys **sure** you wanna help me? We could get into *huge* trouble again, and we're already on thin ice with Willow.
Maya, how many times do we have to tell you? We're friends, and friends help each other out! Right, Nico?
Right.
D
Thanks, guys!

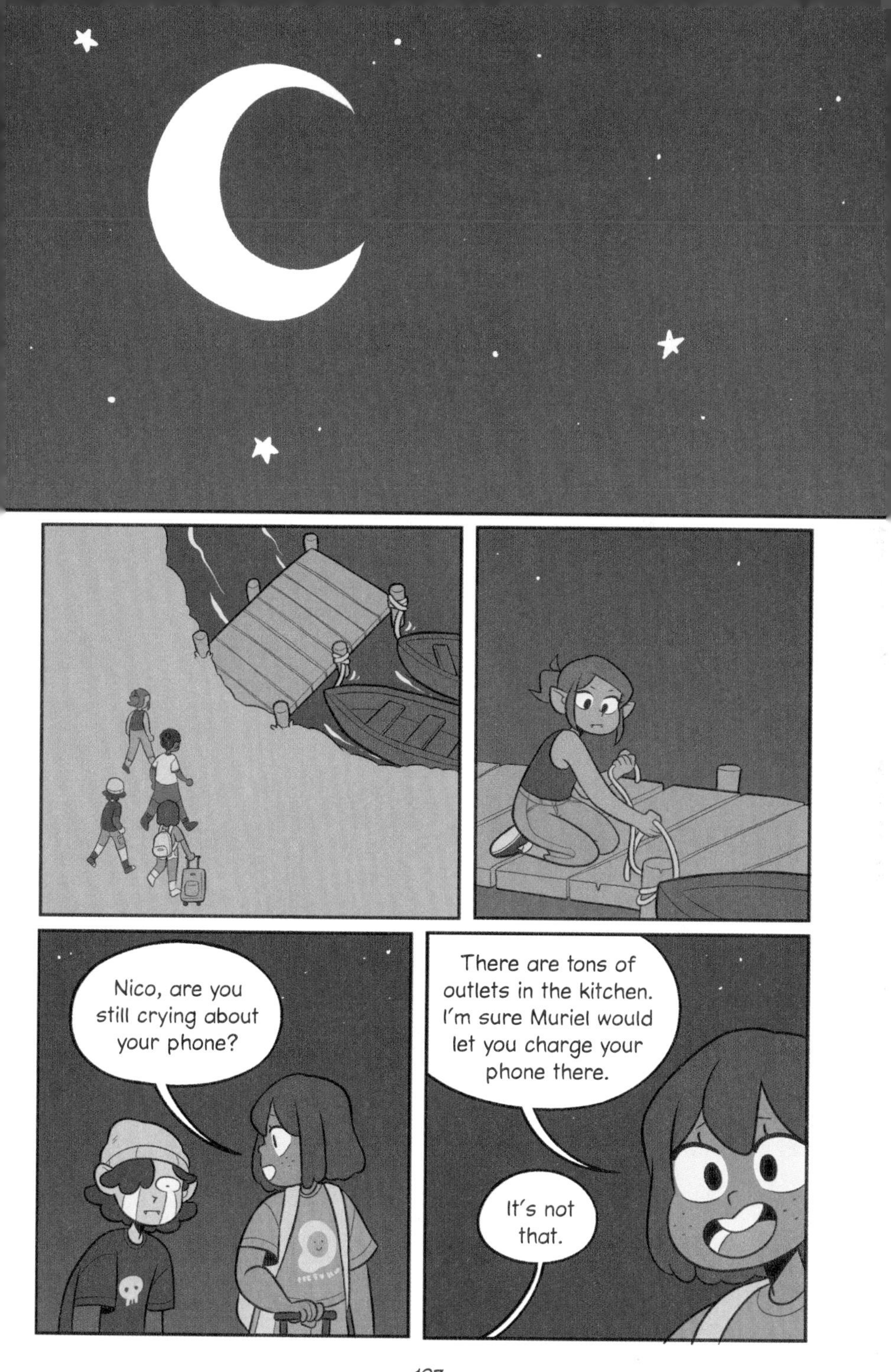
Nico, are you still crying about your phone?
There are tons of outlets in the kitchen. I'm sure Muriel would let you charge your phone there.
It's not that.

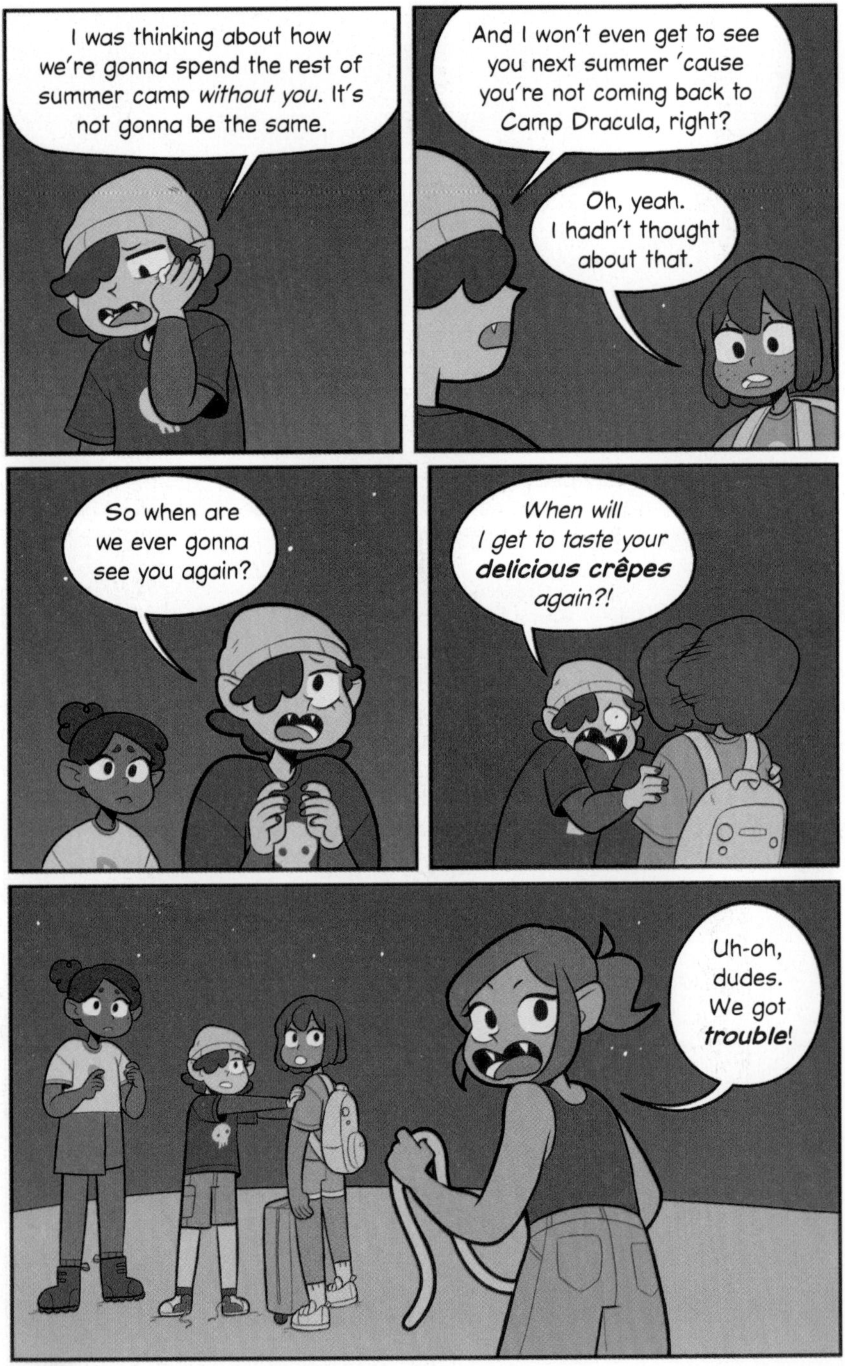
I was thinking about how we're gonna spend the rest of summer camp *without you*. It's not gonna be the same.
And I won't even get to see you next summer 'cause you're not coming back to Camp Dracula, right?
Oh, yeah. I hadn't thought about that.
So when are we ever gonna see you again?
When will I get to taste your ***delicious crêpes*** *again?!*
Uh-oh, dudes. We got ***trouble***!

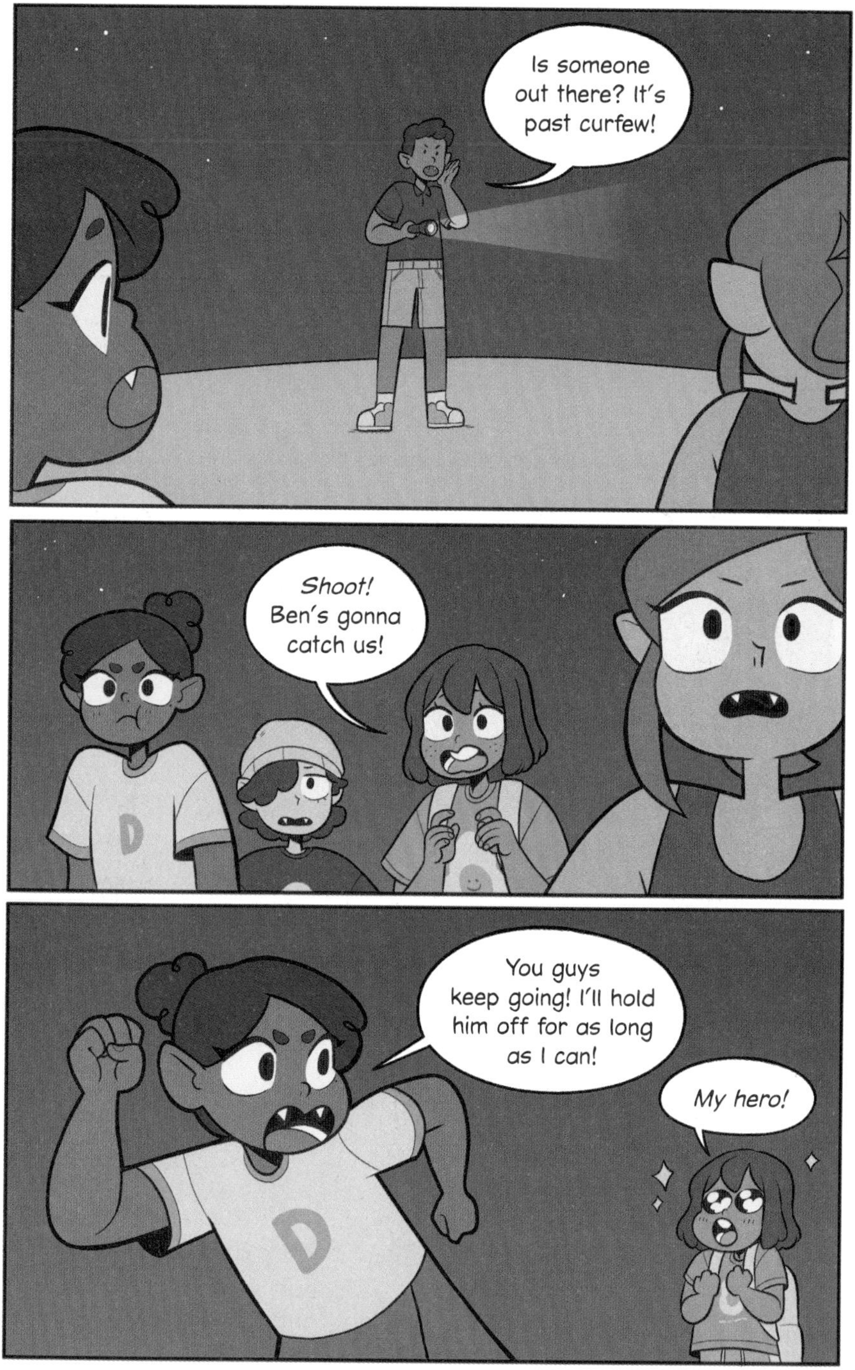
Is someone out there? It's past curfew!
Shoot! Ben's gonna catch us!
You guys keep going! I'll hold him off for as long as I can!
My hero!

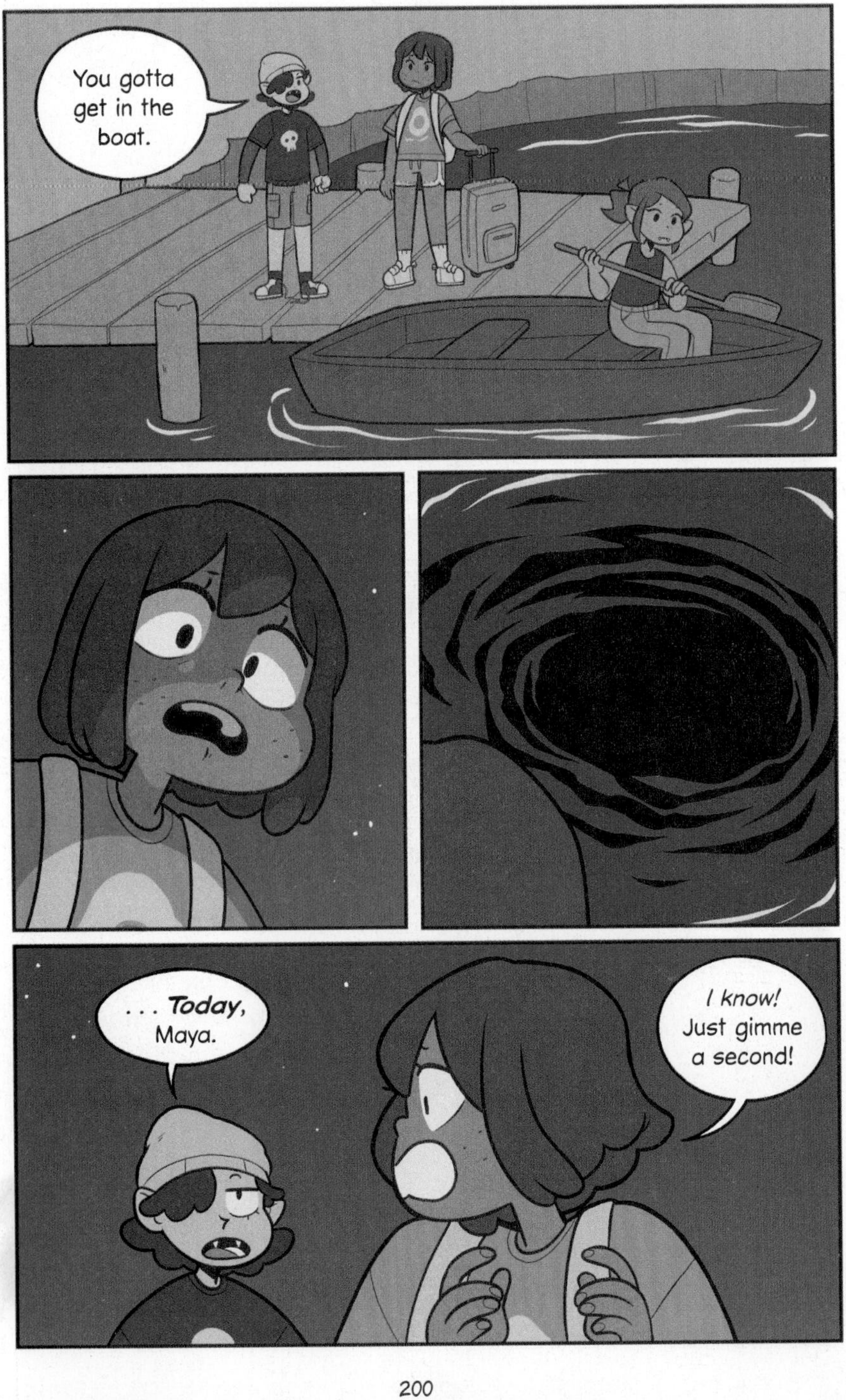
You gotta get in the boat.
. . . *Today*, Maya.
I know! Just gimme a second!

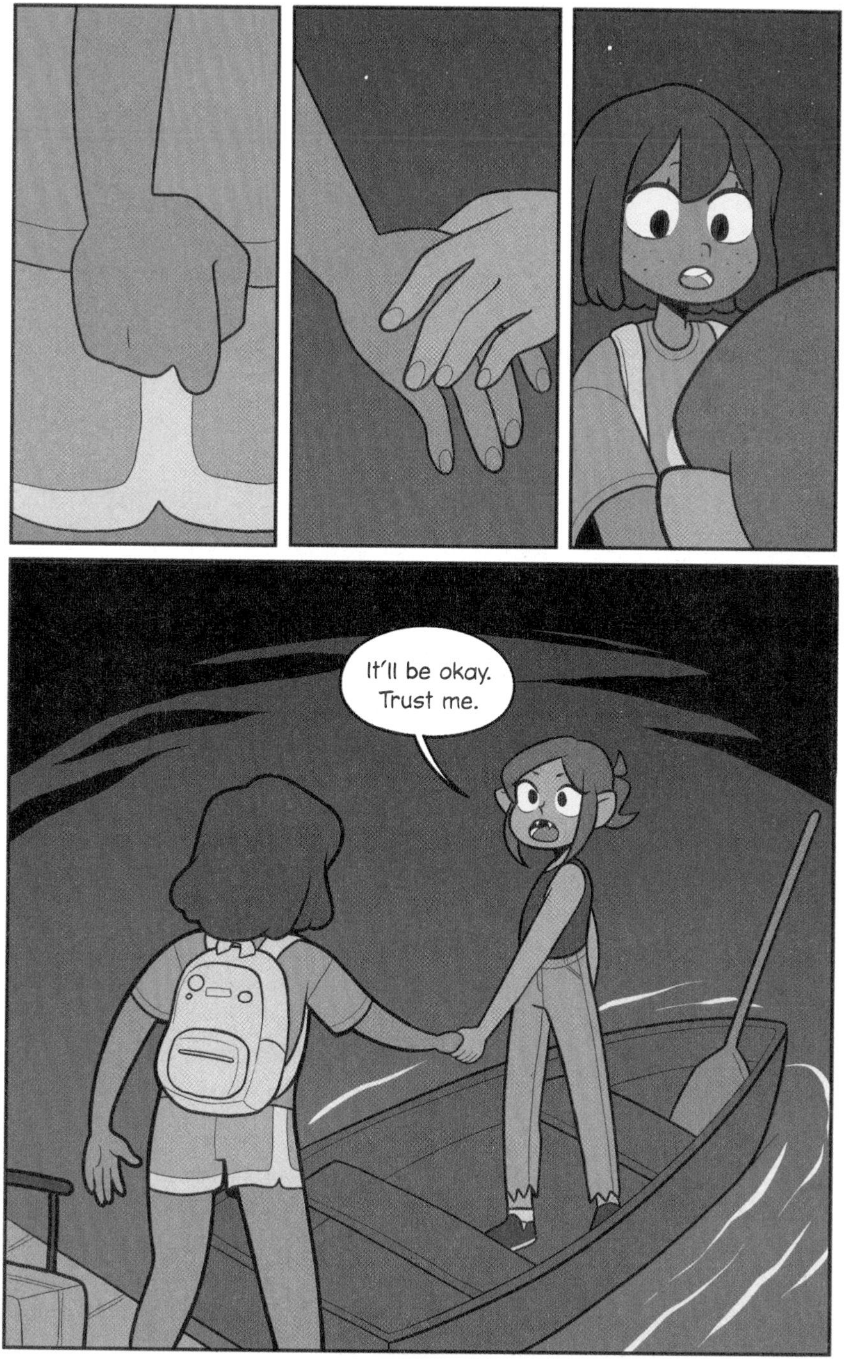
It'll be okay. Trust me.

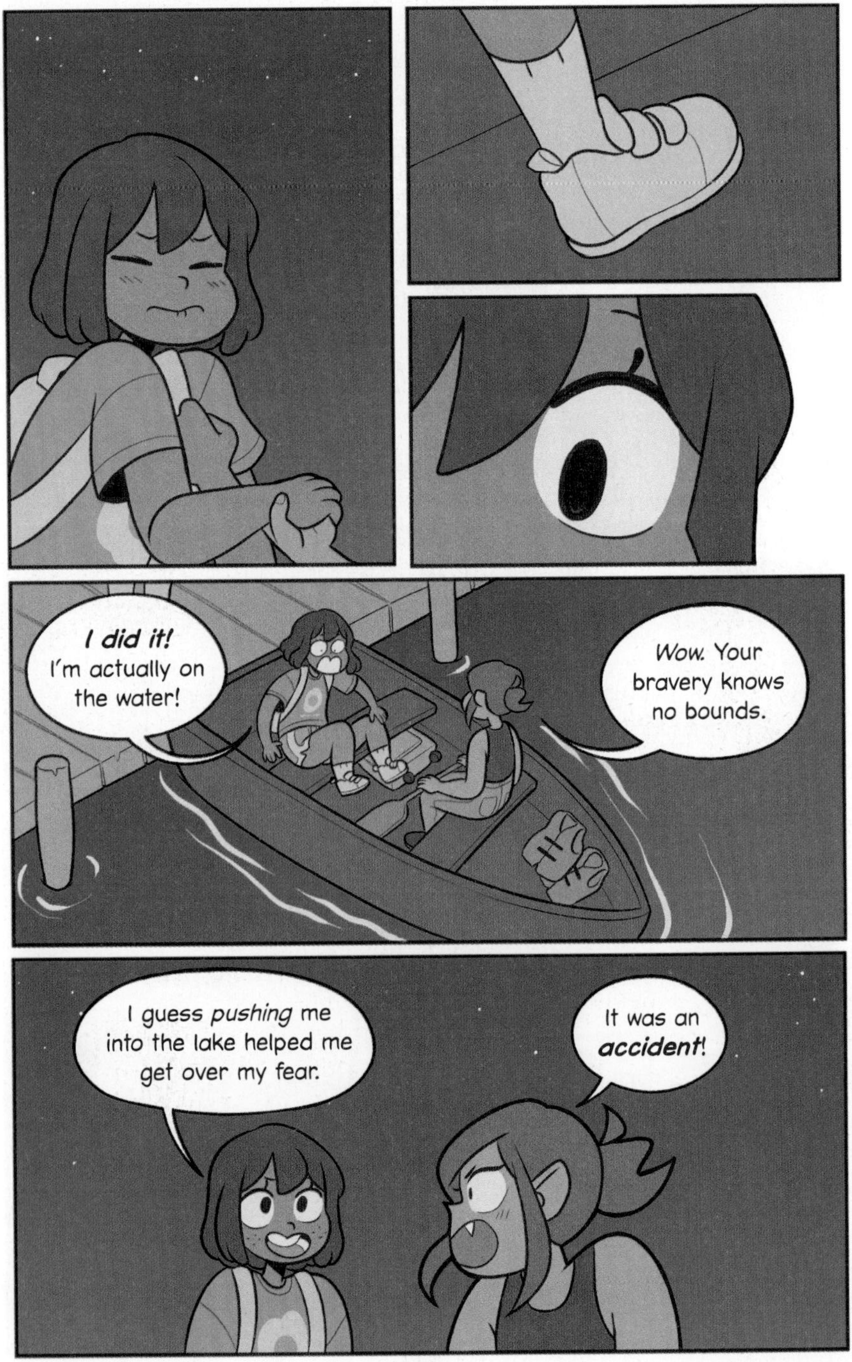
I did it! I'm actually on the water!
Wow. Your bravery knows no bounds.
I guess *pushing* me into the lake helped me get over my fear.
It was an ***accident***!

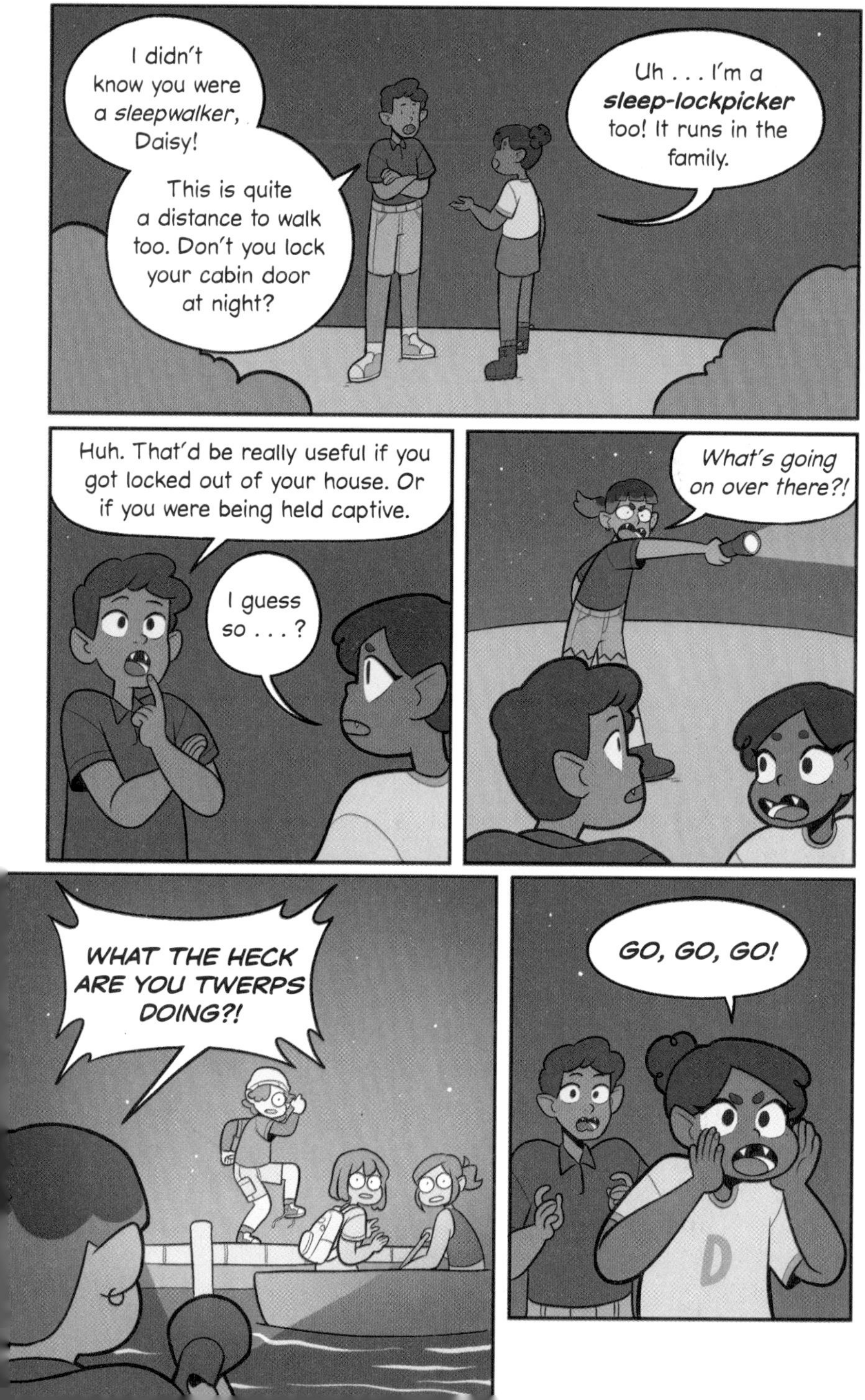
I didn't know you were a *sleepwalker*, Daisy!
This is quite a distance to walk too. Don't you lock your cabin door at night?
Uh . . . I'm a ***sleep-lockpicker*** too! It runs in the family.
Huh. That'd be really useful if you got locked out of your house. Or if you were being held captive.
I guess so . . . ?
What's going on over there?!
WHAT THE HECK ARE YOU TWERPS DOING?!
GO, GO, GO!
D

Hurry, Nico! Get in the boat!

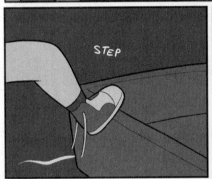

STEP

KICK!

Go on without me! I'll only add deadweight!

I'll never forget your sacrifice!

Bumblebees for life!

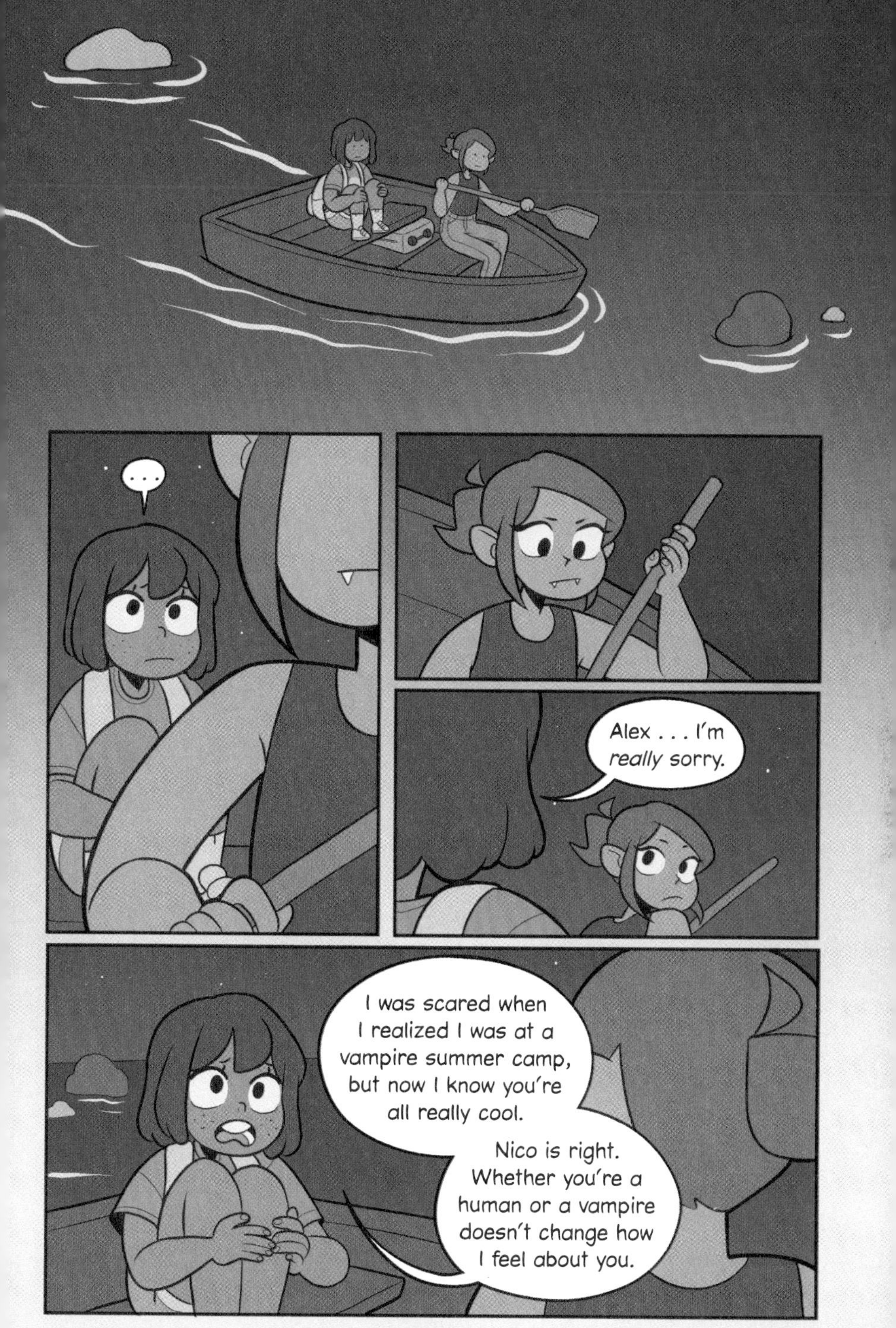
...
Alex . . . I'm *really* sorry.
I was scared when I realized I was at a vampire summer camp, but now I know you're all really cool.
Nico is right. Whether you're a human or a vampire doesn't change how I feel about you.

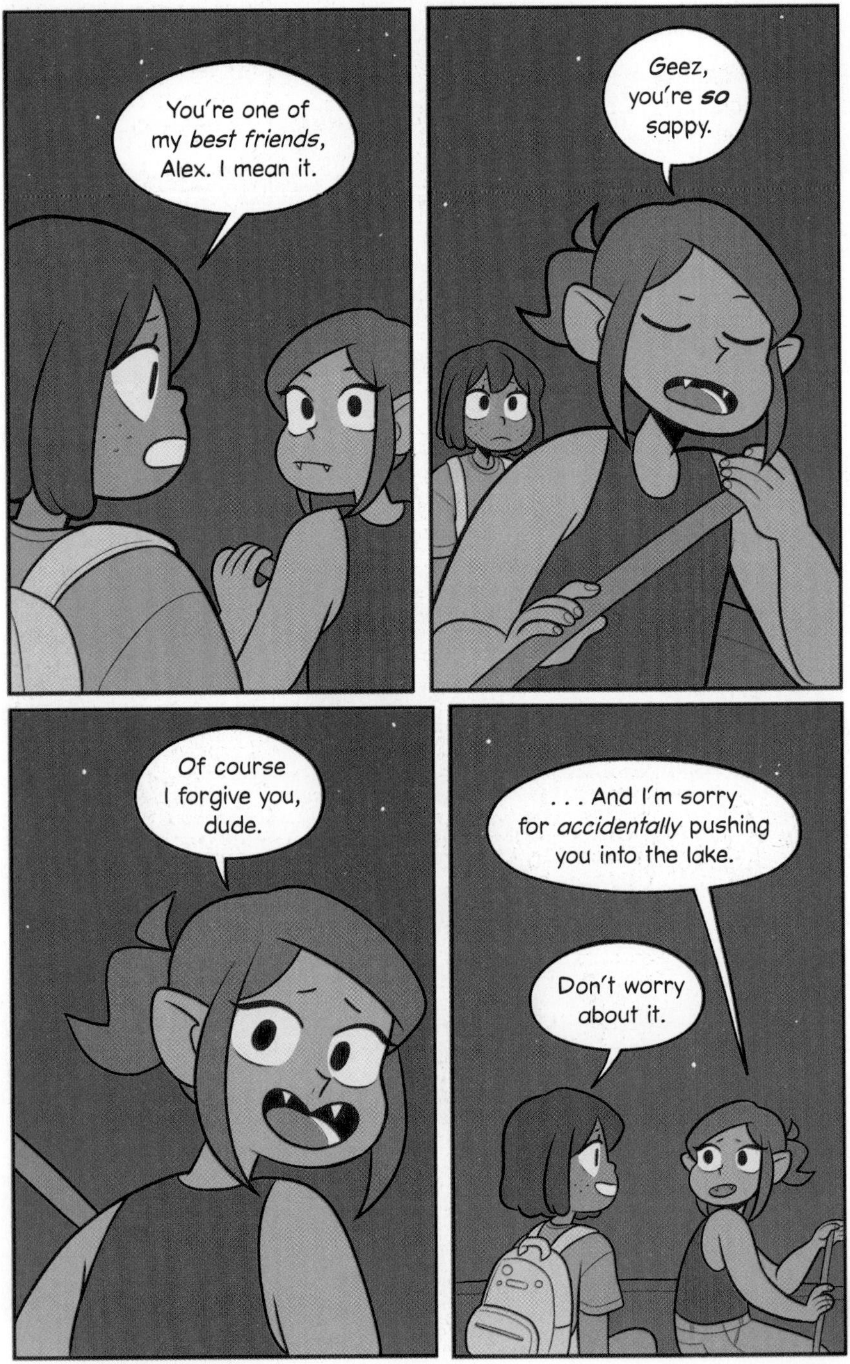
You're one of my *best friends*, Alex. I mean it.
Geez, you're ***so*** sappy.
Of course I forgive you, dude.
. . . And I'm sorry for *accidentally* pushing you into the lake.
Don't worry about it.

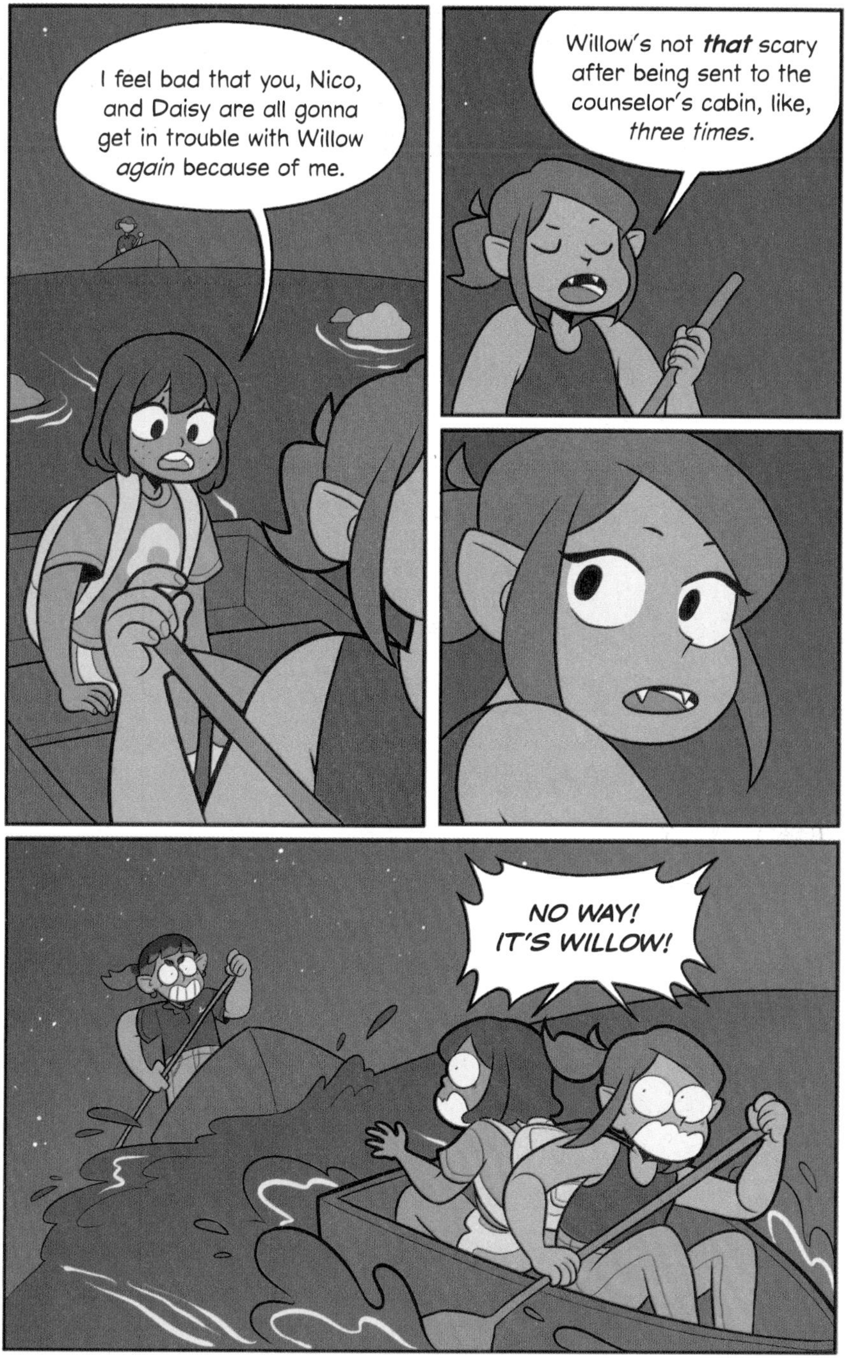
I feel bad that you, Nico, and Daisy are all gonna get in trouble with Willow *again* because of me.
Willow's not ***that*** scary after being sent to the counselor's cabin, like, *three times.*
NO WAY! IT'S WILLOW!

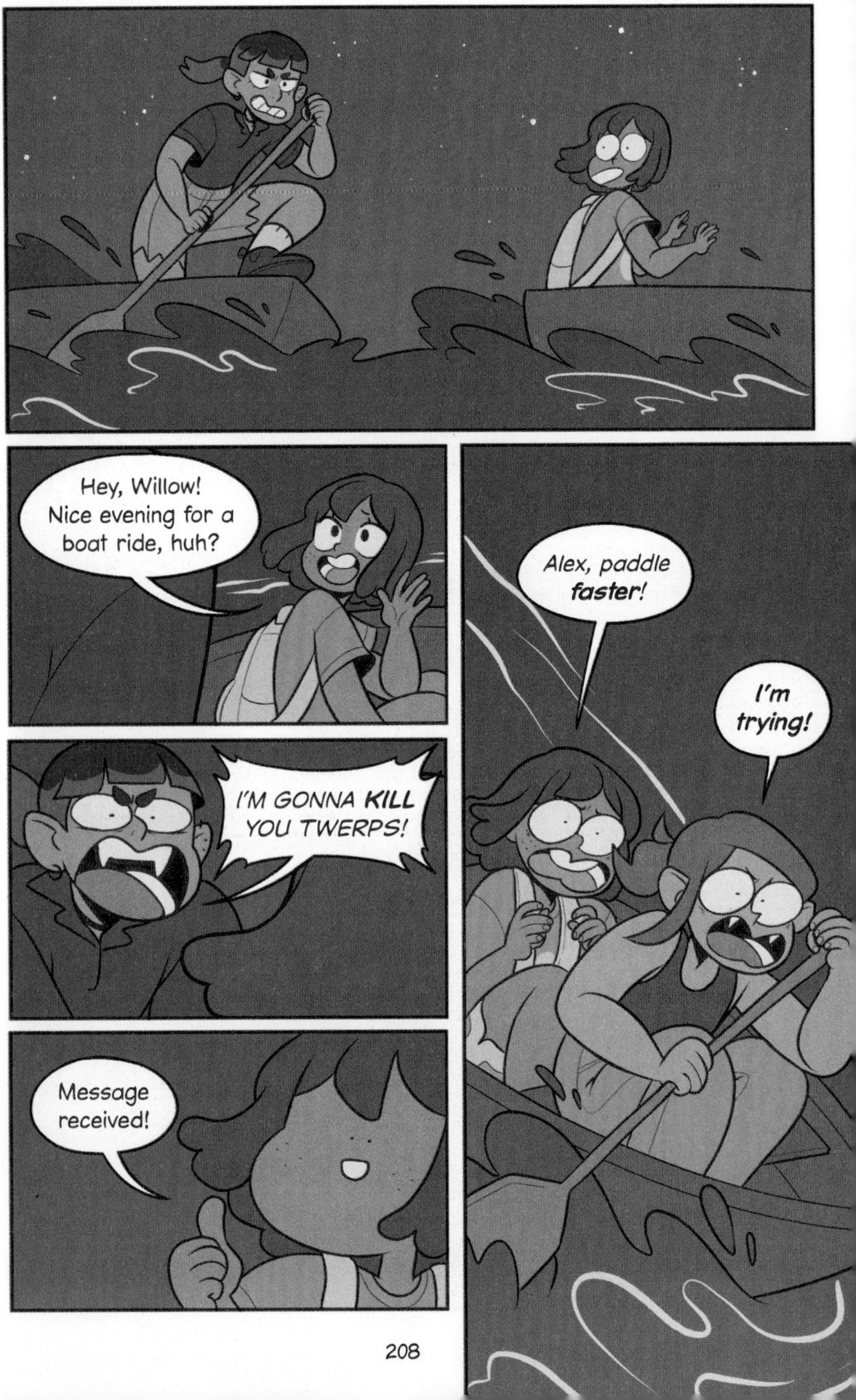
Hey, Willow! Nice evening for a boat ride, huh?
I'M GONNA **KILL** YOU TWERPS!
Message received!
Alex, paddle **faster**!
I'm trying!

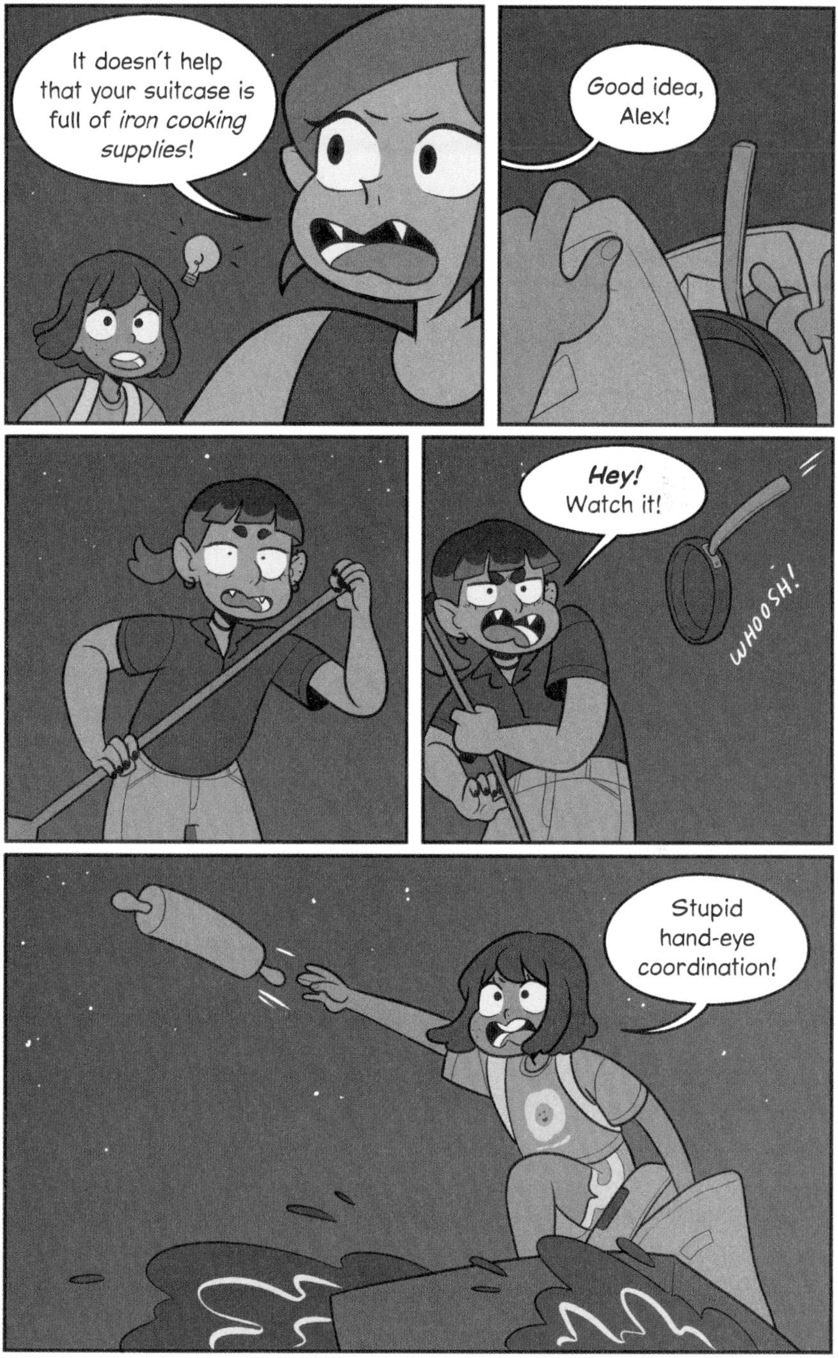

It doesn't help that your suitcase is full of *iron cooking supplies*!
Good idea, Alex!
Hey! Watch it!
WHOOSH!
Stupid hand-eye coordination!

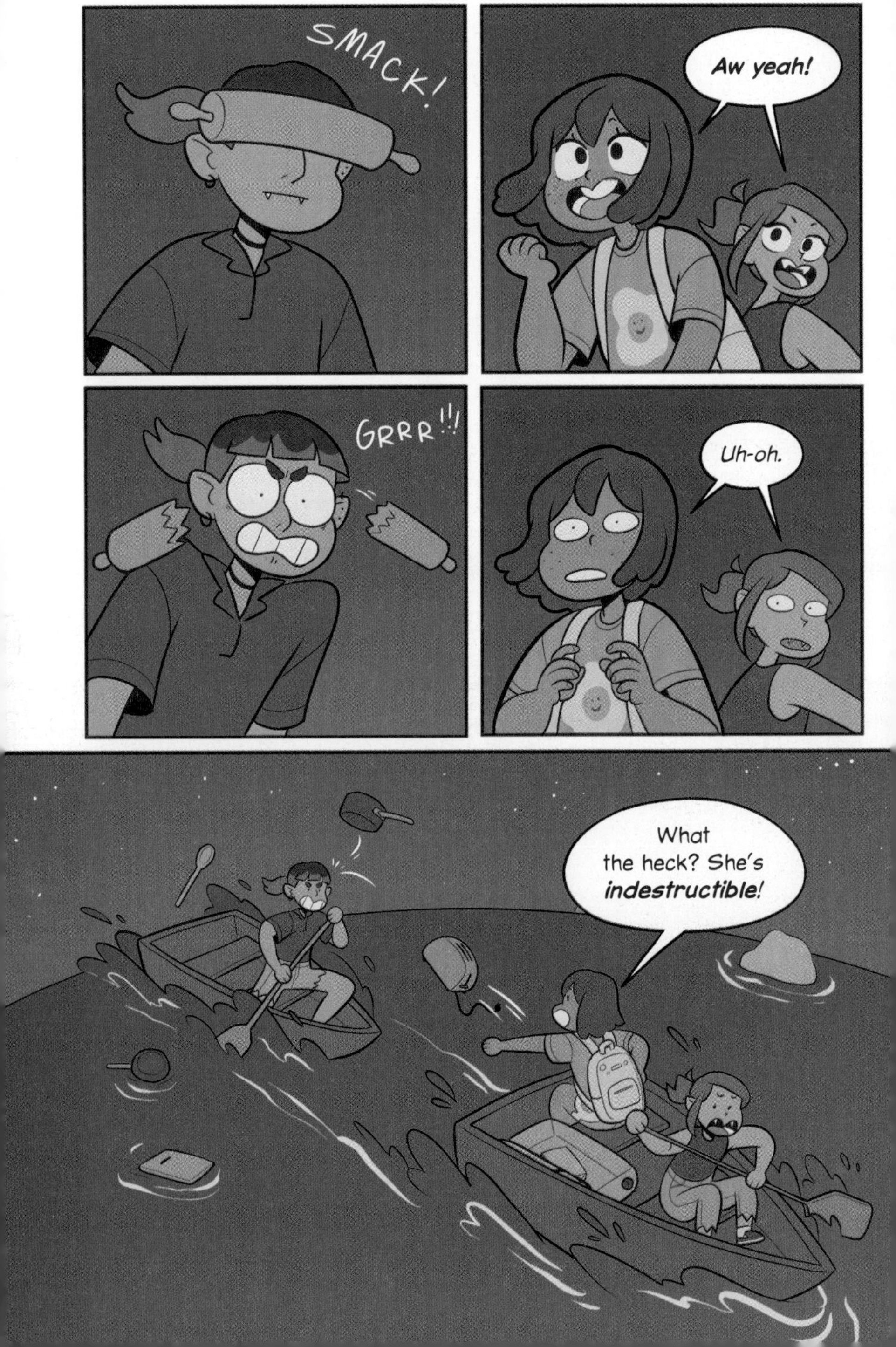
SMACK!
Aw yeah!
GRRR!!!
Uh-oh.
What the heck? She's *indestructible!*

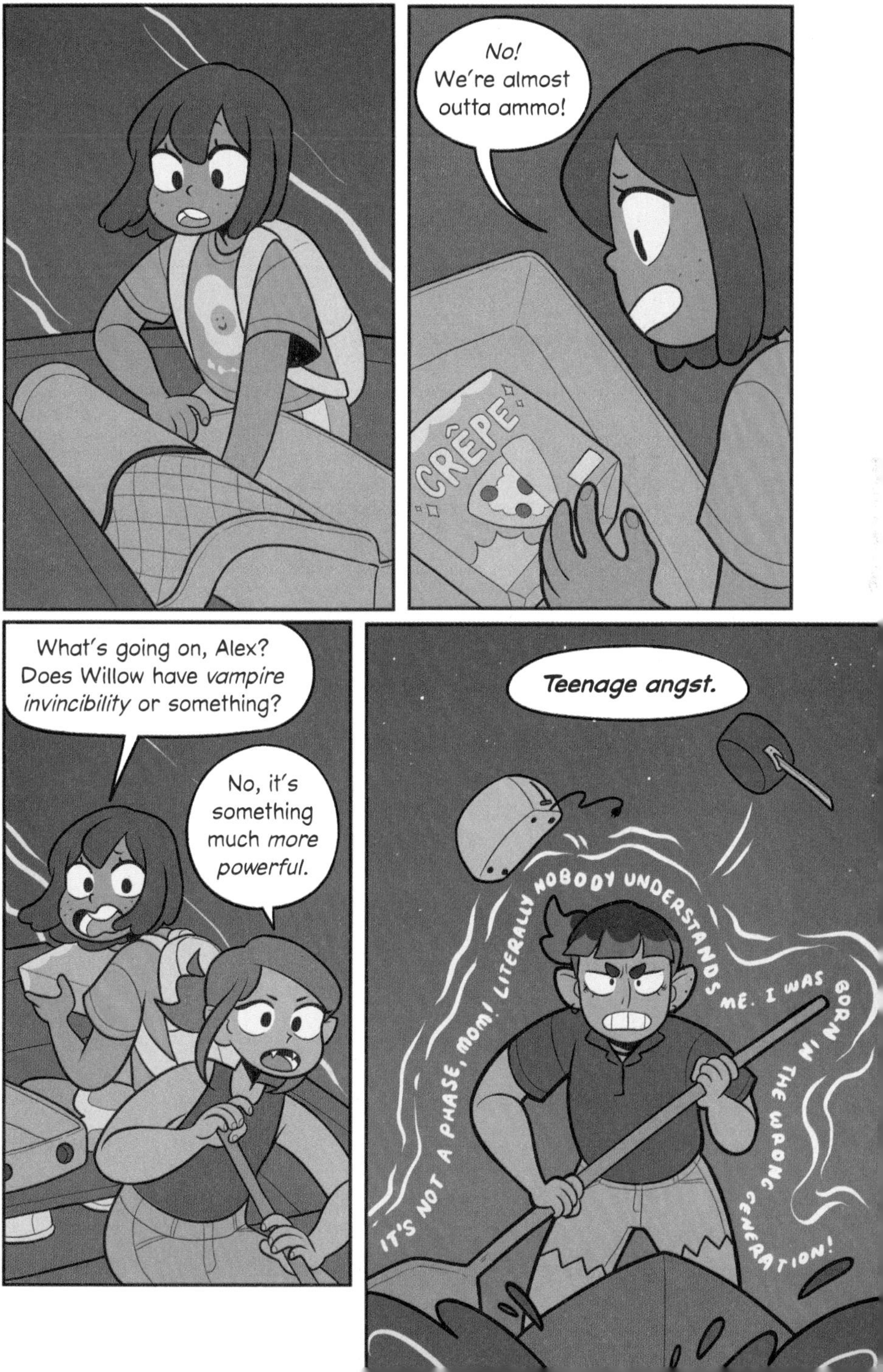
No!
We're almost outta ammo!
CRÊPE
What's going on, Alex? Does Willow have *vampire invincibility* or something?
No, it's something much *more powerful.*
Teenage angst.
IT'S NOT A PHASE, MOM! LITERALLY NOBODY UNDERSTANDS ME. I WAS BORN IN THE WRONG GENERATION!

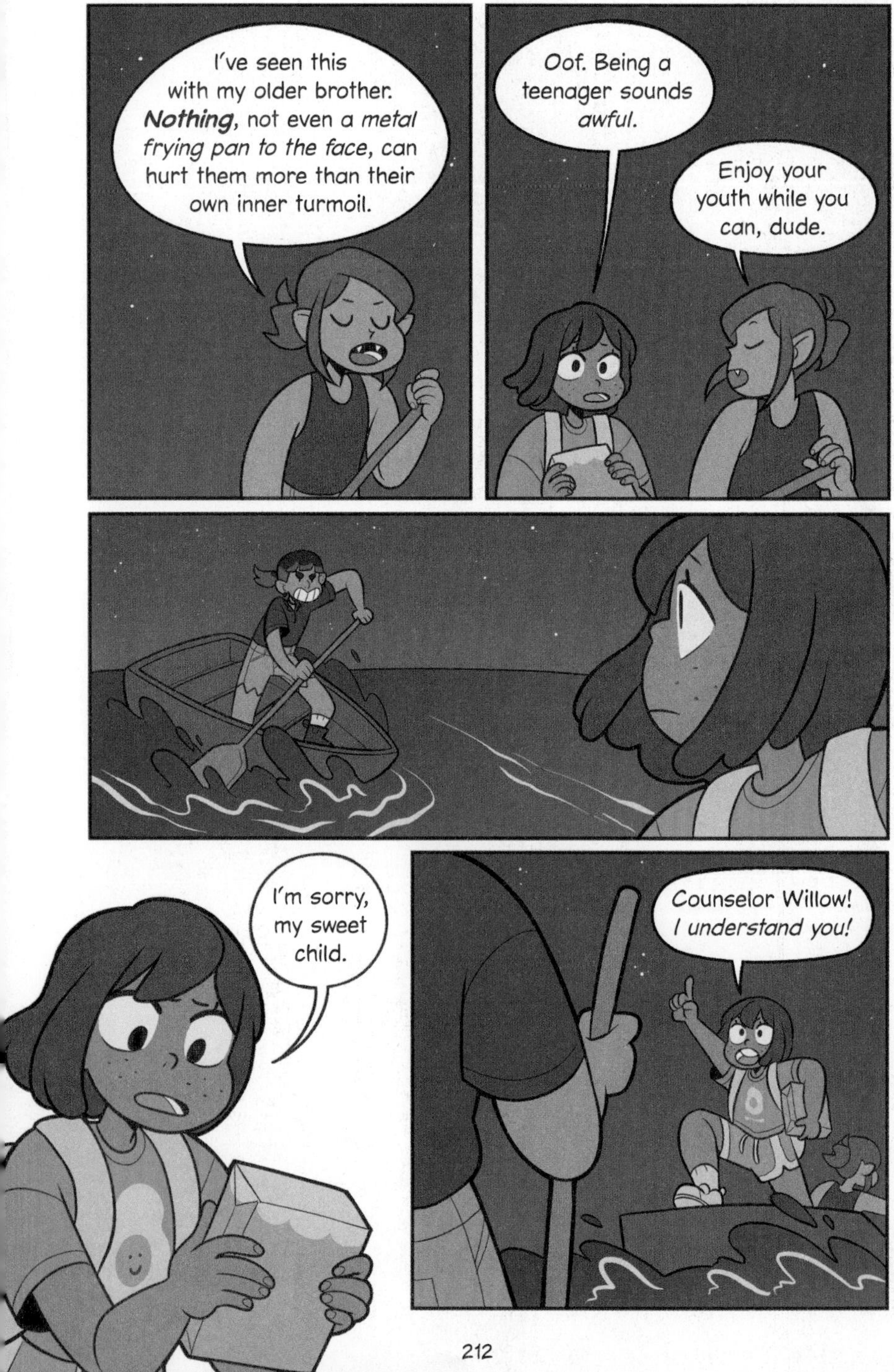
I've seen this with my older brother. **Nothing**, not even a *metal frying pan to the face*, can hurt them more than their own inner turmoil.
Oof. Being a teenager sounds *awful*.
Enjoy your youth while you can, dude.
I'm sorry, my sweet child.
Counselor Willow! *I understand you!*

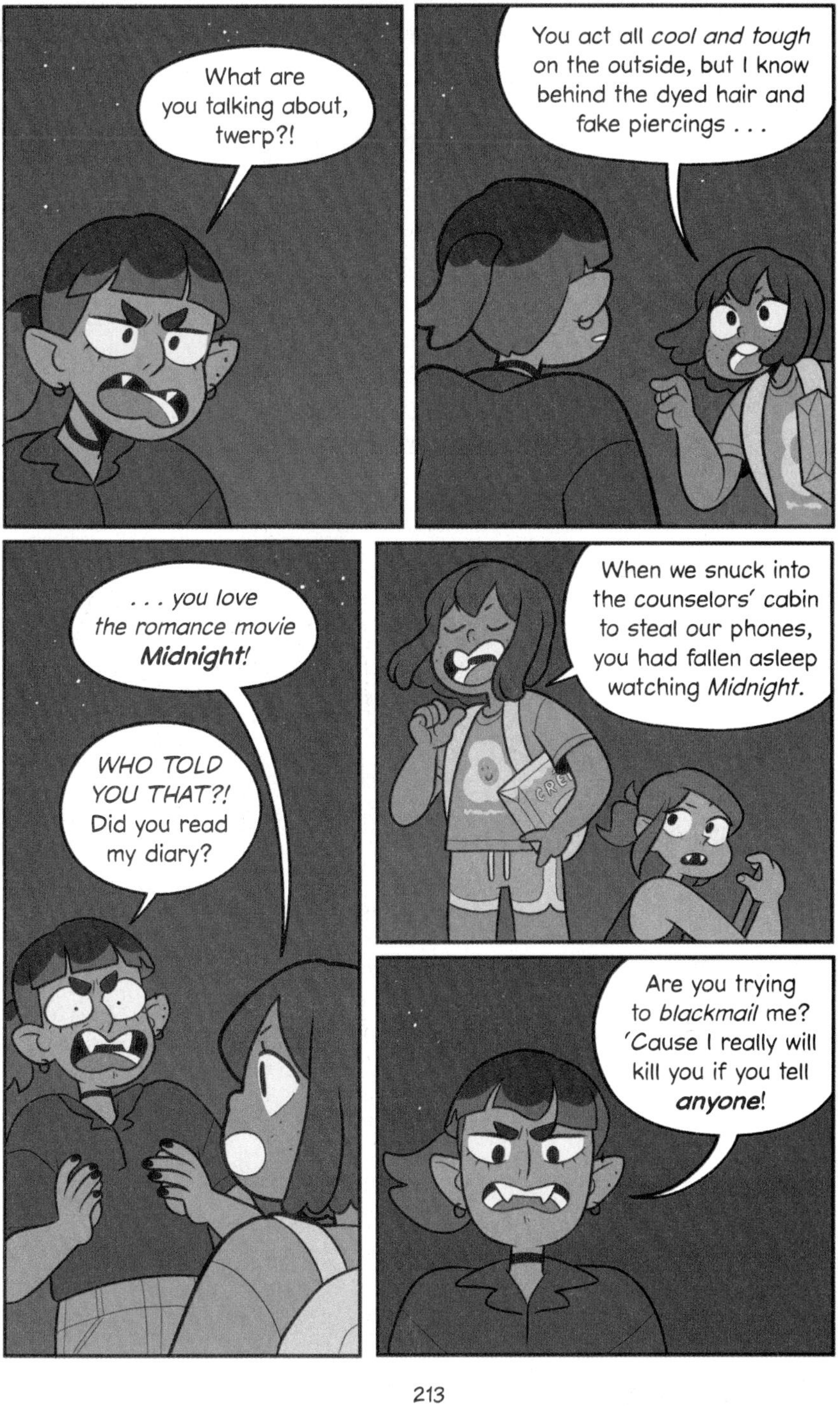
What are you talking about, twerp?!
You act all *cool and tough* on the outside, but I know behind the dyed hair and fake piercings . . .
. . . you love the romance movie ***Midnight****!*
WHO TOLD YOU THAT?! Did you read my diary?
When we snuck into the counselors' cabin to steal our phones, you had fallen asleep watching *Midnight*.
Are you trying to *blackmail* me? 'Cause I really will kill you if you tell ***anyone***!

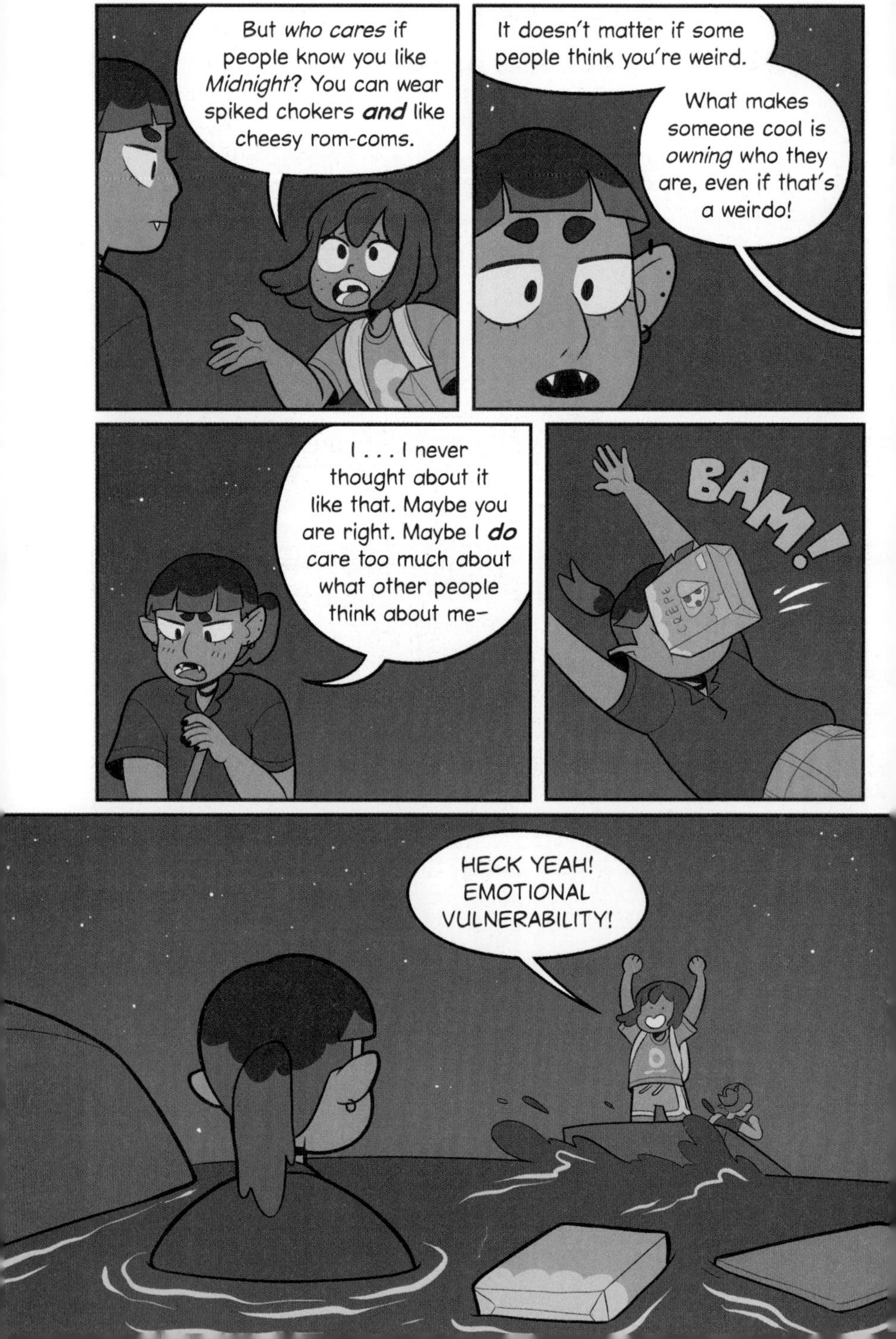
But *who cares* if people know you like *Midnight*? You can wear spiked chokers ***and*** like cheesy rom-coms.
It doesn't matter if some people think you're weird.
What makes someone cool is *owning* who they are, even if that's a weirdo!
I . . . I never thought about it like that. Maybe you are right. Maybe I ***do*** care too much about what other people think about me–
BAM!
CREPE
HECK YEAH! EMOTIONAL VULNERABILITY!

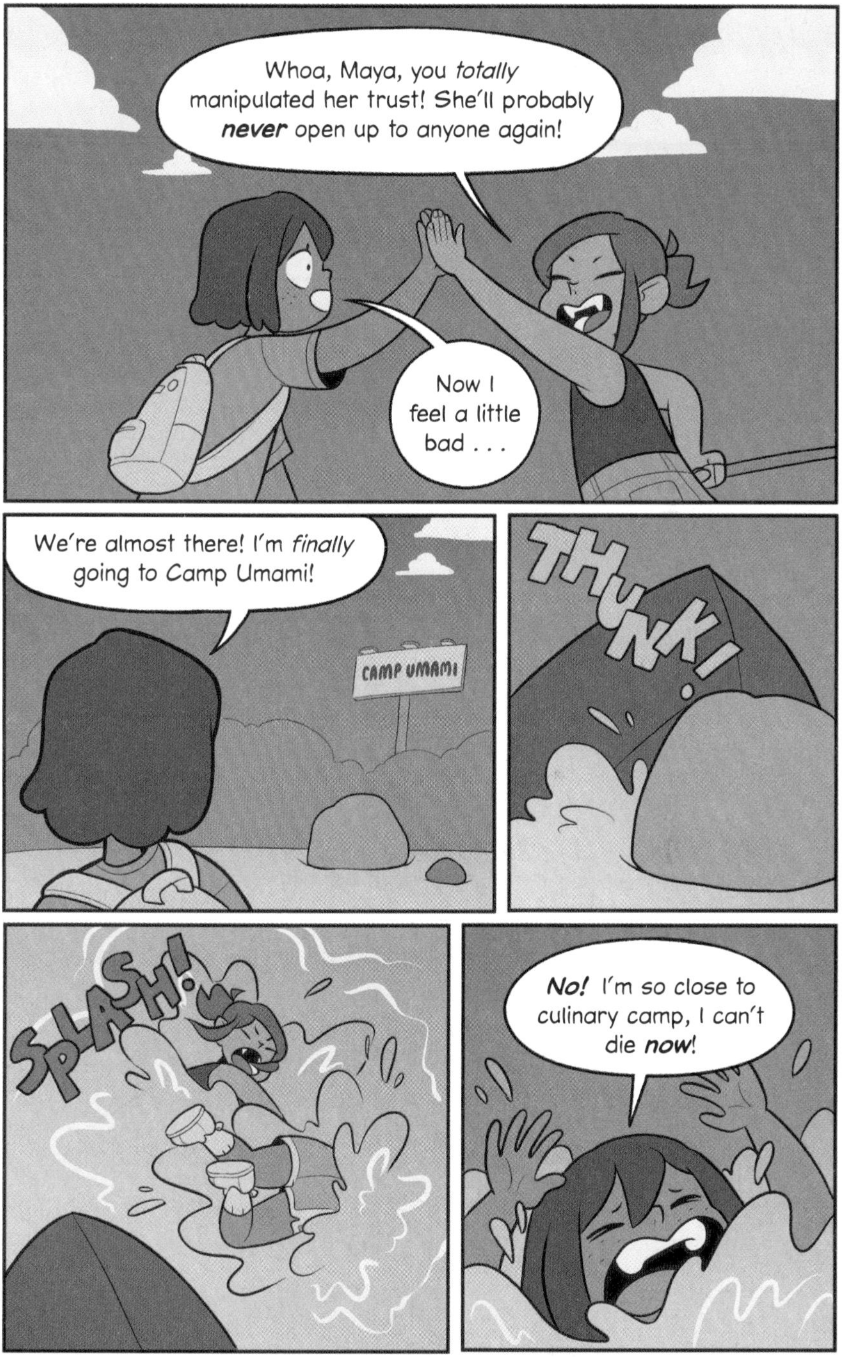
Whoa, Maya, you *totally* manipulated her trust! She'll probably **never** open up to anyone again!
Now I feel a little bad . . .
We're almost there! I'm *finally* going to Camp Umami!
CAMP UMAMI
THUNK!
SPLASH!
No! I'm so close to culinary camp, I can't die **now**!

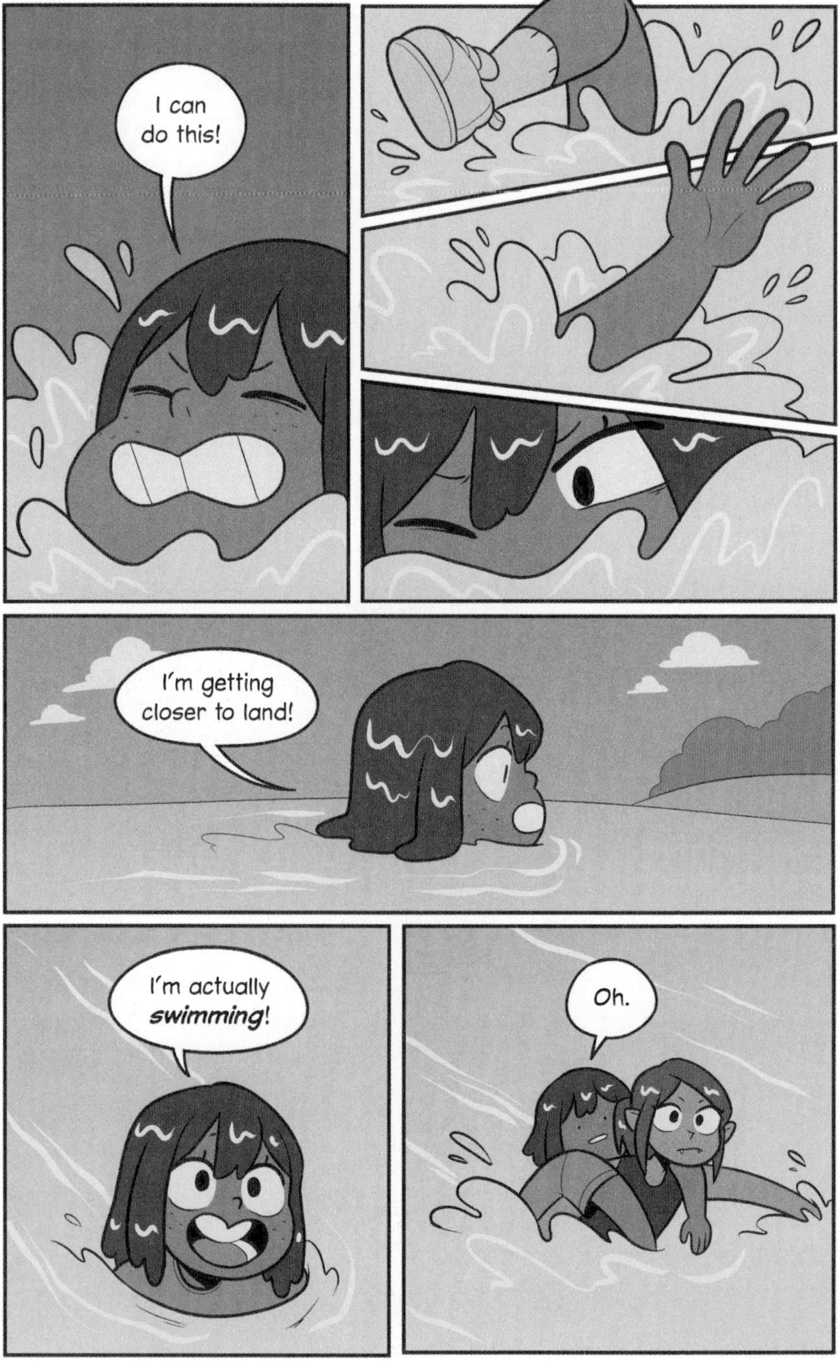
I can do this!
I'm getting closer to land!
I'm actually **swimming**!
Oh.

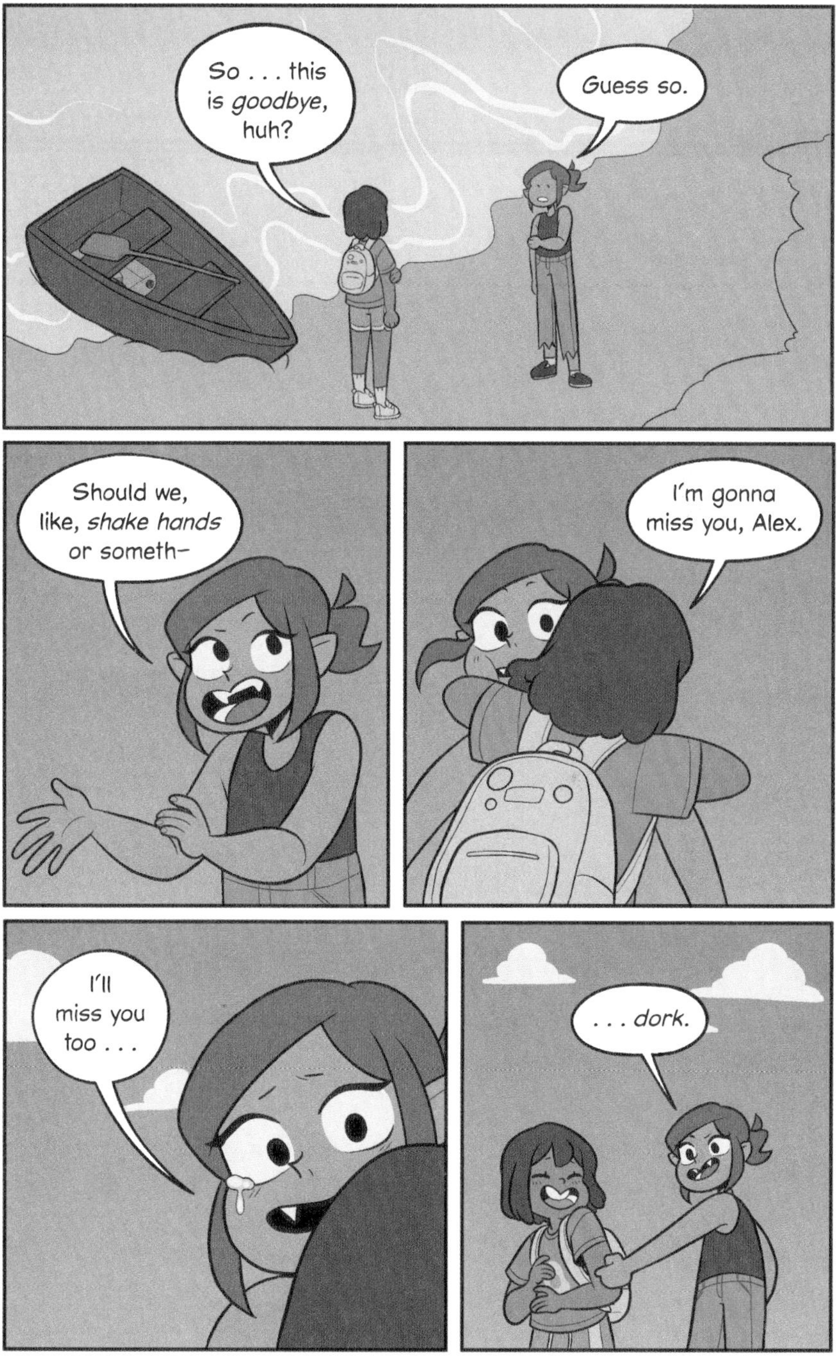
So . . . this is *goodbye*, huh?
Guess so.
Should we, like, *shake hands* or someth–
I'm gonna miss you, Alex.
I'll miss you too . . .
. . . *dork*.

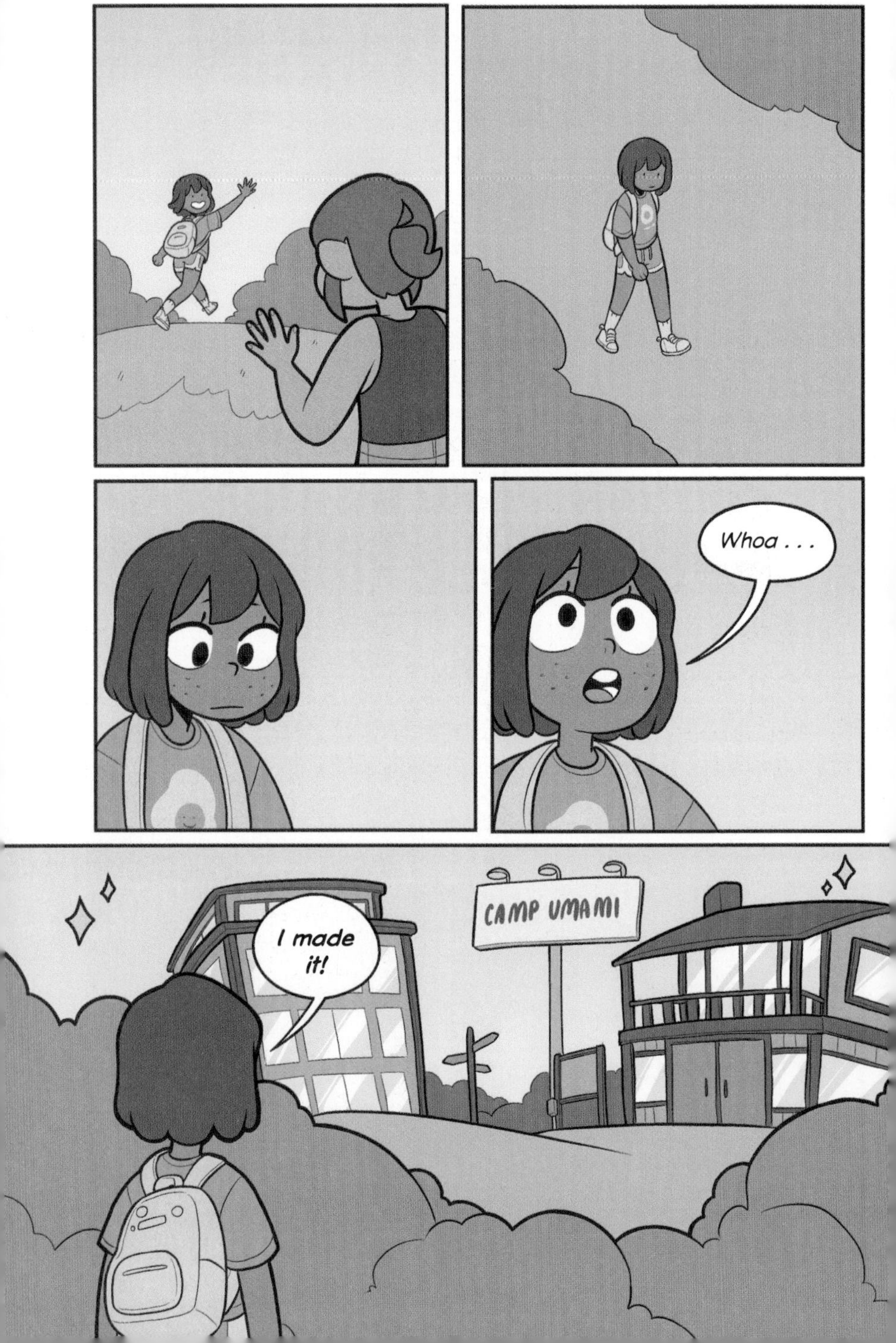
Whoa . . .
I made it!
CAMP UMAMI

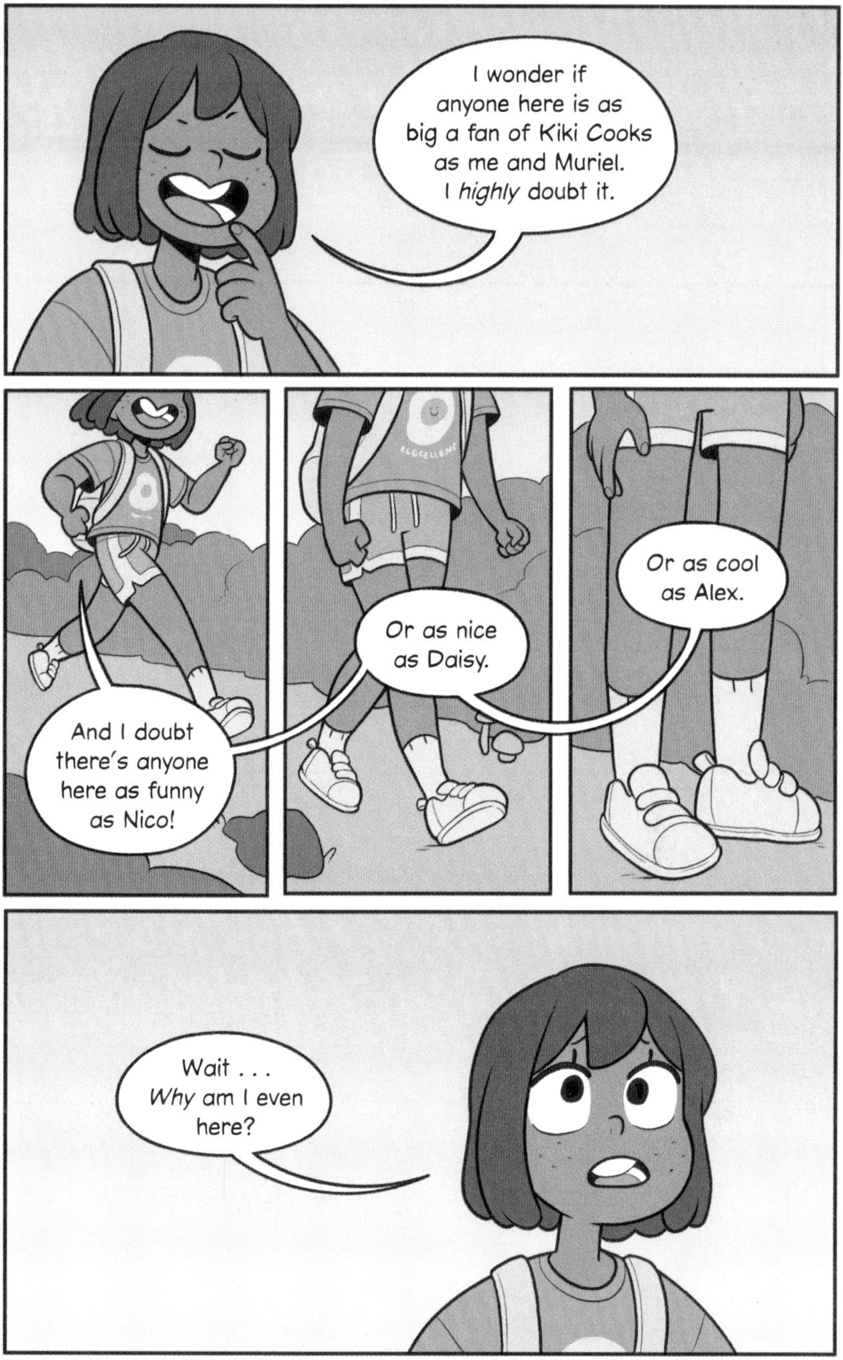
I wonder if anyone here is as big a fan of Kiki Cooks as me and Muriel. I *highly* doubt it.
And I doubt there's anyone here as funny as Nico!
Or as nice as Daisy.
Or as cool as Alex.
Wait . . . *Why* am I even here?

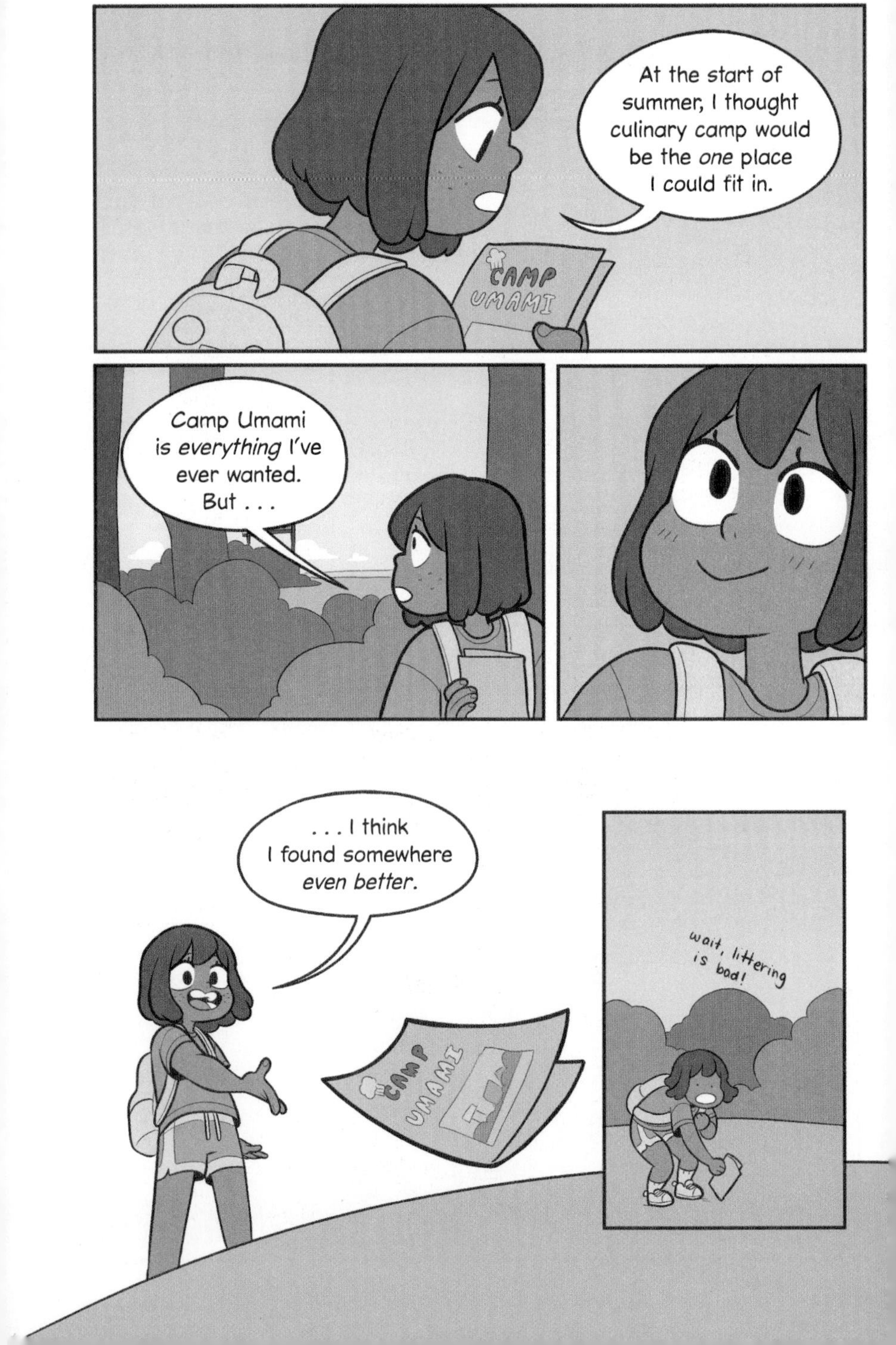
At the start of summer, I thought culinary camp would be the *one* place I could fit in.
CAMP UMAMI
Camp Umami is *everything* I've ever wanted. But . . .
. . . I think I found somewhere *even better.*
CAMP UMAMI
wait, littering is bad!

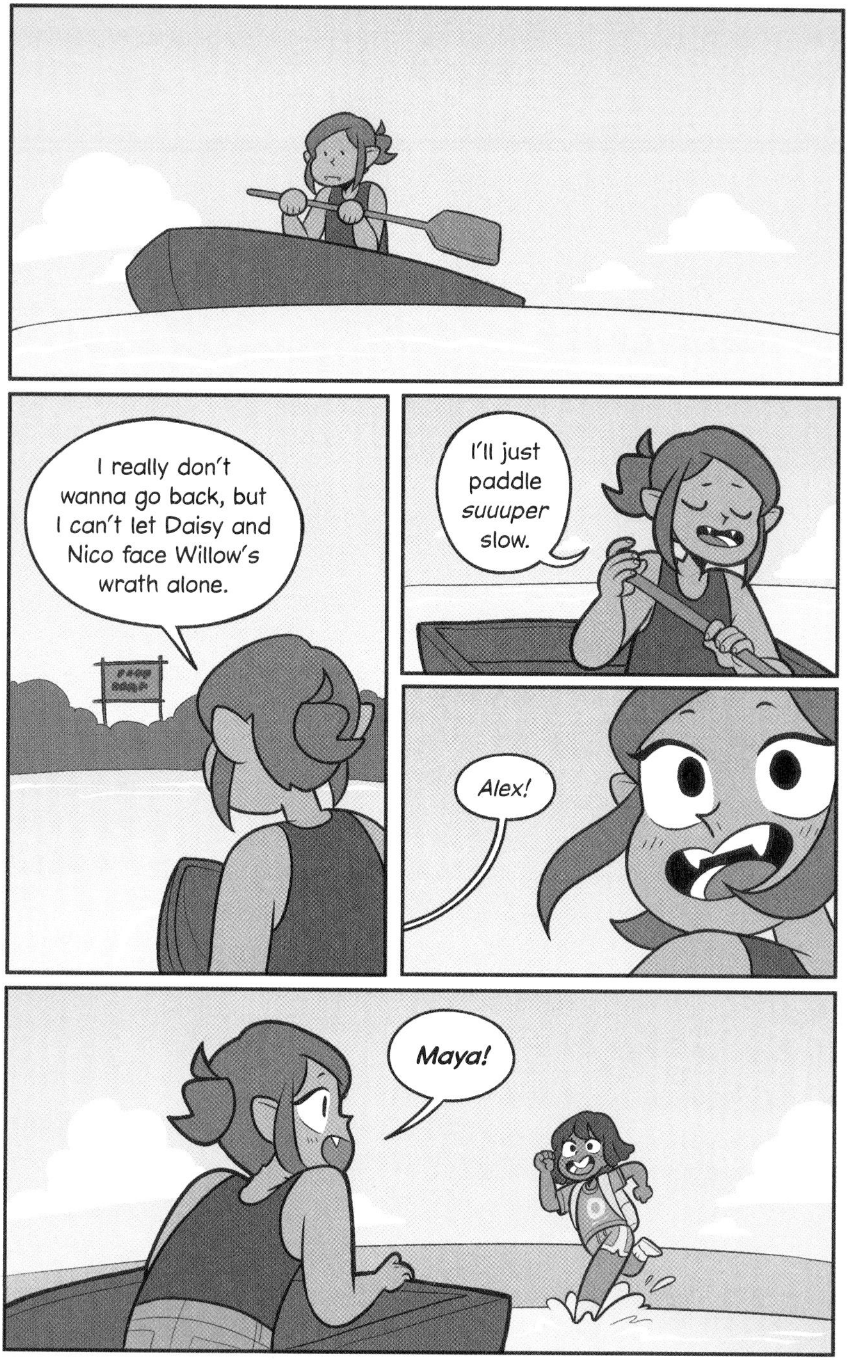
I really don't wanna go back, but I can't let Daisy and Nico face Willow's wrath alone.
I'll just paddle *suuuper* slow.
Alex!
Maya!

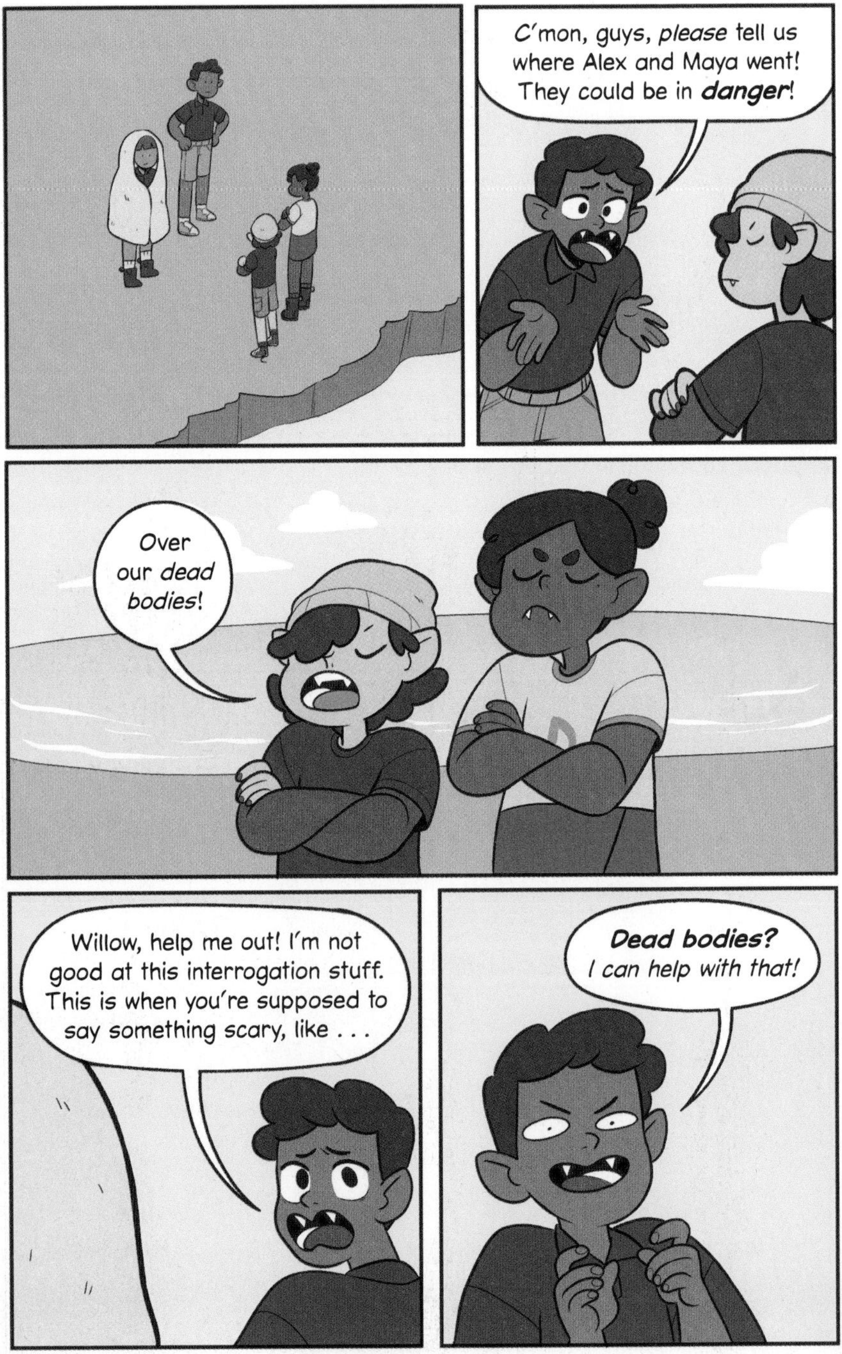
C'mon, guys, *please* tell us where Alex and Maya went! They could be in ***danger***!
Over our *dead bodies*!
Willow, help me out! I'm not good at this interrogation stuff. This is when you're supposed to say something scary, like . . .
Dead bodies?
I can help with that!

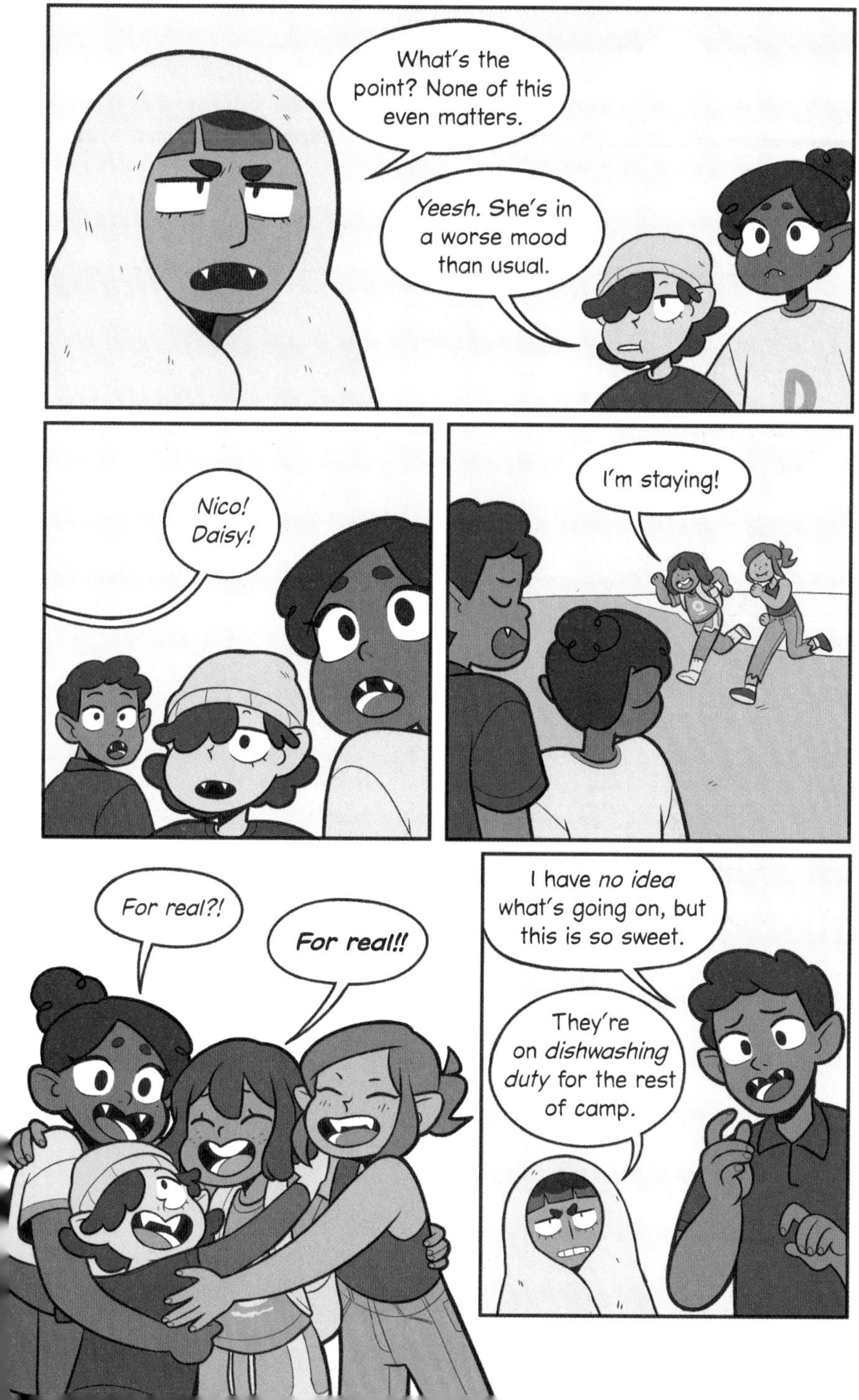
What's the point? None of this even matters.
Yeesh. She's in a worse mood than usual.
Nico! Daisy!
I'm staying!
For real?!
For real!!
I have *no idea* what's going on, but this is so sweet.
They're on *dishwashing duty* for the rest of camp.

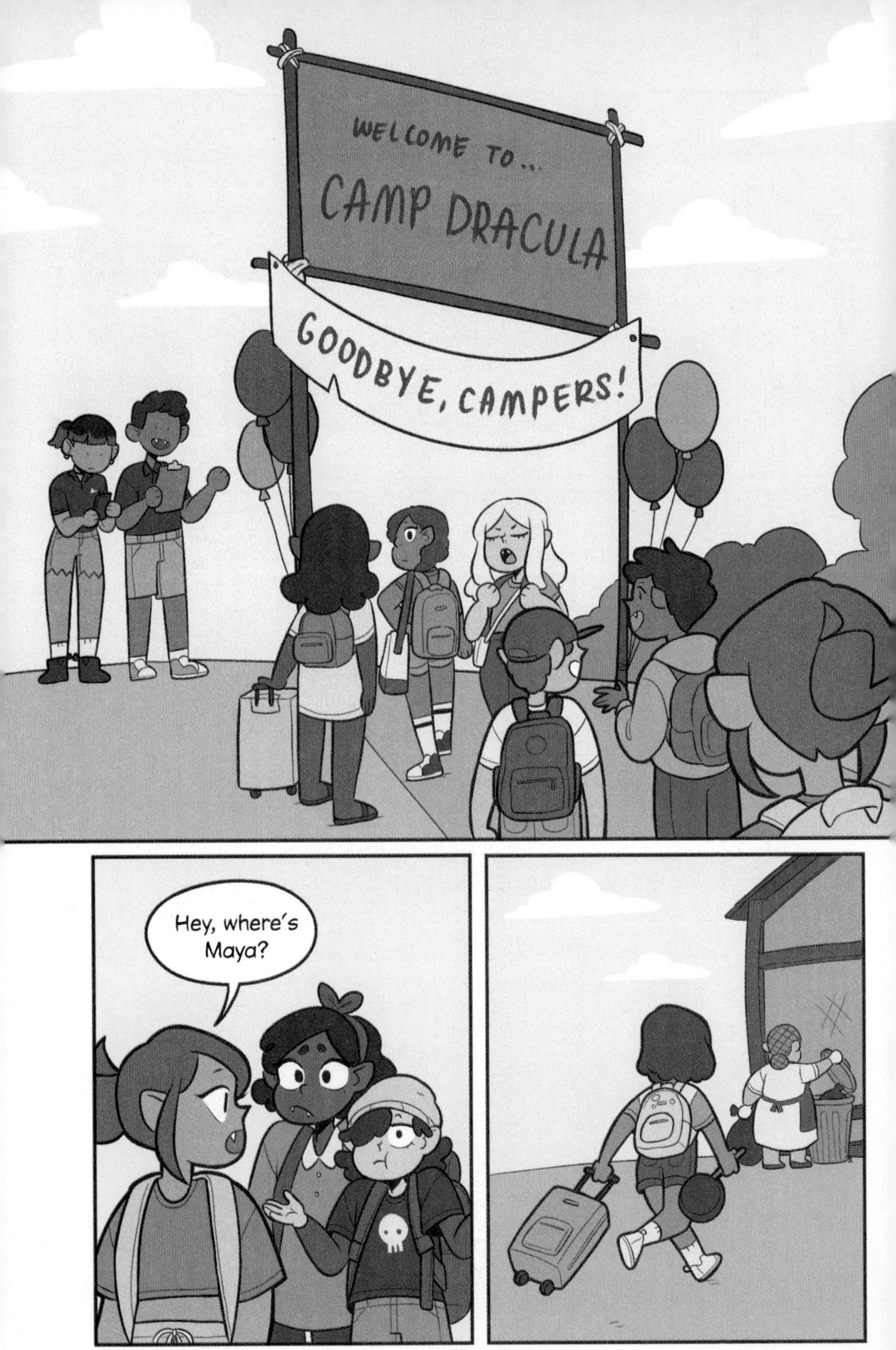
WELCOME TO...
CAMP DRACULA
GOODBYE, CAMPERS!
Hey, where's Maya?

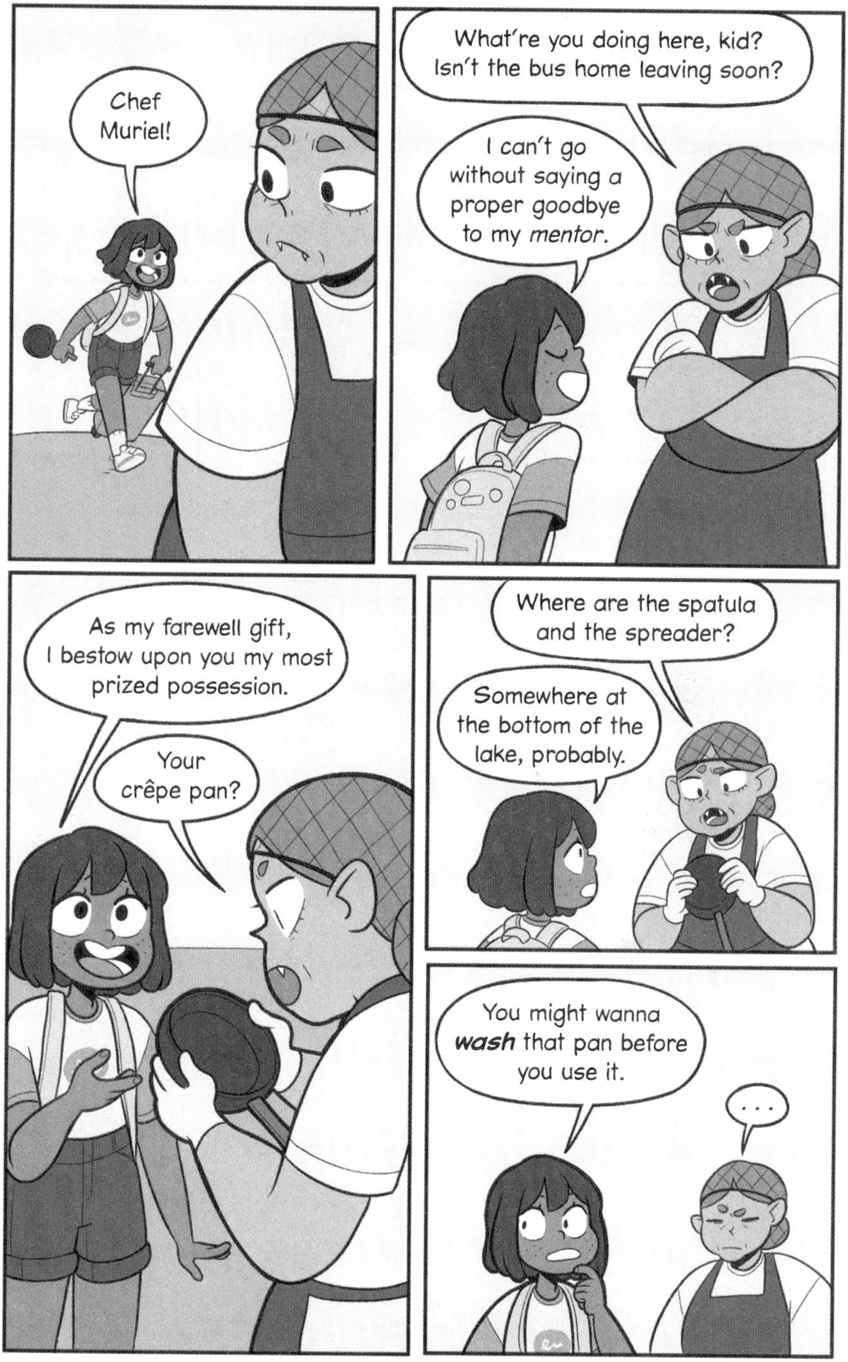
Chef Muriel!
What're you doing here, kid? Isn't the bus home leaving soon?
I can't go without saying a proper goodbye to my *mentor*.
As my farewell gift, I bestow upon you my most prized possession.
Your crêpe pan?
Where are the spatula and the spreader?
Somewhere at the bottom of the lake, probably.
You might wanna **wash** that pan before you use it.
...

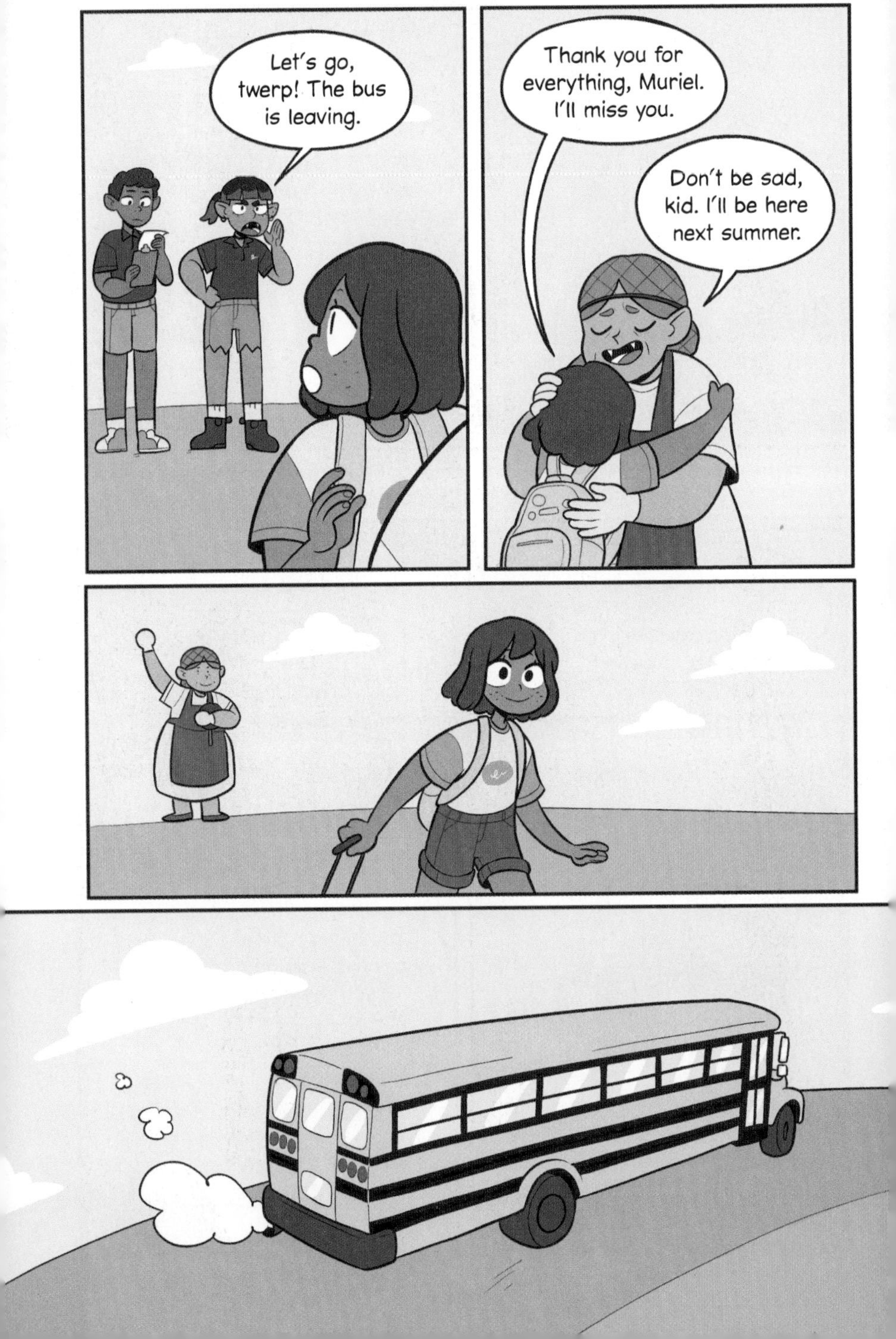
Let's go, twerp! The bus is leaving.
Thank you for everything, Muriel. I'll miss you.
Don't be sad, kid. I'll be here next summer.

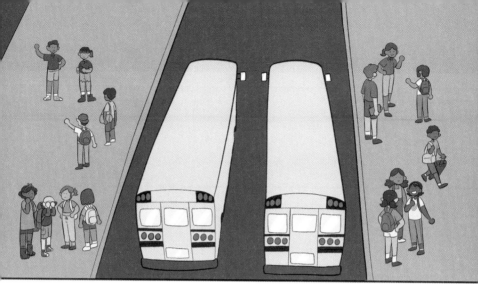

Aw, can you cheer her up, Maya?

This is so cool, Mia!

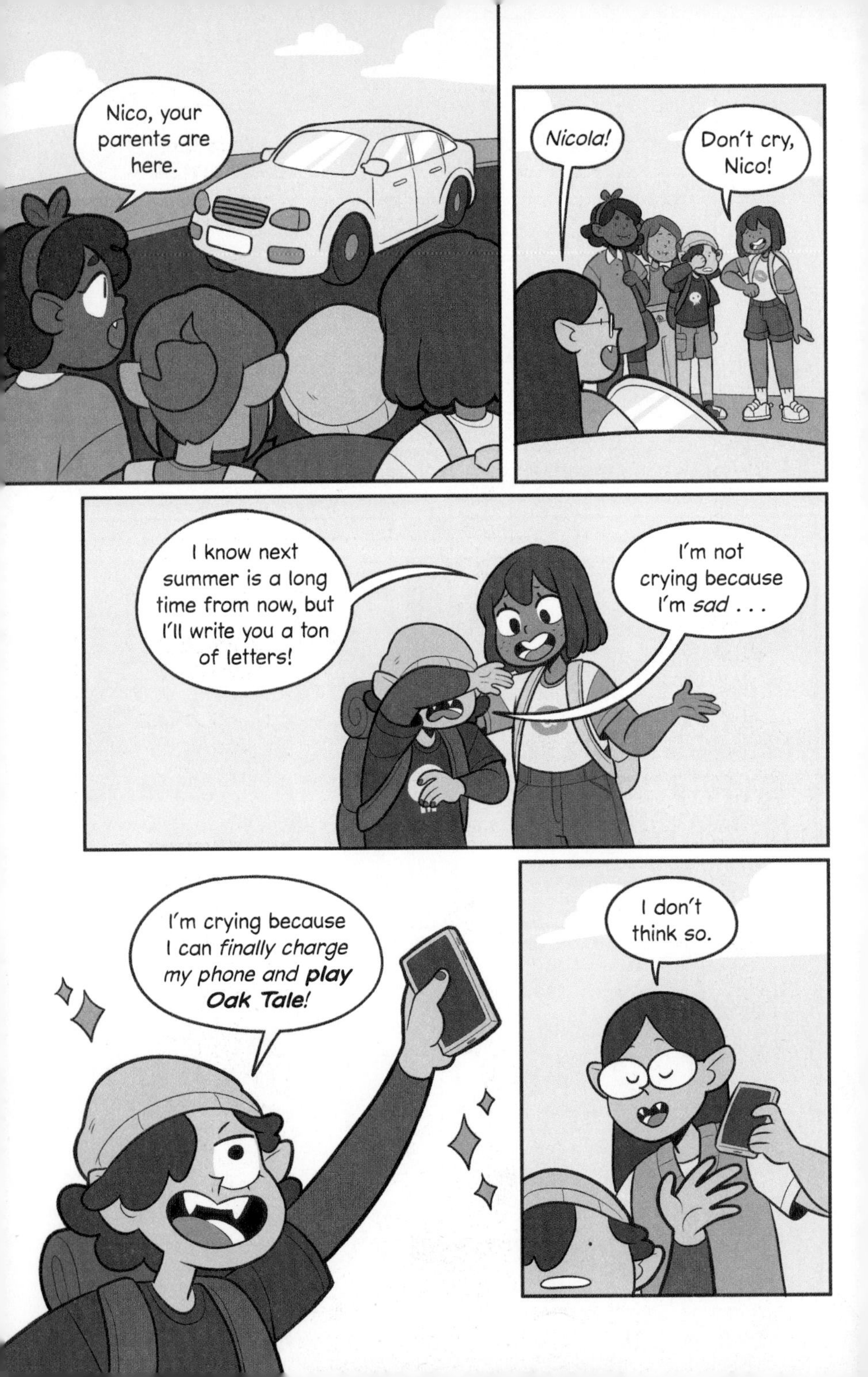
Nico, your parents are here.
Nicola!
Don't cry, Nico!
I know next summer is a long time from now, but I'll write you a ton of letters!
I'm not crying because I'm *sad* . . .
I'm crying because I can *finally charge* my phone and **play Oak Tale**!
I don't think so.

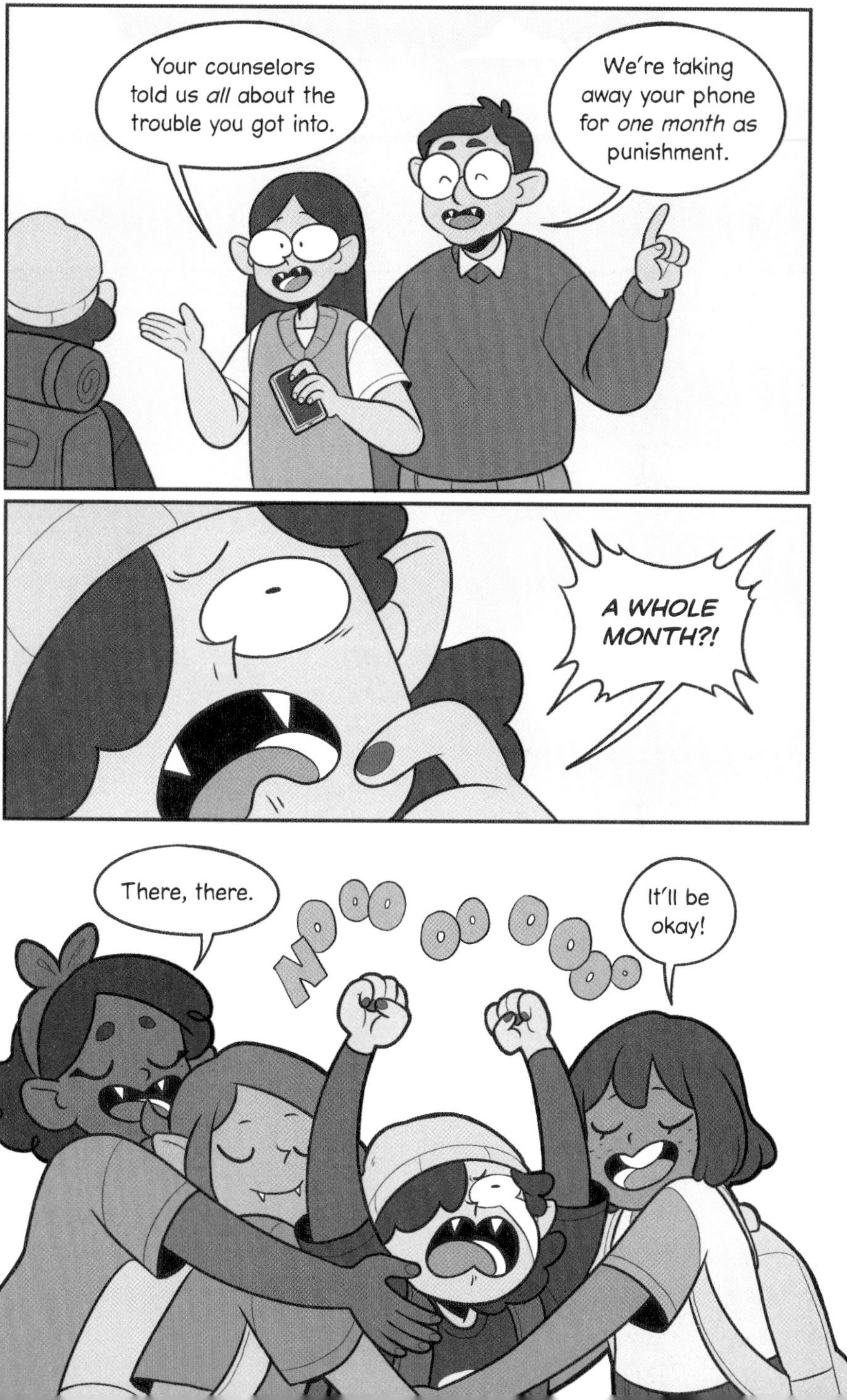
Your counselors told us *all* about the trouble you got into.
We're taking away your phone for *one month* as punishment.
A WHOLE MONTH?!
There, there.
NOOOOOOOOOO
It'll be okay!

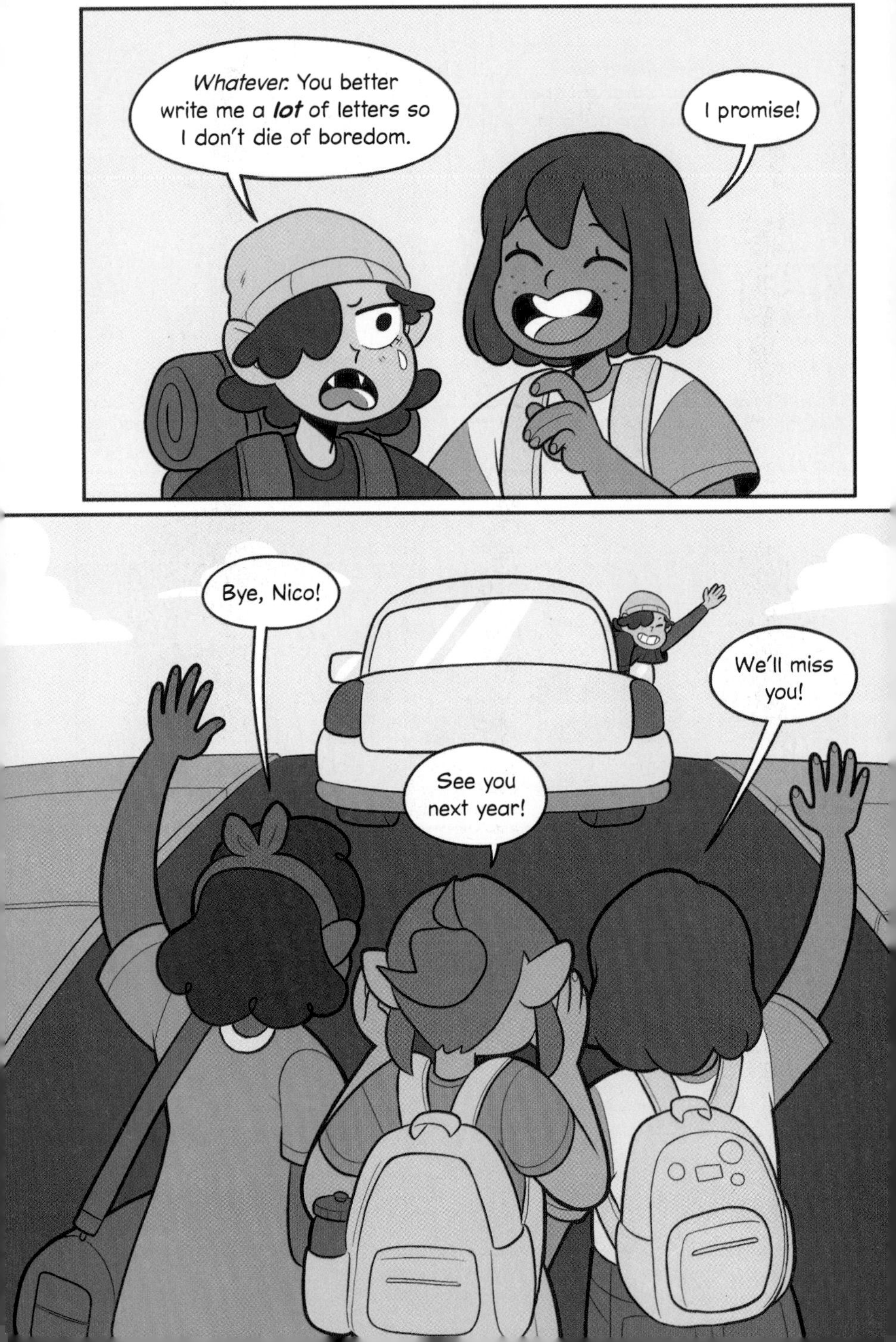

Whatever. You better write me a ***lot*** of letters so I don't die of boredom.
I promise!
Bye, Nico!
See you next year!
We'll miss you!

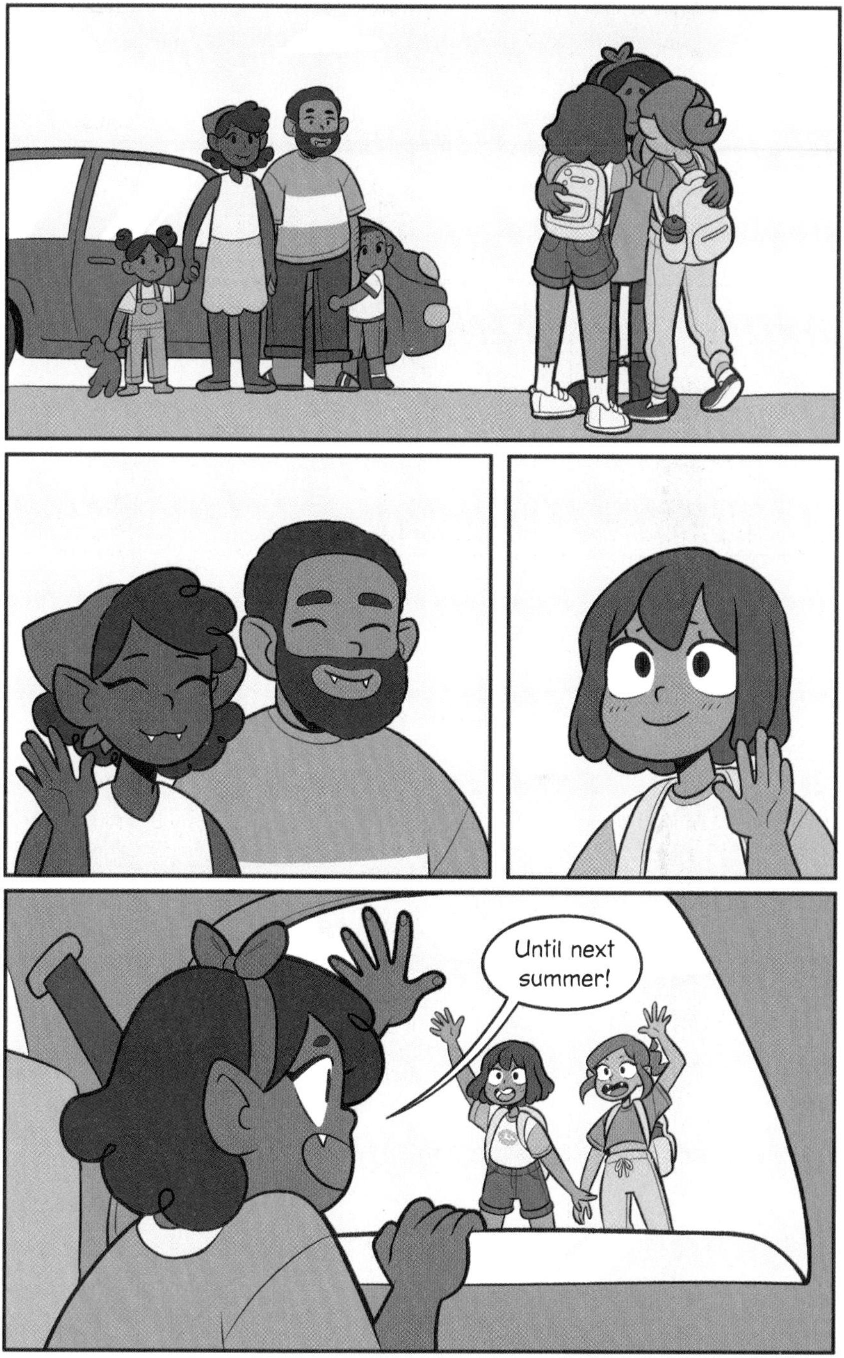
Until next summer!

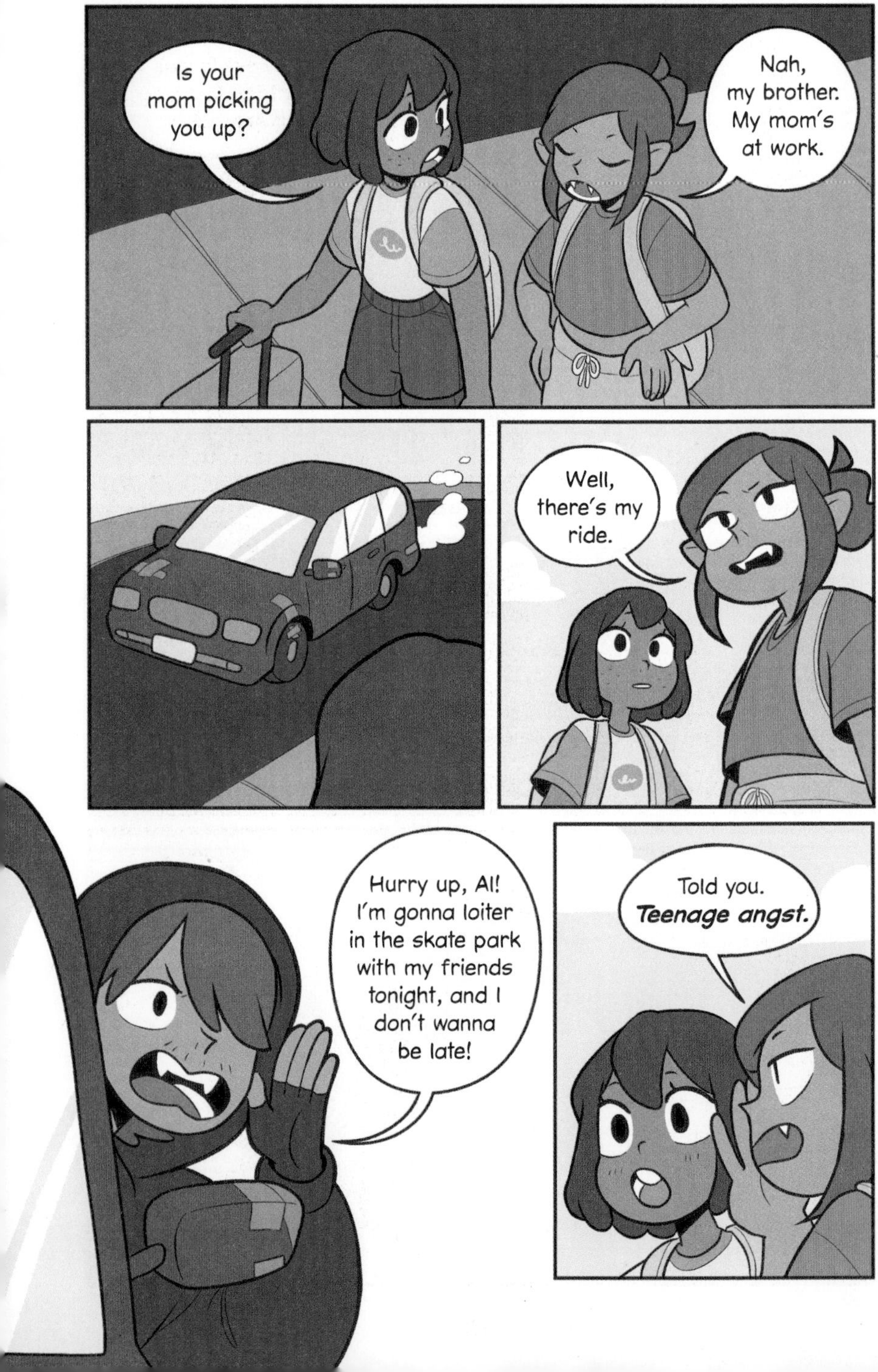
Is your mom picking you up?
Nah, my brother. My mom's at work.
Well, there's my ride.
Hurry up, Al! I'm gonna loiter in the skate park with my friends tonight, and I don't wanna be late!
Told you. *Teenage angst.*

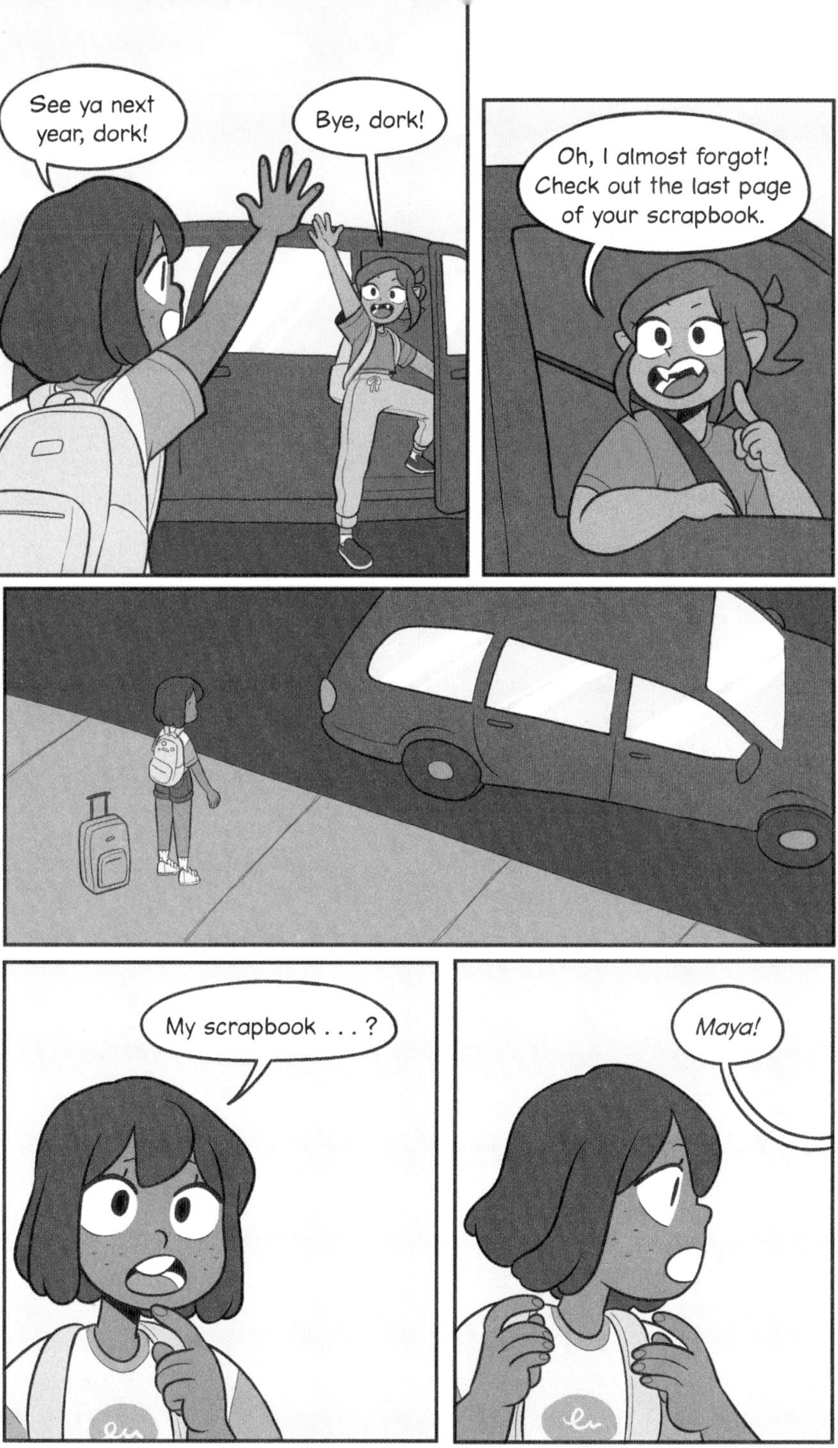
See ya next year, dork!
Bye, dork!
Oh, I almost forgot! Check out the last page of your scrapbook.
My scrapbook . . . ?
Maya!

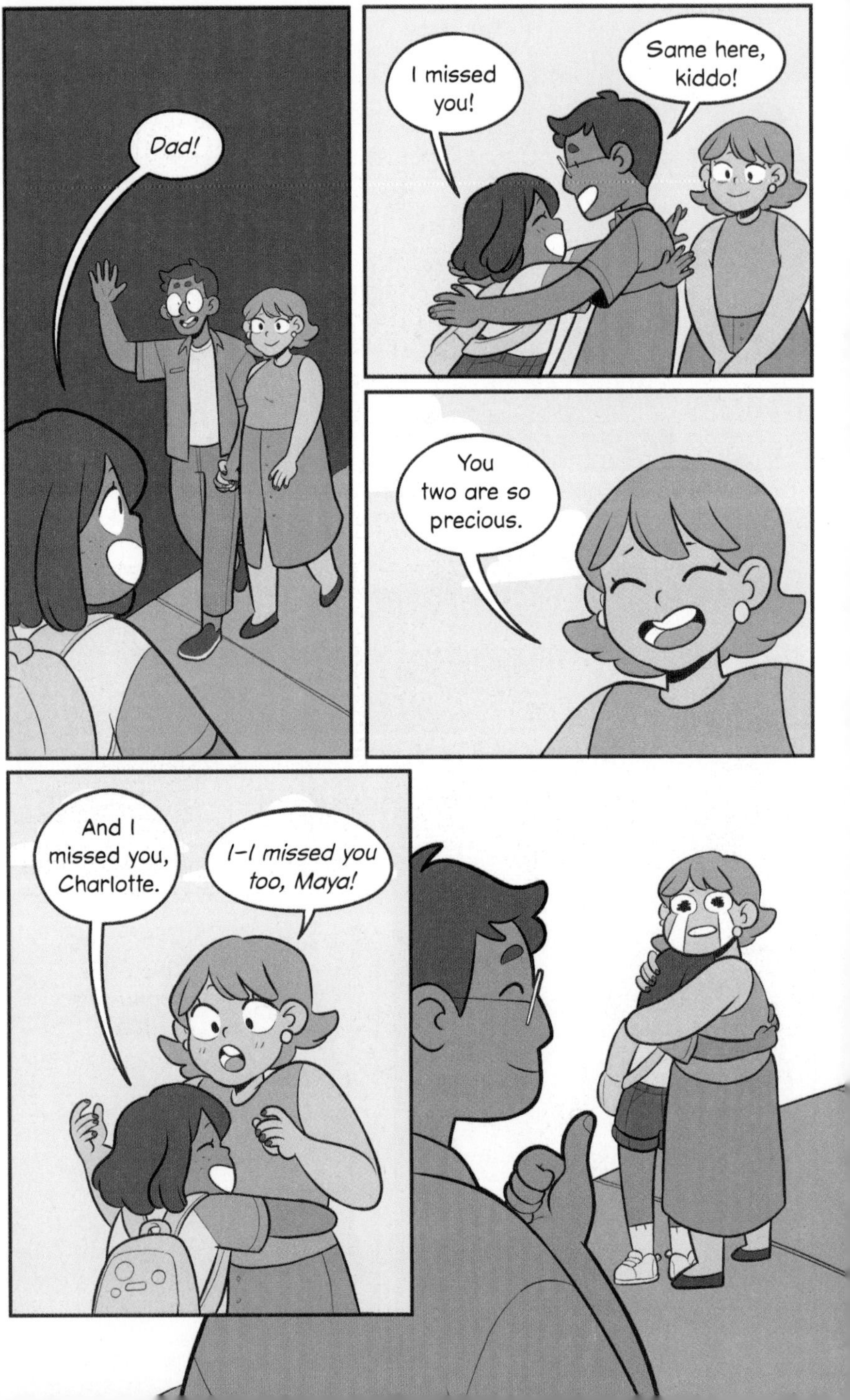
Dad!
I missed you!
Same here, kiddo!
You two are so precious.
And I missed you, Charlotte.
I-I missed you too, Maya!

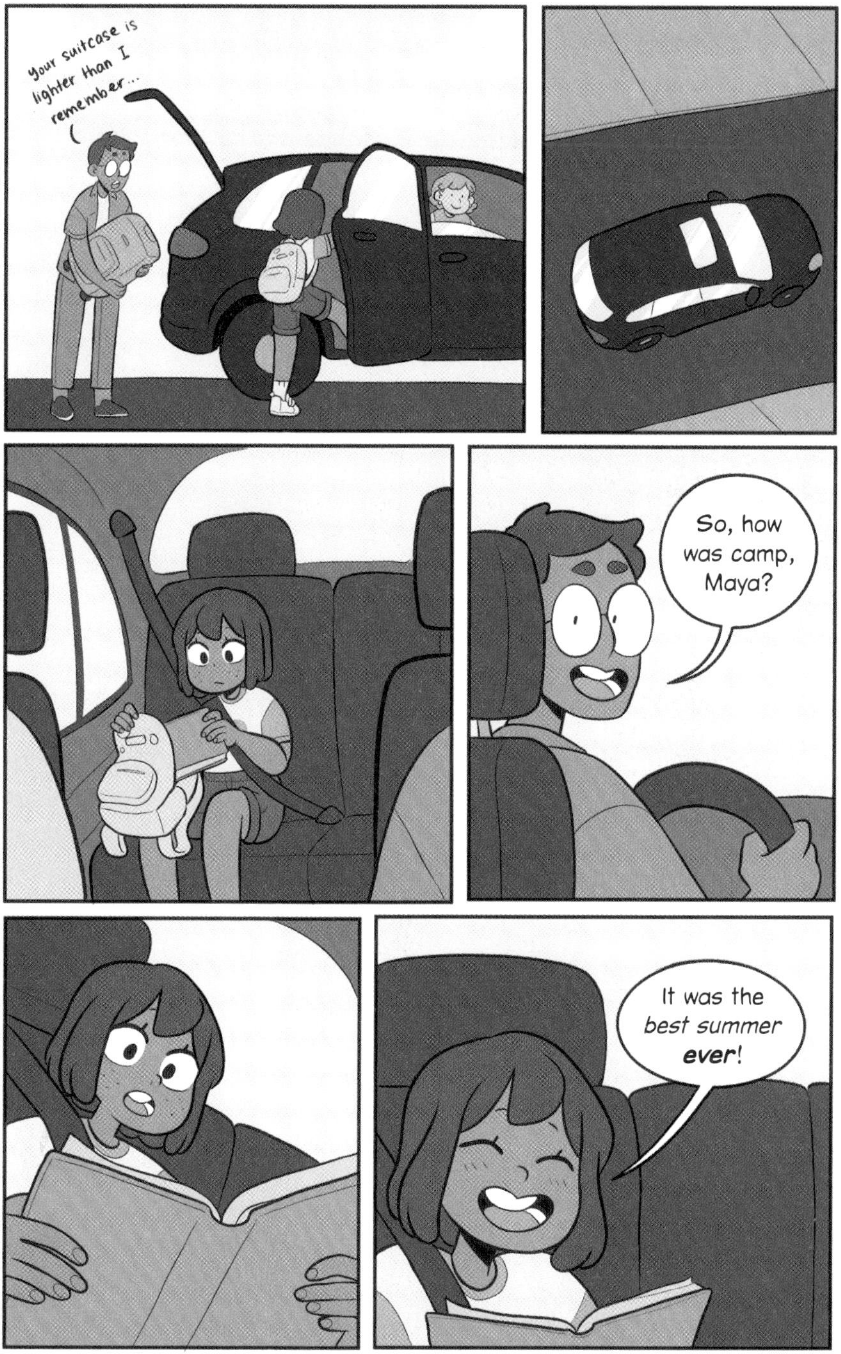
Your suitcase is lighter than I remember...
So, how was camp, Maya?
It was the *best summer* ***ever***!

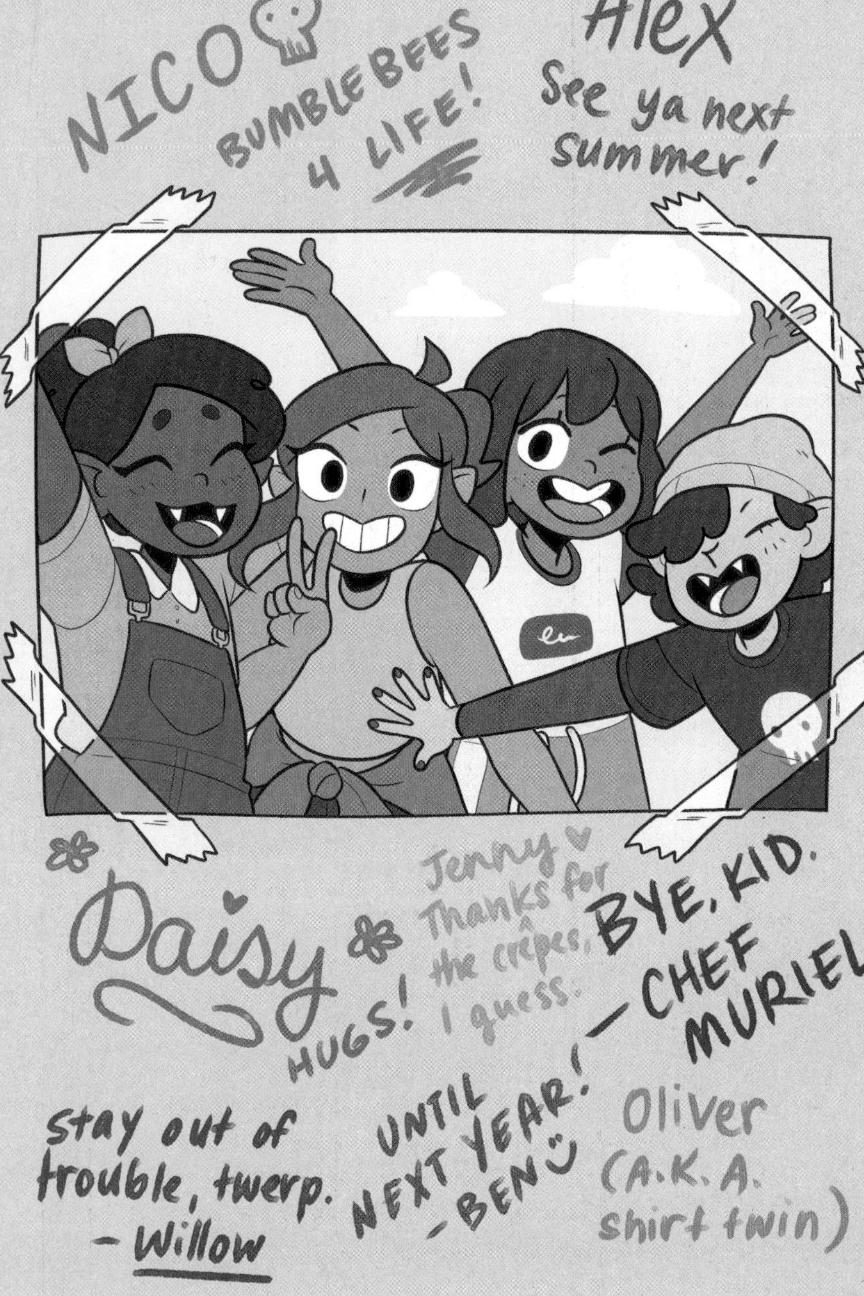
NICO
BUMBLEBEES 4 LIFE!
Alex
See ya next summer!
Daisy
HUGS!
Jenny
Thanks for the crêpes, I guess.
BYE, KID.
— CHEF MURIEL
stay out of trouble, twerp.
— Willow
UNTIL NEXT YEAR!
— BEN
Oliver
(A.K.A. shirt twin)